REVENGE OF THE MALAKIM

To Adam

Best Wishes

[signature]

ABOUT THE AUTHOR

Paul Harrison is a retired police officer with a successful career that spanned three decades. During that time he worked on some memorable high profile investigations, and interviewed countless criminals who operated within the darker side of humanity. Paul began writing and had his first book published during his time in the police. Since then, he has gone on to publish 34 books, mainly in the field of true crime. Now he has turned all that experience into writing crime fiction.

On retiring from the police, he spent time working with the English Judiciary, at the Royal Courts of Justice, London. During which time he gained what he describes as 'an eye opening insight' into what really happens behind the scenes of a criminal trial or civil hearing.

The vast majority of Paul's professional career has been within the criminal justice system. He's worked in many varied and interesting roles throughout his life, and he cites as his greatest achievement to date unanimously winning The Centre for Crime and Justice Studies Outstanding Individual of the Year Award 2009 by a panel of assessors that included the Lord Chief Justice of England and Wales. This primarily was for his voluntary work in the field of child and male abuse.

He's passionate about writing, and his first crime fiction novel trilogy is based on genuine experience. It is the first in a series of books that will feature lead detective, DCI Will Scott, and his trusted sidekick, DI Daisy Wright. This crime fighting duo will, throughout the series, find themselves not only investigating mysterious murders, but embroiled in the world of police, legal and establishment corruption also.

Currently based in the North, and describing himself as a true northern lad, Paul is regarded as one of the UK's leading experts on the subject of serial killers. He has interviewed many such offenders, which has provided a unique insight into their psychology, and all importantly, how and why they select their victims. Detail that will be used within future crime fiction novels.

Paul has made guest appearances in several true crime documentaries on both television and radio. He is a popular and entertaining public speaker, and has talked at many high profile crime writing festivals and conferences, both at home, and on an international stage.

Revenge of the Malakim

Book One

Of

THE GROOMING PARLOUR TRILOGY

Paul Harrison

Williams & Whiting

ACKNOWLEDGEMENTS

I would like to thank two wonderful people who have helped me in the writing of this book, and in the development of the characters contained within it.

Great appreciation goes to my publisher, Mike Linane, for believing in me, and giving me the freedom and opportunity to write crime fiction.

Huge thanks go to Mandy who has acted as a sounding board for my imagination.

Finally, to my readers, thank you for purchasing this book. I hope you will embrace DCI Will Scott and his team, and follow his policing pursuits and adventures over many more volumes.

Paul Harrison

A child screams and spills its tears

The innocent the Malakim hears

Double the damage it inflicts

On abusers and defilers in its midst

Malakim or *Mal'akhei/Malakhim*: An angel employed by God or an angel of higher authority to wreak destruction on mortals who intentionally harm children.

CHAPTER ONE

'This is bloody ridiculous, we aren't a fucking child minding service, we should be able to charge these people with child neglect or something. It happens every summer when the tourists come to the seaside, they seem to leave their brains at home,' Clive Wilson, the tall, slightly overweight copper sat in the police canteen of Bridlington police station. Looking remarkably pissed off as he talked to a new uniform recruit about the number of children, every tourism season, that the police 'baby sat' at various police stations around the town, as a place of safety. Jamie Benton looked slightly intimidated by his tutor constable who went on, 'Honestly, you wouldn't believe it, I'll bet you a fiver that in the majority of these cases, mum and dad have wandered off into a pub and left the kids playing in an amusement arcade. They have the cheek to seem surprised when they return, an hour later, and there's no sign of the kids! That's when they end up here. We waste our resources looking after these kids. It does my head in, honest it does.'

The police radio suddenly burst into life, crackling out another message. This time asking for any officer in the Marshall Avenue area of town to attend a public order incident which was believed to be drug related. Wilson jumped up from his seat, tapping his apprentice on the shoulder and barking out the command, 'Come on, we'll take this shout, I could do with a good ruck.' Slamming the canteen door open, he added, 'We could get tied up

1

with some other dross job if we don't grab this one. Hurry up!'

The two officers were gone, leaving another figure sat alone in a quiet corner of the canteen. Detective Inspector Will Scott wasn't really interested in operational workings of the uniformed branch. Unlike many of his colleagues in Bridlington, Will was a local man, born and raised in the town. Now in his early forties, his family had moved here from Garforth, Leeds, back in the 1970's. There was very little he didn't know about the town, including the local criminal fraternity. He had recognised that the shout on the radio was more than likely just some druggie visiting the town for the weekend or maybe on his holidays, doing a bit of dealing on one of the local's territory. One of his team of trained detectives would, depending upon the circumstances, pick up the aftermath of the arrests a little later, interviewing the alleged offender and sorting out what crimes had been committed. Will knew that experienced dealers wouldn't operate so openly and as close to the sea front, therefore a large recovery of drugs was unlikely.

Looking down, he checked his watch, it was close to six o'clock, knocking off time, he could then head to his home in Marton Gate, and spend some quality time with his two children, Ellie and Danny, and his wife, Mel.

He quietly made his way from the canteen, climbing the stairs that led up to the senior management floor and which also housed the CID offices. Arriving at his desk, he checked his computer one last time for any messages that might need an urgent response, before closing everything

2

down. He picked up a police radio and slipped it into his jacket pocket along with a pager and mobile phone before heading home. He was the duty officer this weekend, on call for any serious incidents, not that there were many, but in recent times there had been a few murders to investigate. By and large, duty officer weekends tended to go by smoothly and without any issues. On his way out of the nick he logged off duty and notified the control room staff that he was making his way home.

As he drove through the busy streets of Bridlington, he could hear the wailing of police sirens in the distance, this was quickly followed by a radio shout for 'Police back up' at the Marshall Avenue incident. From what he heard, the situation had well and truly kicked off and was fast becoming a major public order incident. The urgency in the voice of the radio caller made Will think twice about diverting to the scene. He thought again, that wasn't his role, he was a detective, not uniform, and the thought of missing out on valuable family time swayed his decision as he continued on his way home through the busy traffic on Sewerby Road. A few minutes later, the sound of police sirens were a distant reminder, the radio transmissions had all but gone quiet, the incident was over, dealt with effectively by the uniform officers. Will drove his blue Audi A4 through the double gates of his detached home. The sun was still shining and it was a warm summers evening, life felt good for Will Scott, even on duty officer weekends.

As he stepped into the front hall of his home, he was greeted by the excited cries of Ellie and Danny who ran up to him, hugging him tightly. They missed him when he was at work. He loved these sort of greetings, a loving, caring family helped put into perspective the utter madness that could often reign in his working role. From the kitchen, Mel waved to him and held up a large glass of red Shiraz. He could smell the aroma of his favourite meal, spaghetti bolognese, being cooked. The children returned to the tv in the living room. Will walked through into the kitchen and cuddled up behind his wife, kissing her gently on the back of her neck. Mel turned around and the pair hugged.

'Don't forget I'm duty call this weekend, so I can't have too much of this stuff,' he muttered, as he took hold of the full glass and sipped from it. 'Can we eat in the garden this evening, it's beautiful outdoors?' he asked. Mel agreed and suggested he go upstairs and shower, by which time she would have dinner ready. Will grabbed the glass of wine and took it with him upstairs. Throwing his dark blue two piece work suit onto the bed, he had a quick refreshing shower, and changed into more relaxing clothes, swilling a mouthful more of his wine before returning downstairs for dinner.

Mel had everything set out on the patio table. She could tell Will was tired, he was a dedicated and hard-working copper and a man who genuinely tried to do his very best for the people of Bridlington and its surrounding areas. He hated the tourist season, it brought all kinds of undesirables to the town, and everyday life for local people was made all the more difficult by the sheer quantity of people, cars, caravans and motorhomes during the summer months.

With the couple's house backing onto tree lined fields, the rear garden was a sanctuary for the family, private and peaceful, just the way they liked it. Mel dished up dinner as the family sat down to enjoy the meal together.

Will and Mel had met when she joined the Eastborough Police force. Tall, slim and with auburn shoulder length hair, Mel was attractive in every way. She was the ideal companion, best friend and wife for Will. From the moment they had first met as uniform officers, he was blown away by her intelligence on all subjects. She held the same interests as he did, reading, writing and watching Formula 1. He knew it was their destiny to be together when he told her he was travelling to Monaco to watch a forthcoming Grand Prix. Mel had replied, 'Me too, I'm flying from Gatwick.' On the same flight as Will, and since he didn't believe in coincidence, he recognised it as fate.

After something of a whirlwind romance, the couple were married in Bali 18 months later. Mel had resigned from the Police force within a year. She felt the position was too political and common sense policing had disappeared, now replaced by diversity awareness, and partnership corroboration that effectively gave the local politicians too much of a say in how the Police operated and what their priorities should be. Catching criminals was secondary to meeting statistical targets and achieving performance indicator figures, this kept both the local council and its councillors content.

Will had been sensible enough to get out of the uniform branch as quickly as he could. He had hated walking the streets of Bridlington with a police tit on his head. After serving his probation he had branched out into the intelligence field. He had made such a name for himself by the accuracy of his reports, and the quality and quantity of criminals he had brought in, that a move into CID was a natural progression. Wanting to better himself, he sat his promotions exams as soon as he could. Passing for Sergeant at the first attempt, a short time back in uniform was inevitable to provide career experience. A spell at Driffield followed by a year serving in Beverley, he was soon back in CID in Brid.

With the Inspectors exam under his belt, he was given the nod to sit promotion boards, which led him to his current rank of Detective Inspector.

Will rarely took his work home, he didn't want his family involved or to know of who or what he was dealing with. He protected his children at all costs. Occasionally they brought friends home for tea and some of these children were from recognisable criminal families. He never discussed this knowledge with his children, nor did he prevent them from visiting. It was a difficult balance to maintain in such a small place like Bridlington, yet most people who knew him socially or professionally, including some local criminals, liked Will because he was decent, and those who knew the family felt Mel and Will had found their true soul mates in each other.

With dinner over, Will helped Mel clear the table and sort the kids out, ready for bed. Soon it was just him and Mel, he poured them both another glass of wine, as together, they sat and watched the sun disappear into the distant horizon. They talked of the jobs they wanted to get done in the rear garden.

'Can you hear something buzzing?' she asked Will, looking back through the patio doors into the house. 'I think it's something in the kitchen,' she said.

Will leapt from his seat exclaiming, 'Christ it's not my pager is it? Fucking hell, where did I put the bloody thing?' Frantically looking in all the wrong places, he eventually found the pager where he had left it, next to the sink!

'I've got to call in, something must have happened.' He had a look of resignation on his face as he punched the control room number into his police mobile.

'Thank fuck I didn't have too much wine, I bet they want me to go in,' he said to Mel as he waited for his call to be connected.

'Is that DI Scott?' said the female voice on the other end of the phone.

'Yes, I can confirm that it's me, is there a problem, what have we got?' said Will with a tone of authority and urgency.

'Sir, I think you would be best going direct to the scene, there's been a murder. Only it's not as straight forward as that, it's a difficult situation,' the control room operator replied with a slight tremor in her voice.

Will clicked into business mode. 'Right, give me the location, victim details and what resources have been called to the scene already. Is the Duty Superintendent aware?'

'Yes sir, the Duty Superintendent has been made aware. He has asked me to tell you to attend in Senior Investigating Officer capacity. He's unable to get there. You can page him on 546 if you want to speak with him direct. We have serials deployed from Bridlington, Hornsea and Driffield, two dog handlers and armed response is on standby. Crime Scene and Forensic Investigators are en route and the entire street and surrounding area has been cordoned off. The deceased person has been found inside a house in Kent Road. A neighbour noticed the front door has been ajar overnight, and the curtains drawn, so phoned it in. No confirmed identification yet, other than the deceased is a male.'

'Okay, thank you. Call out DS Wright and ask her to meet me at the scene. Are we definite it's a murder and not accidental death or of natural causes?' he enquired hopefully.

'It's definitely a murder, sir. Can you give me an eta for you to get to the scene? The police surgeon is on his way, they really need you there soon as.'

'Yes, I'll be there within 15 minutes. In the meantime, no one enters the property or garden. I don't want a crowd of onlookers blocking everything up either. Get any available uniform officers to clear the street if necessary. Oh, and get someone to speak to immediate neighbours or potential witnesses, we need to clarify who lives at the address. Do a voters check for me, I don't want anything getting out. It's a complete information blackout where the media are concerned, at least until we have something to say.'

Will ended the call and tossed the phone onto a kitchen worktop in an act of frustration.

'I have to go in, darling. There's seemingly been a murder at a house in Kent Road. I bet it's another bloody drugs related incident. Sounds like they need someone to make a few decisions. Typically, the Superintendent has passed the buck down to me. I'm sorry I better get ready and get myself there.'

Mel stood up moving towards Will, wrapping her arms around his body and giving him a loving hug. 'Take care won't you, darling. Keep me posted as soon as you know if it's going to be an all-nighter.'

Will ran up the stairs two at a time, threw on his blue suit, shirt and tie, and quietly sneaked into both of the children's bedrooms. Bending over the forms of their peaceful sleeping bodies, he kissed each of them goodnight and crept back out before returning to his wife in the kitchen. He kissed her, reminded her that he loved her and left.

CHAPTER TWO

As he turned into Bessingby Gate, Will was confronted by a crowd of people who were stood across the road and effectively blocking it. Most of them were morbid onlookers satiating their sanguinary desires, and hoping to get a snippet of detail, no matter how farfetched it might be, that they could turn into fact.

'Why the fuck are these people here?' he muttered to himself, giving his car horn three distinct blasts in an attempt to get people to move. The assembled throng begrudgingly parted, allowing his car to slowly move between them and up to the police cordon. As he parked up and got out of his car, he heard a voice he instantly recognized. 'Will, Will, DI Scott.' Looking up, the detective saw his good friend and local journalist on the Bridlington Free Press newspaper, Lucien Palmer. The two men had grown up as friends, both respected each other's professional position and never pushed the respective boundaries. Lucien wanted a story, whereas Will didn't yet have a story to give him. He gave the journalist a nod of acknowledgement as he ducked and moved through the stream of blue and white police cordon tape.

It was a warm humid night which didn't help with the behaviour of the crowd, many had been drinking and were full of Dutch courage, shouting obscenities at the officers guarding the property. Jeff Powell, an experienced uniform sergeant, moved forward to greet the detective. 'Sorry to call you out, sir, but we had no option.'

'No problem, Jeff. We need to get this crowd pushed well away from the scene, get the dog handlers down here to help move them.' Both men moved slowly towards the front garden of the property.

'Right, run me through what's happened, who was first on scene and make sure we have full details of everyone who has been inside the house.'

'Okay, sir, the first officers to arrive were PCs Wilson and Benton. Benton is a probationer, he's sat in the back of the police car. He passed out when he saw the body.'

This prompted a smirk from Will Scott. 'Probably his first dead body, eh? Always memorable. So where is PC Wilson, I will need to speak with him?'

'He's standing by the front gate of the house, he's protecting the main crime scene. He's the officer with the beard. The only people to have entered the house are those two PCs and myself.'

Will approached PC Wilson, and recognised the officer as one of the two he had seen in the canteen a few hours earlier. 'Is this related to the drugs incident you attended earlier this evening?' he asked him.

'No, sir, that was something and nothing, a public order incident caused by a mix of drugs and alcohol. We've got three banged up in the cells for that. This is a totally separate incident, fucking grim it is in there, too,' he said, nodding towards the house. Will frowned and thanked Wilson for his thorough appraisal of the situation and turned to speak to the uniform sergeant.

11

'Jeff, can you arrange for a forensic tent to be erected outside the front door. Without seeing the internal layout, is it worth having a second one set up at the rear?' he asked his colleague.

'Yes, sir, I'll get forensics to sort that once they get here.'

The detective was deep in thought. 'I don't suppose you know who the victim is, it's probably going to be one of our usual CRO's, isn't it? So next of kin are bound to be local. Can you get someone to speak with the immediate neighbours on each side of the property, Jeff? Once they know anything, come directly to me. I don't want loose talk so the officer is to tell no one else.'

'He's not CRO, sir. I've never clapped eyes on him before this evening. I'll get all of that done straight away. Do you want me to take you into the crime scene and show you the body?'

Will was showing a little reluctance in entering the house. He wasn't good with the unique smell of murder, nor with dead bodies, yet he knew he had to confront this one as Senior Investigating Officer.

'Yes please, Jeff. If you go and get an officer to speak with the neighbours, and I will grab us a couple of Tyvek suits.'

Minutes later, Will Scott and Jeff Powell were donning the high density polythene forensic suits, very similar in style to HazChem suits. They were anything but flattering, yet they were super-efficient at keeping crime scene areas sterile and free from cross contamination. As they walked towards the bright red front door, Powell grabbed the detective by the left arm and stopped him in his tracks. 'Sir, you need to know, it's like PC Wilson said, it's fucking gruesome in there, and it stinks to high heaven.' Will nodded his head to acknowledge his understanding of the statement, in his own mind he thought the sergeant meant the house was unclean and smelt dirty.

He followed the sergeant into the house, first passing through a tiny front hall and through a door on the left that led to the living room. He was surprised at how clean and smart it was. He couldn't smell anything and wondered whether the uniform boys were taking the piss out of him. As he moved into the central area of the room, Jeff Powell stepped to one side, and pointed to an area directly in front of Will. 'Here he is, the poor bastard really suffered.'

The detective's eyes were darting around the room, scanning his surroundings until they finally came to rest on the back of a man's head. The body was seated in a wooden chair facing away from him. 'Christ, what's that fucking smell, has he burnt his bacon sarnies under the grill or something?' Will involuntarily gagged before stepping closer to the body finally moving to a position where he was stood in front of the corpse. The sight caused him to take a deep breath. 'Fucking hell, Jeff, what is this? It's like a scene from a slasher movie,' he exclaimed as he ran from the room, out into the front garden and projectile vomited his spaghetti bolognese dinner into the manicured green grass.

Jeff Powell emerged from the house soon after, and stood beside the detective, giving him a reassuring pat on the back. 'I told you it was bad, sir, it's a little bit easier to stomach the second time you see it, you can kind of prepare yourself for the horror. Sir, DS Wright is here, I think you need to stand up.'

Daisy Wright was a Detective Sergeant and Will's sidekick. The pair had worked together for almost two years. She was a slim and attractive woman with blonde hair that was neatly tied in a bun on top of her head. Daisy had transferred on promotion to Eastborough from Northamptonshire Police two years previously. Like her boss, Will Scott, she was sharp, eagle eyed and intuitive with very little getting past her.

'You okay, boss,' she asked as she approached the doubled up form of DI Scott.

'What do you think?' he replied sarcastically. Jeff Powell walked away and left the detectives to talk between themselves.

Daisy was already writing down notes on a clipboard she carried with her.

'What have we got here, sir, another druggie related overdose?'

Will took a deep gulp of the warm night air and looking at his fellow detective said, 'I don't know, I'm really not sure what it is just yet. It's anything but normal. Fuck, to be honest, I've never seen anything like this before!' He was shaking his head in disbelief. 'Get suited up, Daisy, we are going back inside, but be warned, this is the most sickening sight you will ever see. This bloke has suffered, he's a real mess.'

Daisy had never seen her boss so shook up, and could not imagine what it must be to affect him so badly. Within moments, the pair entered the house, this time Will led the way. As they moved through the rooms, Daisy busily took down notes and points of interest that were identified by her boss. These areas would be further examined by forensics when they arrived. Reaching the body of the man sat upright in the chair, Will tentatively moved around the corpse until he was stood directly in front of it. He then gestured to Daisy to join him, advising her to get out of the house if she thought she was going to be sick. The smell was overpowering. It wasn't bacon as flippantly suggested by Scott a few minutes earlier, but burning human flesh.

'Think of it as an object, not a human being,' he told his sergeant. 'You must detach yourself from your emotions.' He glanced towards her, and was surprised to see that she didn't seem fazed by the horrific state of the body. 'What do you reckon, what're your thoughts?' he asked her.

There was so much to take in. The corpse in front of them had been nailed to the chair and the floor, two large nails through the back of each hand and a further two through his feet, the carpet and into the floorboards were enough to keep him firmly in place. The body was entirely naked, his clothes neatly folded lay on a sofa behind him. Dark red blood covered his groin area and had pooled on the seat of the chair before dripping onto the carpet beneath. Moving up the body, his stomach had rows of symmetrical gouges removed from the skin. On his chest area, both nipples had been removed, cut away by a sharp implement, probably with a knife or scalpel. His face was simply a mess. Protruding from each eyeball was a slim wooden kebab stick, not that the eyeballs were recognisable, they had been burnt like the rest of his face. On a table nearby, both detectives had noticed a small hand held kitchen blow torch, the obvious cause of the burning. Beside that was a cheese grater with what appeared to be human skin hanging from its rough cutting blades. The remains of the eyelids were open, only because they had been stapled into that position. As Daisy looked more closely at the face, she thought his mouth had an odd shape about it. 'There's something in his mouth, I think,' she said as she pointed to a small trickle of blood running down the dead man's chin. Both officers knew not to touch anything until the forensics team had done their work.

Daisy took countless photographs of the scene and of the body in situ. She knew that forensics would be hours taking the crime scene and surrounding area apart, so it was useful to have something to work with. As she photographed all areas of the room she saw a flicker of light on a table full of papers. It was a laptop computer.

The computer lid hadn't been closed properly, the machine was still on. She called to Will and told him of her find. The two officers carefully opened up the screen part of the laptop, gently lifting it away from the keyboard, causing it to spark into life.

'See if you can see what it is he's been looking at, it might give us a clue what this bloke was up to and a motive for his murder.'

As both officers peered at the white screen they saw a word document that held nothing more than lists of names, dozens of them, none of them were readily recognisable. 'We need to seize this, Daisy, take plenty of photographs of it as we found it, make sure you record its exact position on the desk. This is so fucking weird. This guy must have been a dealer, I reckon, maybe that list is all of his clients? I can't think of anything else that might warrant such a bloody awful death.'

Daisy agreed. The pair were suddenly interrupted by the presence of a third person in the room.

'Sir, I think we have a name for the victim,' said a slightly agitated Jeff Powell as he stood in the entrance to the living room. 'He's not CRO but he is known to us.'

'Who is it?' enquired Daisy.

'Allan Roberts.'

Will looked bemused. 'Who the fuck is Allan Roberts when he's at home?'

'He's a local councilor, sir, you must know him, he's the Crime and Disorder portfolio holder, a Conservative I think?' Powell felt slightly foolish at his last remark since it made no difference what his political leaning was.

'Do we have a wife, a family, any relatives?' asked Will.

'Not that I know of, sir. The neighbours say he lives here alone, although he does have regular visitors, but they don't seem to stay long. He was last seen alive at about 3pm yesterday afternoon, carrying shopping from his car into the house.'

Behind Powell a crowd of forensic officers all suited up arrived at the front door of the house. A gruff Yorkshire voice enquired, 'Who is the SIO here? What have you got for us?'

Will stepped forward and ushered everyone outside the house while he briefed Mark Daniel, the Senior Crime Scene Officer. He instructed that the body should remain in situ until he authorised its removal once everything else had been forensically achieved.

'I want you to give this place a thorough going over please. The offender or offenders must have left their DNA all over that room. The victim has been tortured, he's nailed to a chair, his eyelids have been stapled open and protruding from each eyeball is a partially burnt barbecue skewer, also his hair and upper face has been torched. There is no way on earth that all of those injuries could be inflicted without leaving some trace behind. I've seized a laptop computer from a table in there, it may help us identify the killer or killers. I'll show you where it was, Mark, okay.'

The forensics team were left to their scientific processes and given full access to the scene. The sheer logistics of this crime would cause man power issues for the general policing of the town, and it was summer, the place was packed with tourists.

Acknowledging this, Will again approached Jeff Powell. 'I want uniform to protect this scene until further notice, 24/7. Have we got any PCSO's on duty or can we call some Specials out to cover this, Jeff? We don't want to tie you down or your teams. We can clear away the onlookers, take the road cordon right back in all directions and control entry and exit for the local people living in the street. I'd better get back to the nick and make some phone calls, and arrange a briefing for the press. I'll get some CID and spare uniform resources down here for house to house. They can liaise with you, okay?'

Jeff Powell nodded.

In the crowd of onlookers Will saw his friend Lucien, the journalist, still waiting to speak to him. Walking towards him, he beckoned him a few feet through the cordon, away from the inquisitive ears of those gathered. 'Lucien, mate, how are you?' he said gripping the journalists outstretched hand firmly and shaking it.

'I'm fine, Will, but how about you? I take it you are duty officer this weekend? What's going on in that house then, surely with all this fuss it's got to be a murder? Another druggie, I suppose?'

'I'll be honest, Lucien, I don't know. It's early stages yet. We're obviously treating it as a suspicious incident, but I cannot say any more than that. I'm heading back to the nick to organise a press conference. I'll get the press officer to give you a call when it's all arranged and we have something to say. Please don't promote any theories about murder or anything else, we don't want panic on the streets. The bloody town's busy enough already with tourists, we don't want the curious and the morbid swarming in. I promise, once we know anything, you'll be made aware. I'll have to go, my Superintendent is waiting

19

for me and I have a stack of notifications to make back at the nick. Be safe, mate.'

As he made his way back to Bridlington police station, a hundred thoughts were spinning through Will's mind, primarily he needed to call Mel to let her know he wouldn't be able to get home until tomorrow at the earliest. As he pulled into one of the police parking bays in Ashville Street, a pale looking Daisy Wright was waiting for him.

'Christ, boss, I'm shaking like a leaf. What we just saw back there has just hit me, who the hell would do something like that?'

Will placed a supporting arm around her shoulder and guided her inside the police station and up to the CID office. 'Well, what the hell do we do now, who do we notify first?' she asked.

'Okay, Daisy, first things first, we have a mug of tea, and then we make phone calls home. Your fella is going to need to know that you won't be home until god knows when, and I'm going to ring Mel. Then we prioritise our calls thereafter. We need a script to report it to the Chief and the governors. They'll ask the same questions and want to be absolved of any ownership or responsibility for the investigation, so we make it clear that everything is under control and we will keep them updated with all progress.'

'I tell you what, boss, if it is that Councillor Roberts, there'll be loads of media enquiries, political interest and without doubt, interference.'

Will agreed and questioned the motive for murdering a mere councillor in such a horrific manner.

'If it is that bloke, then he must have seriously pissed someone off. It's not like his position is full time or controversial even, he's an amateur politician living in Bridlington. He's hardly likely to be involved in anything of national importance. I always think that people connected to the local authority tend to be a bit wishy washy. Once we've notified everyone that needs to know we can start digging into his background. It would be a whole lot easier if he had previous for something.'

CHAPTER THREE

Hours later, the CID office was humming with officers of all ranks making telephone calls and arranging to speak with callers who wanted to report suspicious activity across all of Bridlington. News had leaked out that it was a murder, and everyone was assuming the identity of the victim to be Allan Roberts.

'Boss, the pathologist wants you down the morgue straight away, he has something he wants to discuss with you,' shouted a uniform PC drafted in as support for the inquiry.

'Okay, I'll make my way there straight away. Daisy, I want you with me. Come on, the mystery deepens,' he said light heartedly.

On the journey to the hospital both officers talked of every eventuality, the next step of the investigation and the need to get a close knit team together to progress every aspect of the inquiry.

'We should be able to determine identity and cause of death here, Daisy, that's a starting point at least.'

Daisy agreed, 'I have a horrible feeling about all of this, boss. This is Bridlington, for heaven's sake, nothing big happens here, it's hardly like Hull, crime bloody central. But that body, it was deliberate torture. Whoever that bloke is, he suffered. It's like a professional hit, gangster style!' Both officers, somewhat nervously, laughed at the thought.

'The Mafia in Brid,' suggested Will, 'whatever next DS Wright.'

As they walked through the cold echoing corridors leading through the hospital to the morgue, the sickly sweet smell of death filled their nostrils. Daisy let out a little cough as the whiff caught the back of her throat.

'Here we are, Daisy. Let's hope it's straight forward and we don't have to go through the entire autopsy. Dylan is normally shit hot with his findings.'

The pair stopped at the secured double swing doors of the mortuary, and looked through the port hole glass window for any sign of forensic pathologist, Dr Dylan Haynes.

They didn't have to wait long before Dr Haynes appeared and welcomed both officers in.

He instinctively led them through to the changing area and handed medical smocks to each of them. 'You have to come inside, I want to present a number of issues I have about the remains. I hope you aren't squeamish.'

As they walked into the cold white room, before them lay the body they had last seen in murder pose at the crime scene. A white sheet, spotted with blood covered the remains. Dylan Haynes didn't waste any time, and whipped off the sheet exposing the partially forensically butchered body. Both police officers took a step back. It was even more gross to look at in this state.

'Don't worry, it won't bite you, he's definitely dead,' Dylan said with a laugh. 'First thing, his eyelids, they have been stapled back. I thought it was pins, but the upper lid has been stapled back on both sides of the head. Whoever did this wanted this man to suffer and see what was happening to him next. The wooden kebab skewers

23

were carefully inserted through the retina while he was alive, likewise, most of the other injuries. The burns had caused the eyeball to partially harden before melting so the heat must have been ferocious. Moving down to the groin, his is minus the penis and testicles, these have been removed, judging by the cuts, with a small sharp instrument, possibly a scalpel.'

DI Scott groaned, 'This is awful. What kind of nutter would do this to another living person? Do you think they took the penis and testicles away with them as a trophy? Our forensic team haven't found anything like that at the scene.'

Dylan Haynes coughed. 'No, they didn't take them away. Look here,' he lifted a stainless steel bowl containing what looked like entrails and pushed it toward them. These are the contents of his stomach. See these chewed up things here, they are his testicles. Whoever did this made him eat them.'

'Jesus Christ,' blurted out Will, 'this gets worse by the minute.'

'Yes, detective, it certainly does.' He moved his attention back towards the victim's head and focused in particular on his mouth.

Taking a stainless steel spoon like tool, he inserted it into the mouth and prized it open.

'Look here, look inside the mouth.' Both officers bent over to look inside, neither quite certain what they were looking for or at.

'What is it?' asked Daisy inquisitively.

With the jaw open, Haynes inserted a pair of tongs into the open mouth and extracted a piece of flesh that to all intents and purposes looked like a rancid sausage.

'It's his penis. It was removed and stuffed inside his mouth while he was alive.'

'How do you know he was still alive when that was done?' asked Will.

'Because, if you look closely at it, you will see teeth marks. Whoever killed this man, cut off his penis, inserted it into his mouth, and made him bite into it. If you are looking for a cause of death, I would have to say heart failure. The amount of pain this chap went through was enough to stop his heart. I noticed abnormality and weakness in the ventricles, his heart gave out due to the strain. He was heavily overweight at 19 stone 8 lbs, and judging by the state of his lungs, he was a heavy smoker. Although it hasn't been confirmed yet, I can tell you who he is and a little more about him. His name is Allan Roberts, a local councillor and Freemason. He's a member of my lodge. Allan was a loner. He mixed socially at Masonic events, however, I suspect he had a very private side to his life. There was never a close woman, or man, come to think of it, that I ever heard of. He was an only child and both his parents passed away years ago. I confess, I have never before seen such gruesome and horrific injuries on a cadaver.'

'Dylan, you mentioned the Mason's there, you don't think there could be a connection to his death, do you?' said Will.

The question aroused a short sharp response from the doctor. 'No, absolutely not,' he snapped.

'Then why mention it?' asked Daisy, who was scribbling everything down on her clipboard.

'I mentioned it, young lady, because I wanted you to understand how I knew him. I wasn't close to him! As I said earlier, he was a bit of a loner, other than the Masonic connection, I had nothing in common with the man. In fact, whenever he was interviewed in the local paper, I found his comments about how he intended to lower crime and disorder within the town to be farcical. He talked as though you were his private police force, and those idiots at the paper played to his ego and printed everything he said. I dare say, crime and disorder got worse during his tenure as portfolio holder. The man was regarded as something of a joke around the town. Who in their right mind wanders round fun fairs on their own, or hangs around the arcades with teenagers, I think it shows an immature side to him. I once fronted him about his behaviour. He said it helped him understand the problems facing the youth of the town and to make it better for everyone. Peculiar if you ask me.'

Will interjected the discussion. 'Doctor, when will you be able to officially confirm the cause of death?'

'I'll write up my report now, it will be with you later this afternoon, okay? I can confirm to you now, unless I find something else during the remainder of the autopsy that it will be down to heart failure.'

Daisy blurted out, 'You mean he was frightened to death?'

'If you want to sensationalise it, then you could say that, but I wouldn't advise on that course of description. Whatever, his heart failed. There will have to be a coroner's hearing and they wouldn't take kindly to you making such fantastic suggestions.'

'Thank you, Doctor Haynes,' said Will as the two officers left the autopsy room and made their way back to the car. Neither of them spoke another word whilst in the hospital, both knew there was much to discuss in the privacy of the car.

'Do you know what, Daisy, I feel a bit peckish after all that. Are you hungry? I could really eat a bacon sarnie.'

Daisy looked at her boss with an air of disbelief. 'Why would you want to do that when we've just been looking at a disembowled corpse? Honestly, boss, you certainly pick your moments.'

Will drove his car out of town and pulled into a lay by on the Beverley Road, where a fast food van was regularly parked. There was no queue and he was soon back in the car munching away on his breakfast.

Daisy meanwhile was looking at her notes. 'Did you hear what the doctor said to us back there? This Roberts bloke was a bit of an oddball. How come he's never been on our radar if he is so odd and how did he get to a position where he was controlling the Crime and Disorder Partnership?'

'I don't know, Daisy, I think we need to speak with Superintendent Clegg about that. He sits on that partnership as well, I think. We need to take Roberts' life apart. Doc Haynes mentioned him hanging around fun fairs and with youths at arcades in the town. What's that all about? I'll tell you what I think, it's an easy way to sell drugs, no one would ever suspect him as a councillor, and even when the Doc fronted him on his behaviour, he produced the perfect excuse, engaging with the youth of the town to look at what problems or issues they faced. I bet he was a bloody dealer and that's what this is all about. Spaced out druggies killed him in his own home? I'm just putting that theory out there, Daisy, it's not that unbelievable.'

The moment they got back to the police station, Will made an appointment to speak with Superintendent Clegg to update him and ask a few questions about the victim. Clegg called them both to his office immediately.

'I don't understand,' said Superintendent Brian Clegg in response to Will's update. 'Allan Roberts was a good fellow. He was honest, Will, not at all offensive and everyone seemed to like him in the partnership. He got things done, particularly for the youth of the town. Yes, he could be a bit vocal in his opinion and that rubbed people up the wrong way, but surely not to the extent that he would be murdered in his own home. This has all the hallmarks of a politically motivated crime, if you ask me. I will speak with the leader of the council and come back to you. I take it the council have been made aware?'

'Err, not yet, sir, we are still awaiting DNA confirmation that it is him. We are 99% certain though.'

'Keep me appraised at every stage, do you understand? I don't want any nasty surprises that could

28

cause political embarrassment. Now get out there and catch me that killer.'

Will stopped as he made his way to the office door. Looking back at the Superintendent who already had the telephone receiver in his hand he said, 'Sir, one more thing before I go, apparently Roberts was a Freemason, so we may need to interview members of the local lodge.'

Before the Detective Inspector could utter another word, Clegg interrupted. 'Before you do anything like that, you contact me first. The last thing we need is bloody complaints from the brotherhood. I'll deal with anything like that, okay.'

Will nodded and left, the Superintendent's response was no less than he anticipated. Clegg had a nickname in the job, Teflon. This was because no crap ever stuck to him, he always made sure someone else was at fault, and first and foremost, protected his own position.

Returning to his office, Will was met by Daisy. 'Boss, we've had it confirmed, the victim is Councillor Allan Roberts. Crime scene forensics also say that no sign of forced entry was made to the property, so Roberts either let his killer in or the killer let themselves in. However, the front door lock doesn't close properly so it may be that it was ajar, meaning anyone could have walked in. Also, it's believed from blood spatter, and the location of body fluids found on the carpet of the lounge, that he was killed while sitting at his desk, probably looking at his laptop computer. Forensics are looking at the laptop now, so we can perhaps find out the time he was last using it, and identify any communications from that.'

Will was deep in thought. 'This is crazy, everyone I talk to tells me this guy was okay, no known enemies and he was honest. Nice people don't get killed like this, do they, Daisy?'

'No, sir, they don't. The press office want to call a media conference, we have to put together the salient facts and send it over to them. We have to keep the state of the body to ourselves.'

An hour later and DI Will Scott was sat in front of a crowded police station office that had been commandeered and transformed into a media briefing room. Dozens of reporters were present and cameras and microphones were all directed towards him.

'Ladies and Gentleman, I can confirm to you this evening, that we are investigating the death of Councillor Allan Roberts at his Bridlington home. Inquiries are at an early stage and we ask for your co-operation in supporting our investigation. We would like anyone who saw Councillor Roberts yesterday afternoon or early evening to come forward and let us know please. All information will be treated with integrity, so please contact us with any details you may have. Thank you. I cannot answer questions at this time since there is little more to tell you. Be assured we will keep you appraised of any progress.'

Will quickly left the room and the barrage of press questions that were eagerly fired towards him. He was shaking, not through nerves, but from exhaustion. He hadn't slept for 24 hours, nor had Daisy.

In his media briefing absence, Daisy had pulled together a team of detectives to work the case. In her opinion, the four chosen officers provided individual policing skills that would enhance the investigation. She knew the boss would agree. The team weren't close, but they were effective and efficient at what they did. She noted down on a sheet of A4 paper their details and left this on Will's desk, with a quick note explaining why each officer was selected:

Detective Sergeant Steve Fletcher - Trustworthy and intelligent, good interrogator

Detective Sergeant Barry Smith - Motivated and a good investigator, trustworthy

Detective Constable Amber Taylor - Exceptionally intuitive, trustworthy

Detective Constable Paula Jay - Rigorous investigator, entirely trustworthy

'Boss, I know you are busy, so I've pulled together this team of officers to support us. You'll see I've put trustworthy by every name. These officers can be relied upon and trusted to work as a team and not to gossip in the canteen or to other officers about the investigation. Steve Fletcher can be trusted to give cover when we are out of office or away. I've told them all that they are to report here to you without delay, and to expect to work long hours until the case is cracked.

Daisy W'

As Will returned to his desk, he saw Daisy and called her over.

'Thank you for doing this, Daisy, when these officers arrive I want them to go to the Senior Officer briefing room, I've been told we can temporarily have this as our base. First things first, I think both you and I need to go home and catch up on some shut eye. I'm knackered and you must be too. Steve Fletcher can keep things ticking over until we report back here later this evening. How do you feel about that?'

'I'm so glad you said that, boss, it's been a stressful 24 hours and I'm shattered.'

Within the hour, the entire team were gathered in the briefing room and the status of the investigation outlined. Everyone was allocated a specific piece of the investigation they were responsible for, and told that no information was to be communicated to officers or persons beyond the team. Will instructed Steve Fletcher to contact him at home should any senior officer ask questions, or if there was any furthers news gleaned from the lines of enquiry being followed. He was specifically not to contact or discuss with the local council any aspect of the case.

Will and Daisy both returned home, buzzing from the adrenalin pumping round their bodies, yet mentally exhausted from the stress of the situation. 'See you later this evening, Daisy, I'm looking to report back here in about eight hours. It'll give us a chance to work things through in our own minds and hopefully by then, we'll have some results from the forensics examination of the laptop. Uniform are doing house to house, so we'll maybe get more from that as well. Anyway, get yourself home and I'll see you later.'

CHAPTER FOUR

Mel had taken the kids out shopping to allow Will to catch up on some hard earned sleep and said she would bring something home for dinner. Will loved the way she was so supportive and caring about him. He had barely dropped off to sleep when his work mobile rang. He reached out and answered it.

'Hello, this is DI Scott.'

It was Steve Fletcher. 'Sir, sorry to bother you, I think you'd better call Detective Superintendent Kilpatrick straight away, he's asking to speak with you directly. It sounds extremely urgent.'

'Sure, okay, I'll do that. You got his pager number Steve? Did he say anything else?'

'No, sir, just that you were to call immediately. He sounded as though he was in a good mood if that means anything? He's on pager 314.'

Will made the call knowing that the DS would be questioning him about all aspects of the case, and reminding him that the first 48 hours are the most important in any investigation.

'Sir, it's me, Will Scott, you okay?'

'Hi, Will, yes, I'm fine. I gather you've got your hands full at the moment with this murder. Are you getting all the support you need from the Divisional Superintendent?'

'Yes, sir, he's fine. It's the Chief Inspector whose acting like a spanner. He's already tried to pull rank about resource issues and uniform overtime budgets. He doesn't seem to understand the practicalities of policing, he's a number cruncher.'

'Well, that's easily sorted. With immediate effect, I'm temporarily promoting you to Detective Chief Inspector, that's backdated pay and pension wise from yesterday when you took control of this case. I will circulate a memo to all senior officers and staff right away. I've spoken with the Chief and he agrees. This is your case, Will. I'm off on holiday for three weeks from tomorrow, so the decisions are all yours. Don't let them bureaucrats grind you down, Detective Chief Inspector Scott. Understand?'

Will wasn't sure what to say, but needed some assurance that he would still be allowed to lead the CID team from the front. 'I don't want to be one of those desk bound Chief Inspectors, boss, pushing paper around all day and with no real purpose. I am at my best out on the ground working with the rank and file, catching crooks.'

'Will, if that's what you want to do, then go ahead, be my guest. I never have liked the rank of Chief Inspector, it's neither something or nothing. A halfway-house which sits uncomfortably on the police landscape. You make the role what you want it to be.'

Will thanked his boss for the opportunity. The call ended. His mind went into overdrive. The promotion was great but he still had a murder case to solve. He was certain that somewhere within Roberts' background there was likely to be something that would help crack the case. The phone buzzed again, this time it was a voicemail message.   'Sir, it's Daisy Wright here, sorry to disturb you, but I can't sleep. I'm heading back into the office now. If anything major comes up I'll call you on your home number. If you need me to come and pick you up later today, let me know. Bye.'

'Fuck it,' Will exclaimed. Daisy wasn't the only one who couldn't sleep. He quickly showered and got dressed before making his way downstairs to the kitchen. Making himself an expresso, he felt restless yet excited.   He needed a reassuring hug from Mel to help gets things into perspective. Promotion and Senior Investigating Officer in a murder case in less than 24 hours, it was too good to believe.

He was pacing around the house, constantly clock watching. The minutes seemed to be dragging by. He recalled a time when a now retired DI had told him that every minute is valuable in a murder investigation, yet here he was, drinking coffee and doing nothing remotely useful to catch Allan Roberts' killer. The decision was made. He had to go back into work.

He picked up the phone and called Mel. 'Darling, it's me, how are you?'

His wife was surprised by the call, she expected him to be sound asleep in bed. 'I'm fine, so are the kids, why are you up?' The sound of his wife's voice gave him a warm feeling inside.

'I can't sleep, there is so much going through my head, and ... guess what? Detective Superintendent Kilpatrick has just rung me, he's given me temporary promotion to the rank of DCI, and I'm being paid at that rate.'

Mel was thrilled by the news and at the same time she was aware that her husband was pushing himself extremely hard, promotion and to be in charge of a murder investigation was of huge kudos. She also knew that Will wouldn't want to let anyone down and would push himself to the very limits. 'Will, that's fantastic news, but listen to me for just a moment. You need to rest. Can you remember the man who told me, I work to live, not live to work? That was you, don't make yourself ill over this murder, please, promise me. You have a wife and two children who love and adore you very much, you mean everything to us, remember that. I know what's coming next, you are going back into work aren't you? Well, listen to me for once, take it steady, don't damage your health over some filthy dead paedo.'

'What did you just say? Paedo, where did you get that from?'

'I met Jenny this morning, she said it to me, apparently some of the local kids called him the kiddie fiddler. It seems it was common knowledge in the town, but no one had the balls to report it. It's probably nothing, Will. The bloke was odd looking and morally very different to most folk, so it's natural, that kids being kids, they pick up on things like that and they give him a nickname. Please tell me you knew all of this?'

Will laughed, 'No, I didn't, not until you just said it. We have very little to go on at the moment and every lead is important, so it's something I can look into. It's like I say, I can't sleep so I'm going to head back into the

37

office, I'll leave the Audi here and get Daisy to pick me up in the work car. Okay, darling, I love you.'

He didn't hesitate to make his next call. It was to Daisy, telling her to come and pick him up from his home straight away.

While he was waiting, he mulled over the paedophile suggestion mentioned by Mel. The more he thought about it, the more unlikely it seemed. Surely a paedophile working in the Crime and Disorder Partnership would have to go through checks and would get noticed? He laughed at the thought of all those high ranking bureaucrats working alongside a paedophile, now that really would be politically and professionally embarrassing for all concerned.

Will recognised the blue Vauxhall GTC as an unmarked police car as it pulled up outside his house. He could see the smiling face of DS Wright behind the wheel. Throwing on his jacket, he rushed out to the car and jumped into the passenger seat. 'What you looking so happy about?' he asked.

'Well, Detective Chief Inspector, I believe congratulations are in order? Fucking hell, boss, that was sudden, wasn't it? The whole nick is talking about it. You are hash tag trending in the canteen gossip. The only one who's not so happy is Chief Inspector Hayes, he's well fucked off by the news. That bloke always struck me as a bit weird. He could be a bloody paedo with those freaky glasses and the curly hair, skinny rake of a man, yuk he makes my skin crawl thinking about him. Have you seen him cycle into work in those lycra shorts? The man's got issues I can tell you.'

Will sat bolt upright, that's twice in the space of a few minutes that the term paedo has come up in conversation, he thought. Dismissing it from his mind, he explained what had happened with his telephone call to DS Kilpatrick. 'I expect we can celebrate once we've got the nutter who killed this councillor banged up,' he responded.

At the Police Station, two booted and suited forensic officers were waiting to speak with Will, one of them was Mark Daniel. 'Detective Chief Inspector Scott, we need to speak with you, it's about this laptop you seized from the crime scene. We've uncovered quite a bit of detail from it. For a start, it's council property. It's been set up by their IT department, so there's confidential information stored on it. Christ only knows why it's not encrypted. Typical council, doing things on the cheap.

'We've also found 41 names listed on a word document, there is no other detail or reason for these names being there, it's simply a list. Curious, don't you think?'

The DCI couldn't see the importance of what forensics were saying. 'Can you get to the point? Why do you think the list so important?'

'Well, ordinarily, it wouldn't be. However, when it's taken in context with what else we have found, then it has a sinister aspect to it.'

The forensic officer spun the laptop screen to face Will. 'Oh, for fucks sake, no. Please no!' he yelled out in anguish. Before him was an image of a naked young child being sexually exploited by Councillor Roberts.

'There's over 5000 similar images on the hard drive. They get progressively more horrific, filth and depravity at its very worst. We think the list might be connected to these photos. I can also confirm that Roberts was looking at a child porn website just before he was killed, this being the last image he viewed.'

'That's fucking sick! Is this for real?' Will pushed the laptop away. 'What about emails and websites, do we have anything there?'

'The odd thing is, the only emails on here relate to council business. The pornographic images and the list are stored in files separate to the council communications. We cannot find any emails sent to anyone on this list, and none of the names seem to be council related.'

Will called Daisy over and pointed to the laptop screen. A look of disgust filled her face. 'You have got to be kidding me? Please, no, that's not real, it can't be! The evil fucking bastard, they're children. Oh God, I wish I'd never looked! That image will remain with me forever.' Holding her hands up to cover her eyes, she let out a scream.

'Might I suggest, Will,' said Mark Daniel, 'that we return to the murder scene and lift the floorboards throughout. I think he's the sort who might have various hiding places around his house, secret places where he stashed his pornographic images.'

'This gives the investigation a whole new dimension. Yes, let's get that done straight away. Get me a full report on the findings from the house examination.'

He moved through to the briefing room where his assembled team were busy compiling information and intelligence from officers on the ground and those carrying out house to house enquiries. Calling for everyone's attention, he said, 'Our victim was a paedophile. There are over 5000 child porn images on the laptop, chances are he's been at it since who knows when. I want us to speak with every nonce in the district. Question them and ask what they know about Roberts' activities. This bastard could be worse than the Murray case we had in the town a few years ago!'

'What was that about boss?' asked Amber Taylor.

'Have you not heard of that case, Amber? Christ that was as bad as it gets. This perv lived in Bessingby. He was well liked in the town, a bit of a character according to many. He was an expert groomer. He had something like 2000 child victims. When police raided his home they found stacks of indecent images and thousands more on undeveloped film. He drugged his victims, stripped them naked and then photographed them in explicit poses. Worst thing about it was that he often wore a mask during the photographic sessions. I think it was similar to the one worn by the killer in the horror film *Friday the 13th*. Murray had written '*Child Killer*' across his mask. It must have been terrifying for those poor kids. Twisted git even photographed himself wearing the mask next to one of his victims. The investigating team thought he had murdered a child, but they never progressed that from being just a belief. Anyway, the bastard was sent down, but not anywhere near long enough.'

'I was part of the Chris Cressey enquiry,' interrupted DS Barry Smith. 'He was another child abuser. He got away with it for donkeys years. Cressey was a sick bastard, a big Hull City supporter as I recall. He groomed kids to come back to his flat where he had CCTV secreted in various rooms. The arsehole filmed himself sexually abusing kids there for years. I was involved in one of the early investigations against him. We could never quite pin anything on him. Social Services were involved. I think there were nine different investigations before we managed to nail the bastard.'

Will Scott broke the flow of the discussion by coughing out loud, 'Christ, Barry, I love the Hull City link, we don't have his sort at Leeds United you know,' he said with a wink. 'Right, that's enough of the anecdotes, let's look at what we know about our killer and his victim. This Roberts bloke seems to have avoided being on our radar, so we are going to have to build a profile on him. Where's a forensic psychologist when you need one? Not the sort of thing we have access to in Bridlington.'

DC Paula Jay was a Leeds lass. She had qualified as a DC in 2013, whilst serving in the West Yorkshire force. Her track record was impeccable, with four Chief Constable commendations already on file for outstanding police work in bringing a gang of armed robbers, operating across the North of England, to justice. Married, with two children, she had diversified her specialism and was now working within the field of Child and Vulnerable Adult Abuse investigations.

As Paula listened to her boss she was searching through house to house enquiry forms that had been returned by the uniform officers.

'Have you got anything for us, Paula?' asked Will.

'Actually sir, I have and it fits with paedophile activity. It appears that some of the neighbours occasionally saw children going to the house. They were varying ages, but it's only guess work, they think the age range was between 5 - 13 years, male and female. Other than that no one seems to have paid too much attention or seen anything suspicious. It seems the whole local councillor thing threw everyone off the scent. Nearly everyone says he was a decent, inoffensive bloke who wouldn't hurt a fly. He had worked hard to sort out anti-social behaviour in the area, using council funded PCSO's. He told one neighbour that he knew everything the police did and that the local Chief Inspector, Pete Hayes, went out of his way to keep him sweet, Hayes was answerable to him as the Crime and Disorder port-folio holder.'

'That last comment doesn't surprise me. Hayes is completely wet when it comes to sucking up to local politicians. Without doubt, he's their bitch,' added Daisy. Everyone laughed at the suggestion, which was closer to the truth than most knew or appreciated.

Paula Jay continued, 'There is one other thing of note boss. You know you said you wanted a forensic psychologist? Well, there just happens to be one living in Beverley. I kind of know her. We met at a prison officer's

43

party last week. She seemed nice enough, a professional sort of woman, I think she said she worked at HMP Wakefield. I have to admit, I don't like talking to shrinks or people of that nature, because I kind of get the impression they are analysing me.'

'You are joking, Paula?' asked Will, 'We genuinely have a working forensic psychologist in the area? I don't want one of those old retired duffers who think they know everything. I need an active skilled professional. Can you get me her contact details, and leave them on my desk.'

'Yes, sir, will do. Do you want me to pay her a visit and speak to her?'

'No, not yet, Paula. That will be a political nightmare trying to get her to work with us, but it's handy to know. I think we would need to speak with the Governor of Monster Mansion to get his permission, and then there's the question of funding, who would pay for her services? All too complicated and time consuming, we haven't got that amount of time to play with, but it's good to know she's there.'

Daisy Wright stood up and moved towards the white board, which had different scribbling covering its surface. These were the independent thoughts on the case, of each officer. Daisy, like a school teacher, wiped the board clean and turned to face the team. 'I have the crime scene photographs. I'm going to put them up here. I want everyone to step up and examine them. Look for anything out of place or suspicious. The house is still sealed off and under police cordon, so nothing will have been removed.   Our killer or killers have acted methodically, they must have been aware of Roberts' movements.   Burglary doesn't appear to have been a motive, the victim's wallet and other valuables were left in the house. So we are looking at Roberts' political and private activities. I've requested full financial background checks, they should be with us within 24 hours. Forensics have stated that there was no sign of drugs or illegal substances within the house.   I've got drugs dogs available if we require them to carry out a search. Then we have this whole paedophile thing. I find it hard to believe that he kept his perverted mind and activities quiet from everyone who knew him. Somebody must have known.

'The first port of call has to be the IT bloke at the council. We want to know when he last checked Roberts' laptop. That individual is a person of interest. Then we have to check out the Masons from the local lodge, is anyone here a member?' No one showed a hand.

'Good, I find that sort of thing a bit peculiar as well, grown men having to be part of gang, it's odd. So we need to check out everyone in that lodge.'

Will stepped forward. 'That includes fellow police officers, including the powers that be. If they are involved in the Masons then they are potentially a source of intelligence. No one escapes our attention. I am going back to the scene with Daisy. We can look through his possessions and when we leave, the drugs dogs can go in again, I don't want us to miss a thing.'

In the background, a phone rang interrupting Will's briefing.

Paula Jay answered it. 'Boss, it's for you, the person has asked for you by name.'

Will took the receiver. 'DCI Scott here.'

'Hi, Will, it's Lucien. DCI, eh? When did that all happen? Congratulations anyway, mate. Have you got any updates for me? I've kept the detail low key in our paper, but I think some of the nationals are trying to big it up. I thought I'd better tip you off. Word on the street is that Roberts was a kinky fucker, into kids seemingly. By the sound of things he's a real piece of work. How come this deviant stuff only comes out when someone dies? Anyway, I have plenty of people willing to speak with me about your victim being a kiddie fiddler, oh, and apparently, he was a good friend of one James Savile. I expect you are getting the same info, so I won't bore you.'

Will took a deep breath before responding, 'I'll call you later, Lucien. Thanks for the tip off.' He slammed down the receiver in frustration.

'For fucks sake, why is it that the local press knows more about our victim than we do? Christ, what have we got here? There's a bloody connection to Jimmy 'fucking' Savile now. The local paper, apparently, have people coming out of the woodwork wanting to talk about Roberts being a kiddie fiddler. Why has none of this come our way? Right, I want you all out there, walking the streets, and gathering real intelligence about our victim. Not fucking speculation, but fact. Paula, Amber, Barry, I want you to speak with every informant you've got, and get in amongst the uniform officers and get them talking to us. We want to know every snippet of information they've got, everything is important now. By the sounds of it, some of tomorrow's national papers are going to lead with this story, so I need more than speculation to tell our governors. I also want someone to do some digging around to find out who, locally, were friends with Jimmy Savile. It might be that if we can find criminal associates then we might find our killer. Come on people, we can do this, I want us to break this case superfast.'

Turning to DS Wright, Will barked a reminder. 'Daisy, you and I are going back to the crime scene. Come on, every minute counts.'

The pressure was seriously on, and suddenly Will felt as if the whole town was working against him. The case was moving at break neck speed, it wasn't being driven by the police, but the media.

CHAPTER FIVE

Back at the crime scene, Will and Daisy were greeted by a PCSO who was stood in the street guarding access to the murder property. He wasn't the greatest example of a professional police officer. He looked more akin to a scruffy bus driver. His cap precariously perched on the back of his head, his shoulders rounded, he was wearing no tie and his hands were stuffed inside his un-pressed trouser pockets. To complete the disinterested look, he was sat slouched on the wooden garden fence of the property. The officer didn't bat an eyelid as the two detectives approached the house.

Daisy was angry by what she saw and marched right up to the PCSO, looking him straight in the face and demanded to know his name, and the reason why he was improperly dressed in his police uniform. The PCSO stuttered and made some attempt to redeem himself by standing up. Offering a lame apology and in justifying his slovenly appearance he used boredom as his excuse. Will shook his head disapprovingly and asked the officer a relevant question. Who has visited the scene during his tour of duty?

'Just the press really, sir. No one has been inside since forensics left three hours ago.'

'Okay,' said Will, 'you need to remember officer that you are representing Eastborough Police Force. Tens of thousands of people are going to see you stood in front of this property on television and in newspapers. They will form an opinion of the entire force by looking at you, so get your fucking hat back on your head properly, put your tie back on, and get your bloody hands out of your pockets. Is that understood?'

'Yes, sir, sorry sir,' said the reprimanded officer.

As the two detectives walked up the short path that led to the bright red wooden front door of Roberts' property, Daisy remained incensed by the PCSO. She commented: 'What a perfect bloody example of a plastic policeman that guy is. I question the validity of some of these PCSO's. They only do it for the money, lazy tossers. Why the hell the Home Office can't just fund more real police officers, I'll never know. Policing on the cheap. It's ironic that Roberts was right behind the PCSO movement, the wanker.'

At the front door, Will produced a key and inserted it into the Yale lock. As the door swung open the smell of blood and burnt flesh filled their nostrils. 'Yuk,' he exclaimed, 'that smell is rancid.'

Before they stepped inside, he said to Daisy, 'I want to check everything in the house. This pervert didn't have those evil images on his computer for fun, he was well into child porn not just as a voyeur, he was an active participant in child sexual abuse. There has to be more evidence somewhere in this shit hole. Forensics will be coming back again to lift and examine the floorboards, so let's get this done before they get here.'

The two officers disappeared inside, closing the front door behind them.

In the entrance hall they saw several coats hanging from a rack. 'Go through his pockets and the linings please, Daisy. I'll go through to the living room, starting from the front window end and working my way to the rear of the room, okay.'

The DCI stepped to his left, passing through an open doorway that led into the lounge. It was clear that the forensics team had gone to town on the house, furniture had been moved and rearranged in the search for vital clues and evidence. Will was pleased by this.

He went through the contents of a wooden writing bureau that housed the dead man's mail and hundreds of pages of laborious minutes from council meetings. He looked through everything but found nothing that resembled a clue or of evidential value. Thereafter, he systematically made his way to the rear of the room and the house arriving at a circular dining room table that stood in front of two locked, double glazed patio doors. The table was covered in papers and spatters of dried blood.

Daisy had joined her colleague at the table having completed a full search of the hall and the upstairs rooms, with nothing to show for it. Both were scanning their eyes over the table when Will suddenly told her to stop.

'Daisy, look, what's that over there?' he was pointing towards a notepad. Carefully Daisy lifted the paper pad from the table, and beneath it they found a small metal, silver angel figure. 'It's a trinket of some sort, I think,' said Daisy holding the tiny object in the palm of her right hand and offering it to the DCI.

'It seems a little out of place don't you think? Why would he have something like this, do you think he might have removed it from a child, or maybe used it as some kind of grooming tool?'

'I'm not sure, boss, but you are right, it doesn't fit in with everything else in this place. He doesn't seem the type to collect angel trinkets. I'll bag it as evidence anyway, sir, it might open up new lines of enquiry,' she replied.

The chair on which Roberts had been tortured before his death was a grim reminder of what had happened in this room. It was now covered in dried blood and had scratch marks on each arm, presumably made by Roberts' finger nails as he was in the throws of agony.

Will moved the chair to one side and bent down to look inside the small cupboard of a dated wall unit which stood near the table. He removed several books and a photograph album.

'What have we here?' Will asked in a suspicious tone.

'It's covered in fingerprint dust boss so forensics must have checked it out,' Daisy commented.

Will flipped the large hard backed album cover open. Quite incredibly, the page it fell open at displayed photographs of Allan Roberts standing with the late Jimmy Savile and other town dignitaries. There was one black and white image in particular that leapt out at both officers. It showed Savile and Roberts standing together in a room, in the background there were children, the look upon each and every face of the children was not one of joy or happiness, but rather of fear and sadness.

'Boss, those children, look at their expressions - the whole group were clearly frightened by something or someone. The photographer certainly didn't ask these kids to say 'cheese' when he took this photo. What the hell would cause them to look like that?'

'Bloody hell, Daisy, it's a terrible image. We'll take this with us. I wonder if we can identify any of the kids in the photograph, or maybe the place where it was taken. Could it be local?'

Both officers were overcome with a feeling of absolute sadness and grief. Will placed a reassuring arm around his colleagues shoulder and told her that she didn't have to be strong, she needed to let go of her emotions if she could. Both officers cried at the thought of the horrors that those, and many more little children had endured at the hands of Allan Roberts and other sick individuals just like him. 'Come on, Daisy, let's get back to the station and see what the rest of the team have got for us.'

Daisy replaced the paper tissue she had been using to wipe her eyes clear of tears, into her bag and offered a suggestion to the DCI, who was likewise drying his eyes.

'I do wonder, sir, whether this is the first time our killer has taken someone's life? It all seems a bit too personal for my liking. Why go to the extent of torturing him so much, unless Roberts knew something that was valuable to someone else? It doesn't add up. The killer must have known Roberts' movements and felt comfortable that he wouldn't be disturbed during the attack. If that is the case, then it's likely to be a local and maybe a family member of one of his victims, do you think?'

'That's good thinking, Daisy,' said Will as he stepped out of the dark house and inhaled the fresh Yorkshire air, clearing the aroma of death from his nostrils.

'Raise that during the briefing at the nick. Don't forget though, with the amount of transient tourists, visitors etc to the town, it could be any one of those people, or maybe a few of them acting together. Our killer or killers aren't necessarily local.'

The PCSO stood to attention as the two detectives walked past him, he threw up a lame attempt at a salute. Will stopped and addressed him. 'Excuse me, officer, just so you know, you salute the uniform not individuals. Thanks for the effort anyway, glad to see you are dressed more correctly,' said Will with a wink as he walked away.

Back at Bridlington Police station, the investigation team gathered to provide their individual situation reports, better known in police circles as 'sit-reps.' It soon became evident that Councillor Allan Roberts was abusing his position as a member of the local authority, in gaining access to local schools and clubs used by younger children. Worse still, he had played 'Santa Claus' at several council Christmas parties. There were countless images of him dressed in Santa's festive attire, with children, and mothers, sat on his knee.

The council IT officer who was responsible for the issue and servicing of laptops for everyone within the local authority had explained to a detective how Councillor Roberts always made excuses when his laptop was required for council network updates. Roberts had not handed his computer back since the date of issue, five years previously. The officer justified this by saying 'he was rushed off his feet and it had been an oversight.' This oversight became more of a huge failure when it was later highlighted during the investigation, that a total of seventeen council laptops were unaccounted for. In the council officers own words, 'they had simply gone missing, or were more likely, stolen by thieving council officers and politicians. You can't leave anything of any value in the council offices, because someone is guaranteed to nick it.'

The leader of Eastborough Council requested that this information should remain confidential since it portrayed councillors and council staff as being dishonest. Revealing such behaviour 'would damage the very fabric upon which society is based,' he claimed. Will, along with the rest of his team, laughed at the suggestion that anyone in today's society took local councils as being genuine or honest.

'It certainly isn't going to help when they find out that one of their most experienced councillors is a bloody paedophile,' muttered Will.

Meanwhile, full reports had been received from forensics and from the police surgeon that helped determine Roberts' death. Will studied the documents, which made grim reading. He skim read the salient points to his team.

'Two small circular spots were found in the hairline on the back of his neck. These were taser marks from a stun gun that had temporarily incapacitated Roberts, who had been sat with his back to the entrance door into the lounge from the hall. He had been sat at his desk using his laptop computer. Research into the computer's history dictated that he had been looking at Category A child abuse images at the time of the attack. The killer had entered through the front door, which had a faulty latch and was probably open. There were no other possible means of entry since, other than the front door, the house was secure.

The victim had slumped forward in his seat and a second bout of electricity had been thrust into his nervous system causing further paralysis. The perpetrator had worked quickly and efficiently, first stripping him and then restricting his movement by cable tying his wrists to the arms of his chair, and his ankles to the chair legs, his mouth was filled with cotton wool as he was gagged with gaffer tape to prevent him from crying out. His attacker then began the torture. First nailing his hands to the arms of the wooden framed chair quickly followed by nailing his feet to the floorboards. Next, his genitals and penis were removed causing him to go into a state of shock. Removing the gagging material, the killer had replaced the cotton wool with his testicles, forcing him to eat and digest them. This was followed by his penis which had been forced between his teeth. His jaws had been forced tightly closed, leaving bite marks on the penis which remained in his mouth.

A stainless steel cheese grater had then been used to damage his skin, slicing chunks of it away and exposing bloody flesh beneath on his chest. The face received the same treatment, the wounds to his body and face were then bathed in petrol. The eye lids were stapled open and wooden barbecue skewers had been forced into each eyeball, sufficiently to cause blindness and not pervade beyond the back of the eyeball. Finally, the skewers, which had also been doused in petrol, were lit, probably with the kitchen blow torch when it was used to burn the flesh. Each of the injuries were endured while the victim was alive. Time of death was estimated at around 8.30pm. The entire episode was likely to have taken no more than twenty minutes. Semen stains were located on the carpet throughout the crime scene. All samples were analysed and belonged to the victim. The most recent sample had been deposited at around 4.30pm on the day of the crime. Historical traces of semen had also been found on the computer keyboard. The computer had been taken offline and the 'documents' folder had been accessed by someone, presumably the killer, at 8.55pm on the day of death. The list of names that remained visible on the screen had been added two months earlier. There does not appear to be any obvious link between the names, certainly not locally. The list might well be unconnected to the crime.'

With the room in total silence, Daisy Wright seized the opportunity to discuss her findings and theory. 'The findings from the medical and forensic reports seem to justify my belief that this attack was personal. The killer took way too much time in torturing Roberts, so it sounds very much like a revenge attack. It's possible that the killer knew him and, dare I say it, had a serious grudge against him. We know that the victim in his capacity as a

Councillor, had opposed the opening of an Eastern European fast food outlet in the town, his objections had prevented the business from trading. At an open council meeting, one of the owners of the business was sat in the public gallery, and on hearing his application fail, he shouted abuse and placed a curse on Councillor Roberts. The leader of the council had brought the meeting to a halt, while the man was escorted from the premises. And, guess what? No one from the council thought about letting us, the police, know of this matter. It wasn't even reported in the local press. I guess this Eastern European guy has to be of interest to us, so we need to ascertain very quickly, who he is and where he is.'

Will Scott resumed ... 'I want checks carried out on this person ...'

'Sir, sir, can I interrupt your flow for a moment please,' said DC Amber Taylor. 'I've got the name of that suspect here in front of me. It's on the applications area of the council website and I've run him through Interpol. His name is Viktor Klimes, date of birth: 31.08.1955, a Czech. He is 6'2", weighs 17 stone, and has a scar on the left side of his face from a knife attack in 2006. He has previous for sexual assault x 2, rape x 2 and one count of murder.'

'What? How the fuck is he walking the streets of Bridlington, let alone setting up a business here? Right, he sounds like he could be a serious suspect. Get Interpol and Europol to send through everything they have got on this Klimes fella, and any images they have of him. We need to track him down immediately.'

'Sir, sir,' Amber was holding her hand up again for attention like an excited schoolgirl who knew the answer to a problem. 'I have his address here, too, he's local, in Skipsea.'

'Amber, you're an absolute star,' said DCI Scott.

'Right, let's get firearms involved, and dog handlers. I'll ring the Deputy Chief Constable and give him an update and get his authorisation to deploy at the same time. Let's go get our killer, people.'

Will and the whole team were excited by the quickness of the breakthrough.

With all the force notifications made, and authorities granted, within half an hour, the smart semi-detached house in Skipsea was effectively surrounded by police officers. Moments later, the front door of the house was breached by heavily protected uniformed officers in body armour. The peaceful village was stunned into life, by the sounds of barking police dogs and shouting. 'Police! Police! Armed Police! Drop your weapons!'

A team of officers filed in through the front of the property, inside, there was no sign of life. However, it was clear that someone lived at the address, that someone was very quickly identified as Viktor Klimes.

'It's all clear boss,' reported the lead officer of the entry team on his police radio. 'There's no one here.'

Moments later a uniformed officer protecting the outer scene called in on his radio. 'All units, all units, I have the named suspect in custody. I am on the village green. He's been in the village pub, not armed, but I am requesting back up.'

On arrival of police back up, Klimes, who was far uglier than his police photographs credited, became agitated and violent. He was restrained, handcuffed, put into the rear of a police detention vehicle and transported to Bridlington police station for further questioning. Within minutes, a team of forensic officers were combing through his home, seeking vital evidence or clues that might link him to the murder of Allan Roberts. Will advised the search team that he would hold the suspect in police custody awaiting the outcome of that search which would assist in their interrogation and questioning.

Two hours later, Will received the call he had been waiting for, the news wasn't good.

'DCI Scott, its forensics here. Along with your uniform officers, we've completed the house search of the Skipsea address. It's negative, I'm afraid. There is nothing to directly link your prisoner with the Bridlington murder. In fact, I would say his property was 100% clean of any criminality whatsoever.'

'Okay, thanks.' Will replaced the handset and felt a heavy wave of disappointment engulf him. He looked up to see a dozen uniform and detective officers looking directly at him, all waiting to hear the news from Skipsea.

'He's clean. The house gave up nothing, so we will have to interview him based on our suspicions. Daisy, can you and Barry interview the prisoner right away please?'

Barry Smith had spent 15 years serving in the Royal Military Police before joining the Eastborough force in 2009. He moved into CID in 2013. He was a resilient, reliable, no nonsense sort of detective, who, in his short time in the Police, had received three individual Chief Constable's commendations, one of which was for bravery. Like most police officers, he had a serious dislike for offenders who were active in the world of child abuse. He always said it as it was, wearing his heart on his sleeve, he was open in his opinions of certain types of criminal.

'Daisy, Barry, explain to the custody officer that the delay has been caused as a result of a property search, and that we had to wait for the outcome of that search. Make sure you cover the threats in the Council Chambers at the public meeting when his application was rejected. We need to know his connections locally and where he was at the time of Roberts' death. Keep it brief and to the point please, and keep me updated if he coughs to anything, even a sodding parking ticket.'

Will returned to his desk and contacted the force control room, and the respective Senior Duty Officers, updating them with details of the incident and investigation. With the calls complete, he sat down with a cup of black coffee and reflected on the evidence available. He desperately tried to read his own gut instinct, but was unable to sense, with any conviction, that Klimes was their man. Sat there, he contemplated what the killer was doing at that very moment, worried, and in all probability, looking over his shoulder, he mused. His eyes felt dry through tiredness, he had been on the go and without sleep for the best part of two days now. However, he had a suspect in custody and plenty more potential leads to follow.

CHAPTER SIX

Sat at his desk and staring blankly into space, Will somehow knew he was going to have to concede that currently there was insufficient evidence to hold Viktor Klimes in custody and that he would have to be bailed pending further enquiries. That in itself was problematic since the likelihood was that Klimes would flee the country. Will hoped that the two detectives would be able to break him down and get a confession.

The telephone on the desk next to his burst into life causing Will to snap out of his deep thoughts. He answered, 'DCI Scott speaking.'

Will was surprised to hear a voice he recognised but was unable to put a name to.

'Hello, DCI Scott, this is Stuart Levy, leader of the local authority here. I understand that there may be some suspicious background to Councillor Roberts' lifestyle. That he was an active paedophile and in addition, you have found graphic child pornography on his laptop. We really don't need a scandal like this getting out, so can I ask that you don't put it into the public domain?'

'How have you become aware of this?' asked the DCI.

'Superintendent Clegg just called to let me know, how else do you think I'd get to know? You are aware that you are playing with serious politics here. I'll have to make the Conservative Party Leader and the Prime Minister aware. The first thing she'll ask is if it's likely to cause a scandal and how it might affect her position. I can tell you here and now, she'll demand that all scandalous talk is suffocated. She will want to entirely disassociate herself from Allan Roberts, and a statement will be crafted to distance herself from him and the case. I'm certain she will say, that you, as in the police, will receive all the support you need to solve the murder. What I'm dictating to you is, make sure you and your team don't have loose lips. Allan Roberts will be a sacrificial scapegoat, there will be no digging around looking for any other dirt to dish on the council, do you understand what I'm telling you? Back off.'

Will was shocked by the content of the outburst. He had previously heard tales of how the establishment closed ranks when faced with scandal, however, he had never believed such stories to be true. He felt resentment at being told how to conduct a police investigation.

'Councillor Levy, I won't have you, or the Prime Minister telling me how to do my job. I can't control how the press might report and comment on the case. Please be assured that none of my officers have, or will, leak any details about this case until it's heard at trial.'

'Thank you, DCI Scott,' said Levy ending the call with no further comment.

Cheeky bastard, thought Will, how dare he think he can control me, and why the fuck was the Superintendent telling him confidential information about the investigation?

Will was seriously tired, he needed to go home to see his wife and children. He needed a comforting hug from Mel. With a suspect in custody and about to be interviewed, he seized the window of opportunity to go home and give himself some head space away from the investigation.

A few hours later, having gone home, hugged, showered and eaten, the time taken away from the police station helped him put matters in perspective. He returned to his office, full of motivation and renewed enthusiasm. He had managed to snatch a couple of hours sleep and felt refreshed. The interviewing officers had completed their interrogation of Viktor Klimes. They couldn't break him down and having checked out his alibi, he said he was with friends in Rothwell, Northamptonshire, at the time the murder happened, found this to be true. Albeit, he did say during the interview that he wasn't sad that Councillor Roberts was dead, since his bullying of fellow council members, to get them to oppose his application to open a business, had effectively stopped him from providing for his family. Roberts, he claimed, was a racist and anti-East Europeans. Viktor Klimes was released on police bail.

The investigation team regrouped in the briefing room of Bridlington Police Station. Will instructed Daisy to go home and rest, and if she could, catch up on her sleep.

'I need every one of us to be at the top of our game throughout this investigation, so make sure that you all take regular breaks, and keep DC Taylor aware of your movements. Klimes might not be our man, but he sure as hell has associates in this area, some of whom are capable of murder, so we need to clarify their movements now.'

Will was interrupted by a uniform officer who burst into the room.

'DCI Scott, you have to call DI Bell at Driffield, as a matter of urgency,' said the nervous looking constable, 'There's been another one, another murder.'

The briefing room fell quiet as Will made the call.

'Hello, Will, its DI Jack Bell here. I understand you are heading the murder investigation in your area, the Divisional Commander has told me to contact you and ask that you attend the crime scene here. I don't know whether they are connected or if the modus operandi is similar, but I can tell you, this is a gruesome piece of work. I've not seen anything like it in twenty years of coppering.'

'Christ, Jack! What is the location of the crime and have you called forensics?'

'Sure have,' said DI Bell as though dealing with a murder was a normal procedure for him. 'The victim is a single white male, a local school teacher. He is not known to the police. His name is Charles Peter Hooton, DoB: 18.07.1970, in Stockport, Cheshire. Seems he moved here five years ago to take up the teaching role. Neighbours say he was a bit of a loner, no girlfriend or boyfriend, just kept himself to himself.'

'Okay, I'll be with you in half an hour, Jack, and we can take it from there. I doubt the murders are linked, timescales are too close, but it's right that I view the body and the crime scene.'

Will looked at his team, and glanced towards Daisy in particular.

'It's another murder and the powers that be want me to go to the crime scene in case they are linked. Daisy, you look shattered, I told you to go home. Barry, you come with me to Driffield. Steve, can you see about getting some additional resources and man power support while I'm gone. It might just be that we have to pick up this additional murder as a matter of course, so we'll need extra resources to cover. Ring Superintendent Clegg please and get his authority and can you update him for me?'

Will and DS Barry Smith left Bridlington and made their way to the murder scene in Driffield, which was situated on the eastern peripheries of the town. Curiously, it was on the road to Skipsea. Both officers were quiet throughout the thirty minute journey, each of them consumed with thoughts of the initial murder on their own patch. As they pulled up to the scene, the area was typically flooded with nosy people and uniform police officers, most of whom seemed to be wandering around aimlessly. The house at the centre of the crime scene had been taped off and had a police dog and handler stood by the access gate. The two Bridlington officers parked up nearby, and approached the property on foot. They were met by a tall, bearded man, wearing designer glasses and a well cut suit. He was a well-groomed individual with a confident manner.

'DCI Scott,' said Jack Bell, shaking Will's outstretched hand, 'I hate to say this, but this body is a real bloody mess. This isn't a spur of the moment murder, it's been carefully planned, the killer has spent some considerable time with the victim to achieve the level of mutilation he has. I hope you aren't squeamish, because what's on display in there is going to turn your stomach.'

'Thanks, Jack. No need to tell me anymore, it's doesn't do to embellish the crime scene. I'll take a look and judge for myself.'

Will approached the forensics crime scene manager. It was the same officer, Mark Daniel, that had covered the Bridlington crime scene. 'How are you, Will?' he enquired.

'I'm good, Mark, how's yourself? What have we got this time? Are both murders linked, do you think?'

'Too right they are, Will, although this time, the killer or killers have been a bit more creative in the damage inflicted on the victim's body. Poor bastard, I can't even begin to imagine how much he suffered.'

He handed Will a Tyvek suit and another to Barry Smith. Both officers dressed quickly and were guided through the crime scene by Mark.

'It looks as though the victim let the killer in, since there is no sign of forced entry throughout. The rear of the premises are locked and secure.'

Moving through the hall, they entered the kitchen of the house. There was no sign of disturbance in here, but two mugs had been placed on the worktop as though a drink was being prepared. As they left the kitchen, an all too familiar smell filled the air, it was burnt flesh. Barry Smith was unaware what the smell was and commented, 'I think he may have eaten a bacon sandwich, can you smell that?'

Will put his detective right, explaining that it wasn't bacon but human flesh.

As they turned into the lounge, they saw the remains of Charles Hooton laid out on the floor in front of them. Barry Smith reacted badly, and pushed Will out of the way as he darted back into the kitchen where he threw up in the white plastic sink.

The scene was indeed grim. Hooton lay on his back, his trousers and underpants had been pulled down to his ankles. Blood covered the entire genital area. His hands were folded across his chest. The skin from each finger had been sliced from its very tip down to the hand knuckle, there it had been peeled back to form collectively, what looked like a bloody flower. His lips had been removed from his face, exposing his yellowing teeth which bore the appearance of neatly lined up rows of sweetcorn. As with the Bridlington body, the eyelids had been stapled open, and two wooden skewers had been forced into each eyeball. These had burnt down so much that just an inch or so protruded from each eye ball.

Will looked towards Mark Daniel. 'Is there anything in his mouth?'

'I haven't looked, but the testicles and penis are missing. They have been crudely removed, this time with a pair of blunt scissors,' he said, pointing to the heavily bloodstained instruments laying on the carpet nearby.

'Can you look in his mouth please, it's important.'

'No, I can't. Sorry, Will, you need the pathologist or an authorised medic to do that.'

Barry Smith had composed himself and returned to the corpse and interjected the conversation. 'Boss, the police doctor is here, he could look.'

The doctor obliged, prizing open the dead man's jaws, revealing the tongue, this had been split in two, straight down the middle, causing the muscle to fork.

'No penis?' asked Will.

'Not in his mouth,' replied the doctor.

'Where is the smell of burning flesh coming from, I can't see any sign of burning flesh on the body itself? It appears to be restricted to his hair,' asked Will.

'Maybe your killer has taken the penis as a trophy,' said Mark Daniel.

The doctor pointed out that there was an excess of blood on the carpet, too much to have bled from the visible wounds. 'I think there may be injuries to the back of the body,' he commented. 'Shall I roll it over and take a look?'

'As long as forensics have done with crime scene photographs. We will need to take a look and photograph the back too,' replied Will.

The body was gently rolled onto its side, exposing a huge area of burnt skin on the back. Yellow puss covered the open wounds. The smell of human excrement filled the group's nostrils.

'What the hell is that? asked Barry. 'He's shit himself, it's still coming out of his backside,' he said, pointing to the victim's anal area.

The doctor looked more closely at this region and observed. 'The sphincter has been sliced open. I think you'll find that's his penis protruding from it. Well, it's made it easy for me to pronounce life extinct anyway,' he added sarcastically.

Mark Daniel asked everyone to leave and instructed his crime scene photographer to capture images of the back of the victim's body.

'Will, I think you are dealing with a double murder. I can only conclude at this stage that the man has been overpowered here, in this room. The blood spatter on the carpet and wall dictates that the attack occurred on this spot. We will systematically search the property for fingerprints, alien DNA and points of interest. It's going to take at least 24 hours, maybe 36 before I can get a report to you, will that be okay?'

'Yes, do what you can and keep me updated please, Mark,' said Will as the police officers made their way out of the house.

Outside, Mark asked Jack Bell to contact his Divisional Commander and to update him on the situation. 'I'll ring the Deputy Chief Constable and ask about overall command of the murder investigation. We urgently need resources and support staff if this is a double murder.'

The telephone call with the DCC was as Will had imagined. The senior officer didn't want to get physically involved in the investigation, and instructed Will that he was to take overall command of both murder investigations, forming them into one team, especially so since the killers MO dictated that both victims met their fate by the same or similar hands. Resources would be provided by the various sub-divisions, with the most appropriate officers being designated to the team.

'I will have your resources in place by 9am tomorrow morning. Will, you will operate out of Bridlington and answer to me only. If anyone in this force objects, then direct them to me,' confirmed the DCC. 'I suggest you go home and get some rest before tomorrow morning's briefing,' he added before ending the call.

As he walked back to the unmarked police car, Will felt like the weight of the world was on his shoulders. Barry Smith asked if he was okay and if there was anything he could do.

'No, thanks for asking though, Barry. It looks like we have a double murderer on the loose, and we haven't yet got a motive for these killings. Whoever this guy is, he has to be some sort of psychopath to inflict that much pain on a living human being. We maybe need a psychological profiler to help us. Like they are ten a penny in Bridlington,' he said with a note of anguish in his voice.

'Actually boss, didn't DC Jay say there was one living in Beverley? Maybe we should have a word with her to see what the protocols are for employing her to work for us. Whoever is committing these murders is seriously unhinged, so how are they camouflaging this lunacy? Surely they should be sticking out like a sore thumb?'

'Good thinking, Barry. I'll pay her a visit for an informal chat tomorrow morning, I think. We can take it from there, let's hope that there won't be too much bureaucratic shit to jump through.'

As both officers entered the briefing room, every telephone in the room was ringing. Everyone but the telephone on Will's desk, which had rang just twice, and both calls had been to report a murder. 'It's been like this for the last half hour,' said Steve Fletcher. 'Fucking nightmare. Everyone wants to speak with you, boss. What's going on?'

Will's response was short and concise. 'We are in battle with the devil himself, that's what is going on. Hell has descended on Eastborough.'

CHAPTER SEVEN

The murder incident room temporarily closed down at 7.00p.m. that night. Tomorrow was a new day, bringing an increase of fresh resources and inquisitive minds to the double murder investigation. Will advised his current team to go home, switch off and chill out. He wanted his officers back in the office at 7.30 a.m., well in advance of the new team members, so that a full and comprehensive briefing could be delivered to all officers.

'I'm giving you each a different area of responsibility, so it will be your role to keep me updated and of any new lines of enquiry. Daisy, will be working alongside me, and after tomorrow's briefing, we'll be paying a visit to this forensic psychologist in Beverley, to see how, or if, we can get her on board. I'm hopeful that forensics will get back to me tomorrow morning with either a report or at least an update. There's sure to be some alien DNA at the scene. Well done guys for all your efforts so far, see you all tomorrow morning.'

Will advised the control room and duty officers that the murder incident room was closed for the night. However, he was available by pager and work mobile in case of emergency only.

Having left his car at home, Will took a taxi home that night. He now regretted not driving into work. The journey home was a quiet one and the taxi driver barely spoke, other than to ask for the fare. The early evening traffic had quietened down and the taxi breezed through the drizzly rain that had descended on Bridlington town centre. The taxi's windscreen wiper screeching with every stroke kept Will awake. His mind was entirely focused on the dreadful state of the two victims and what type of person could commit such a horrific crime against another human being. The second victim, Hooton appeared to be a clean living professional, if the murders were connected, then what could the motive for that crime be? He had barely run through those thoughts when the taxi pulled up outside his home.

Mel came out of the front door to greet him, smiling from ear to ear, she was pleased to have her husband home. Looking at him getting out of the taxi, she was reminded how handsome he was, his broad shoulders carried many burdens, not least those of keeping the streets of Bridlington safe. Will smiled at Mel and gave her a healthy embrace, hugging her tightly and gently kissing her soft smooth neck.

'I've missed you, darling,' he said.

'I've missed you too, Will. You must be exhausted! I'll run a nice warm bath for you. Maybe we can send out for an Indian home delivery, then settle down together for an early night in bed?' Mel replied.

Will nodded in agreement. 'Sounds wonderful.'

Mel poured Will a large glass of wine and asked if he wanted to talk. Taking the glass he took a sip and closed his eyes savouring the wonderful flavours of the Shiraz.

'Well, we've got two murders now, judging by the state of the bodies, they were killed by the same person. We haven't officially confirmed that. One of the dead men is a school teacher, goes by the name of Hooton.

Not sure what school he teaches at, but he's clearly upset somebody to be butchered like he was.'

Mel stopped in her tracks, and returned a look of shock to Will.

'Hooton, did you say?'

'Yes, Charles Peter Hooton. He was about 46 years old I think.'

'Will, Ellie's form teacher is called Charles Hooton. We've met him before. Surely you remember? It was at a parents teachers meeting we attended. I told you I didn't like the look of him. He looked like a bit of a perv! You ended up talking to him for ages - he supported Leeds, that's why you liked him.'

Will frowned before mental recognition caused his eyes to widen into a stare, 'I remember the bloke you mean now. No, it can't have been, the fella I'm thinking of didn't look at all like the dead body I've just seen, I would have recognised him.' Reflecting on the ghastly state of the Driffield body, Will realised what a ridiculous statement he had just made. 'Well, at least I don't think it was him, but then again it might be.' The thought that his family had a loose connection to this murder gave Will a sense of ill feeling. He went upstairs and looked in on Ellie and Danny, both were pretending to be asleep, but the thought of dad being home was so exciting that sleep could wait just a little longer, at least until after they had seen him and he had told them both about his day and they had told him how school was. Will enjoyed telling his children exciting adventure stories that he had made up. The thrill of seeing them taking every word in, then, as his voice softened, watching them fall asleep was one of the best feelings in the world for him. His stories were good, and always ended on a moral high, so it was educating Ellie and Danny too.

With the kids asleep, Will slipped into the piping hot bubble bath that Mel had prepared for him. It was a good feeling, and he let the warmth envelop his body as he relaxed and laid back, keeping his head just above the bubbles. Mel popped her head round the bathroom door, 'I've ordered your favourite, Garlic Chilli Chicken, is that okay? The food should be here in fifteen minutes.' Will could hardly speak and instead of doing so he gently nodded his head to acknowledge his wife. He felt supremely lucky to have met and married his soul mate, she had the knack of knowing what he was thinking and at times she protected him when he was feeling low or upset. He smiled to himself as he recalled how Mel was able to put life into perspective, no matter how great the trauma, she was able to come up with positive solutions. There wasn't an ounce of ill feeling or bitterness in her body. He liked that about her, she didn't judge people.

The sound of the door bell ringing snapped Will back into reality, that must be the food he thought to himself as he stood up in the bath tub and began to dry himself on a fluffy blue towel that had been left out for him by Mel. Rushing through to the bedroom, he threw on his favourite set of Batman pyjamas, bought for him by the kids, slipped into his dressing gown and meandered down to the kitchen. Mel was serving up the food, it was a huge plateful and it smelled delicious.

After dinner, the couple, as they always had, washed and dried the dishes before they retired to their bed. Will had love on his mind, Mel was more practical and was concerned about him getting a good night's sleep, and up and ready for work the next morning. In bed, Will watched his wife undress and put on her nightie, 'You are so beautiful,' he proffered. Mel laughed and called him a 'charmer' before advising him that nothing was going to happen between them that night. She slid into bed beside him, gave him a loving hug and kissed him gently on the lips, Will was almost asleep. She gave him another kiss on the cheek as his head sank into the pillow and his breathing grew deep, a sure sign he was drifting off into his own dream world.

The erratic sound of the noisy alarm on Mel's I-phone dragged them both from a deep sleep. Will sat up, thinking it was a telephone ringing, he was up, out of bed and looking for his own mobile, which, by accident, had remained in his jacket pocket along with the work pager and mobile. Almost apologetically, he removed them from his jacket and looked at each of them. He was relieved to see that there were no missed calls or messages. It was 6.45 a.m. Mel went downstairs to prepare some breakfast, while Will showered and dressed. Over breakfast he barely spoke a word, his mood was serious, as he considered the days that lay ahead. As usual, Mel told him to stay safe and to let her know if he was going to be late.

'I'll do that,' he said. 'I think it's going to be really busy today, so I'll ring or leave you a message. I've got about twenty officers working on the murders from today, so it should be less for me to physically do, I'm going to be delegating boy today,' he said with a grin. Mel was sat at the breakfast bar, Will bent over her and kissed her cheek and reached out his hand to gently and sensually caress hers, lightly stroking it with his fingertips.

'That's enough of that, Will Scott,' she said, 'now get yourself off to work and catch that bloody murderer.'

Will laughed at the suggestion, gave Mel one big kiss on the lips, and left the house.

Mel heard the Audi fire up outside, followed a few seconds later by the crunching sound of the car's tyres rolling over the gravel. Will was gone. She couldn't help but feel a little bit special, after all, not many wives could tell their husband to go to work and catch a murderer.

CHAPTER EIGHT

The briefing room at the police station was busy. Daisy, Amber and Paula had got into work early and had created individual whiteboards covering what they knew about both victims. This included graphic images from the death scenes and the last confirmed sighting and movements, associates and details of their personal lives. A third, and potentially the most important whiteboard on display remained blank, except for the word 'Suspect' which had hurriedly been scrawled across its top.

As he walked into the room Will felt focused and ready for the challenge that lay ahead. He announced his arrival with a friendly 'Good morning all, how are we today? Wow, you've been busy. This looks great, and you've got a timeline together, too.' He was genuinely pleased and as a reward got teas from the canteen and brought them back for each team member who was gathered around.

'Have we had anything new come in overnight?' he queried. Daisy responded by pointing to a thick paper file that lay on a desk at the front of the room.

'That's what we got overnight, boss. We have more details about the victim Hooton. He worked at the local secondary school, there's nothing about him on our systems, he seems clean enough. Plus, we've had that photograph from the Roberts crime scene looked into, it was taken at a Council Christmas Party held in Scarborough. That's why Savile was pictured in it. He had a house there and was big friends with some of the local key decision makers. I've passed it onto the right people at the National Crime Agency, they can check it out, it's doubtful that it holds any connection to our murders. They said they will let us know if anything does come up that might assist us.'

Paula Jay interrupted, 'Hooton might be clean, but clean people don't generally suffer the sort of death he endured. I'm sure once we can get into the school and speak to his colleagues and staff we might find something dark and sinister about him.'

Will spoke to DC Jay. 'Paula, I want you to pursue that line of inquiry today. Speak with the head teacher first, try to take a look at his personnel file and get as much detail as you can. Once we have that and we can confirm it is him, then contact the local police for their area and get them to pass on the death message to his family. We'll need to speak with them at some point, to see if they can shed any fresh information on known enemies or anyone who would want to hurt their son. I'll leave it to you, Paula, okay. Don't worry about this morning's briefing, if you can get onto that straight away, please.'

Paula nodded her head in recognition of understanding the brief and made her way to the school. Twenty minutes later, DC Jay was sat in the head teacher John Bett's office of the girls school. She had been professional and careful in everything she said. Somehow, she felt uncomfortable by Mr Betts' demeanour. He seemed altogether too confident and full of himself. He was eyeing her up and down and flirting with her. Paula used this to her advantage, and she was soon noting down the professional history of Charles

Hooton. Betts was a middle-aged, bald man with an excuse for a goatee beard and pencil thin moustache. His most memorable feature being his bow legs. 'Couldn't stop a pig in a passage,' she thought to herself. Betts was keen to volunteer much information about how popular Hooton had been among the pupils and staff, though there had been a recent allegation made against him that he felt was without foundation.

'What was the allegation, Mr Betts?'

The head teacher suddenly looked and acted nervously. 'Well, you know what young girls are like, they get a crush on their teacher, you know, fancy him. They fantasize and make things up. All perfectly normal behaviour.'

'Carry on, Mr Betts, please tell me more,' said the detective with an almost sarcastic tone to her voice.

'It seems that one of the girls had been out late at night, after school you know the girls tend to play together, they are teenagers and they want to act like adults. This girl, Elizabeth, she had been out very late for three nights in succession. When her parents asked where she had been she told them she had been with Mr Hooton. Highly irregular and most unlikely. They complained to me, so I spoke with Charles and he of course denied it. I have to say I believe him too. This girl, Elizabeth Bower, she's more than a bit untrustworthy in my opinion. The whole family seem to have issues.'

'Has there been any other complaints of a similar nature against him?'

'Actually, yes.   One of the teachers approached me last week as she felt he was too personal with a pupil, an 11 year old called Becky Jones. The teacher thought he was too touchy feely, but you know he's young, he can associate with this age group, it probably wasn't anything untoward.'

'Okay, thank you, Mr Betts. I'll need to speak with the teacher and the parents of Elizabeth Bower, so can you give me their address and contact details please.'

'Yes, sure, officer, speak to my secretary in the other office, she will supply you with all the details you require. Is it possible we can keep this out of the press for half a day please, I'll need to inform the school governors?'

'I doubt it. I think you'll find the local press are already running something on it.   We won't be making any comment until we know more detail, so please don't make a statement on behalf of the school just yet.'

'Is this connected to the murder of that awful councillor fellow? You know the paedophile chap who was found a couple of days ago.   It was all over the national newspapers yesterday, sounds a dreadful sort of person, probably deserved it, don't you think?'

'I couldn't possibly say, Mr Betts, unless of course you think there may be a link?'

'No, but to have two deaths so closely together in the Bridlington area, it's unheard of.'

DC Jay thanked the head master for his time and information and left his office, calling into the school secretaries office on the way out. The information she had requested was already waiting for her, the secretary had very obviously been listening in.

'Thank you, most efficient,' Paula commented as a brown envelope was passed to her.

'I think you'll find all you want to know in there, detective. These walls are paper thin, I heard your request so thought I would have it ready for you. I don't think Mr Betts was totally open about what he told you regarding Charles Hooton. There was something about him, he was a bit strange if you know what I mean. I think you'll find most female teachers in this school thought him to be something of a pervert. He constantly made unnecessary comments that made my skin crawl. Not the sort you want to be left alone with, if you know what I mean?'

Paula knew full-well the type of person she meant. There were plenty of police officers who played on sexual innuendo, she avoided that sort of man at all costs. 'What about the school girls, was he the same around them?'

'Not all of them. He was discreet in his personal contact with the children, saying that, we had a few in-house complaints about him walking into the girls changing room when he knew they were in there getting changed. The complaints were from the girls themselves and he was instructed to stop doing it by Mr Betts. I have to say, I thought the way Mr Betts handled that was completely inappropriate. He told the girls he disbelieved them and it reflected poorly on them for having such filthy minds. He made it difficult for anyone to speak out.'

Paula grimaced at the thought and dutifully thanked the pleasantly faced, grey haired secretary and left with a disturbing image of the dead man at the forefront of her mind.

In the briefing room at Bridlington Police station, twenty-five officers had gathered, ten detectives from various CID departments around Eastborough, and fifteen uniform officers.

Will Scott appraised the officers of the up to date status of the investigation. Daisy Wright identified the facts and the obvious gaps in intelligence that needed to be filled to progress the inquiry. Will added that the major piece of the jigsaw that was still missing and needed to be confirmed was a motive. At the time, the crimes couldn't be officially linked, though it was likely they would be. He then formed the officers into individual teams, with differing responsibilities. A sergeant was placed in charge of each team, however, Will commented, 'Listen up everyone, this is a major enquiry, we are one team, we keep everything in this room, nothing is leaked until it's run by me and I give approval. We're in it together, I'll cover your backs, so don't worry about anything. Let's work together, keep talking and let's catch this bastard before he kills again. Think of him as our prey, let's hunt him down as a pack, and nail him.'

The officers collectively cheered Will in appreciation of his team ethic, there was much in the way of high fives as a display of unity. The motivation and support the team felt filled the atmosphere, everyone was focused on one thing, the same thing, catching the killer.

As Paula Jay walked back into the briefing room, everyone was busy with their own enquiries, she moved through a group of officers looking at crime scene photographs, and approached her boss.

'Sir, I think you need to hear this, Charles Hooton has had allegations made against him that appear more than a little sinister. He's been paying attention to at least one of the girls at the school and that girl has told her parents that Hooton took her to his home to listen to music and hang out. There were other girls present at the house too apparently. As well as that, the school secretary told me, on the quiet, that some of the women teachers thought Hooton was a bit of a pervert. I've an odd feeling that Betts, the headmaster, knows more than he's letting on. He's one we need to watch.'

'Christ, well done, Paula. I want you to cover this area of the investigation. Take a female uniformed officer with you, speak with the girl's parents and get what else you can out of the school. This is beginning to ring a few alarm bells. Daisy, before we go and visit the forensic pathologist woman, you and I are going back to Hooton's home in Driffield, I think we need to seize computers and start looking into his extra-curricular activities.'

As Will and Daisy left the office, the telephones were busy with calls being received from the regional and national press, all seeking updates, and officers making calls delving into the victims' backgrounds. In Driffield, uniformed officers were diligently carrying out house to house enquiries, the double murder investigation was now in full flow.

As they pulled up in front of the murder house in Driffield, Will saw a crowd of local women looking anxiously at the house and on their arrival, at him and Daisy in particular.

'Worried neighbours I think, boss?'

'I think you are right, Daisy, let's go and have a quick chat. We want them to feel safe and know that we are there to help them. I know it's good PR but I really want these people to know we care.'

The group were pleased to speak to and hear what the detectives had to say and offered to make tea for the officers on duty outside the house. Both officers assured the women that Eastborough Police were working round the clock to keep the streets of the area safe and if they had any suspicions at all they should contact the local beat officer or call the usual police number and ask for the Bridlington Investigation Room direct. The women promised to let the police know if they heard anything suspicious. On hearing this, Daisy produced three business cards bearing her contact details. 'Let me know if you do hear anything, please,' she said handing each woman a card.

The pair then walked the short distance to the crime scene, where they again donned their forensic suits and entered. Some forensic officers were still working in the upstairs of the house. Will announced his presence by shouting out at the foot of the stairs, and asked if the down stairs rooms were all clear. 'Yes, it's all done down there, you can go through,' came the muffled reply as the forensics officer spoke through his paper mask.

Will and Daisy gently pushed open the door into the living room. They were instantly hit by the smell of death. Pausing for a moment, Will turned to his colleague.

'Keep an eye out for any computer equipment or communication devices, mobile phones or anything of that sort, or things that look out of place.'

It took Daisy but a few moments to notice a laptop computer that was sticking out from behind a brown fake leather sofa. She photographed it, removed and placed it in an evidence bag, noting down the time and location of the item as she did so. Will, meanwhile, had moved to a cheap looking desk that sat at the far end of the room. It was littered with papers and letters, mainly bills. Moving an envelope to one side, he saw something that caused him to take a deep intake of breath. Bending down to look more closely, he saw it was a silver metal angel figure, matching exactly the one he found at the Roberts murder scene. He pointed it out to Daisy, who photographed it in place, and bagged it as evidence.

'It looks like we have the killer's calling card,' he commented. The remainder of the search offered very little, other than an address book and a mobile phone, minus its sim card, which seemed odd to both officers, since it was plugged into a wall charger. 'Looks like someone's deliberately removed the sim card, why would Hooton charge a phone without that?' queried Daisy. As they were about to leave, the forensic officer called out to Will and advised him that a kitchen blow torch had been found. This had been photographed and taken away for fingerprinting and examination.

'That's curious. The victim, like the previous one, had all his hair burnt off, and burn marks on his back. Keep me posted on what you find, and if you can remind Mark to have a full report with me as a matter of urgency please.'

Will felt a vibration in his inside jacket pocket, it was his mobile phone. He quickly removed it and snapped into the mouthpiece, 'DCI Scott, how can I help?'

'Hi Will, it's Lucien here, what's going on?   The big boys from the nationals are all over us like a rash. Sky television and the BBC are covering the Hooton murder in their news bulletins and sending reporters to the scene in Driffield. My editor is giving it large and wants to know why we aren't getting a scoop on this story. Come on, mate, give me a break, just a little something to tease our readers into buying our paper. There has to be something you can give me, were both victims killed by the same hand do you think?'

'Lucien, slow down. When I'm able to, I will make an official statement to the media, I'll make sure you have a copy first. You need to give us some space to do our jobs. How many times have the press fucked up an investigation because they want to get their version of the story out there first? All I can say is we are currently looking into two murders which happened within a close space of time and within the Eastborough policing region. Both victims are male. There, will that do? Now do me a favour, mate, and let me get on with solving these crimes. I'll be in touch, okay?

Will turned to Daisy, 'For fucks sake, the press and the media are swarming the area looking for salacious gossip relating to the two victims. There's a Sky television van setting up outside the house right now. Our press office need to get their bloody finger out and send out another press release. Now let's get back to the nick and get that laptop and mobile phone examined before we get collared by that television crew. We need something to fall into place to help us move this investigation forward. Maybe a press release would be useful and open up new lines of enquiry?'

As the pair drove back to Bridlington, Daisy ran through her mind what type of person would be able to commit such atrocities to another human being? 'Boss, this killer of ours, he has to be covered in blood when he leaves the crime scene, so maybe he drives a car? We really need to review CCTV footage to check on vehicle movement and registered owners?'

'Let's face facts, Daisy, you don't get many people walking through the streets of Brid or Driffield carrying a kitchen blow torch. The killer has to have some form of transport. When we get back, get one of the investigation teams to contact the local council and to view relevant CCTV footage. I'm going to see what Paula has found out and take a look at the forensics report. I want checks done on those metal angel figures too: Who makes them? Are they available locally? They look like cheap mass produced tat, so I would think they are easily acquired. Our killer clearly has access to them.'

CHAPTER NINE

The investigation briefing room was buzzing on Will and Daisy's return. Officers were busy taking notes from telephone conversations with witnesses, associates of the dead men, and from outside police forces keen to know what was going on. It had been confirmed that Allan Roberts had no living family or next of kin, therefore notifications of death were restricted to the local council and neighbours. The most expedient and efficient manner to achieve this was through the pages of the local press and in local media reports. His final remains were to be left in the morgue until both the police and the Coroner were satisfied that they could be released for burial or cremation.

A death message had already been passed to the family of Charles Peter Hooton, and there would be no movement on his remains in the foreseeable future. Hooton's family were due to make a flying visit to the region to identify the body once a full post mortem had taken place. Photographic and medical evidence shown to the relatives, indicated that the victim was who the police believed it to be, so his name could be released to the press and media. In the interim period, his family were advised to remain in Stockport until such a time as the entire crime scene was cleared and cleaned and access agreed with Eastborough Police. It was a difficult time for the family in particular, and Will took it upon himself to personally call them and explain the situation. As part of this caring approach he provided his direct line telephone number and told them to call if they had any concerns. He advised them not to read or believe anything said in the media relating to the police investigation, and that he alone would provide them with accurate details, not anyone else.

Unfortunately, local reporter Lucien Palmer had written a little too much detail in his reports on both crimes. Much of it was pure speculation, some parts were accurate, the vast majority were comments made by local people regarding Roberts' dark side and his unhealthy interest in young children. Such speculative reporting had engaged the imagination of the national and international press, especially when an online version covering Bridlington news mentioned that Roberts was a good friend of Jimmy Savile. It became open season for conjecture that Savile and Roberts were part of the same gang of paedophiles. Seldom had the town of Bridlington received so much media attention. At times, it seemed as though the world's media were focused solely on the darker side of the town, as historic tales of local child sex offenders and abuse were suddenly being reported alongside these murders.

Will was a well-known face in the town and region. He had never previously encountered the type of mass reluctance from local people to help, instead, they were distancing themselves from the police. It was as though, in certain quarters, the police had become the enemy and people preferred to speak with the press and media news teams, granted, most press informants remained anonymous. It hurt Will, and the rest of his team, professionally and personally, that people they thought they could trust as a good source of intelligence, had suddenly abandoned them, preferring to place their trust in the media instead.

Will couldn't understand it. The local council had become a stranger, closing ranks on the instruction of the Chief Executive and the Leader, neither of whom wanted their inefficiency and corruption highlighted. Access to council CCTV footage and anything pertaining to Councillor Roberts had first to be cleared by the CEO. It was a ridiculous situation. Partnership working had gone out of the window. A leaked internal council memo instructed that: All council employees should refrain from engaging in conversation or discussion with the local police about any investigative matter. If such discussion was requested by the police then the individual council officer must immediately report it to their line manager. It felt like a case of them and us.

Will called another briefing for teams and officers to update the investigation, the latest forensic reports had come in and further detail about each victim had been identified during examination of the laptops.

Mark Daniel, the Forensic Team Manager, stood before the room full of detectives and uniformed officers. He was a tall, good looking man in his early thirties, his boyish appearance disguised the fact that he had already viewed more gruesome crime scenes and bodies of murder victims during his professional career than most general practitioners see in a lifetime. Despite such experience his hands were trembling as DCI Scott introduced him to the team, and asked him to discuss the linked findings from the first two crime scenes. A blank white board stood behind him, and to the right of that stood Paula Jay. She was waiting to write down in bullet point form critical detail that would help the investigation team understand what they were dealing with.

'From initial investigation of the crime scenes in Bridlington and in Driffield, I can formally advise officers that both murders were committed by the same killer or killers. More importantly, the information extracted from the laptop computers belonging to both victims, indicates that they were both active and predatory paedophiles. Both used similar child pornography websites on the dark web, and both had approximately 13,000 indecent images between them, the vast majority being in Category A. We are talking about two seriously sick people here. At both locations, the killer has entered the property without forcing entry. Both victims were tortured before death, the severity of the injuries indicate that the killer or killers may be known to the victim, hence the piercing of the eyeball with wooden barbecue skewers.

It appears from two small circular marks identified a few millimetres above the nape of the neck, that both men were incapacitated by some kind of stun gun, allowing the attacker to restrain them. Curiously, an identical list of names has been found on each victim's laptop, at this stage, we don't know what the list relates to, it could be other paedophiles, or it might be quite innocent, I think that will be for your investigations to determine.'

The room fell silent for a few moments, with every officer present trying to gain some comprehension of what they were dealing with. Will Scott took to the floor and thanked Mark for his update before providing further insight into the crimes.

'I've deliberately kept my own counsel on this until now. The killer has left his signature or whatever they call it, at both murder scenes. I don't mean by the manner in which he kills, in both instances, a small silver metal angel trinket has been found hidden beneath unassociated documents. Clearly, it's some kind of message. Until we know more about the type of person who is capable of committing these murders we can't begin to guess what the meaning of the angel is. It may be totally unconnected. However, as you all know, there is no such thing as coincidence, so it's my belief that this is the killer's calling card. Who'd have bloody guessed we'd be dealing with this kind of thing in Eastborough? Listen up, everyone, I don't want anyone to mention the angel trinket. I'm keeping it back from the press, and we aren't discussing the mutilations to the bodies. The press are running with the paedophile theory for both victims. Let them have their day, we make no such connection beyond the confines of this room. I'm expecting the usual loonies to surface with their own theories and insider knowledge, let's just keep everything in perspective, listen to everything that's being said and double check every detail.

'I want Klimes brought back in and his alibi checked and checked again. If he's clear, then he's released with no further action, a full intelligence log is to be submitted to both Interpol and Europol.

'On the topic of suspects, I want all known violent offenders across the area listed on the whiteboard. Someone has got to know who this bastard is, you don't become a double killer overnight. Our killer has gradually built up to this level of viciousness, so check CRO, local intelligence and PNC details on anyone you consider a potential suspect.'

One of the seconded officers, DC James Baty spoke up. 'Boss, might I suggest we draw up a list of all known nonces and convicted paedophiles in the district? If this tosser turns out to be a serial killer then he might be picking off these freaks one by one.'

'Good call, James,' said Daisy in a more than appreciative tone, 'Can you take ownership of that and post it up for everyone to see, include home address and date of birth details, that way we can identify any patterns in the killer's behaviour. Can I just say to everyone, I've organised a duty roster so that we can give 24 hour coverage to the investigation, so please check the roster before you leave here tonight. Some of you will be on twelve hour nights tomorrow, and some on twelve hour days.'

The closure of the briefing signaled the end of another long day for the investigation team. For Will Scott it meant a 6.00 a.m. start the following morning. His head was swimming with so many questions and very few answers. The murder of a teacher at his daughter's school made it all the more personal. Inside he worried whether Hooton had approached or groomed Ellie. There was only one way to deal with such a question. That was head on. Though he knew Mel would deal with it so much better than he could.

The drive home that night was prolonged by the media, some of who had set up camp outside the police station. Like every other officer on duty, Will had to force his car through the crowd of journalists and camera men blocking the road to start the journey. He briefly rang Mel to let her know he was on his way, the soft tones of her voice made everything feel that much better.

As he walked into the kitchen of his home, Mel was busy preparing dinner, she turned to her husband. He looked tired. The couple moved towards each other and embraced in a long and reassuring hug.

'Well, mister important detective, your investigation has been all over the television. The phone hasn't stopped ringing with friends and neighbours wanting to know what's going on. Don't worry, I've said absolutely nothing to anyone. Ellie wants to speak to you though. That Hooton man, he was her form teacher. She's really upset about it. Apparently, the head teacher, Mr Betts, called a special assembly and told the pupils not to speak to anyone, especially not parents or the police before speaking with him.'

'What? Did he really say that? The bloody tosser. Mel, I need you to speak with Ellie. This Mr Hooton, he was into odd stuff. He was a paedophile and you know, I can't get it out of my head, if he's touched or said anything to

Ellie, well I just need to know, okay. Can you ask her please, it'll be better coming from you?'

'Will, Ellie would have told us if he had done anything to her. I'll ask her but I think you might be being just a little paranoid.'

Mel disappeared into the other room and returned to the kitchen a few moments later with Ellie closely behind. 'It's all okay, Will, nothing has happened to Ellie, but she is a little sad about what happened to her form teacher. She wants to say something to you.'

Will looked on anxiously as his daughter made eye contact with him.

'Dad,' she said, 'I want you to catch whoever killed Mr Hooton and lock him up forever. Mr Hooton was so kind and caring to us all, he was the best teacher in our school. He wasn't a nasty man at all like people are saying, he wouldn't hurt a fly. Why do you think he was murdered, because he was so kind?'

Will thought carefully about his answer. 'I'll do my best to catch the man who killed him, darling, don't worry. Sometimes, good people get killed for no reason, I think that may be the case with Mr Hooton.'

He picked Ellie up and gave her a long reassuring cuddle. He welcomed the strong embrace she returned. 'I love you, dad.'

'I love you too, Ellie,' said Will in reply.

CHAPTER TEN

As the investigation team gathered the following morning, the mood in the briefing room was one of unease, when the first disappointing news of the day was revealed that suspect, Viktor Klimes, had been released with no further action. His alibi was cast iron, he was, on this occasion at least, an innocent man. The day shift officers hardly had time to consume that news when Daisy Wright took centre stage and revealed that information was coming in that a further murder had occurred on their patch. Details of the matter were sketchy and the crime scene hadn't yet been visited by police officers. The body of a woman had been discovered at the foot of the cliffs on North Landing Beach, Flamborough Head.

Daisy told her colleagues, 'Potentially, it could be an accidental death or suicide, and, of course, there is a small likelihood it may be murder. However, officers are visiting the scene as I speak to determine the identity of the victim and the circumstances surrounding the death. We'll be the first to know if it bears the hallmarks of our killer. Who knows, it might even be our killer?'

By 8.00 a.m., that morning, Will and Daisy were at the Flamborough Head beach crime scene. Without any shadow of doubt, their killer had struck again. The body bore signs of torture and mutilation. This time, there were no eyes in the head, and the fingers had been entirely removed from the hands. A row of forensic tents had been erected on the sandy beach to the right of the tight slipway. Inside one of the tents, lay the dead body of a woman, on her back, and just a few feet in front of a small cave formed in the rocky cliff face.

As well as the two lead detectives, Mark Daniel, Senior Forensic Officer was present, as was the pathologist and Police Surgeon, Dr. Dylan Haynes. Uniform police officers in marked cars had cordoned off the road giving access to the beach. A few tourists and ghoulish sightseers had gathered there in the hope of catching a glimpse of the gruesome scene down below. Overhead a police helicopter hovered noisily, scanning the coastal area around Flamborough, in search of further bodies, or perhaps, a lone curious observer watching and enjoying the official reaction to his handy work. Some killers, the police believed, like nothing more than savouring the mayhem and confusion their crimes have created. The aerial commotion caused by the police helicopter aroused the interest of the local media, as the police and emergency service activity was reported on local radio.

Local reporter Lucien Palmer was laid in his bed when his mobile phone rang at 8.35am that morning. It was one of the directors from the local radio station.

'Do you know what's going on at Flamborough Head, the North Landing Beach? Apparently there's a shit load of coppers up there and forensic tents have been erected on the beach. There's a police helicopter circling the area.'

'What? I haven't got a clue mate. I'll get myself up there though and give you a call once I know anything.' The journalist was dressed and in his clothes within a few minutes, personal hygiene wasn't important when a decent news story was breaking. He jumped into his old style Mazda 6 estate and made his way to the scene. By the time he had arrived, his mobile phone was ringing non-stop, as news of what was happening was spreading and being reported farther afield.

Parking up in the main car park, he walked along to the cordon tape and pushed through the crowd to get to a police officer. 'Can you tell us what's happened, officer?' he enquired.

The burly looking police officer seemed in no mood to be talking, he was more concerned on keeping the ever increasing crowd of people from breaking the cordon. Those who stood alongside Lucien claimed to know what the fuss was all about. One middle-aged woman who had brought her pug-like dog to the scene told him. 'It's a suicide. A jumper from the top of the cliff. I think, from what I've heard on the police radio, it's a Scarborough man who has been missing for several days.'

If it was a suicide, then the story wouldn't be anything like as sensational as the current copy Lucien was working on, the two local murders. Most of the people gathered were uttering the word 'suicide' and so Lucien made the first of his news desk calls, to BBC Radio Eastborough, informing them of the police presence and that it was likely to be a suicide. Local people and tourists were therefore advised to keep away from the North Landing Beach area. Lucien followed this call with the same update to local media, each time he informed the different news rooms that the incident was nothing of note. As he began to walk away from the scene, his mind turned to more important things in his life, like climbing back into his bed and catching up on some much needed sleep.

Looking back towards the crowd, he gave one last glance down at the beach below to see if any potential photograph opportunities might arise of the death scene. He felt a shiver run down his spine as he spotted the 6 foot 2 inch athletically built frame of Will Scott standing on the beach, he was talking to Daisy Wright. 'What the fuck are they doing there?' he said to himself. 'Surely, those two are heading the murder investigations, they wouldn't be at the scene of a suicide unless it was connected to the murders?'

Taking his mobile phone from his coat pocket, he dialed Will Scott. Sure enough, the figure on the beach removed a telephone from his pocket, looked at it, then replaced it inside the same pocket without answering it. 'It is them!' Lucien said out loud as he ran to his car. He was deeply offended that his best friend would so readily dismiss a call from him.

Whether it was through misguided desperation, or a desire to stake a claim on the double murder news story for himself, Lucien launched into the realms of supposition, as he spoke into his digital voice recorder and created an ending to the murder story.

'My name is Lucien Palmer, I'm reporting to you direct from the scene of a male suicide at North Landing Beach, Flamborough Head. There is a heavy police presence at the scene, including the lead detective of the recent double murder enquiry in the region, DCI Will Scott. I haven't been able to speak to him yet, however, sources close to him have confirmed that the body of the male person found on the beach, is likely to be that of the man suspected of the two murders. This is breaking news, more detail to follow once we have been able to confirm the details of the victim's identity. He is, however, believed to be a local man from the Scarborough area.' Within minutes, the recording was being distributed to news sources across the UK. Lucien felt smug. At last, he had beaten the media big boys to a real news story. The nations media sources would soon be beating a path to his door wanting more information, which, he thought to himself, they could have, but only if the price was right.

He returned to the police cordon and waited for his phone to ring, which it did, continually, for an hour or so after he had released his story. Within that hour, television news teams from the BBC, Eastborough TV, and from countless digital TV news channels arrived at Flamborough Head, set up cameras and started filming the scene below, each one reminding their viewers of the two local murders, and that the dead man's body on the beach below was that of the killer.

Will was oblivious to the media events that were breaking a few hundred feet above him on top of the cliff. With the murder scene being in such exposed territory, the crime scene examination had to be efficient. The dead woman was identified at the scene by her driver's license which was found inside her purse, which lay beside her on the beach along with an I-pad computer tablet. She was 46 year old Enid Shuttleworth, a nurse at a local old people's home.

The initial examination of the remains, by Dylan Haynes, had confirmed that the woman had been stunned before being hit on the back of the head with a ball peen hammer, causing a large hole in the cranium and unknown damage to the brain. Brain matter was present on the beach close to the skull, which allowed the experts at the scene to determine that she had been mutilated, tortured and killed where she lay on the beach. The hair had been completely burnt from her head, and she was completely naked, except for her shoes, which were still on her feet. Her legs were laid wide apart, 36 inches from heel to heel. Both hands were folded over her abdomen, each hand was minus all fingers and thumbs. These had been forcibly inserted into her vagina and rectum.   Both breasts were minus nipples, these having been crudely chopped from the body and dropped into the sockets where the eyeballs once sat. The eyeballs themselves were found inside the victim's mouth, as with previous victims, each one had been skewered, the tiny wooden shafts were sticking out of her mouth between her lips.   The examination also discovered that the tongue had been sliced in two, making it into a distinct fork shape. Evidence of glue like substance on each cheek, close to the mouth, revealed that the woman had at some stage had gaffer tape placed over her mouth, presumably before the eyeballs were inserted.   The injuries to her tongue would have been sufficient to have made her gag, and forced her to remain silent throughout the torture. There was no sign of the gaffer tape anywhere. The skin on the lower abdomen had been torn using a cheese grater, this had pubic hair attached to it that had been ripped from the body. The grater was left at the scene by the killer and was free from fingerprints.

When the shoes were removed from the woman's feet, it was discovered that the sole of each foot had been burnt with a portable kitchen blow torch, which, like the cheese grater, was minus any sort of fingerprints.

Beside the body, the woman's clothes, a nurse's uniform, pullover, and a pair of tights had been neatly folded into a pile. Laid on top of the clothing was a tiny silver metal angel trinket. The killer had scuffed the sand to destroy all evidence of footwear prints, and there was no sign of any tyre tracks on the beach close to the murder scene. It was evident that the killer and victim had walked down the slipway. Death was estimated as having occurred around 6.00am that morning, meaning the body had been found before any natural disturbance, wind, rain or tidal water could destroy the scene.

Will's phone suddenly burst into life in his pocket. He looked at the screen. 'It's the fucking Chief Constable,' he remarked before answering it. 'DCI Scott here.'

'DCI Scott, what is going on? Why the hell are the media reporting the death of our killer on Flamborough Head before I know anything about it? I want a written update immediately, and you damn well better justify why I've been left out of the loop on this one.' The phone fell quiet.

Will was confused by the Chief's comments, and he repeated what had been said in the call to the three members of the investigation team stood beside him.

'I think the Chief's lost the plot basically,' said Daisy.

'Unless he's been fed the wrong information?' Mark added.

'Well, there are only four of us here who know what's happened with this body, and she's definitely another victim. So unless a further body has been found, you can rule out any information from this crime scene being passed to the media.'

Will checked the BBC news website on his smart phone, and read out the headline story: Eastborough double killer commits suicide at Flamborough Head. Police murder investigation team at scene and making enquiries into man's identity. Story by Lucien Palmer.

'What the fuck is this shit?' said Will angrily, punching the reporters telephone number into his phone, moments later, the call connected. 'Lucien, what the hell is going on? Why are you reporting that our killer has committed suicide at Flamborough Head? Where has all this crap come from? We've got a serious incident here, it's not our killer I can assure you of that! Why are you doing this, you prick?'

'Will, listen, I know you're upset but you've got to understand, I have a professional responsibility to report news stories in a factual and unbiased manner. I got the facts and I recognised what was happening and produced the news story. Don't be having a go at me, because I've done everything by the book. It was you who didn't, or wouldn't update the press, so we beat you to it. It was either me or some other reporter. Can you give me the killer's identity or are you going to hold a press conference soon? How about a quote? If so it needs to be today because the national media are already hunting around Scarborough to find out who he is.'

Will was stunned. 'What are you going on about, why are the media hunting round Scarborough? What's Scarborough got to do with anything? Lucien, listen to me, this body isn't that of our killer. Our killer is still very much at large, so whoever has claimed this body to be that of the killer has made a complete professional twat of themselves. Number one, it's female, number two, she's been murdered. You are a fucking clown, Lucien. A full press briefing will follow later this morning.' The call ended, Will was shaking with anger, while Lucien Palmer was shaking in the realisation of making the greatest blunder of his journalistic career. He had no idea how he was going to recover from such a dramatic error.

With crime scene evidence recovered and photographs taken, the team left the beach and returned to Bridlington police station. The body was recovered by a local undertaker and transported to the morgue at Bridlington hospital. Search teams were allowed access to the crime scene and remained there for several hours, before the beach was reopened to the public later that afternoon. CCTV footage was recovered from the public car park above the beach, and from nearby roads which may identify a suspect vehicle. Will instructed that all vehicles were to be traced and their owners spoken to about their reasons for being in the area.

At the police station, Will contacted the Chief Constable and explained the situation to him. The senior official was more concerned about how it looked and the embarrassment it had caused for him. He advised Will to 'unofficially' warn the reporter that he could be charged with 'perverting the course of justice' or 'obstructing a police officer in the course of duty.' Will agreed, but felt it better to leave it where it was and to focus on matters of real importance, like catching the killer.

'We've got three victims now, sir,' he told the Chief Constable, 'The killer is organised and extremely confident. This latest one was killed in broad daylight on a beach. Anyone could have stumbled upon the crime during its commission, so there must be local knowledge that this area was generally very quiet at such times. I'm guessing here, but I think the killer might have an awareness of human anatomy, maybe a doctor or medical student or something like that. The most recent victim had all of her clothes neatly folded up into a pile beside her body. What kind of person is cool enough to do that then torture someone to death?'

'Will, I understand. Thank you for the update. Get the press office to sort out a media briefing for you, put the bastards straight on the non-news story. Be blunt and say it was all lies, name the reporter, just get it away from my door.'

The conversation over, Will spoke with the police press office and requested an urgent media briefing. He wanted to keep it precise and concise so worded it himself. Two hours later, he was sat in front of 52 reporters, photographers and film crews from across the UK.

The room was quiet except for the noise of automatic cameras clicking.

'Ladies and gentlemen of the press, thank you for attending this briefing at short notice, we have further news relating to the recent murders in the region. This morning, the body of a woman was found on North Landing Beach, Flamborough Head. From the details we currently have, this woman is the third victim of the same killer. We would ask that as members of the press, you report only the facts we have told you, and that you report responsibly. An unnamed journalist today reported grossly inaccurate detail that had been fabricated by him. This has hindered our investigation, since it has taken time to formally correct his copy. I would remind you that we do our utmost to maintain a proactive relationship with you all, however, serious matters of misconduct such as that reported this morning will not only fracture our relationship but allow a dangerous killer greater time to avoid capture. I will not answer any further questions. This ends the media briefing.'

Mel Scott was sat at home watching live coverage of the briefing on local television. She was astounded by the harshness with which her husband delivered the briefing. He looked every bit the professional detective and someone people would have confidence in. 'Will Scott, you handled the situation supremely well,' she whispered to herself.

As he made his way back to the murder investigation room, his mobile phone began to ring. It was the Chief Constable. 'DCI Scott, that was an amazing media briefing. I'm sure the watching nation will hold you in great respect for the way you damned the press, yet kept them onside. You did a marvellous job, well done.'

Further calls were received from senior police officials of the Eastborough force, all were congratulatory. Will recognised that he had taken ownership and full control of the murder investigation that day, the press briefing was his own and it was that of a leader. Now all that remained for him to do was catch the killer.

He called Daisy, Paula, Barry and Amber over to his desk and sat them down. 'We need to make inroads into these crimes. It feels like the killer is giving us no time to dwell on their past deeds, so we must make time. We need to get inside the bastard's head, think what he is thinking, understand why he is killing, and why the killings are so bloody ghastly. Seriously, I can't even begin to think of someone local who would be capable of something like this. Our CRO's are druggies, drunks or paedo's or twockers. Let's be truthful, they are crap burglars as well. That makes me think our killer must travel, maybe from Hull, Goole, York, Leeds?'

'I can see where you are coming from boss,' said Paula Jay, 'but surely the killer is taking some time killing these people. He must be comfortable in the locality and to a certain extent he has to have local knowledge. Leaving any of the crime scenes he is surely going to be covered in blood and guts. To my way of thinking, he wouldn't want to drive far in that state. He's likely to contaminate his vehicle too. I think he's too clever for that. Maybe he's a visitor staying on a caravan holiday park?'

'Okay, Paula,' said Will, 'you've talked yourself into another piece of work. Visit the local holiday parks, particularly that awful place run by real dross, you know, the one where the beach huts are and the huge inflatable caravan sits outside during the summer. The manager is the porky looking fat guy, pale complexion, fancies himself, reckons he's an ex-squaddie or something. He genuinely looks like a pig. He always strikes me as peculiar in a not very nice way.'

'Give him a bit of a grilling please, Paula, pardon the pun,' said Daisy with a wink.

Will addressed the group. 'Right, the rest of us, I want to pull together some kind of profile of the type of person we are looking for, so that means going through every piece of evidence, crime scene images, geographic locations, the works. The laptops must hold something to help us. Barry, you and Amber work with forensics to extract every detail you can about our victims. I can't see Enid Shuttleworth having any links to child porn websites, so maybe the victims are associated through another link. I want every e-mail they ever sent or received in the last 12 months, checked and checked again.

'Daisy, find out the details of this forensic pathologist woman in Beverley. I want us to arrange a visit, or for her to come here. I'd like to know if she can help us in any way, profiling is part of what they do, so let's see if she can help. We'll reconvene at 5.00p.m. this afternoon, okay?'

Daisy checked the paperwork on Will's desk and quickly found the contact details of the forensic psychologist that had been left there by DC Jay. 'I've got those details you were after, boss. Do you want to call her or shall I?'

'We'll visit her, Daisy. Come on, let's do it straight away before I get caught up in something else.'

It was a reasonable drive from the police station in Bridlington to Beverley. As the pair pulled up outside the Victorian terraced house they were struck by how spacious and grand it looked.

'Must be a lot of money in the psychology field?' said Will.

Daisy nodded in agreement, 'I think they get lots of consultancy work, so they get to charge whatever they want. Probably some rich bitch who doesn't know the first thing about murder,' she said dismissing the strengths of the psychologist before meeting her. 'So you don't forget, boss, the psychologist woman is called Amanda Ward.'

Will knocked on the front door rapping three times with sufficient force to ensure anyone inside heard. Seconds later, the door opened and a tall, elegant, good looking woman, with brown shoulder length hair, blue eyes and a welcome smile answered. 'Yes, can I help you,' she said with an air of confidence.

The detectives introduced themselves and explained why they wanted to speak with her. She seemed a little embarrassed by the request and her face momentarily blushed as she welcomed them inside her home. Will asked if she would be prepared to professionally assist them with the investigation, using her forensic and profiling skills. He was reluctant at that stage to go into any detail about the murders, this was more of a fishing expedition to explore the possibilities of getting her involved.

'Well, I'd love to, but I'm employed by the Prison Service. I work at Wakefield Prison.'

'Ah, Monster Mansion, we've got a few of our prisoners banged up in that place,' said Will.

'I think you would have to speak with the governor of the prison to see if they would be prepared to release me on attachment to your unit. There will be all kinds of administrational implications, who pays me, whether my pension will remain as it is, you know the kind of stuff I mean. Whatever, I'd love to work with you. Are you thinking the person who killed the councillor might be a multiple murderer, or a serial killer?'

'We can't honestly answer that question right now, Amanda, everything will be made more clear when, or if, you can join us. Can you give me names and contact details of the people I need to speak with, the decision makers.'

Amanda moved to a writing bureau and wrote down the details, handing them to Daisy who had intentionally stood up to take the paper. It was clear to Will that Daisy had taken an instant dislike to the woman. 'Please, you can call me Mandy, I prefer it to Amanda,' she told the officers as she escorted them to the front door.

'I'll be in touch once I hear anything,' said Will, 'You'll probably know before I do, so give me a call if you do hear something. I'll be making the calls first thing tomorrow, so hopefully by tomorrow evening we'll know if it's possible.'

As the two detectives drove back to Bridlington, Daisy commented on how attractive the 'Psychologist Woman' was. Will now detected an air of jealousy in her voice and smirked. 'To be honest, Daisy, I don't care if she's Miss fucking World, as long as she can help us catch our killer, then, frankly my dear, I don't give a damn.' Both officers laughed at Will's dodgy impression of Rhett Butler from *Gone With The Wind*.

Back in the incident room, Will had a team of officers all keen to provide updates that would narrow down current lines of inquiry. DC Jay had collected a complete list of visitor's names and addresses and vehicle details of people who had stayed at the Sandskipper Caravan Park. DS Smith and DC Taylor were armed with data recovered from each of the victims' computers, including that of Enid Shuttleworth. Will brought the entire day shift team together, and took time to thank each one of them for their hard efforts before telling them to go home, rest, and return tomorrow morning when they would review everything they had collated. He handed over the night shift responsibility to Detective Sergeant Ian Simpson, whose own team had responsibility for intelligence gathering and lead pursuance for the day shift to follow up.

As he left the building, Will felt comfortable that matters were progressing and he was achieving as much as he could. Officers were pursuing leads and information relating to the latest victim overnight, and tomorrow, he thought, might well bring a criminal profiler into the equation. That's when he would really get inside the mind of the killer he so desperately wanted to catch.

CHAPTER ELEVEN

That evening, Will felt the need to treat his wife to a night out. He rang home and asked her to book a babysitter and get dressed up to go out, as he had managed to get hold of tickets, at the Bridlington Spa, to see what was described as a spectacular evening of Tamla Motown with hits performed by tribute bands. He relied very much on Mel a great deal more than he ever showed, tonight he wanted her to know that he appreciated her and that he would never take for granted, her support, love and devotion.   She was thrilled to hear the news and organised for the children to stay at their auntie's.

As Will walked in the door she was pulling on her coat ready to leave the house. There was just enough time for a quick hug and a kiss, before they both left the house excited about an evening out. For Will it was a welcome relief from the intensity of a murder investigation, for Mel it was great to spend some quality time with her husband away from the realities of his everyday professional life. Policing at the level Will performed could be exciting, rewarding and financially beneficial, it could also be onerous and tended to take its toll on the individuals health. Mel had an understanding of the way the job operated, so she saw it as her role to make sure Will understood where his priorities lay, his family came first.

When the show ended, the couple sang the words to the Smokey Robinson hit 'Tears of a Clown' as they strolled, and occasionally skipped, their way along the promenade towards the car park in the harbour where Will had left the Audi. They were happy, and remained very much in love. As they jumped into the front seats Will kissed Mel on the cheek. For a moment he felt his heart miss a beat as he was reminded of her beautiful looks and personality.

'Will Scott, remember where we are. Don't you start your sexy boy antics with me in a public car park. At least do me the service of taking me home first,' said Mel bursting with contentment. That night was one of sizzling passion for the Scotts. The lovemaking lasted until the early hours of the morning as they gently caressed and sexually teased one another culminating with Will howling like a werewolf as he achieved full satisfaction. Mel, on the other hand, arched her back, tilting her head back onto the pillow, as she gasped several times during her climax. Afterwards, the couple shared a shower and soothingly washed each other, before patting themselves dry and climbing back into bed together, this time, to sleep.

The following morning Will was up at 5.00 a.m. He took Mel her usual hot cup of lemon water before making himself a coffee and some toast, which he ate seated at the breakfast bar in the kitchen, while checking his personal emails on his laptop computer. It didn't take him long, his mind was very much elsewhere, he was in the zone, the murder investigation zone. Nipping back upstairs to give Mel a kiss before he left, Will wondered what, if anything, had happened overnight. Suddenly, Bridlington had become crime central of England with every television news show giving a mention to the murders in the region.

Twenty minutes later, he was sat at his desk in the police station, ploughing through dozens of intelligence reports and investigation updates. Of greater concern was the forensic report covering the detail recovered from the latest victim's laptop computer.

As he scanned the three page document, his inner concerns were evident by rows of deep furrows in his brow. He was frowning in disbelief at what he was reading. Two paragraphs in particular resonated with his darkest fears:

'Some three thousand child pornography (Category A) images were stored on the hard drive, around eight hundred of these had been downloaded from various 'disguised' internet websites, in other words, the dark web. Many of the images show Shuttleworth participating in unusual sexual activity with male and female children ...

'Shuttleworth spent some time as a nurse in a hospital that officers working on Operation Yewtree investigated. There are seven individual images on the computer showing her in the company of a well-known celebrity, suspected of being a paedophile. Clearly, she is the second victim to have been a known associate with this individual.'

Will was unaware of the presence of Paula Jay stood by his desk. 'You okay, boss?' she asked.

Will shook his head, 'Christ, this latest victim, Enid Shuttleworth, she was an active paedophile, Paula. Someone is mightily hacked off with these perverts. Now, to make matters worse, we have a celebrity connection to two of our victims. We need to pull Shuttleworth's employment records, can you check with her current employers and go through her file with a fine tooth comb. I want to know every aspect of her life. Can you make it urgent, please? I'd like to have the employment records for the 10.00 a.m. briefing.'

The DCI turned his attention to a stack of intelligence reports and skim read through them, looking for anything obvious that might provide a suggestion of a clue. So far, he had three dead paedophiles and a raft of Chinese whispers circulating throughout the region to work with. As he looked more closely at the data removed from each victim's computer, the more confusing matters became. He hadn't a clue about what type of person he was dealing with, although the killer's motive appeared a little more clear, whoever the killer might be, was obviously targeting active paedophiles and users of child pornography websites. Those websites, he suspected, might well hold the answer to the killer's identity.

Daisy Wright breezed into the office clutching a further pile of documents which she dropped onto her desk and announced, 'I requested details and modus operandi of all known violent sex offenders who remain active across the north of England. I thought it pertinent to check them all out to see if there are any links to our region. They say birds of a feather stick together and all that. The link is tenuous, however, it might throw up something of interest. I'm going to allocate the work to the station local intelligence officer, so don't panic folks.'

The news of the latest victim's involvement in paedophilia rocked the entire murder investigation team.

Will Scott reaffirmed to each officer, the point that this information had to be suppressed and kept from the media.

'It might well be that we have a group of vigilante killers, our victims are clearly linked to the child sex and pornographic industry, however, there's also a link to Savile in two of the cases. I hate to say this, but we need to look into the background of his known victims, check to see if someone is aggrieved and taking out revenge on others, nonces and pervert types. I want someone to double check with officers who were on the Operation Yewtree investigation, for details of all known paedophiles in our police area with Savile connections.'

Will left the remainder of the briefing to Barry Smith and Daisy Wright, he had to update police senior management, and contact the Governor of Wakefield Prison and discuss the process of getting the forensic psychologist, Mandy Ward, working with the investigation team. That situation became less of an issue when the Governor agreed to second Mandy to the team for the period of one calendar month with immediate effect. Eastborough Police were responsible for all financial aspects of the secondment and DCI Scott was her immediate line manager during her time with the force.

The ink had hardly dried on the agreement when Mandy Ward rang Will to tell him she was outside the police station and ready to start work. He asked Daisy to go down to bring the psychologist upstairs where they could sit down and brief her on what would be expected of her during the investigation. Her presence as part of the team was unanimously welcomed, and as she was introduced to the staff, she wondered to herself whether expectations of what she could deliver were too high? While being introduced by Daisy, she seized the chance to address the team collectively, and to make sure everyone knew what was possible and what was impossible. She oozed self-confidence and level headedness.

'First up, I want everyone to call me Mandy, no nicknames, no derivatives, just Mandy. I am fully qualified as a psychologist and I specialise in forensic psychology, that includes offender profiling. To produce an accurate profile, I require complete access to every piece of information regarding each crime. So if it's possible, I'd like to attend the crime scene alongside the senior investigating officer, see what he sees, and know what he knows. I've worked with some of the countries' worst serial offenders of our time. It isn't common knowledge, however I am regarded as something of a guru on the subject of child sex offenders and what makes serial killers tick. Also, my boyfriend is a freelance writer. He's a criminologist. He's interviewed just about every serial killer in the UK during the past two decades and what he doesn't know about serial killers isn't worth knowing. Naturally, I have access to all his data, so if required, we can use that. Right, what I'm not. I don't do psychic shit. I'm not a Mystic Meg or a fortune teller. My profiles come from the data and detail you collect and from my own experiences. If we can get everything right, I'll be able to produce a profile that will be effective, efficient and fit for purpose. It's not a one size fits all profile, but one that will be bespoke to each murder collectively linking them all to the offender or offenders.'

The personal introduction received a round of applause from the officers who had gathered to listen. Daisy raised her eyebrows towards Will, in acknowledgement that she was slightly impressed by the 'forensic woman's' performance. The DCI smiled at her and beckoned her over to his desk, along with Mandy Ward.

'We have to sit down and go through everything with you, Mandy. From now on, you are part of our team. You will be working with Daisy and I. Where do you want to start? I can give you the crime scene images from each of the three murder scenes and the accompanying pathologist's report. I think you need to read up on the cases then come back to us with any questions you might have, that way you are right up to speed with everything.'

Daisy produced the three victim case files and placed them at one end of her desk. Pulling forward a chair for Mandy to sit on, she said, 'We'll be sharing a desk, Mandy, is that okay? You probably don't know how these things work, so I'll tell you. We don't reveal every single part of our investigation to the media, we keep things back, important things that only the killer and us can know. Everything you see or hear is 100% confidential, and mustn't be repeated anywhere beyond these four walls. Not even to your boyfriend. We don't smoke, we don't drink, we don't have fun or play games, so forget all that shit you read about in books or on television. Our offenders are live and active on the streets, not locked up in some cell bored shitless waiting for academics to come and have a social chit chat with them. Our role is to catch this bastard or these bastards whoever or whatever they may be. We'll do whatever it takes to do just that, so anything you can do to support us will be appreciated. Forgive me for sounding less than inspired by your introduction into the team, but I'm not here to make friends. I'll give you my full respect once I see something tangible from you. I'm not absolutely sure profiling a complete stranger is possible, so we shall see.'

As Will looked on, the air was filled with tension, the two women sat before him were clearly uneasy with each other's company.

Mandy broke the silence. 'That's no problem, Daisy. As I say, I'm not a psychic, I don't foretell the future and I don't speak with the dead. Everything I produce is based upon the facts you provide or the killer leaves behind. I'm up for everything you say, catching whoever is committing these crimes is my primary goal. I'm here in a professional role only, and please remember, it was you and your boss who asked me to get involved, I didn't offer my services like some teenage groupie desperate for attention. So get me the evidence and I'll create you an accurate profile of the person you are after.'

Will intervened. 'Right, ladies, can we please crack on and start pulling together the sort of information Mandy needs to build the profile. Daisy, I want you to work with Mandy and give her access to everything we've got. I'm going to update the Chief's office and keep him off our backs.'

As he sat at his desk, Will heard in the background the crackled tones of a police radio communicating a message. His ears pricked up as he thought he recognised the voice, it sounded like Barry Smith. The DCI moved towards the desk where the unattended radio sat. As he neared the handset he heard 'Can you let DCI Scott know immediately, we will need him down here at the scene, as a matter of urgency.'

Will grabbed the radio set and spoke into the mouthpiece. 'This is DCI Scott speaking, what have you got, Barry? Can you call me on the mobile, don't relate any information over the radio net.'

Seconds later, the phone on Daisy's desk rang. Will picked it up.

'Boss, it's Barry here, we've got another, another body. I think you'd better attend, this one is badly burned, the eyes have been mutilated and the fingers are missing. The penis is in the victims mouth.'

'Okay, stay calm, whereabouts are you?'

'I'm with DC Jay, at Sandskipper Caravan Park. We found the body in a caravan on the site. We checked the visitors register and found the name of a convicted nonce staying here, so we went to speak with him. He's been here during the time of each murder. His name is Gary Tilley, a close friend of one of the two managers here. It looks like the same M.O. boss. When you get to the site, go down Central Avenue, turn left after the roundabout, and the caravan is on Barn Fields. It's caravan number 62, right on the end, backs onto trees. The main road runs right behind the trees. Any fucker could get in and out of this place without being challenged. This is bad boss.'

'Okay, Barry, I'm on my way, I'll be with you in twenty minutes. I'll arrange for a couple of police dogs and handlers, forensics and the police surgeon to attend, okay, and I'll get uniform back up to set up cordons. In the meantime, until I get there, no one enters or goes within fifty feet of the caravan. Evacuate people from neighbouring caravans if you have to.'

Will took a deep breath, the murders were happening quickly, with little respite between each that would allow the police to focus on one specific crime, instead they were jumping from murder to murder, confusion could easily reign. Knowing that the investigation might easily become side tracked, he had to rethink his investigation strategy, now, individual teams within the unit were made responsible for investigating each murder. That way, he was covering all of his bases. He approached Daisy and Mandy, both of whom were reading the murder files. He tried to stay as calm as he could when he delivered the news of a further murder.

'Daisy, Mandy, grab your coats, we're off to Sandskipper Caravan Park. Barry and Paula have found another body inside a caravan. It's a male, his name is Gary Tilley. Sounds grisly so make sure you've got sick bags to hand. Mandy, you'll be expected to look at the crime scene alongside us, so it's time to use your skills and tell us what detail you are looking for. Stay close to us throughout the tour of the crime scene investigation, please.'

As they pulled into the caravan park in an unmarked police car, crowds of holiday makers blocked the route to the Barn Fields area of the site. It was a disgraceful scene, with young children holding mobile telephones and taking photographs of the happenings in the area. Some were sitting on the shoulders of adults who were in various states of undress, all seemingly desperate for a glimpse of the crime scene or those attached to it. Will forced the police vehicle through the excited throng until he finally reached the police cordon. The crowd were agitated and demanded information, the false belief that the body of a young child had been found was popular.

As he stepped out of the car, Will turned to what was rapidly turning into a mob and shouted out. 'Ladies and gentlemen, can we please have some calm. I cannot tell you what has happened here, not until I can go inside and investigate. Please allow us to do our jobs. Once we have done this, police officers will visit you in your caravans and where necessary ask for your assistance. You will be helping us by returning to your caravan homes and waiting there.'

A short, fat, man, with dyed peroxide blonde spiky hair, dressed in a cheap grey suit pushed his way through the crowd and asked to speak with DCI Scott. Will approached the middle aged man who clearly had ideas above his station about his self-importance.

'Officer, what you have just done is going to cost us a fortune in lost revenue. You are telling people to return to their caravans when we have on site facilities open for our holiday makers. Who is in charge here, I want to speak with them. You have no right to make decisions of that nature on this site, it isn't a prison camp, it's a holiday camp, our aim is to make as much money as we can. Your presence here isn't appreciated, so I'm a bit pissed off that you are stopping my business from trading by telling people to stay in their caravans. I demand to speak with whoever is in charge, immediately.'

Will stepped closer to the man who had unwittingly rattled the detective's cage. He bent down and looked directly into the face of the man who had irritated him. 'That'll be me, sir, now remind me, who did you say you are? I'd be interested to know your movements over the last 48 hours?'

The man twitched nervously and took a step back from Will. He wasn't used to people standing up to his bullying ways and speaking to him like that, his mouth fell open.

'I asked you two straight forward questions, sir, who are you and can you tell me your movements over the last 48 hours?'

By now the man was trying to make himself invisible and moved back into the crowd. Will stepped forward, 'Right, sir, I'd like you to step inside the cordon and talk to me instead of cowering like a rabbit caught in headlights.'

The man stepped through and immediately apologised for his bullish attitude. 'I'm sorry, Chief Inspector, my name is Andy Hanson, I'm the site sales manager and everything else for my sins. The problem is, this is the summer season, the time when we make an absolute killing from our punters. Most of them are a bit geriatric, you know, older people looking for a place to retire to, so we have to be clear with our instructions to these people, tell them what we expect and want from them. We feed them drink and cheap food in the bar, put on a bit of entertainment, then turf them out, back to their caravans at the end of the day. That's all they want from a caravan holiday. Tonight, the bar is empty, we're not selling anything, because of this, our holiday makers think it's like *Midsomer Murders*, they think its entertainment. Our takings are going to be down massively, how long before you clear up and get off the site? We can't lose money like this.'

'Andy, your attitude stinks mate, if I'm to be honest. I'm here because a body has been found in one of your caravans, very possibly a murder. Yet all you worry about is fleecing these fucking holiday makers. If I want to, if I deem it necessary, I can demand that you shut the entire site down. Do you understand that? What I'm going to do, is ask one of my officers to interview you and record a statement of your movements covering the last 48 hours, is that clear enough for you? I suggest you return to your office and wait there for a detective to visit you. Now kindly leave me and my officers to get on with our work. The quicker you do that, the sooner you can start taking money off these poor bastards again.'

Hanson, puffed his fat chest out and did as he was asked, strutting like an overblown pigeon he left the scene without any further delay. Daisy, who had witnessed the conversation between the two men, asked one of her team to go and interview Hanson and to

126

determine more about his movements over the last two days and to carry out a full PNC check on him.

Will, Daisy and Mandy quickly dressed in the Tyvek suits and entered the caravan. On doing so, Will noted that it's make was a Hymer. He thought the name sounded familiar and recalled his parents once owning a camper van with a similar title. Stepping inside, the trio realised how little space there was to move around, let alone commit a brutal attack on someone and torture them. The inside of the caravan was as tacky as the site itself, full of cheap looking ornaments and furniture.

The victim lay at one end of the caravan. He was on the floor, naked and on his back next to a seating area. The body was just as Barry Smith had described it, with all the hallmarks of the previous murders. The smell of burnt flesh indicated to Will and Daisy that the victim had likely been tortured before death.

Will looked at the forensic pathologist to see how she was coping with the carnage that lay before them. She confirmed she was okay and continued to scan the crime scene for any sign of a clue. 'What's that over there, boss?' she said pointing toward a cushion that had been laid beneath the victims head.

Will carefully bent over the body to see beneath the cushion. He couldn't reach to remove the object so asked Daisy to retrieve it.

'It's a silver metal angel, so it's our killer alright.'

Mandy asked the officers of its significance.

'We have found one of these at each crime scene. We don't understand its significance yet, maybe that's something you could do?' enquired Daisy with a tone of sarcasm in her voice.

The forensic pathologist was quick to respond. 'The killer or killers are toying with you, teasing you. I'm not certain about the meaning of silver angels, I'd have to research that, but clearly it's the killer's calling card. This is someone supremely confident and aware of their surroundings. Until the cause of death has been determined, I'm reluctant to confirm anything, however, I think the killer might be acting alone. Leaving a small angel is definitely significant. The killer is leaving us some kind of message.'

'Why do you say that, Mandy, that's quite a profound statement to make after visiting just one crime scene, the killer is acting alone?' asked Will.

'I'm basing it on the lack of space within this caravan. We are struggling to move around in here, so if the victim has been killed where he lays, then there is room for just one person to overcome, torture, then kill him. Obviously, with the angel trinket, that is his calling card, you are meant to find it, that's a direct message from the killer to you.'

Daisy stepped forward and moved a towel that lay upon the seating above the body, beneath it was a laptop computer. 'Here we go again, boss. What's the betting there's child porn on here?' she said taking possession of the laptop and placing it into an evidence bag.

'I think you may be right, Daisy, our killer is able to move about the area, so he has to have a car or vehicle of some nature. So we can check vehicle movement in and out of the site from this dump's CCTV system.'

'Will, there's one other thing I'd like to point out before we leave here,' said Mandy. 'The killer could be left handed. If you look at the positioning of the body and some of the items used to torture or kill him, the majority have been laid on the left side of the remains. That indicates a left-handed person, surely?'

Will and Daisy both looked down at the area around the body, 'You could be right, Mandy, we need to check images from the other crime scenes,' added Daisy.

As the three left the caravan, they were greeted by Mark Daniel and Dylan Haynes. 'I'll leave it to you guys to sort this out,' said Will to the two experts. 'It's bloody in there, we've removed a laptop from inside. We'll get it over to your team as soon as we've made a cursory check of the browsing history.

'Get your reports to me as quickly as you can. This killer isn't giving any of us chance to breath, let alone investigate each murder. I genuinely believe that whoever it is, is leaving no time between crimes, knowing very well that it will stretch our resources to the maximum and provide no window of opportunity for us to get close to, or apprehend him. We've been playing catch up until now. I want you both to meet Mandy Ward, she is a fully qualified forensic pathologist attached to the investigation. Mandy will be trying to complete an accurate profile of the killer, based on the evidence we identify. Christ only knows, we need all the help we can get with these crimes.'

As they moved back towards the police vehicle, stripping off their Tyvek suits, Will caught sight of Lucien Palmer who was frantically waving at him in an attempt to attract his attention. Will told his two colleagues to go to the car and wait for him.

He made his way over to his friend who looked anxiously at the detective. 'Lucien, how the hell did you find out about this? You know what, if you dare write a load of shite about this then I'll personally run you in. Before you ask, yes it's another murder. We'll be making a full press release in due course. Don't you dare go interfering, or meddling into our investigation, you've caused sufficient damage as it is.'

'Will, no, it's not that at all. I'm here to give you a tip off, mate. There's a story circulating that there's been another murder, this time in Leeds, not sure of anything else really, I just wanted to give you a heads up on it. Remember, Will, I'm your mate, I don't want to stitch you up or make you look stupid. That's why I'm here, to tell you about the Leeds murder. We've got local press over there looking into the report. Have you heard anything about it?'

Will shook his head, partly in disbelief that their killer might have struck again, and partly because the press were again finding out intelligence before the police. 'No, Lucien, I hadn't heard that, thanks for letting me know though. Keep me updated if you hear anything further okay?'

Will looked a lonely and dejected figure as he walked over to join his colleagues in the unmarked police car. As he climbed inside he gave out a huge long sigh.

'What's up, boss? Don't let the press wind you up, you know what they are like, pack of troublemakers and bloody liars the bloody lot of them,' said Daisy without a hint of caring in her voice. Mandy was sat in the rear seat of the vehicle and remained silent, sensing that now was not the time for her to make any sort of comment.

After a few moments of painful silence, Will spoke. 'Lucien informs me that there's been a murder over in Leeds, for some reason he thinks it may be connected with ours.'

'He talks rubbish boss,' said Daisy, 'Look what he wrote about the Shuttleworth woman. Christ, they have murders every week in Leeds don't they? He's testing the waters, looking for a reaction from you, that's all.'

Will agreed.

As the three left the Sandskipper Caravan Site Mandy spoke. 'I'm so glad I don't have to go on holiday to somewhere like this, it's more akin to a Ministry of Defence base than a holiday camp. The staff look a right rum lot, who was that little fat guy, what planet was he from, telling the police what they can and can't do on his caravan park. I bet you know most of that lot professionally?' she said laughing at her own comments. The rhetoric she had hoped might exist didn't materialise, she still felt like an outsider, as the three of them made the journey back to Bridlington police station.

As Daisy sat down at her desk, the telephone on Will's desk rung, she reached out to answer it. 'DS Wright here,' she said in an officious no nonsense tone. Like her colleagues, she wasn't in the mood for talking, she needed head space to allow herself to take everything in. 'Hello DS Wright, it's DS Jon Sharp here from Leeds CID, West Yorkshire Police Force. We are investigating the murder of a woman over here, she has links to your region. I know you've had a couple of murders over there recently, so we are looking at any potential links. Can I give you our victim's details, we thought you might be able to help us, and have some local intelligence on her?'

'Sure, give me her details and I'll check for you straight away,' replied Daisy, checking first the coding authenticity to confirm DS Sharp was who he said. With that confirmed, Sharp continued.

'It's a female, DoB 25.05.1970, Irene James, a taxi driver, born in Howden, with family links to Burton Agnes. She was married to a convicted paedophile, Andrew Sinclair, who is still banged up, so not a person of interest. She reverted to her maiden name when he was sent down on a thirteen year stretch. To be honest, she's been butchered. The hair has been burnt from her head, the eyes pierced with wooden barbecue sticks, the tongue's been removed, the breasts removed, and worst of all, expanding foam has been pumped into her vagina, anus, nostrils and throat. It's an absolute bloody mess. Whoever killed her knew what they were doing.'

Daisy put the phone on loud speaker and alerted Will and Mandy to listen in. 'Where was she found?'

'Of all places, in Killingbeck, Leeds. She was left in a graveyard,' replied Sharp.

'Have you found anything at the scene, any kind of calling card?' she asked.

'What do you mean, calling card? It's a murderer we're after, not a travelling bloody salesperson.' The Leeds detective appeared confused by the question.

'I mean, did the killer leave anything behind at the crime scene, and was there a laptop nearby?'

'Yes, we have a laptop, it's being examined by forensics as we speak. Do you think we have a link then? We've obviously got more available resources than you, and this one's on our patch, so we'll take priority on the investigation front. If the crimes are linked, I think we might be in a better position to solve this one and by association the murders in your area.'

Will took exception to the remark and introduced himself to the conversation, instructing DS Sharp to get the Senior Investigating Officer in Leeds to contact him urgently. With that done, he ended the call.

'Fuck them with their shit attitude, who do they think we are, country bumpkins? We are twice the force than they are in every department. The fucking wanker, how dare he?'

Mandy seized the opportunity to calm things down by offering to go and make a pot of tea for them. She didn't really understand the competitiveness of police forces, she'd always thought they worked together as one. Clearly, this was not the case. 'I know Leeds fairly well,' she said, 'my sister went to University there. I've spent many a night in the city while visiting her.'

The pressure was getting to everyone involved in the investigation. Never before had any police force been bombarded by killing after killing on an almost daily basis. Eastborough had a serial killer on the loose, not just any serial killer, it was one who had everything meticulously planned, right down to timings and discovery of the bodies. It was the killer who was calling the shots, not the police, not the media, and not the public. Despite the high level of media coverage, the public hadn't yet become outraged by the police's failure to capture the killer. Indeed, in the case of Allan Roberts, Will had heard of comments posted on social media congratulating the killer on getting rid of one Bridlington's dirtiest old men. The comment itself hadn't disturbed him. What did was the fact that the police were so far removed from knowing anything of the man's disgusting habits. He wondered why local people hadn't communicated their concerns about the man. It was a worrying detail that police intelligence within the area wasn't sufficiently focused to cover every type of crime. Before the murders, every morning he would read up to twenty intelligence reports submitted by officers with details that covered drug and substance abuse, car theft, shoplifting and the odd burglary. None, if any, mentioned sex crimes of any description. Surely to god, he thought to himself, child sex abuse hadn't so much stigma and taboo attached to it that it caused police officers to feel scared of mentioning it within intelligence reports?

The sound of his desk telephone ringing snapped him back to reality. It was Detective Superintendent Norton from Leeds. 'Hello, Chief Inspector, I think we need to have a conversation about this murder in our area. Are you able to discuss this matter now?

'If it is determined to be the same killer, then we need to discuss who leads the investigation. Naturally, I'm a Superintendent and you're a temporary Chief Inspector, so, essentially, you're an Inspector, two ranks below me. If the crimes are linked, then rank pulls, I'm afraid. That said, we have more experience in the realm of investigating serious crime over here, so we'd be better placed to deal. Send me over everything you've got on the killer, okay?'

Will took a deep breath, he felt himself filling with anger about the manner this senior officer was dismissing not only his experience, but that of the Eastborough force as a whole. 'Sir, with all due respect, I'm going to speak with our Chief Constable about this, ownership is very much a decision for that rank. I'll get back to you directly. In the meantime, I'm busy investigating murders in our area, so until I hear otherwise, that's what me and my team will continue to do. Oh, and it's a matter of opinion if you are better placed, experience wise, to deal with this set of murders. Remember the Yorkshire Ripper investigation?'

Will calmly ended the call, replacing the receiver, before immediately picking it up and calling the duty officer, who just happened to be Deputy Chief Constable Wood. Will explained the circumstances and his belief that the killer had potentially strayed into another force's area. He didn't want to obstruct another force's investigation, however, he needed confirmation as to ownership of the overall investigation. The response he received from DCC Wood was unexpected.

'Will, it's your case. We've had four murders on our territory, Leeds have had one. Experience is fine but you know more about this series of crimes than anyone. I want you to continue. I am in the office first thing tomorrow morning so I will have a word with the Chief Constable and get him to speak to the West Yorkshire Chief. In fact, bear with me a moment please, Will, yes, I have it here. I'm going to pass this directly through to the Home Secretary's office and that of the Justice Secretary for clearance. If they authorise it then the investigation is all yours. Can you manage it, Will? Don't say yes if you have any concerns.'

'Sir, I want to catch this killer. My team are wholly focused and working their socks off to get us closer to nailing whoever it is. There's no better, more determined investigation team in the whole of the UK to deal with these killings. What concerns me most is whether Leeds or other police forces will play ball, and provide us with everything we need. We need access all areas. It could be a political minefield.'

'Nonsense, Will, you leave that with me. I will get you the clearance and authority you require to lead nationally on this if needs be.'

There was no other way of describing how Will felt at that particular moment, elation at being so trusted and respected. He could barely believe that the Home Secretary and the Justice Secretary would be giving authority to his leadership. It was the lift he needed, as he spoke to the day and night shift investigation team, his mood was buoyant and again his speech inspired the team when they most needed it.

'Everyone, listen in to what I have to say. It appears that a body has been discovered in Leeds. It bears all the hallmarks of being a victim of our killer. The DCC of our force is speaking with the Home Secretary first thing tomorrow morning. That's right, I said the Home Secretary. I don't even know who the present Home Secretary is, however, it seems highly likely that we'll be leading the investigation until we catch the bastard who is committing these crimes. So we keep doing the same things, nothing gets past us. The murderer is out there now, he maybe killing again. Whatever he's up to, he'll be looking over his shoulder because he knows we are catching up with him, and soon, there'll be nowhere left for him to run and he'll be ours. Great work so far people, so let's keep it going. I'm heading over to Leeds now to take a look at the crime scene and the body. Daisy, Mandy, are you okay to join me? It's going to be a late night I'm afraid. Paula, can you contact Leeds, and let them know I'm on my way over to them. If they get arsey about it, tell them to contact our Deputy Chief Constable.'

The two women wasted no time in confirming their commitment to the investigation, and desire to see the Leeds crime scene. Soon, the three were on their way to Leeds. During the journey, Will seized the opportunity to call Mel and to let her know he was going to be late home. As usual she was understanding and supportive. He felt content knowing she was fully behind him in everything he did. He noticed that neither of his colleagues called their respective partners, and wondered how their relationships were. For certain, they would be spending less time at home during the murder investigations.

CHAPTER TWELVE

The journey into Leeds was straight forward, and one Will had traversed many times on his way to watch his beloved Leeds United. Passing Killingbeck Police Station on their right by the old Charlie Brown's roundabout, they followed the inner ring road into the city for a distance of about 100 yards, before turning off to the right and into the cemetery grounds. A line of eight police cars were parked on the grass verge leading into the burial grounds.

'Christ, how can they afford to have so many officers tied up with this one incident?' exclaimed Will. 'We are lucky to have ten bobbies on duty at any one time,' he continued.

'Welcome to big city policing,' Daisy responded.

As they parked their unmarked police car, a uniform officer approached them. 'You can't park there, madam' he ordered Daisy. 'This is a police crime scene, no unauthorised persons are allowed to enter this area.'

Will flipped open his warrant card and displayed it to the officer. 'DCI Scott, DS Wright and forensic psychologist Amanda Ward, the Home Secretary has approved our attendance,' said Will with a serious tone to his voice. 'Where is the SIO, I'd like to speak with him, please?'

The officer spoke into the police radio attached to his stab vest. 'Message for Superintendent Norton, we have three Eastborough officers here. They wish to speak to you, shall I send them up?'

A brief response, which Will recognised as an 'affirmative' crackled back over the radio. They were pointed in the direction of a blue and white forensic tent that had been erected over a number of headstones. It was raining quite heavily and the scene in the graveyard had an altogether eerie appearance, as forensic officers dressed in all white, scurried about like ghosts, under the illumination coming from temporarily erected artificial lighting.

'Shades of the Yorkshire Ripper,' commented Mandy, 'I bet most officers here have had that thought.' Will and Daisy ignored the comment and were met at the door of the tent by a tall thin man, with a goatee beard and a worn face that looked like it had seen a thousand dead bodies.

'Detective Superintendent Norton, you must be DCI Scott,' said the officer in a broad West Yorkshire accent, shaking Will's hand in a tight grip. Will made his own introductions and explained to his Leeds based colleague what had been said during his conversation with the Eastborough DCC. He was quietly surprised by Norton's response. 'Yes, I understand. Our Chief has told me to provide you with all the help and support you need. Our local intelligence might offer some further details. This woman, she's a bit of a mess if I'm to be honest. In twenty plus years of policing, I've not seen anything as gruesome as this. What kind of sick bastard would attack, kill and leave a woman in such a horrific state, in a graveyard of all places?'

The Eastborough officers donned their forensic suits and entered the scene accompanied by Superintendent Norton. The body was still there and looked badly deformed, virtue of the expanding foam that had enlarged and bulged various parts of the face and body, it oozed out of its orifices. The woman was completely naked, and like all the other crime scenes Will had witnessed, a small kitchen blow torch had been used to scorch off her hair and burn part of the body. This was sat on the ground, on the left hand side of the body as Will looked at it face on. A curious gurgling noise coming from behind him alerted Will that someone was about to be sick. He turned around to see Mandy shoot out of the tent and projectile vomit onto the grass outside.

'Sorry everyone, I couldn't stop myself. That poor woman,' she said, wiping her mouth with a clean tissue.

Looking back towards the body, Will saw something partially buried in the earth beside the right buttock, it was precisely what he had been looking for, a silver metal angel trinket. He reached down and collected it, placing it inside an evidence bag.

Norton availed further information about the victim. 'We are fairly sure she was driven here by someone, since she had a tablet and bag with her that's been recovered and is being examined. The clothes she was wearing are, as you see, neatly folded nearby.'

'Is the gravestone significant?' asked Will.

'It doesn't appear to be. It dates back to the 19th century. Belongs to a Graham Savile, so no link with the victim. Anyway, she's been living in your neck of the woods,' he added.

Will gave Norton a stare. 'What do you mean, the gravestone doesn't appear to be significant, read it, it's a fucking Savile, it's been selected by the killer because of that connection. Our killer has been picking off paedophiles. This lady was married to a convicted nonce, I believe? Does she have any form or is she known to you locally?'

Norton took a deep breath, the Savile connection had bypassed him. 'Savile, that's a bit tenuous don't you think? Christ, get real, this isn't an Agatha Christie novel you know, this is the real world. Killers don't preselect murder sites in order to leave us a sodding clue. Whoever did this, carried out the attack and fucked off as quickly as they could, more likely to be an opportunist I believe. Yes, this woman is known to us. No convictions though, however, when her husband was lifted, she was believed to have been working with him to groom the kids and invite them into their home. We couldn't prove it for definite though. She gave evidence against her husband at Leeds Crown Court. I'm sorry, but honestly, I can't believe you genuinely think that the killer selected this grave specifically because of the surname and its connotation to paedophiles?' Norton was laughing and dismissive of the suggestion.

'It's not a joke mate, so stop laughing. Yes, I do believe the gravestone is of significance, and for me, it shows that our killer may well live on your patch. How many people would know a gravestone bearing that name was to be found here? Granted, the occupant of the grave probably has no family connection to the 'Jimmy Savile', it's the surname that's the important detail for the killer and us.

'Can you ask your forensic people to email me the report on their investigation into the tablet and any other details that might prove useful? I'll also need the police surgeons report and time and cause of death, once it's ascertained please. If your guys can carry out the usual investigations into her last known movements, associates and enemies, though I think because of who she was married to, that list might be lengthy. Also, check CCTV footage covering the York Road area leading up to the cemetery opening, both directions. Someone must surely have seen something?'

Norton nodded his head to acknowledge Will's instructions and offered his hand to him as they walked away. Will snubbed the gesture and turned his back on the Detective Superintendent, making his way back to their car. Within half an hour the Eastborough officers had left Leeds and were on their way back to Bridlington. The conversation in the car during the journey was deep. First to deliberate was Will.

'So, what did you make of that dick? He didn't think the name on the gravestone was relevant. No wonder they didn't catch the Yorkshire Ripper, it took South Yorkshire officers to do that for them.'

Daisy spoke up, 'Now then, boss, don't get all childish, it was the blokes opinion that's all, it doesn't really make any difference to us, does it?' she said in an almost motherly manner.

Will returned to talk of the killings. 'Anyway, we have a killer who might well be from Leeds, or at least they knew Killingbeck cemetery well enough to know that grave was there. We know for certain he is mobile, and carries tools for the killings in a vehicle. They obviously have some kind of vendetta against paedophiles and anyone involved in the child porn industry. They are potentially left-handed, and strong enough to overpower a man or a woman. Then we have the silver angel calling card, what's that all about? I'm seriously confident it's a man, based purely on the level of torture that's being inflicted on the victims.'

Mandy Ward stopped him there. 'Boss, can I just say, I think you are wrong there. The key aspect of the crime scene isn't the state the body is in, or the torture, it's more likely to be the neat arrangement of the victim's clothes and the angel trinket. Whoever the killer might be, they are calm enough to be able to torture someone, then neatly fold up their clothes into a pile. Then, they take time to hide a trinket somewhere around the crime scene, not so it's obvious to all and sundry, it's kind of secreted away. I can tell you now, the killer wants you to find the Angel thing, no one else, it's for your benefit Will. It's relevance is anyone's guess, but it's important enough for the killer to leave at the scene. How many men do you know who would be spiritually connected with angels? A man in touch with his feminine side perhaps? I think it may go deeper than this, there might even be some kind of religious connotation to all of this.'

Daisy agreed with Mandy. 'Our killer might be a religious nut job, I'd never considered that before. What with the angel connection, it makes sense to me now. Glasgow had a killer known as Bible John in the 1960's, now Eastborough has its own religious killer. What shall we call ours, something catchy, like the Archangel Arsehole.' The team momentarily laughed, yet deep inside they knew they might actually be onto something. As they neared Bridlington, a wave of tiredness wafted over the three of them. In the car park outside the police station, Will told both women to go straight home and to be in work for 8.00am the following morning. He returned to the briefing room, signed the vehicle keys back in, and gave a brief update to DS Simpson. As he moved to leave the building, he turned back to the DS.

'Ian, unless it's another murder, don't bother me this evening, I'm shattered and I need some timeout. It's been another long day, but I think we are starting to get somewhere at last.'

He couldn't wait to get home that night. He needed room and time to get his head around the day's activities, and yesterdays. The body count was piling up, and the clues were few and far between. Despite that, there was a real belief that they were onto something with the angel trinkets, it was something he could look up on the internet that evening.

Mel was pleased to see Will return home, the kids hadn't long been in bed, so he had a chance to go and have a chat with them, and hear how their day had been. Ellie seized the opportunity to ask him if he had caught

Mr Hooton's killer yet, this was something she was to ask every day. Will knew it was important for her to know that her father could protect her and others from the person who had killed her teacher. He was almost her guardian angel, someone who could right a wrong. It had been traumatic for her and her school friends, so Will reassured her that all the policemen and women in Bridlington and elsewhere, were out looking for the murderer night and day.

Eventually he returned downstairs where Mel had prepared a special dinner for them both to sit and enjoy, her plans were for them to have a relaxing evening, away from dead bodies, serial killers and murder investigations. An evening where they could simply enjoy each other's company. The dinner was eaten with hardly a word spoken between the couple, a sure sign that the food was good. Afterwards, Will helped with the washing up and general tidying up.

Mel poured them both a large glass of wine and told Will that he was going to sit together with her on the sofa and chill out. The conversation soon turned to the subject of the murders, but not in a way that Mel could ever have anticipated. 'Tell me what you know about angels?' asked Will as he slipped his arm around her shoulder and cuddled her close.

'Angels?' responded his wife. 'What the hell are angels to do with the murders?'

'Well everything and nothing really. It might be a clue, it might not. I know you're into some of that stuff, so I wondered if you might understand why our killer leaves a small silver angel trinket at each crime scene. The forensic psychologist seems to think it is the killer leaving some kind of message for me to find. I don't naturally buy into that kind of belief. So who better to ask for advice, other than you.'

'Well, it depends what kind of angel it is. It could be an archangel, an angel or a fallen angel. Are you convinced that the killer is focused on child sex offenders only?'

'Yes, he is. All the victims so far have been paedophiles. Why?'

'Well, it could be that the angel might represent something sinister, or something good, you know, like a St Christopher charm brings good fortune to travelers. It's a bit too deep and maybe a bit too much like the movies, however, the angel might represent some form of revenge attack being played out on the victims. There is an archangel of children you know. She is charged, by Him from above, with protecting children all over the world. Particularly children who have been abused. I can't remember her name, just give me a minute and I'll look it up on the internet.'

Mel reached over for her laptop computer and entered Archangel of Children into the search engine. Will was astounded by the level of knowledge his wife had about all things. Moments later she had uncovered a wealth of information.

'Here we go, Will, the Archangel's name is Naarai. This is the one I was looking for, Malakim. This title basically means angel. Malakim was one of Naarai's angels and

147

she 'delivers double damage to anyone who has intentionally harmed or abused a child'.'

Will sat up. 'What the hell! That's just a little too close for comfort. Delivers double the damage to a child abuser? That's exactly what our killer is doing to the victims. Christ, Mel, you've got something there. Malakim. It sounds kind of serial killer-ish, doesn't it?'

'Listen, Will, you need to put some space between you and this bloody investigation. You're at home now, your two little angels are upstairs sleeping, and your big angel is right here wanting her husband to talk about anything but paedophiles and murder. So come on, snuggle up here beside me and we'll watch a film together. A nice film, with no violence or mystery attached to it.' Mel scanned the TV listings and found a film they both fancied and settled down to watch it. Within twenty minutes, Mel could hear the faint breathing pattern that she recognised as Will sleeping. She cuddled up to him as the overwhelming feeling of being safe in his arms made her smile. Soon both were fast asleep.

CHAPTER THIRTEEN

As the early morning sun rose on the horizon, it shone directly through the vertical blinds on the living room windows of the Scott home, awakening the sleeping couple curled up in each other's arms on the sofa. Will strained his eyes in an attempt to open them in the direct light of the sun. He was momentarily confused, finding himself asleep downstairs, more curious to him was the sight of Mel sound asleep beside him. The last thing he could remember was discussing the angel that Mel had identified, and a real feeling that it was an important detail that he shouldn't ignore. In the cold light of day, it seemed less so. That said, he couldn't remember its name anyway.

Mel stirred, and stretched. 'What time is it, Will?'

Her husband wasn't yet quite with it, he was still half asleep. Looking at the clock on the mantelpiece, he saw it was 7.15am. 'I better get showered and ready for work, I'll stick the kettle on as I go upstairs,' he said disappearing from the lounge.

A quarter of an hour later he came back downstairs and into the kitchen. The kids weren't yet awake, and Mel was preparing a toasted bacon sandwich for him.

'Don't suppose you can remember the names of those angels we were talking about last night, can you?'

His wife, as usual, was one step ahead of him. She handed him an A4 piece of paper. 'I've printed the names and their brief meanings off, so you can take it into work and read it. Just remember, I've got those details from the internet, and not everything is accurate on there. Though I am reasonably certain that what it says about the Malakim is correct.'

'I don't suppose you know if Malakim are male, or female, angels do you?' asked Will.

'It's all in the paper I printed out. Malak is a Semitic word, meaning angel, so when the Christian bible refers to angels it's referring to Malakim. They can be male or female and not all of them are good. To be honest Mister Detective Chief Inspector, I don't think you'll get away with trying to pin these murders on an angel,' laughed Mel as she pushed his bacon butty towards him.

Within a few minutes, he was heading out of the front door and back to Bridlington Police Station. His mind was spinning with thoughts about the Leeds murder. He mulled over reasons why the killer had chosen to move farther afield. From Brid to Leeds was a good 60 miles to drive, so maybe the killer was Leeds based, and had been visiting Bridlington, or perhaps there was family in Bridlington? There was too much missing detail for the investigation to truly make progress. He wondered whether that level of information would ever be revealed, almost everything they had, clue wise, was guess work and assumption. Will noted in the 'to do' part of his memory, to task Daisy with listing and detailing the known facts in a new timeline.

With that thought, he pulled his Audi A4 into the police station car park, and parked up. He was surprised, because he had no recollection of the journey he had just taken through the town. He raised his eyebrows, causing his forehead to momentarily furrow as he realised how fortunate he had been not to be involved in any kind of vehicle accident during the journey. As he plodded up the cold sterile stairs that led to the investigation room, the only sound he could hear was that of his footsteps echoing off the walls. As he reached the top landing, the building suddenly sprang into life, and he could hear the busy sound of people talking, the different tones and accents creating somewhat melodic tunes to his ears. All peaceful thoughts vanished from his mind as he entered the room.

Daisy stood waiting by his desk, she looked a little nervous, anxious even. 'Morning, boss, I'll let you take your jacket off before I hit you with this.'

Will felt the fluttering of butterflies in his stomach, if this was something that had caused alarm to his DS, then it must be something grave indeed. 'Right, Daisy, what have we got, girl?'

'Well, forensics have recovered identical word documents from the laptops of each victim. It's the same list of names every time. We can find no valid reason or explanation for the lists being there. There is no title or name for the document in any of the hard drives of the computers. The documents, we are now told, were created at the time of the murder, so our killer has very likely added them. Why they have done this is another question. Forensics were wrong with the early analysis of these lists, when they said they were added some time before the murders. That's not all boss, we have now identified a website that each victim had visited hours before their death. It's called *'A Step In The Dark.'* It's based overseas, however the owner lives in Ireland. He's an ex-fireman who's done time for defrauding his own family. A horrible piece of work, he stole hundreds of thousands of inheritance from his relatives. We've researched him. He's driven by hatred of the establishment, a really peculiar bloke in every sense. He's astute enough to know how to hide his business activities online. It takes dogged perseverance finding anything out about him, but when you do, it's all damning stuff. I should mention that his brother is a convicted paedophile, name of Liam Burton. He doesn't appear to have left Ireland during the timeline of the murders so I guess that gives him a cast iron alibi, but I have asked the local garda to check him out and see what they can find out about the website. The other thing, you have to give some Superintendent down at the National Crime Agency a call. He's asking loads of questions and wants to speak to you direct. He's talking about getting the Child Exploitation Online Protection team involved as well, I believe.'

Will was impressed by Daisy's ownership of the investigation. 'Okay, good stuff, Daisy, do we have a name and number for the NCA? I'll give this chap a call and see what assistance he can provide. CEOP is a resource we can tap into. I'll let them know about the *'Into The Dark'* website and the Burton fella. I'm certain he'll be on their radar. Then maybe we can get on with investigating our murders. This bureaucracy shit is really doing my head in, having to feedback updates to the powers that be all the bloody time. It feels like every officer above the rank of Superintendent wants to know what's going on, best of it is, most of its out of pure nosiness.'

Will made the call to the NCA in London, and was soon speaking with Superintendent Guy. He expected the senior officer to pull rank on him, instead, he found him to be supportive, understanding and helpful. 'If there is anything we can do to help, just give me a call, Will, we are here to help where we can. As long as you keep us informed of what is going on up there, then we'll leave you to it. Our intelligence system is far superior to what you will have at station level, we have Europol access too, added to which, we have bespoke investigation tools in our armoury, all of which are at your disposal. If you can copy everything to CEOP as well, because they clearly have a vested interest in this.'

Will agreed, and for the first time in days, he felt as though everything was heading in the right direction and that the breakthrough they needed to identify and catch the killer was not too far away. He called Paula Jay over to his desk and informed her that she was the official liaison officer with CEOP and the NCA. She was to compile and distribute daily update logs for those agencies, to be sent out at 10am, each morning. 'Nothing, I repeat nothing, gets sent out without my approval, please Paula.'

DC Amber Taylor approached the group carrying a pile of documents. Amber had transferred to Eastborough in 2012 as a substantive Detective Constable from

Merseyside Police. A born Liverpudlian, she was married with no children. Amber specialised in domestic abuse investigations and was regarded, by all who knew her, as a professional and extremely focused officer. Her determination and perseverance in the most challenging of cases was a real asset. It was Daisy Wright who recognised her as an asset to the CID team at Bridlington.

'Boss, these are the forensic reports from the Shuttleworth and Tilley cases and the James case over in Leeds. It's the same M.O., and from the wounds inflicted, it's the same killer, forensics believe. Unfortunately, they've found no alien DNA present on either corpse or at the crime scenes. Tilley had a family relation who was an active member of the Paedophile Information Exchange between 1974 and 1984. His name was Neil Ross, now deceased. Our killer, it appears, is smart and maybe, because of the knowledge of the PIE group, might be close to middle age?'

Daisy Wright interrupted the conversation 'Sir, I've got the Chief Constable on the phone, can I put him through to you?'

'Good morning, DCI Scott. This isn't an official call, so please make sure no one else can hear our conversation.'

Will motioned away the officers stood by his desk. 'You are free to talk, sir,' he replied.

'Will, I've had my bag carrier harping on at me about finances and costs. I don't want this to turn into another fucking Yorkshire Ripper scenario where the money is concerned. Wherever you can, stick to the budgets. I'll keep you all on the 12 hour shift pattern for a further month, that includes rest day working. Thereafter, if we still haven't got the killer, then we review it as a cost cutting exercise. Does that sound fair?'

'Yes, sir, extremely fair, I'm hoping we'll have our killer behind bars within a month.'

Finally, the SIO and Daisy could sit down and go through what facts they knew of. They were joined by Mandy Ward who held in her hand a typed paper which she put before Will Scott. 'This is what I've come up with overnight. It's not science, more gut feeling than anything, I thought it might help.'

Will thanked the forensic psychologist for her efforts and read through the document which outlined the known facts that he was about to analyse with Daisy. 'This is great, Mandy, just what we needed.' It was hardly ground breaking content. However, it showed that Mandy had clearly identified the important factors at each crime scene and attempted to put them into perspective alongside each murder. The important fact that stood out from everything else was the evidence that each victim was a predatory paedophile, with an active interest in child porn.

Will decided it was time to take a gamble, and to use the power of the media to distribute news stories that would be to the police advantage. He discussed the details with the police press office and received official clearances to make a press announcement. Rather than hold a press briefing, Will determined that Lucien Palmer would be the ideal vehicle to disseminate the story for them.

The local reporter couldn't believe his luck when Will called him, and invited him to a meeting at the police station. The investigation team believed that the public needed to be made aware that the killer was identifying and sadistically killing active and known paedophiles. It would create a moral juxtaposition, promoting an element of calm among the greatest section of society, while causing sheer panic among the child pervert community. In turn, this might encourage, or force witnesses to come forward, especially so if they are part of that child sex group.

Lucien, for his part, would not be aware that he was being used by the police. In essence he wasn't, however, it was common knowledge that he needed to rebuild his reputation after his reporting debacle surrounding the Shuttleworth murder. So Will believed he was doing his friend a favour, and an opportunity to build bridges with the local constabulary and the people of the region.

Lucien avidly lapped up every detail the DCI imparted to him, leading him towards the conclusion about the killers selected victims. 'Can I give the killer an identity, all serial killers have a press created pseudonym? I'm thinking 'the paedo preyer.' Would you object, Will?'

'Lucien, you're the journalist not me. So long as you don't print untruths or anything that is likely to affect our investigations, then call the killer what you like. It would make a good title for a book though. Lucien, play your cards right and you could have a book on your hands as well. So play ball with us, don't shit on us. We want the good normal people of the region to feel safe and secure in the knowledge that it's 'paedophiles' and child pornography perverts only our killer is hunting down and butchering. We have four mutilated bodies across our police area, and one in the Leeds area. You can also quote that I am the nominated senior investigating officer for all the murders, that decision has come direct from the Home Secretary, I am asking anyone in the region who holds suspicion about someone locally to get in touch with us. Integrity will be 100% maintained.'

By that afternoon, the nation's media was filled with stories about the 'paedo preyer,' linking historic cases to the most recent murders. The press release had the desired effect. The investigation room telephones rang constantly with people volunteering information about friends, neighbours and in some cases, family members who showed a physical hatred towards paedophiles. The counter effect, which was still viewed as a positive, was fifteen fresh cases of historic child abuse were reported, five of which involved high profile personalities.

No one involved in the investigation could have pre-empted the media onslaught that followed the news story. Sky television news were unrelenting in their desire and requests to interview DCI Scott on camera, live from outside Bridlington Police Station. Eventually, Will rose to the challenge and delivered a first class interview, fending off many leading questions about the investigation and his experience in heading it. One thing Will could not disguise was his passion and determination to find the killer, this enhanced the public image he portrayed. As one Sky news reporter put it, 'Detective

Chief Inspector Scott is the detective every individual in the country would want to investigate such crimes.'

Inside the investigation room, Mandy Ward had pulled up details of a number of support groups who work in the field of child abuse. One in particular stood out as being different, it offered confidential support to paedophiles.

Paula Jay noticed Mandy looking at the group's website. 'That's a bloody weird bunch of people, if you ask me. Why would you want to help paedophiles? I rang them yesterday and asked how many paedophiles they had absolutely cured, that they felt confident wouldn't reoffend. The answer was nil, none, zilch. Apparently it's not about curing them, it's about helping them manage their illness.'

Barry Smith was equally as shocked. 'Illness? Did they call it an illness? It's a choice these people make, it's not an illness. From what I know, most of them are vile predators, with no conscience or care for the children they abuse or the impact it has upon them later in life.' Smith seized the opportunity to look over at the webpage being displayed on Mandy's computer. 'I tell you what, while agencies exist such as this bloody lot, it empowers the paedophile. They will, and do, say at trial, that they sought addiction management training to help deal with their child pervert issues. The Judiciary, being so far removed from reality, listen to the defendant, and accept that this bloody agency is working towards helping them, so administer a reduced sentence. I have no time for these do-gooders and it beats me why the government provide hundreds of thousands of pounds worth of funding to them. An absolute waste of good financial resources.'

It was a passionate discussion that got others in the team questioning whether paedophilia was a personal choice or an illness. The overwhelming belief among the investigators was that it wasn't an illness but a personal choice. Statistics were banded about. Two in every six children are abused in some form or another, 70% of child victims are female, 90% of victims know their abuser, 95% of abusers are family members of the victim, and it wasn't true that abused children themselves become abusers later in life. Surprisingly, two detectives in the team, one male one female, were brave enough to stand up and admit they had been abused as children.   DC Ron Prudham, a vastly experienced detective, explained how he had first been groomed then sexually abused by a church minister when he attended Sunday school aged just seven years old. The abuse had stepped up a level when he went away with cub scouts on a trip to the Lake District. The minister was on the same trip, and had raped him during the week-long stay.

'It was dreadful, there was no one I could tell, and he continually told me that no one would believe me. I felt so alone. The abuse continued until I was about ten. I never did tell my mum, I think my father knew something was wrong, because he pulled me from all interaction with the church and the minister. I'd find it really hard to report it to the police now that I've got my own family. The shame and guilt lives with you forever, and there's not a day goes by when I don't think about it.

'I can't believe I've just told you lot all this right now. There's no need to pussyfoot around me or anything like that, I'm still the same Ron Prudham you all know. I manage my issues by suppressing everything, bottling it up inside me. God, if I was ever to let it all out, it would overwhelm me. I have nothing but the highest respect for those people who are strong enough to reveal everything about their abuse. It takes some guts and courage and if I'm honest, I don't think the police service or the judiciary truly understand the impact it has on victims lives.'

The investigation room fell quiet, no one knew how to respond to DC Prudham's revelation. Then Constable Alison Poulter stood up. 'Ron, you're not on your own. I know exactly where you are coming from. I was abused as a child too, a family relative. It went on for about six years, I was just eight when it started. I told my mother and father, neither of them believed me and I was punished for telling horrid lies about my uncle. Not being believed scarred me for life. My uncle was eventually arrested and charged for raping other girls. My mum and dad could never look me straight in the face after that. My uncle, the coward, hung himself before any of his victims could get justice and closure. There's something about people who have been abused as children, I can spot them in a crowd. I never broach the subject, but there is a certain manner about them. I expect I have it too. I joined the police because I wanted to make a difference, and help catch these abusers, and in doing so help protect children. I'm sorry if I've upset some of you, I didn't mean to, and like Ron said, just because you know

I was abused as a child, it doesn't make me a different person.'

There was barely a dry eye in the room, hardened police officers stood in admiration of the strength of their colleagues speaking out in such an open and candid manner. Slowly, every officer in the room rose to their feet a round of supportive applause gathered pace among them, in appreciation of the two officers' bravery for opening up to them. Such detail cemented relationships and a closeness throughout the team which didn't go amiss by their leader.

As Will entered the room, he asked the team the reason for all the clapping? When he was told, he nodded in appreciation. For a moment, he stood in silence before revealing, 'I'm not one for letting people get close to me. However, I want you to know, I too understand what it's like to suffer abuse as a child. I was a victim, survivor, or whatever the academics want to call people like me. It doesn't make me a bad person, the stigma that attaches itself to you as an abused child never leaves you, it sits there every day. Saying that, you lot have empowered me to reveal my inner self, I'm not ashamed, it doesn't make me different, it makes me stronger to succeed in everything I do. If emotions played a part in this investigation, off the record, I'd probably say the killer is doing the public a good deed and I'd shake his hand in appreciation. However, emotion doesn't play a part in policing today. It's all about being impartial, professional and treating everyone fairly and equally. Truth is, nobody likes a paedophile, yet the saddest fact is, they are free to walk among us. Maybe, just maybe, these killings will get people reacting differently and working together not only to catch our killer but to report their suspicions about paedophile activity. God, listen to me, I sound like a government propaganda machine.

'Right, enough of the emotional stuff, we've got to nail this bastard soon, we need to stop this glut of victims we are stockpiling, so get out there and get some serious police work done. Someone told me just now that the number of victims we have, five, in the space of less than one week, is a record, so we are up against it. It's my opinion that our killer isn't righting wrongs, as he first might have been. He is playing a game with us, creating pressure through the body count, giving us no respite, or time to investigate. He's careful where he kills. Each kill site has been pre-selected, he's also done his homework on each victim, he knows how to win them over and manipulate them before committing carnage on their bodies. I firmly believe, that the killer is spiritually aware, the wrath of God and all that, since he has left us one clue at each crime scene, the silver angel trinket. Listen carefully, the angel is otherwise known as Malakim and 'the attack of Malakim has double the damage to anyone who intentionally abuses or harms children'. That is precisely what each of our victims have a history of doing.'

The mention of the word Malakim swept through the team like an icy blast of winter wind. It left them cold in disbelief, yet aware that many serial killers carry out rituals that have biblical connotations on their victims.

The honesty of three of the team, including their leader, DCI Scott, emotionally connected the group. An invisible bond of respect was forged. Now they had a name for the evil they pursued, Malakim.

CHAPTER FOURTEEN

With the world's media alerted to the sinister activity of a serial killer active across the north of England, the news stories relating the crimes became more sensational. As each media source attempted to produce sanguinary details that might satiate their reader's appetite. With that came an avalanche of anonymous mail addressed to and for the attention of DCI Will Scott. Every letter had to be read, the content examined and assessed for credibility. The vast majority had genuine intent, but some were spiteful and vindictive, abusive even. These wasted valuable police time and resources, as innocent people were maliciously named as the killer, and all such reports had to be investigated.

The media had not the faintest inkling about the severity of the injuries each victim had suffered during the fatal attacks. Had that level of detail been made public, mass hysteria and public panic would most certainly have followed. Will had made huge efforts to deter any kind of reference to the killer being some kind of vigilante. He reiterated to the media throughout, that it was the duty and responsibility of the police to investigate the murders and bring the killer to justice.

The different squads within the investigation team continued to identify fresh leads, in particular from careful scrutiny of local authority CCTV footage, they were able to identify three different types of car as being potentially suspect. The black and white footage had been blurred. However, it was sufficient for officers to glean that all the vehicles were silver in colour, four door models, and either a Ford Mondeo, Audi A4 or a Volkswagon Passat. Number plate recognition camera footage wasn't available, due to council cut backs that didn't deem it necessary. If it had been, then it was highly likely that suspects would have been brought in and questioned and potentially, the killer could have been identified and caught. It annoyed Will that the same council had spent £3 million pounds on car park CCTV cameras to catch unsuspecting motorists, who outstayed their timed parking limit by a minute or so, and fine them. When he questioned this with the council CEO, he was told that parking enforcement was an important and integral part of the council's revenue. Whereas automatic number plate recognition cameras, brought no revenue to council coffers at all, the fines resulting from vehicles having no motor vehicle tax went direct to central government.

The concentration of the investigation team was shattered when the usually composed DS Smith called out with a sense of panic in his voice, 'Boss, you've got a telephone call. DCI Mattock from Northamptonshire Police would like to speak with you as a matter of urgency. It sounds serious.'

As Will took the call, the investigation room again fell silent, every officer in the room had one ear listening to their DCI's comments during the conversation. A tangible feeling of dread pervaded throughout the room.

'This is DCI Scott from Eastborough Police, how may I help?'

'Yes, I understand you are investigating a series of murders,' said the voice at the other end. 'I have a feeling we have one of your bodies here in Kettering. It's a savage piece of butchery that's been committed to this corpse. Never seen anything like it before, and I've seen some grisly old murders. I guess this one is ritualistic. His hair has been burnt off, right down to the scalp, the eyelids are stapled open and each eyeball has been stabbed through the cornea with a wooden barbecue skewer, the fingers have been chopped off, and the genitals and penis removed, the penis was inserted into the victim's mouth, and his jaws were clamped shut, forcing the teeth to bite into it. We haven't yet found the rest of his genitals. Does it sound familiar to you?'

Will fell silent, his brain frantically tried to rationalise the information he had just received.

'Yes, it is familiar. Do you have the victim's identity, the time of death and where the body was found?'

'Yes, his name is Martin Newell, his date of birth is 14.07.65. He is known to us and he's CRO. He's a sex offender. He likes children, preferably older boys, a convicted pederast with a string of convictions. Until recently he was employed as a librarian. We've just ascertained that he was sacked two weeks ago for exposing himself to a group of boys in the library building here in Kettering. A tad weird by all accounts. He was found in his home, a two up, two down, terraced house off Rockingham Road in Kettering. He's been dead for several days, three to four, according to the pathologist. The body had begun to smell a bit, that's what alerted the

166

neighbours to call us. The house reeks of death, so we assume the killer must have put the central heating on to help decomposition, because we're in the middle of a really warm spell here. There was also a dog who had produced a litter of recently born puppies in the house. Strangely, someone had been in the house and fed and watered the dogs, caring for them, while the body rotted away in the living room. We can only think the killer must have returned and fed them.'

'Do you want to visit the crime scene directly or can I get the body removed and the house made secure? Our forensic people have been all over it already.'

Will took a deep breath and glanced at his watch before randomly asking his team, 'Does anyone know how far Kettering is from Bridlington?'

DCI Mattock on the other end of the telephone answered. 'It will take about four hours to drive, bearing in mind you'll be coming through the rush hour traffic on both the A1 and M1, I'd avoid the A14 at that time day too, they're all bound to be busy.'

'Okay,' said Will, 'I'm on my way with a couple of my investigation team. Can you leave the body in situ and maintain a police presence at the property? No one goes in or out without my approval, through you, does that sound feasible?'

'Yes, of course, we'll protect the scene until your arrival. Don't forget to bring plenty of Vick to rub under your nose, you'll need it in that house.'

As Will replaced the receiver, he looked up at his investigation team, his body language said everything

167

there was to say. 'You've probably guessed by now, however, to make it clear, we have another body, this time in Kettering, Northamptonshire. Makes me wonder if our killer is a travelling bloody salesman or a truck driver like Peter Sutcliffe. Whatever, he's struck again, a bit further from home this time, but it's got his trademarks all over it. Daisy, we are going to Kettering. Why the hell did he have to kill in Kettering? It's bloody miles away. Can you call Mandy and ask her to come to the nick straight away, explain what's happened, and inform her that we require her attendance. Tell her it's urgent. I'll ring the Chief and update him, this whole investigation is fast becoming a bloody farce. We aren't getting time to properly look into anything before another bloody body turns up. Amber, can you contact the NCA and CEOP, let them know of this latest murder. DCI Mattock is faxing through all the details, so pass those on please. Everyone else, stick with your current enquiries, until I advise differently.'

Daisy was quick to remind her boss that she knew Kettering extremely well having served there during her time with Northamptonshire Police. 'Sir, Kettering used to be my patch, so I know how far it is, and the quickest way to get there. Chances are, I've dealt with this victim previously. If he's a Kettering con, then I'll know him.'

An hour later, the three colleagues were headed down the M1 towards Kettering. The journey was made all the more stressful by the thought of the carnage that awaited. Of the three, Daisy seemed more focused on the logistical aspect of the killings. The killer was indiscriminately leaving bodies in random geographic locations. He was on the move and no one, it seemed, could predict where he would kill next. Daisy studied the pages of an atlas which she had laid open across her knees. 'There doesn't seem to be any logic to the murder spree, the only thing I can come up with is that the last victim was found in Killingbeck, Leeds, and this one is in Kettering, Northamptonshire. Both locations start with the letter K. It's a complete mystery to me.'

As Will drove, he asked Mandy for her take on the randomness of the crime scenes.

'It's a tough one to understand, I tend to side with Daisy, at this stage of proceedings it's a mystery. It makes sense that the killer will be a driver of some description, I also question whether he is acting alone. The Leeds victim had been killed at a specially selected site, showing that the killer possessed local knowledge. It's natural to consider therefore that the killer had to be local to Leeds. Now we have a body in a house that is over 120 miles from Leeds. Are we also to believe that the killer has returned to the Kettering crime scene several times post murder, to feed the dog and its puppies? Again, it's a natural assumption that the killer must live in the Kettering area. From a sensible perspective, the question that must now be asked is, do we have two killers acting wholly independent of each other, or have we two, or more, working together? I don't think we can rule out an entire network of vigilante type killers, who have connected through the dark web and are planning this entire thing. There's a whole raft of so called 'paedophile hunters' cropping up all over the UK. They are non-violent, and intelligent people who plan and research their targets before tricking them into a meet. Once there, the paedophile is confronted and the police called. The hunters then hand all the evidence over to the police. Could it be a rogue element of these hunters has taken it a stage further, and is killing paedophiles?'

'Fucking hell, Mandy,' said Will gripping the Audi's steering wheel tightly and fidgeting uncomfortably in the driver seat. 'What are you suggesting, we have a nationwide army of vigilante murderers trying to extinguish every known paedophile in the country? That's outrageous and totally inconceivable.'

Daisy did her best to calm her angst filled police colleague down. 'Boss, I think what Mandy is trying to say is that we cannot rule anything out. The killer is unpredictable, and to be honest, I think it's a good shout that we may have more than one killer bumping off paedos. For me, the real question is more of a moral one, are these killers carrying out a public service getting rid of these sickos? There hasn't been too much public outrage so far, and I guarantee in most homes across the country, people will be privately accepting of a serial killer in these circumstances. I know and understand all that protection of life shit, but let's be honest here, kiddy fiddlers are the lowest of the low, no one likes them and no one seems too bothered that they are being hunted down. I don't have much sympathy for them as victims, it's a hard call trying to feel anything but loathing for them.'

The car fell quiet, as each occupant wrestled with their own conscience and opinion of how Daisy Wright had been brave enough to state her feelings. 'I think you are right, Daisy. However, we swore a solemn oath as police officers, we cannot let personal opinion blind our judgement or stop us doing our utmost to catch whoever it is committing these murders. We have to detach ourselves from the victim's criminal past. It's not easy but that's what we get paid to do.'

No one spoke, other than Daisy giving driving directions, for the remainder of the journey to the town, and the crime scene which was off Rockingham Road and very close to the old Kettering Town football stadium. The sight of the four towering floodlights signaled they were close, and caused Will to speak. 'I remember coming here to watch Leeds play the local team in a pre-season friendly. It was 3-3 draw if I remember correctly, I'd never have guessed that one day I would be back here investigating a fucking murder.'

As Will's Audi wove its way through the narrow streets that backed onto the stadium, the rows of dark terraced houses seem to close in on them, forcing them down even tighter car lined streets, and finally, to the murder scene. As they pulled up, no one was in any kind of hurry to get out of the car.

A uniformed officer walked up to the driver's window and knocked on it with an air of authority. 'Who are you and what is your business? This is a crime scene, you can't park here,' he said gruffly.

'I'm DCI Scott and these are my colleagues. I'm the SIO for these murders.'

Will was directed towards the entrance of the murder house, where he could see a group of suited officers stood talking. As the Eastborough team moved closer, one man broke from the group and identified himself as DCI Mattock. There was no time for niceties, as Will was given a full briefing of the crime scene, and the three visiting officials were handed Tyvek suits and shown into a tent where they could change.

DCI Mattock led the team inside the house through the front door which opened directly into the living room. The caustic aroma of burnt hair and putrefying flesh infiltrated the face masks of the officers causing Mandy to cough to prevent herself from gagging. 'The killer gained access through the front door. The back door, which is the only other point of access, is bolted and locked from the inside. All the windows are locked and secured from the inside, our forensics team found cobwebs on the lower floor windows, showing that they hadn't been opened in some time.'

The living room was clean and tidy, a door at the far side of the room led through to a further room at the back of the house. DCI Mattock stopped at the entrance to this, the door was wide open and covered in fingerprint powder from the earlier forensic examination of the property. Standing at the doorway he turned to the group and pointed inside, 'He's in there, poor bastard, no matter what he was in life, he certainly suffered at the end, hard to believe one human being could do this to another. I'll leave you here to get on with your own search for information, it's a square room and the door at the back leads into the kitchen, the other door which runs off this dividing wall takes you to the upstairs floor of the property. The victim is pinned to the floor, nails have been driven through his hands and into the floorboards.'

As the Northamptonshire officer left the group, Will advised his team to stay focused and not to concentrate on the injuries to the body. 'We are looking for additional evidence that might definitely show that this is our killer, look out for the silver angel trinket. Mandy, is there anything specific that we should be looking out for that might help you?'

The forensic psychologist advised that she would be looking at the crime scene as a whole, and the mutilations to the body. 'It's important that I see the body as it was found. It will help determine any consistent behaviour and patterning he has left behind, the ritualistic side of the attack that may also give me an understanding of where it first happened. It's clear we are dealing with someone who is very controlled during the act of killing, they are careful, it's premeditated therefore they are unlikely to leave obvious traces behind.'

The three entered the room, Daisy worked round the room from the left, Will from the right, while Mandy followed taking a central position and scanning her eyes left and right so that nothing was missed.

The naked body was laid out on the floor on the far side of the room, the curtains had been drawn making the area seem cramped and claustrophobic. Will asked

Mandy to turn on the lights from a switch by the door. As she did this the full extent of the atrocity of the attack was exposed to them. A pool of dried, dark blood surrounded the body, the top of the victims head and upper face area had been scorched black and was badly blistered. Daisy pointed to a movement in one of the wounds in his hand, it was a wriggling off white coloured, larvae, the body was under attack from a more natural source that would ultimately emerge as bluebottle flies.

There was no obvious sign of the silver angel trinket around the body mass that the officers were looking for. Will and Daisy seemed perplexed by this, the killing bore all the hallmarks of previous murders, yet the killer hadn't left his signature calling card behind. Will wondered whether it was as Mandy had suggested, a network of vigilantes killing at random, maybe this killer was unaware of the Malakim link? Daisy was busy taking additional photographs of the crime scene and speaking into her digital recorder, numbering each frame, and physically describing each image. Mandy was scribbling down notes and was busy talking to herself, questioning the crime scene and the killer's actions. Will cast a disconsolate figure in the room, utter carnage surrounded him and from this mess he was expected to create a story of what happened, how it happened, and why it happened. For a moment, his mind went blank. He was staring into nothingness when he caught a glimpse of a familiar looking object stood on top of a cheap glass ornamental skull.

'Everyone stop, stand still,' he exclaimed, 'look over there, on the television stand behind you, Daisy, the glass skull, it's got something on top of it.'

'That's it, boss, that's his calling card, it's our killer,' responded Daisy. As Will and Daisy approached the ornament, they could see that the angel had been permanently adhered to the skull using a glue of some sort.

'Seize the glass skull and the Malakim. Mandy, what do you make of this? Why has he glued the angel to a glass skull?'

Mandy moved closer to look at the ornament before revealing her professional opinion.

'It could be a sign of superiority, the killer is seeing this as a game and in his opinion, he believes he is winning, he's outsmarting or out thinking you. I have to say, this whole Malakim thing is personal. It's directed at you, Will, not for any special reason, other than because you are the SIO. Alternatively, he might have stuck it there to let you know that he's watching you, monitoring your movements and the investigation.'

Daisy openly shivered and wriggled her body. 'The thought that he is watching us makes my flesh creep, that's really fucking unnerving. Do you mean he could be physically watching us right now? You don't think there might be hidden cameras in here, do you?'

'There's only one way to find out, let's have a good look for any,' said Will opening up, and checking inside an old wooden wind up clock sat on a shelf. A quick examination of the room revealed no hidden cameras, or

175

recording devices, causing Mandy to reaffirm her professional opinion.

'When I said watching, I should have been more precise and said monitoring the police investigation. That could be through the media, or perhaps from what the killer would believe to be a safe distance. You have to consider the fact that whoever killed this man, returned to the scene several times and fed the dog and its puppies. He therefore knew the body hadn't been found, so he was definitely watching the property.'

Will beckoned Daisy and Mandy to come closer to him, and leant forward down to their height, so he could quietly whisper. 'Listen, it's a fact that some killers like to see the mayhem their actions have caused, our killer might well fall into this category. When we leave here, Daisy, can you take photographs of the ghouls who have gathered at the cordon outside, I want every face captured if you can. If possible, go to an upstairs window and get these images, Mandy and I will leave the house so their attention will be on us and you'll get full on face views.'

'No problem, boss,' replied Daisy disappearing through the door that led to the stairs and the upper floor of the house.

Will and Mandy slowly left the house and moved towards the forensic tent where they could change. A couple of minutes later they were joined by Daisy. 'All done, boss, got every face as requested.'

As they stood inside the forensic tent, Mandy caught sight of the dog and its puppies, laid outside in the garden shed. The shed door was open. 'Aw look, it's the dog and the puppies,' she said with some excitement.

'Yes,' said one of the Crime Scene Investigators, we are waiting for the RSPCA to come out and collect them, they are divine aren't they?' Mandy slowly walked over to the animals. 'Be careful,' said the CSI officer, she's a biter, a new mother protecting her litter, she'll give you a nip if you get too close.' Mandy ignored the warning and as she neared the dog, it suddenly jumped up and ran to her, it didn't attack as she expected, instead it licked her hand and excitedly wagged its tail.

'I'm really good with dogs,' she said, patting the animal and showing it back to its puppies.

'We haven't got time for that, Mandy, come on,' said Will.

Turning to Daisy he said, 'That was great work, Daisy. We have to go to Kettering nick to touch base with DCI Mattock before we leave, so get your directional head on and tell me how we get there.' Daisy was deep in thought, and looking a little perplexed. 'What's up, Daisy, what is it?' asked Will.

'Probably nothing, boss, just my paranoia playing up again. Seriously, it's nothing. Come on, let's get you to Kettering nick.'

The police station was less than a five minute drive, parking the car at the rear, they were soon entering the building by the back door. Daisy took them through a long dark corridor that led past the custody suite and up some stairs to the CID suite. There, DCI Pete Mattock was sat at his office desk, with a pile of document folders in front of him. 'Hi, Will, I've got everything ready in these folders for you to take back to Bridlington. I told you it was a grisly crime scene, how does it compare to the others?'

'Very similar in every way, Pete,' replied Will. 'The killer is methodical and calm in the commission of the crime. I can't help but think he must have ice coursing through his veins and not blood. We've taken loads of photographs of the crime scene, so I'll hand it back to you now, if you can chase your forensic people for the laptop analysis and anything else that you might consider useful. Obviously if it fits with one of your local CRO then let us know and we can come down and give them a pull. Just keep us posted on anything and everything.'

The two senior officers shook hands and wished each other well. The Eastborough team left Kettering behind and were back in Bridlington within four hours. Will dropped Daisy and Mandy off at the police station and went straight home. He was exhausted, mentally and physically, and ready for his bed.

Mel was stood at the front door as he pulled into the drive, it was late and the children were in bed. She was relieved to see her husband return home, and welcomed him with open arms and a kiss. Inside, Will collapsed onto the cream leather sofa in the living room, Mel joined him carrying a mug of hot tea which she placed on the coffee table next to the document folders Will had put there moments earlier. 'So then, how was Kettering?' she asked.

Her husband could barely speak, he was that tired, instead he pointed to the folders, and muttered, 'Those folders contain everything you need to know about my away day.'

Mel picked up the top folder which contained the crime scene photographs captured by Northamptonshire officers. She took one look at the first image, before replacing it inside the folder and placing it back on the pile. 'Bloody hell, Will, that is shocking. How the hell are you dealing with this? You're going to need counselling after this you know, that is serious shit. Christ, who could do that to someone?'

The pair held each other tightly, Mel broke the moment and pulled away, she insisted that they go to bed and sleep. Will was in no place to argue the point and was first up the stairs, checking in on the sleeping children first, before returning to their bedroom, having a shower and climbing into bed. Within minutes he was in a deep sleep.

CHAPTER FIFTEEN

Mel was first to hear the faint drumming and vibration within the room. It was pitch dark and it took her a few seconds to acclimatise to the lack of light. She didn't want to switch on the bedside light and risk awakening Will, so instead concentrated on what was creating the noise. As she gently sat up in bed she realised it was Will's work mobile, it suddenly stopped. The momentary silence was broken in devastating fashion, as the house telephone on her bedside cabinet rang out, the noise in the dead of night seemed deafening. Mel reached out and grabbed the handset, 'Hello,' she said in an inquiring voice, knowing that any call received at this time of night or morning was not going to be a positive one. The person on the other end was hesitant, she could hear him breathing before he spoke. 'Hello, could I speak with DCI Scott please, this is DS Simpson from Bridlington nick, I'm really sorry to disturb him, but it's a matter of urgency.'

Mel explained to the sergeant that her husband was tired and exhausted. Deep inside she recognised that he would have to take the call, but it didn't prevent her from voicing her displeasure at being woken up at 3.33 a.m. 'I'll get him for you, but it better be urgent, his health is more important to me and his family than any bloody police matter.' Will was awake, but barely alert, as he sat up in bed next to his wife. He looked bemused and he was rubbing his eyes as she handed him the telephone. 'It's for you, it's your work,' she snapped.

'Hello, sir, it's Ian Simpson here, sorry to disturb you at home but this can't wait. We believe there's been another one of our bodies found, this one's in Romford, Essex. I've got all the victim details noted down here. It's a female, Patty Quinn, DoB 25-05-68. She's been dead a while, five days Romford reckon. The duty officer has asked me to call you, to see what you want to do, whether you want me to attend on your behalf, or to get an officer to come over and collect you and drive you there?'

'Thanks, Ian, this is getting quite ridiculous now, have you got a contact number for me to call Romford? I'll speak with their SIO direct and make a decision from there. I'll give you a call back once I've spoken to him or her. Can you start an incident log please?'

Will looked at his wife with an air of resignation, he dropped his head into his hands and shook it from side to side in disbelief. 'They think they've found another body, this one's in Romford, it's about five days old apparently. Christ, Mel, this is becoming unmanageable, there has to be some respite when these killings will stop. We haven't got time to wipe our own arses before yet another body turns up. It's too much, it really is.'

'Will, you need to ask for more support if you don't think you can handle it. Don't be stubborn or too proud to ask for help. These killings, they can't surely be the work of one person. What is that person, some kind of machine? Surely the abundance of murders is going to take its toll on the killer as well,' she reasoned. 'It takes time and effort to kill someone. If your killer is torturing them as well, that's going to take a huge amount of energy out of him. If it's a bloke and he's married, his fucking wife needs to have a word with him, and tell him to take a holiday or something. Seriously though, he must be superhuman or some super fit athlete, at the very least to continue the way he has. Have you considered it might be more than one person doing the killing?'

That was the last thing Will needed to hear coming from his wife, 'No I haven't, it's surely not feasible, Mel, or is it?' he asked.

Mel shrugged her shoulders, "If you are struggling to find whoever it is, then I think you need to be open to every suggestion, Will.'

Will nodded in agreement and made the call to Romford CID. The information that was conveyed was everything he didn't want to hear. The body had been found inside a house in the middle class Noak Hill area of the town. The female victim lived alone in a four bedroomed semi-detached house. She had worked in a civilian capacity for the police, so had no previous convictions and no local intelligence was held upon her. Her immediate boss had noticed she hadn't turned up for work and there was no reply when he phoned her home. He sent one of the beat bobbies round and the rest, as they say, is history. There was a suggestion among the rank and file, that she had been in different relationships with a number of police officers over the past few years. The officer he was speaking with, Detective Superintendent Gray, described her to Will, as a bit of a police junkie. Her remains were found nailed to the floor of the dining room of the property, she was naked. Her hair had been burnt down to its roots in the scalp, both eyes had been pierced and she had mutilations to her breasts and the vaginal region. The body remained within the house and local forensic officers were examining the crime scene. It was the duty Chief Superintendent who had read newspaper reports about the spate of murders up north that alerted Gray to contact Eastborough.

Will took the decision to visit the scene later the following day and asked the current SIO to commit and continue with investigations until his arrival later in the day. Finally, he requested that they search the crime scene for a small silver angel trinket that was the killer's signature. If found, it had to be photographed in situ and left where it was found. The Superintendent sounded put out by Will's requests. 'It's a little unusual for us to be temporarily running an investigation for a different force, we'll certainly do what we can, are you certain you don't just want us to deal?'

Will didn't consider the officers suggestion and advised him that Eastborough would be dealing, not Essex, the officer at the other end of the line indignantly hung up with no further comment.

'For crying out loud, what is it with these police forces,' said Will frustratingly. 'They all think they're better at investigating than we are, bloody tossers, especially Essex, they're renowned for fucking everything up.'

Mel laughed out loud and suggested that the officer to whom he had just spoke probably had small man hang up.

'Size matters to those pint size officers down there, darling. That's why they all drive round in big four wheel drives, and everyone is so loud and gobby, they think it makes them look big. Don't let them get to you.'

Will rang Ian Simpson and asked him to inform the Chief Constable's office of what might well be the latest crime. 'Let him know I'll be going down there first thing tomorrow to check everything out, please, Ian.'

He laid back in his bed and thumped his head into a soft pillow, that did its best to envelop him. Turning to Mel, he asked her to switch off the light so they could get some sleep. To consider that he could get to sleep after hearing such dreadful news was, at best ill-conceived and Melanie knew it, but acquiesced anyway. Both of them tossed and turned for what remained of that night's sleep, until finally the sun rose, which was the signal for Will to begin a fresh working day.

As he climbed out of bed he casually glanced at his work mobile. Six text messages and a voicemail message were outstanding. He quickly read through them and replied to the one that warranted immediate attention, they all related to the murder in the Romford police area. The voicemail was the earlier missed call from DS Ian Simpson asking him to ring in as a matter of urgency.

His priorities were a little different this particular morning, it felt like a lifetime since he had spent any time with his children, so he was determined to have breakfast with them, and listen to their stories before going into work. His children could make him laugh (and cry), but they were the perfect remedy to keeping him grounded, and sensible.

Will decided to make the breakfast, but before that he had to make a call to Daisy to tell her of the latest murder and the fact that he would be coming into the office later in the morning. She was to hold the fort until he arrived. Fruit juice and boiled eggs with toasted soldiers was the order of the day, quick and easy allowing the family to spend more time together sat around the breakfast table. There was much laughter and chatter about future holidays, and everyday life. Will felt at ease with his lot, if only he could get a real lead into the murders, his life would be perfect.

Ellie stopped her father in his tracks when she again asked how the investigation into the murder of her form teacher Mr. Hooton was coming along. It seemed so long ago, and several murders had occurred since Hooton had been dispatched. Will recognised its importance to Ellie. He responded with several positive comments that let her know that he cared too. The reality was somewhat different. Little headway had been made into that investigation since the body was discovered. Now Hooton was nothing more than a statistic in the bigger scheme of the murder inquiry. Will momentarily felt guilty that a human life could so easily be forgotten and dismissed. Hooton, for all his sins, had been something important in his Ellie's life, it wasn't his place to crush that belief.

To make life a little simpler for Mel that morning, Will volunteered to drop the kids off at school before going on to work, allowing his wife to return to bed and enjoy a rare, for her, lazy morning. Driving the kids to school was a welcome distraction from his usual thought process which, during the current investigations, tended to be more than a little macabre.

It was close to 9am, when Will arrived at the police station, his mood was much brighter and he was ready to deal with the worst that the Romford murder scene could throw at him.

The officers at Romford had failed to find a silver angel trinket at the crime scene, so thinking back to what his wife had said to him about being open to all possible suggestions, Will again considered Mandy's opinion that it might be a network of killers operating in some kind of synchronicity across the country. As he sat down at his desk, he saw countless post-it notes stuck to his computer screen, most were marked in red as 'urgent.'

Will called the dayshift investigation team together for a briefing and individual updates. Daisy had sorted a better quality unmarked police car as transport to Romford, something that allowed for a bit of comfort, it was the Vauxhall GTC normally used by senior officers on their jollies. Most of the officers on the dayshift confessed to feeling overwhelmed by the quantity of the body count and the frequency in which they were being discovered. Mandy Ward spoke to the team, offering her professional thoughts on the psyche of the killer or killers. When she used the plural term 'killers' she was asked to quantify this suggestion, and when she explained her rationale behind a network of killers working towards the same goal, terrorising paedophiles and child sex offenders everywhere, it produced a unified look of dejection on the faces of the gathered officers.

Will took the floor to lift the spirits of his team. 'How many of you have heard of Occam's Razor?' he asked. The sea of blank faces looking back at him provided confirmation of the answer. 'Well, the theory of Occam's Razor is that the likeliest explanation to a confusing situation is likely to be the best one, the more simple the explanation the better. So, our body count, if the Romford crime is one of ours, currently stands at seven. Theoretically, it is absolutely possible that one individual is responsible for each of these crimes. That individual leaves a calling card for us to find at each crime scene, the MO and the act itself are the same across every murder, no DNA, fingerprints, alien fibres or other evidence, are left at the scene. Therefore, using Occam's Razor, the likeliest explanation is that we are looking for one killer, and not a network, which would be massively difficult to operate and manage. I appreciate that Mandy, our forensic psychologist, is offering us options, but my gut instinct tells me we are looking for one serial killer.'

Daisy Wright looked over towards Mandy, who was standing by a whiteboard covered in various crime scene images. There was a look of indignation on the psychologist's face, this turned to one of sourness followed by anger. Daisy couldn't help but feel a little sorry for her. The boss had rubbished her suggestion in front of the entire team, doing her credibility no good at all. Many of the officers already regarded her as an expensive luxury, one which the investigation didn't need. Daisy, for her faults, was beginning to think differently, she recognised Mandy's skills as being useful, though not a necessity. As the briefing finished, Will called Daisy and Mandy to his desk and told them to get ready for the trip to Romford. Mandy ignored his command and was packing away her personal possessions from the desk she shared with Daisy.

'Mandy, did you hear what I just said, what are you doing?' asked Will. 'I want you with us at the Romford crime scene.'

The forensic psychologist ignored the Detective Chief Inspector, causing him to move towards her. 'Don't you come anywhere near me, or touch me,' she snapped at him. 'How dare you question my professional integrity in front of everyone, my suggestion to this investigation, was just that, an informed opinion. Which is far more likely than your opinion, because you haven't got one. What did you want me to say, DCI Scott? That you are wonderfully insightful and you are closing in on the killer because you are thinking on the same wavelength as him? Because let me tell you this, you are nowhere fucking near catching him. You currently don't know your arse from your elbow, so catching a serial killer who knows what he is doing, is thinking and using his brain, puts him a long way ahead of you. Before you get close to this person, you have to think like him, act like him, live and breathe as he does to understand him. You have to gain an understanding of how he selects each victim, then, and only then, will you be able to get close. I really don't know why you have brought me into this investigation, because you're giving me very little to work with. So I'm pulling out, I'm going back to Wakefield prison where I can work as part of a team and not as some sort of outsider that you use as your kicking post whenever you dislike what's being said, or you feel you are failing in some way. It's about time you stopped running around like a blue arsed fly and got on with what you're paid to do, investigating these bloody murders.'

The forensic psychologist was red in the face and clearly agitated. Will, stood, with his mouth open, his jaw dropped, it was an unexpected attack on his leadership, and he wasn't sure whether to be angry or to just let the woman go.

Daisy intervened. 'Mandy, I'm sorry if that's how the boss made you feel. I think we are all under pressure in this investigation, the last thing we need to be is fragmented. We all respect you, and what you are doing to assist us is unbelievable. You are an integral part of the team, none of us want you to go, least of all the boss.'

Will followed up this affirmation with a full apology, and a genuine plea for Mandy to stay on the investigation. Mandy agreed with Daisy that the pressure of this investigation was difficult to handle, and that she would remain with the team until either she was recalled by the prison service, or the killer was caught. Mandy's outburst, most felt, was warranted, and in truth the majority of the team supported her, and felt that Will had overstepped the mark with his comments.

CHAPTER SIXTEEN

The tension among the three occupants of the unmarked police car as it sped down the A1, M11 and finally round the M25 to junction 28, which led the team through to the Noak Hill region of Romford, was tangible. Tees Drive was a splendid looking road consisting of large semi-detached houses with well-kept gardens. The sight of a parked marked police car outside one of the houses, and a white forensic tent, identified the property the Eastborough officers were looking for.

As Daisy parked up, Will turned to Mandy who was sat alone in the rear seat and as a further apology, offered her his hand to shake as confirmation that they were still a team. Mandy barely spoke, but shook his hand and immediately got out of the car.

Will looked at Daisy, shrugged his shoulders and asked, 'What else can I do?'

Daisy provided a short sharp answer, 'Just be professional, boss, she'll come round don't worry.'

A uniformed officer asked to see Will and Daisy's warrant cards, which they produced from their coat pockets, they introduced Mandy to the officer who registered their visit to the crime scene onto a log sheet along with the time and date of arrival. 'There's no one else here at the moment, other than me and two officers to the rear of the premises. Forensics have left the scene but are coming back later today, and CID are back at the nick in Romford, so you have the house to yourself. Can I ask that you put on forensic suits which are in that tent before entering please?'

Will thanked the officer for his efficiency and, along with his colleagues, moved inside the tent and changed. 'Same format and drill inside the house please. Mandy, if you can identify anything that you feel may be of interest, point it out to us, Daisy will photograph it and you can analyse it later back at Bridlington. I'm looking for the angel of death or whatever they call the bloody thing and, Daisy, I want you to check out the victim's possessions, go through mail, and telephone history. I want to know everything about her. It might tell us why our killer selected her as a victim.'

Mandy, somewhat tongue in cheek, pointed out, 'It's not the angel of death you are looking for, it's a Malakim. If you think it's a clue then at least get it's bloody title correct.'

Will raised his eyebrows to show he accepted the reprimand and immediately moved inside the house.

The body was nailed to the floor of the dining room on the ground floor, the stench was vile, bluebottles annoyingly buzzed around the room, some gathering around a double glazed window, as though they were trying to co-ordinate a mass escape. Will wasn't alone in gagging. Behind him, he could hear the sound of Daisy and Mandy struggling to overcome the sickly yet powerful aroma of decomposition of human remains. He directed Daisy upstairs to begin her search and told Mandy to follow him to where the body lay. His eyes darted frantically from side to side as he scanned around the room and areas close to the body in search of the Malakim.

He jumped as Mandy shouted out 'There! There it is,' she said, excitedly pointing underneath a small table.

Will bent down and recovered the trinket. 'Is there anything else that will add value to your assessment of this crime scene, Mandy?' he enquired.

She shook her head and moved to leave the room. 'If Daisy can take some photographs please, and I'll need copies of the original photographs taken by forensics of the entire scene too. It would be good to know how access was gained to the property by the killer. I expect all that will be in the forensic report you will receive.'

The pair retreated to the living room of the house and began a cursory search of the dead woman's mail and belongings, hoping to fit together her life and movements in the lead up to her murder. Daisy, meanwhile, was upstairs rummaging through personal letters, and important documents including a passport, that could help build a picture of Patty Quinn's life. The team spent a good hour committed to the search before leaving the property, signing out and heading to Romford police station.

'What a grim looking place,' said Daisy, 'this has to win awards for the most miserable looking police station in the United Kingdom.'

Mandy agreed and added, 'The whole town looks like a throwback to the 1970's. The architects must have been grey suited council workers, because they clearly had no idea about style looking at that view.' The view she referred to was gleaned as the police car circled a large roundabout.

'Yes, you're right, it's a fucking depressing shit hole,' said Will, 'Wasn't this Essex boys territory back in the day, you know, drugs and nightclub bouncers and raves and all that. Clearly, by the look of it, the place has never moved on.' Will was forced to suddenly brake, as a black coloured four wheel drive vehicle swerved and pulled in front of him on the roundabout. He blasted his horn at the driver, a woman, plastered in make-up and clearly oblivious to other road users because she was too busy talking into her mobile phone which she grasped in her right hand. Will blasted the horn again, this time the driver responded by sticking her middle finger up at Will and mouthing the word 'wanker' at him. Daisy was first to react, and gave the middle finger salute back. At which the four wheel drive accelerated at speed away from the unmarked police car. 'If I had the time, I'd report that bitch for dangerous driving, she could have caused a serious accident there. What's so important that you need to use your bloody mobile when you're driving?'

'Probably booking in to have her nails done,' added Mandy with a giggle.

As they pulled up at the large electronic gate that when open provided access into the rear yard of Romford Police Station, Will voiced his opinion that the nick looked more like a prison. He stopped next to a push button communication box which looked like a sentry guarding the closed gate. Will pressed the intercom button and identified himself to the machine. There was no response.   Six times he repeated this exercise before giving up, reversing the car back onto Main Road and leaving Romford behind. 'That's piss poor that no one answered the intercom to allow us into the nick,' his dissatisfaction was clear in his voice. 'We haven't time to mess about and wait for those lazy pricks to press a button and open the fucking gate. I expect they've all convened in the gents bog, sorting out the roots of their dyed peroxide blonde hair!' He was clearly hacked off by the indiscretion of the Romford Police Station gatekeeper. 'What's the best thing about Romford?' he asked his passengers.   'The road out of the shit hole,' he proclaimed. 'We'll have to ring them when we get back, explain what happened, and our desire to get out of their concrete jungle and back to civilisation.'

'I take it you didn't like Romford then, boss?' asked Mandy with a hint of sarcasm in her voice. 'You might need to know, I'm originally an Essex girl, I come from Ilford. If you think Romford's bad, then don't even bother looking at Ilford. They used to be nice towns, full of real East End folk who cared about the community, today I doubt there's hardly any orginal eastenders in either place.   What is it the government call it, diversity or something? I liked the Essex I grew up in, far better than the one of today. It may be cosmopolitan and buzzing, but for some reason I constantly feel on edge even when I'm driving through the place. It's way too busy. I doubt whether many folks living here know who their neighbours are. It wasn't like that a few decades ago when communities pulled together and helped one another. My family moved away from Ilford a few years back. They bought a house in Clacton and have been much happier since the move. A lot of the old eastenders are moving out that way.'

'I think it's the same everywhere nowadays,' said Daisy. Multicultural societies are all well and good, but it takes generations for them to gel together and for respect to be born.'

Will's mobile phone began to ring out from the dashboard cradle where it sat. Daisy answered it since he was driving. It was Barry Smith from the murder investigation room. She put the phone on loudspeaker.

'Daisy, can you tell the boss we have someone in custody for the murders up here. He's singing like a canary at the moment, and he appears to know a fair bit of detail about the murders. He was arrested at Driffield Railway Station after he asked a station guard to arrest him for the killings. He sounds a bit of a fruit loop, but to be honest, he is fairly lucid in his recounting of the crimes.'

Daisy asked a relevant question, one that Will would have wanted an answer to. 'Have you formally cautioned him and interviewed him? If you haven't interviewed him leave him in a cell until we get back. What's his name?'

'John Nixon, he's a Driffield bloke, married, with two kids. Seedy looking bloke. He is, however, a transvestite. No previous record. He's not been interviewed yet.'

'Okay, Barry, thanks, just leave him until we get there, we should be back within the hour.'

'Wow,' said Mandy, 'sounds like he could be our man if he's got personal knowledge?'

Will pressed the accelerator as they raced to the north and away from the urban monstrosity that was Romford.

A couple of hours later, as he parked the police car in the street outside the police station, he told both Daisy and Mandy that he wanted them present in the interview with John Nixon. He first went up to the investigation room for any further detail on the prisoner, before returning to the custody suite, which was located on the ground floor. Nixon, it seemed, was unknown in any police capacity.

The custody sergeant released the prisoner from his cell, advising him that he was to be interviewed regarding the murders he was confessing to. Will, Daisy and Mandy led him to interview room number one, a small oblong shaped room, containing, as well as the necessary recording machinery, four chairs and a desk. During the short walk to the room, Will looked closely at the prisoner, whose wiry frame stood at 5' 6" in height, with a mop of dark hair on his head, and a face that reminded Will of a proboscis monkey.

As they each sat down in the interview room, it was clear that Nixon was nervous. His hands were shaking and he was sweating profusely.

'Would you like a solicitor present, John?' asked Will.

'Nope, don't need one. Can we just get on with this so I can be charged and locked up for life?' replied the prisoner. He was reminded that he was under caution and one by one, the interview team introduced themselves and their role. The opening rounds of the interview were fairly basic.

'Where are you originally from, John?' asked Will.

'My family come from a town near Seascale in Cumbria, that's the nuclear place where they've closed all the beaches because of radiation levels,' said Nixon confidently.

'So what brought you to Driffield?'

'Work really. I always wanted to be a writer but there wasn't the options up in Cumbria, so I moved down here and tried to get a job on the local paper. That never happened, so I do seasonal work at one of the caravan parks in the area. Sandskipper, do you know it?'

'John, are you aware of the murders that have been occurring in this region, there was one at Sandskipper last week? Tell me what you know about the murders,' asked the DCI staring deep into the darting eyes of the man sat opposite.

'Well, you know, it was me. I killed them all. My life is fairly shit, I get no recognition from anyone, my wife is having an affair, and my kids take the piss out of me all the time, I've got no friends. So, I woke up one morning and thought to myself, 'I know, I'll make sure people know and remember who I am. I'll go on a killing spree.' So I killed them folk. I stalked them all, and you know, I killed them,' an air of hesitancy was evident during the latter part of his declaration. Will pushed him further.

'John, why did you select those people to kill? Did you know them?'

'No. Actually yes, I knew Allan Roberts, we were lovers. Yes, I'm gay, so go on, it's a moral crime and a sin, lock me up for that as well.'

'I'm not at all bothered by your sexuality, John. I am asking you about Allan Roberts, how did you kill him? In fact, how did you kill any of your victims?'

The prisoner looked forlornly at the interviewing officers before revealing, 'I cut their throats with a knife, then I ate their brains. I posed them all for you to find. I know that's right because it said so in the papers, so don't deny it.'

'John, I have to say, you don't appear to be a violent kind of person, so what drives you to kill?'

'The moon. It's when it's a full moon, I turn violent. I kill anything that gets in my way, people, animals, birds, you name it, I kill it.'

'John, let me put it this way, you aren't the killer, so please tell me what's going on in that mind of yours. Is there something bothering you, that you want to tell us about?'

'Alright, you got me there. I just wanted to know what it would be like to be famous, you know, to have folk recognise you in the street and ask for your autograph, that sort of thing.'

Will ended the interview there and then, switching off the tape recorder and getting up to leave the room. He asked Daisy to release the prisoner with no further action, and to organise a uniform police officer to take him home to his wife. Mandy meanwhile followed Will back to the investigation room and to his desk.

'Why didn't you charge that man with wasting police time?' she asked curiously.

'It's the small man syndrome. He is self-conscious of his less than average stature so he is trying to make himself more of a man by committing to ridiculous behaviour like this. I'm not the psychologist here, you saw and heard for yourself. He wasn't insane, he wanted the attention. We aren't a nursing home, so he needs to go to his doctor and get his inferiority complex sorted out. I won't add to his woes by getting him a criminal record, or waste police resources and court time in pursuing an action that helps nobody. I don't know, maybe the West Cumbrian radiation has affected him, whatever, let's not waste any more time on discussing him, he's not our killer.

'Can you pull together a fact file of your findings so far? I know it's difficult based on the minimal amount of detail we have, but it will help, especially if we can start to build a picture of him. I'm aware that you are being pulled in all sort of directions in this investigation, Mandy, so I need you to start to tell us who and what type of person we are looking for.'

Mandy smiled reassuringly at Will. 'Yes, I'll do that, of course I will. I think you may be pleasantly surprised by the profile I can produce from the definitely known facts. Can I just say, I thought the way you handled that John Nixon character was totally professional, and you showed a great deal of empathy to him, which in the long term he will remember and it will help him.'

'Thanks, though I'm not so sure about the empathy aspect of my decision making. I did what I thought was right for everyone.'

Daisy rushed into the room and stared directly at Will. 'Boss, you better come quickly, the control room want to speak to you, I think you need to hear this direct from them,' she said all breathlessly.

'No, please tell me it's not another murder, Daisy. Right now, at this very minute, I couldn't cope with that. Tell me now, is it?'

'It's not another murder, sir. I think you need to speak with control immediately.'

Will followed Daisy down to the control room where three members of police staff sat manning telephones and the police radio.

'DCI Scott, we've received a call that was meant for you. We were unable to patch it through as you were in interview with a prisoner. A woman by the name of Christine Palmer has asked that you call her as soon as possible. Her husband is the local newspaper reporter apparently, Lucien Palmer. He's gone missing. Hasn't been seen or heard from for three days. Apparently he was following a lead into the series of murders you are investigating.'

Will turned on his heels and left the room entering the first available office he found to use the telephone to call Christine Palmer.

Her telephone was engaged so Will rang Mel, who was a close friend of Christine and explained what he had just been told. 'Can you tease as much information out of her as possible please, Mel? We haven't got the resources available to us to pursue a missing person inquiry alongside the murders. We'll put everything we can into finding him, but he's an adult, he's not vulnerable nor is he suffering from any illness, it won't be given a priority unless we understand what he was dealing with and where he was going.'

Mel was shocked to hear the news and told Will that she would do as he asked, straight away.

Will returned to his desk and told the team to focus on the matter in hand and not what might or might not be a missing person investigation. 'I've known Lucien Palmer since we were kids ... He can look after himself, he's nobody's fool, so I'm certain he'll turn up soon. He's probably gone on a bender somewhere and will return home with his tail between his legs.'

Will felt guilty that he had dismissed Lucien's disappearance as nothing more than an error of judgement on the missing man's behalf. He knew that Lucien had a habit of getting into scrapes, it's part of the terrain for decent journalists. A good reporter won't let a potential story die, at least not until they kill it themselves. Until Will heard back from Mel, he could not make a reasoned risk assessment about Lucien's safety. In truth, it was a distraction he could well do without. The local press were going to be all over the story, and with a weighty national reporter presence in the region, the situation was likely to be blown out of all proportion by media sensationalism.

Will's pager buzzed in his pocket. It was a message from Romford CID asking him to call them as soon as he could. He didn't delay in making the call to his Essex counterpart, Detective Superintendent Gray. The mood between both men was hostile. Gray demanded to know why Will had returned to Bridlington without so much as a thank you or a handover and release of the crime scene. 'As a result,' he went on 'Essex Police have tied up three uniformed officers on nothing more than guard duties, because that house is still officially a crime scene. If you had the decency to notify me that you were finished at the scene, it could have been closed down, the body removed and the three officers guarding the property released and returned to general police duties. As it is, nothing can happen until tomorrow now, you've wasted our fucking time. If you were stood in front of me now, I'd fucking drop you like a brick. I should have known that a country bumpkin force like yours wouldn't know how to deal with a professional force.'

Will took a deep breath, before calmly explaining what had happened at the electronic access gate, how his calls went unanswered on six different occasions. 'The front office had about ten people sat waiting to be seen, they were queuing outside, we could see that. We simply didn't have time to piss about waiting for you lot to let us in, so we left and came back here. I appreciate I should have notified you, but in the circumstances I took what action I thought correct at the time. As a matter of interest, what sort of car do you drive?' he asked Grey. The Romford officer asked why he wanted that information and what it had to do with the murder? 'Let me guess,' said Will, 'my bet is, it's a four wheel drive?'

'It is, but why is that important to you?' reiterated the senior officer.

'No reason, just a question that's all,' said Will. 'I'd like you to send me the forensic reports and a detailed report on the laptop content and usage. I'll need that promptly please. If you can get your forensic people to send it to mine, that will be the most expedient method of getting documents to us. Again, I apologise for not advising you of our departure from the scene, I trust you will keep us informed if anything becomes apparent during your follow up enquiries and the check of all relevant CCTV footage as requested?'

His Essex counterpart slammed down the receiver at the other end, all Will caught was the words 'ignorant fucking northern ...' He laughed at the thought of an irate Superintendent who was hopping mad with a country bumpkin northerner who was in charge of a murder in his police area. It must have been seen as the ultimate insult to an experienced, Essex Police senior bod. Will knew that cross boundary working had never been a willing collaboration between forces, police intelligence often stops at the county boundary line, this though was his first real taste of nastiness. Albeit he recognised that he had caused the situation by not hanging around in Romford and therefore failing to make the correct notifications.

His mobile rang, this time it was the call he had been waiting for, it was Mel. 'Will, I think this might be serious. Apparently Lucien has been working all hours trying to get a lead on the murder investigation. He's been playing around on the dark web, going onto forums and connecting with paedophiles and other perverts. Chris thinks he has given himself an identity and he's trying to find the link between the killer and the victim. He's been gone three days now, and she's not heard anything from him in that time. Worse still, she hasn't got any idea where he is, or even might be. I've got a description of the clothing he was wearing when he left the house, so maybe you can circulate it? I've explained to Chris that you can't drop everything to search for Lucien, and she understands that, but you've definitely got a misper on your hands here, and it's connected to the murders.'

Will asked Mel to email over to him the time Lucien left home and what he was wearing and anything else Chris could remember about his pseudo investigation into the killings. 'I'll arrange for a uniform officer to visit her and to take a full missing person report. In the meantime I'll circulate this locally and to all forces with a marker that it relates to our murder investigation, so it will be prioritised.'

There was no option but to inform the investigation team of the known facts surrounding Lucien's disappearance. On learning this, the team were concerned by his involvement on the dark web and some of the forums. Paula Jay pointed out that a high proportion of vigilante types, who were on crusades to expose active paedophiles, were present on the forums.

These people were skilled in the art of extrapolating information from others in order to gain more detail about who they were, and the region where they lived. 'It's this category of person where I believe we will find our killer. They lurk silently on these sites, picking out likely victims to publicly expose. What's worse, in the mind of the crusading vigilante, anyone on the forums is a target, they are there because they are perverts looking to groom an innocent child. If Lucien Palmer has agreed to meet someone, or has exposed his vulnerability to a vigilante online, then he might well have been pursued and manipulated into meeting them probably at a private location. If he's revealed his true identity, namely an investigative journalist of sorts, the likelihood is he will have suffered a severe beating, or worse, since neither a paedophile nor a vigilante will want to be exposed. I've got to be honest, I really fear for the bloke. This dark web is a vile place, it's one huge hub, where every weirdo in the world hangs out. Most of them are looking for something illegal, be it drugs, firearms, dodgy images, or sex with children.'

Will looked startled by Paula's statement. 'Paula, can you get someone, a uniform officer, to go and speak to his wife please? See if she can remember the names of any sites he had been on, or the pseudonym he might have used on them. His nickname at school was a bit mundane. He wanted to be known as 'LP' but everyone referred to him as 'Loose End.' Maybe we can trace him through his online activities on the forum message board?'

Everyone stood still, as the Chief Constable entered the room. He had a determined look on his face as he stared towards Will, who was back sitting at his desk. The Chief was alone, it was usual for the bag carrier of a Chief Inspector to be hanging off his shirt tail. Will rose to his feet as the force's leader neared.

'All correct, sir' reported Will.

'Thank you, Chief Inspector, can I have a quiet word with you please? We'll use that office there,' he said pointing to a small room where the photocopier was located. Will followed the senior officer inside and closed the door behind him.

'Will. I've had Essex on the phone, claiming you've breached force protocols and were rude to their staff. If it's true, don't do it again, okay? I told them not to be so sensitive and to move on, so they shouldn't bother you again, bunch of southern softy prima donnas. Anyway, that's not the sole reason I need to speak with you. I've had a tip off. Nothing to do with your investigation. It's about a visitor coming to the station tomorrow. The secretary to the Home Secretary. We are talking about a serious civil servant here, an advisor to the government no less. She sounded a right obnoxious so and so on the telephone. She's coming here tomorrow to speak with me and later with you. She said it related to a matter of huge importance that could cause embarrassment to the government. It appears that a local journalist from up here has been ruffling a few feathers at the House of Commons, asking too many questions. He's apparently investigating paedophile activity and the connection to our murders. It isn't straight forward, Will, it seems he's found rogue connections to some senior MP's and it's got the entire house panicking. Quite why she thinks we can stop this journalist from reporting on his findings, I don't understand. Anyway, she's here tomorrow at 11am, so can you be in my office for 11.15 am, please?'

'Yes sir, of course. If this is who I think it is, we genuinely do have a problem. We have just learned of the disappearance of a local reporter, Lucien Palmer, and he's been carrying out his own investigation into the crimes. According to his wife, he's been digging around on the dark web. Nothing's been heard from him for over three days. The press are already aware, simply because he's one of their own, so they are bound to give his disappearance a lot of coverage. I think we need to secrete this civil servant woman through the back door of the nick tomorrow if possible, keep her visit quiet. If the press get a sniff of her being here, they'll know something unusual is going on.'

'Okay, Will, leave that one with me. This journalist fellow, do you think he's likely to have come to any harm, or is he just off on some jape?'

'I know him well, sir. He's an alright sort of bloke, not prone to aimlessly wandering off, he loves his job, some of his work has won national journalism awards. I've already got officers discreetly working on tracing his movements. We are being proactive in an attempt to lessen the hysteria the press are bound to create with their reporting of his disappearance.'

The Chief looked satisfied with Will's response, and before leaving, reminded him that the civil servant's visit was totally confidential, and therefore not to be discussed with anyone. 'I'd like a precis report on the current status of the murder investigation on my desk for 8am. I want this suit to know we are handling this investigation efficiently and effectively. See you tomorrow, Will. Oh, and if there are any further developments overnight, let me know right away can you please?'

'I will, sir, no problem,' replied Will as the force's senior uniformed officer opened the door and left the tiny room. Will took a moment for himself. He was juggling many issues, not all of which were under his control. For the first time in his police career, he felt worried, frightened even, that one of his good friends could be seriously injured, or worse, dead. The thought that followed was of more concern, Will considered that Lucien may have deliberately come to harm or been killed by the establishment, in order to silence him. 'Nonsense, that's the stuff of conspiracy theorists, the government don't really do that kind of thing, that's only in books and films, why am I thinking that load of shite?' he thought to himself as he returned to his desk, under the watchful gaze of several police detectives who were all keen to hear what the Chief had said to him.

Will's mood was dark, he said nothing, instead he picked up his coat and went home for the evening. His mind was focused on his missing friend, he reasoned that away from the murders he could achieve more from home than sat at his desk.

CHAPTER SEVENTEEN

When he got home Mel was out. She had left the kids with her parents for the evening, while she comforted Chris Palmer at her home in Kingsgate. Will made the short drive to join his wife and to try to make some sense of what Lucien was up to in his investigation. He was annoyed that despite requesting a uniform police officer to attend to deal with the case no one had visited the Palmer residence. 'It's no bloody wonder people lose confidence in the police when they get the fundamental basics of policing wrong,' he said angrily. 'An officer should have been dispatched here an hour ago. I'll make a call and get someone here pronto.'

Within two minutes of making the call, a uniform officer was allocated the missing person enquiry and sent to visit Christine Palmer to take the full details and file a report. Realising his own need to gather information, Will quizzed Chris on Lucien's behaviour in the lead up to his disappearance. He explained to her that this information was for his use only. 'I stand a better chance of locating Lucien through my own enquiries, I don't want uniform plod treading all over my investigation and compromising it, so I need to understand what he was working on.'

'You know what he's like, Will,' said Chris sat on the sofa, gripping Mel's hand and trying to hold back her emotions. 'Once he gets involved in something he won't leave it alone, he has to research it to death. He said he was investigating paedophiles and he had found some serious people who were involved in the child

209

pornography and abuse industry. Influential government figures he called them. He said he had found information that would blow the whole Westminster child abuse investigation out of the water and that the Met Police had been wrong to close that investigation down. No names were mentioned by him, but I think he knew who was involved. I think he was heading for London, because he said that he would need to visit and speak to people who knew the inside workings of the Houses of Parliament. He's got his laptop with him, but he did carry out some research on the home computer.'

'Can I go on there and access that please, Chris?' asked Will.

'Sure, it's in the dining room, through that door, it's on the left.'

'Good, please don't mention any of that to the uniform officer who visits. Just keep it plain and simple. I'll be here to guide you through the questions and report when they arrive so please don't worry.'

A short while later, a female police officer arrived at the Palmer home to record the missing person's details and other useful information about his potential whereabouts. The officer was a rookie probationer, so she didn't question Christine too deeply. Nor did she recognise Will as being a detective police officer serving in the same nick as her. When he pointed this out in an attempt to help her, she blushed bright red through embarrassment and apologised. This naivety endeared her to the group, and Will offered to make her a cup of tea which she declined. The officer was efficient, and gathered all the detail required for a comprehensive missing person's report, and all importantly she reached out to Chris Palmer and offered her genuine support and promised to keep her up to date with her enquiries.

Once the officer left, Will opened up the Palmer's home computer. He searched the internet history file and was soon accessing the same pages viewed by Lucien a few days earlier. He had access to the dark web, and what Will saw without using any secure password was heart breaking stuff. Image after image of child abuse and child pornography, some of the victims were very clearly under five years old. The trail went cold when he tried to access forums. He didn't know Lucien's username or password and he had logged out of every one making it difficult and time consuming to try to guess them.

'Chris, I'm going to ask one of our forensic IT fella's to try to access the forums for me. If Lucien has been active on those boards, then we might be able to track his online footprint, see who he was communicating with and track him down that way. Is that okay with you?'

Chris agreed that it was a good idea, and allowed Will to take the computer tower with him. Mel offered to stay the night with her friend, which she gratefully accepted, allowing Will to go home and get a good night's sleep on his own. He wasn't best pleased about it, but he understood the seriousness of the situation for Chris and that she needed someone on hand to help her and to talk to.

It was gone midnight when Will finally climbed into bed. He was exhausted and his mind was racing with thoughts of his missing pal, and each of the unresolved murders. He wondered what the killer was doing at that very moment, 'unlike me, I bet the bastard is probably sleeping,' he thought to himself. Reaching out, he switched off the bedside light and the room fell into darkness. He missed having Mel beside him. It was their personal space and it didn't feel quite right when he wasn't sharing it with her. He could smell her perfume on the pillow next to his, so snuggled up to that as a kind of comfort.

The next thing he knew, was the alarm sounding on his mobile phone. It was daylight and he couldn't recall falling asleep. The instant he was awake, his mind turned to thoughts of the absent Lucien Palmer, the visit later that morning by the secretary of the Home Secretary, and the precis report the Chief Constable had requested on his desk by 8am. He panicked. He had forgotten the report and he knew that the Chief would be, quite rightly, pissed off with him for not providing it. He hastily rushed downstairs, turned on his own computer, and dressed only in his boxer shorts, frantically produced a bullet point formatted report for the attention of the Chief, which he emailed directly over to his office. It had just turned 6am now and to make matters worse he was going to be late into the office for the morning briefing.

He rang Daisy and asked her to cover for him until he got there, he would be less than half an hour. Daisy was her usual calm and collected self, 'No worries, boss, take your time, it's all quiet here, nothing has come in overnight, oh, and the journalist is still missing.'

Will felt reassured by Daisy's cool attitude, he could rely on her to watch his back and he trusted her implicitly. He could never understand why she never had time for a steady boyfriend. Both he and Mel had, in the past, tried to pair her up at dinner parties but she somehow never clicked with anyone. Truth was, she was passionate about her job and she was comfortable in her own company. She had freedom to do as she wished in her personal life, and that's the way she liked it. She recognised she was pretty and carried herself well. However, relationships for her were a bit of a bind.

As Will breezed into the office he handed Daisy a copy of the report he had produced for the Chief Constable earlier that morning. 'Have a read of that, Daisy, tell me what you think,' he said, handing the three page document to her.

'It's good boss. I take it this is a briefing report for the CC?'

'Yes, it is. I realised when I was typing it up, we know a lot more than we appreciate about these murders and potentially the killer. Can you give a copy of that to Mandy? I want her to read through it and to check if I've omitted anything she believes important from the profiling of the killer aspect.'

Mandy was already in the office and was stood behind him. She heard his comments to Daisy. 'I've compiled my own report, boss. Mine is offender focused. Here, take a look. I think it's fair to say we are looking for a man, some of the victims have been too physically large for a woman to overpower.'

Daisy interrupted her colleague. 'What do you mean by that? Are you aware that all but one victim has two distinct marks on the back of the neck? These have been confirmed as Taser shots. If the current is fired a couple of times in quick succession, it can cause temporary paralysis in the target. That way, someone of either sex could pose, attack, mutilate and kill each victim.' Will looked to Mandy for her opinion.

'I agree with you there. However, the likelihood is, it's a male. I just can't see a female committing such atrocities on a human body, particularly on another woman. For instance, it takes a massive amount of strength to pierce an eyeball, the exterior is really tough. Then we have the removal of the testicles in the male victims, only a man would know how painful that could be, then forcing the victim to eat them, again, it would be a really offensive thing to get a man to do. A male killer would understand that and a whole lot more, it would provide the killer with a feeling of power over his victim. So at this stage, I believe we are looking for a male offender.'

'What's the significance of the burning, Mandy?' asked DS Smith who had listened in to the discussion.

'It's the desecration of the human body. Our killer enjoys the feeling of power the mutilations provide. He's also creating something ugly, vile, repulsive, that's for our benefit I believe. He wants those who see the remains to feel disgusted by their appearance. People take time doing their hair, it enhances their look, so burning it all off makes a significant change, it demeans the victim, especially females.'

Daisy expressed a further argument. 'The blow torches that have been left at every crime scene and used in the attacks, they are for cooking in the kitchen, surely only a woman would be likely to have such a thing, I don't know many men who would use them or know about them even?'

Mandy was on form and responded to Daisy. 'You are wrong there, Daisy, my partner knows how to use one, in fact he bought it. They are mass produced, and available in thousands of outlets. They are quite a common item and, of course, there are thousands of male chefs across the UK.' On that point, the discussion ended and Will asked Daisy to update him on that mornings briefing.

The team were busy working on different aspects of the case, some officers were researching the national database of violent offenders, trimming down the list of potential suspects from that. Others were working with CEOP and the NCA, identifying links between the victims and also attempting to highlight potential victims. The national sex offender register was examined. This was in an attempt to identify any pattern to the killings and to check if the lists of names that had been found on every victim's laptop computer were registered offenders. None of the listed names were present.

The forensic reports and crime scene studies were being analysed, with follow up house to house enquiries being carried out in an attempt to locate any further witnesses. A team of two uniform officers were searching through hundreds of hours of CCTV footage covering the areas close to the murders and access routes in and out of the urban regions where the murders had occurred. In an attempt to ease bureaucracy, the local authority had allowed the council Community Safety Manager, an ex-police officer, to work with the unit and to act as liaison with the police. This ensured that the council leader and the CEO had a mole who would keep them fully informed of the direction the investigation was taking. However, the council employee was given no access to confidential information, so had very little to report back to his masters.

What the team believed to be a real breakthrough occurred when an off duty member of the investigation team saw identical silver angel trinkets on sale in a shop in Bridlington, close to the harbour. A visit to the premises revealed that some 100,000 such trinkets had been produced, and sold, by the overseas manufacturer to retail outlets across England and Europe. The minimum purchase quantity was 250, making it virtually impossible to trace every sale, this was exasperated since many were bought by travelling people as prizes on fairground attractions. That in itself had led to enquiries about travelling show people being in specific areas at the time of the murders. This was a slow and laborious inquiry that was proving difficult since travellers, through their own choice and beliefs, didn't work with or help the police.

The wooden barbecue skewers were traced back to a supplier in China. It was estimated that one million similar or identical items had been sold in England alone during the previous 12 months. They were generally available in packs of twenty four, therefore, trying to identify individual purchases was a pointless and hopeless task. Likewise, the staples the killer used to pin back the victims eyelids. It was a common and popular make readily available across the UK.

Will became aware of someone trying to attract his attention at the back of the room. He looked up to see the Superintendent's secretary waving at him, beckoning him over. He looked at the clock on the wall, it was 11.15 a.m., he had to be upstairs at the meeting with the Chief Constable and the civil servant. Grabbing his jacket and straightening his tie he asked Daisy if he looked presentable, before rushing out of the room and upstairs to the Divisional Commander's office, which was temporarily being used by the Chief Constable for the meeting. Stopping at the closed door, he knocked twice and waited. 'Come in,' said a voice from behind the door. As he entered, Will was in no doubt that the civil servant was unlikely to be on their side, they would be bureaucratic, probably bespectacled, wearing ill-fitting clothes, plastic shoes and carrying a cheap black briefcase.

That image proved so wrong. Sat around a coffee table close to the Chief Constable was a glamourous looking woman, with shoulder length red hair and wearing a tight fitting knee length dress. Will instantly noticed her patent leather, black stiletto heel shoes, with the tell-tale Christian Louboutin lacquered red sole. It was his opinion that you could determine the class of a person by the shoes they wore. This woman oozed class.

'Felicity, this is DCI Will Scott, he's the Senior Investigating Officer for the spate of recent murders taking place. Will, this is Felicity Harvey, she is the private secretary to the Home Secretary. Take a seat and join us, please,' said the Chief Constable.

After a little small talk, Felicity took control of the meeting. Will was surprised to hear she had a gritty northern accent, Lancashire, he detected. He'd expected her to have the usual false upper class Southern one.

'Gentlemen, thank you for taking the time to speak with me. I've been sent here because of a rather delicate situation we, as in the government, have encountered. It appears that it may be connected to your murder enquiry. A regional hack, who goes by the name Lucien Palmer, has been digging around in the gutter, looking for dirt on a number of politicians and key local authority figures across London. Apparently he's found explicit material that can be linked to high ranking officials and others.'

Will asked, 'How are you aware of this information?'

Felicity squirmed in her chair and her face flushed a little.

'An undercover MI5 officer was speaking with an informant and happened to hear of his activities, and has reported it back. Our problem is, the journalist has gone to ground and we can't locate him. Naturally MI5 are all over him and his family up here. We are presently monitoring their web use, emails, mobile and landline telephones. We need to get hold of him before he leaks this information, which at the very least, is spurious in its content, and brings embarrassment to the government.'

Again, Will interjected. 'If its spurious, then what damage can it cause? Surely it can be proved to be false?'

Felicity ignored the question and continued. 'From his web activity, it seems he's an active paedophile, so I'm here to ask, no, to tell you that we want this Lucien Palmer arrested and charged under the Sexual Offences Act. He must be discredited, in any and every manner possible. If you can pin anything else on him all the better. It's important we, you, protect the fabric upon which society is based. We don't want the masses losing confidence in that, and believe me, this man is single handedly attempting to do just that. The public reaction if any of the details get out will naturally be 'there's no smoke without fire.' We don't need to be placed in that situation, so its simpler to remove him from the equation. May I remind you both, your principle role is to protect the establishment first, everything else thereafter.'

Both police officers looked at each other in total disbelief. Will was first to break the silence. 'Are you asking me to set this journalist up? Because, if you are, then that is not only unethical it's illegal.'

Felicity Harvey looked slightly anxious. She clearly hadn't received the response she had hoped for. 'I'm not asking you to do anything. I'm informing you that this journalist is an active paedophile. That's official, and it's come from the highest level of intelligence in the land. He's committed various offences under the terms of the Sexual Offences Act. I'm sure, once you find him, you will examine his computers, there you will find all the evidence you require.'

Will was agitated. 'I can't believe you are asking this of me. I seized his home computer last night, it was examined by forensics today. It's clear, there are no illegal images stored on it, indeed, there's nothing sinister on it at all. So if you are hoping to place anything on there, forget it, at least a dozen official persons have checked it in the last 24 hours. Added to which, he's not at home, so how could he have stored any illegal images on there?'

The civil servant backtracked. 'I think you may have misinterpreted what I said. Perhaps it's my mistake. I was under the illusion that when the police had a crime reported to them they were duty bound to investigate it, particularly so when it involves vulnerable persons like children as the victims? Are you now telling me that this isn't what happens, do you have your own set of rules in Eastborough?'

Will wasn't going to allow a civil servant tell him what he could and could not do, and responded, 'I'm more than surprised that MI5 are taking an interest in a missing person and a police investigation, since when did that happen?'

Felicity was uneasy and was squirming in her seat. 'DCI Scott, the investigation you are heading is of national interest, you may not have noticed, but it's being reported in all the newspapers, it's plastered over the internet where every nutcase across the planet is discussing it, and then, if you get bored with that, it's on every main television news channels. Why wouldn't MI5 be interested, a local government official is a victim, he was a well-connected paedophile. It's those connections we need to protect, this bloody journalist has unearthed some filth that no one should be privy too. If you truly value your role as a police officer, then as I say, it's your duty to protect the establishment that pays your wages and gives you a sweet detached home in Marton Gate.'

Will was stunned, the woman sat before him knew where he lived, someone had been digging into his life. Suddenly, it was Will who felt uncomfortable, and instantly became worried about his family. 'Where did you get that information from, why have you been looking at me?'

'Don't worry, your nothing special, it goes with the territory. We need to understand everything about the people we work with, we are very thorough. If you like, I can tell you all about your finances, your holidays, what newspaper you read and every aspect of your life, right down to the content of your telephone calls. Why do you think you got clearance to lead this investigation? Why do you think we are telling you about your friend Lucien, you, more than anyone will know what he's up to and what he's capable of. Now, tell me, would you rather I got MI5 to find him? If that's the case, then there'll be serious consequences for everyone. Now, I'm going to ask you to step outside while I make a call, I'll give you two gentlemen a couple of minutes to think about what I've said, and how we can progress matters before I leave here.'

The Chief Constable and Will stepped outside the office. 'For fucks sake, Will, what the hell are you doing? You're committing professional suicide here. These people, they run the country, she's got the power to destroy you. Think before you speak in future. I'm far too close to getting my pension to lose it because of your pig-headedness. When we go back in there, think carefully about what she has said, don't put up barriers, give her options, alternatives. There's clearly something the establishment are trying to hide and it's not our place, or your journalist friend's, to expose it.'

The door opened, and Felicity Harvey invited both men back inside. 'Well, it seems I am mistaken, please accept my apologies. I was unaware that our target had been officially reported as a missing person, it's put a whole fresh perspective on the matter.'

Will listened intently, before speaking to the civil servant who was looking increasingly more uncomfortable by the minute. 'Could I offer an option for you to consider? It is something that will help everyone and hopefully keep any scurrilous reporting and news stories out of the media.'

'Yes, please do, Chief Inspector, I'm open to any suggestions you can offer.'

'Okay, I know this person well, I grew up with him. He's not a criminal nor is he a paedophile or sexual offender. As you know, he'll listen to me. If I can find him I can stop him from reporting anything. He owes me a few favours, so I know I can stop him from talking. How does that sound? I will use the threat of the Official

Secrets Act on him, he'll believe that. My only issue is, what if the evidence he has is damning and proves that criminal activity has taken place by senior establishment figures?'

Felicity smiled at Will, nodding in approval at what she was hearing. 'I like that option, I like it a lot. If there is any proof of criminal behaviour, then the people responsible will retreat from the public eye and immediately retire overseas. There will be no criminal prosecution against any such person, we will deal with it internally. It's not your concern, MI5 will deal with all of that. How certain are you that you can find and silence your friend?'

Will couldn't disguise his stunned belief of what was taking place and nervously shook his head. 'Jesus, I can't believe any of this is really happening. Is this one of those crappy television shows, where someone is going to jump out on me, and say, you've been caught by Candid Camera?' No one laughed, they just stared blankly at Will.

Finally, Will answered the question. 'I'm 100% certain I can silence him without jeopardising or involving anyone else. Please, before you set MI5 on him, give me the opportunity to sort it out, if I fail and he refuses to keep quiet, then I'll contact you straight away.'

The civil servant stood up, smoothed down her skirt and looked down on the two seated police officers. 'Thank you for your co-operation. It's a hard lesson to learn, but it's life, you don't mess with the system. If you do, then you suffer the consequences. This country is full of people who have tried to take on the establishment, every one of them has suffered professional and personal humiliation, all have been discredited to the extent that they are regarded as what the masses term fruit cakes. Your friend is fortunate to have you, I advise you to make sure you succeed, I'd hate to see your career end before it's really started. The journalist might well turn up tomorrow, who knows? If he does, let's hope he is able to permanently keep his mouth shut. Thank you for your time, Chief Constable, DCI Scott, I hope our paths never again cross.'

Will stood up and left the room, he wasn't certain what had just happened. He was stunned to hear how the establishment could simply jettison individuals who they deemed to be a threat. He laughed to himself at the thought of stupid bloody Lucien being on the MI5 hit list.

He had barely got back to his desk when the Chief Constable appeared behind him.

'DCI Scott, can I have a further moment of your time?' he asked. Will followed him to the photocopying room and closed the door. 'Will, listen to me, you must make this happen, silence your friend. They'll be watching your every move, gathering information to use against you and your family.'

'Family?' Will exclaimed.

'Yes, family. When your friend returns tomorrow, silence him before he lets the cat out of the bag. He has to understand its more than his career that's at stake here. These people are vicious, they don't give a damn about us or the real world.'

'Do you honestly believe he'll come back tomorrow boss?' Will asked.

'If we believe what Ms Harvey said, then yes, he will. So it's important you are ready and prepared.'

'Thanks, sir, by the way, I have a serial killer on the loose and murders to solve. The fucking establishment thinks saving their own arses is more important than catching a killer psychopath. Fucking great isn't it?'

'Will, stop talking shit and feeling sorry for yourself. Deal with it, that's what you are paid to do. Keep me updated with everything, and please, for heaven's sake, do not repeat to another living soul anything about this morning's meeting.'

The Chief Constable left the office, asserting his authority by throwing back his shoulders, raising his head and pulling himself up to his full height, making his walk out of the office more of a march. Meanwhile, Will struck an almost defeated figure, his shoulders were hunched, his head stooped and his face devoid of any expression. He looked for all the world like a beaten man.

'You alright, boss,' said a friendly voice breaking the DCI's train of thought, 'I've brought you a cuppa, you look like you could do with it. That looked a little tense with the Chief?'

'Thanks, Daisy, I really do need it. I'm thinking I need to get a bit more involved with Lucien Palmer's disappearance. Can you keep this investigation ticking over for a few hours? I'll still be local, but I need to speak with a few people like his editor and colleagues. I want to see what they know.'

'Okay, not a problem, boss, I understand. You and Lucien are close, I'd do exactly the same if it was one of my mates.'

Will spent the rest of the day at the offices of various regional media reporters, speaking in depth to Lucien's colleagues, and more importantly to his editor. None of them knew much about what Lucien had been working on, albeit his editor, somewhat tongue in cheek, expected whatever it was to be ground breaking. In exchange for the odd scoop on the murder investigation, Will persuaded the editor not to print any news story that might relate to Lucien's disappearance.

'It could compromise our investigation if you do print anything. I assure you the minute I know more about our killer you'll be the first to know the details. I'll give you the scoop. We need to work together on all fronts.' The editor couldn't believe his luck. It wasn't every day that the SIO of a murder investigation wanted to work with the local press. Little did he know that the Chief Inspector was being entirely disingenuous, he was manipulating the situation in order to protect those closest to him including his friend.

Next, Will visited Chris Palmer at her home. He needed to be the first official that Lucien on his return talked to. He reinforced this detail to her. 'Chris, listen, if Lucien calls you, you must tell him to call me before he does anything else. I need to talk with him before anyone else gets to him. I'm being serious here, trust me, I know what I'm talking about. He might well be in some trouble and I can help him if he comes home tomorrow, make sure he speaks with me first.' Chris was more concerned that Will appeared to know that her husband would be coming home very soon, possibly from the way he was talking, within the next 24 hours.

'Do you know where he is, Will? Has he been harmed?'

'I don't know, Chris, I'm in the middle of a difficult situation, trying to balance management of a murder investigation on the one hand, and find my missing friend on the other.'

Chris assured Will that the minute she had heard from Lucien she would tell him to speak to him as a matter of urgency. There was nothing further Will could achieve until his friend returned, if he returned.

CHAPTER EIGHTEEN

It was 3.00 a.m. when the telephone landline at the Scott residence began to ring. Mel was first to hear the shrill ringing and answered it. 'Mel, it's Chris. Lucien's home. He's just turned up at the front door. I haven't told anyone. Can Will come over straight away please? Lucien needs to speak with him.'

Will took no time to dress and drive over to Lucien's home in Kingsgate. When he walked into the living room he saw his friend sat on the sofa, his face was blooded and bruised, his eyes were vacant, he was pale, and looked like he had received a severe beating. 'Bloody hell, Lucien, where in God's name have you been?' he said walking over to his friend and giving him a friendly pat on the back.

'I can't tell you, Will, it's secret. I've been warned not to discuss anything with anyone, ever! It's serious shit, mate, stuff you don't want to know or get involved in. I'm sorry. Let me put it this way, everything we have learned and been taught all of our lives, about the leadership of this country, and who runs it, it's a load of bollocks. There is another tier of authority that transcends all we believe.'

Will understood what his friend meant, but couldn't reveal what he knew. 'Don't talk shit, Lucien, how far have you got with your investigations into the murder? Did you get any fresh leads for us to use?'

'Will, listen, I'm not talking to anyone about what happened to me. It's not newsworthy to be honest, I've been scratching about in a depraved community. I was threatened with my life if I spoke out about anything I found, I took a number of fucking good beatings. Had my laptop stolen, my notes and my voice recorder are gone and I woke up in a gutter in Whitechapel, absolutely paralytic drunk and terrified for my life. These blokes in suits were stood over me, poking me with their shoes, I don't know whether they were helping me or robbing me. Next thing I know, I'm in a taxi and on my way here.'

Will worried that his friend had been tagged and that someone was listening into the conversation. He was reluctant to say anything that could be construed as suspicious. He told his friend to go and have a shower, and they could catch up when he came back down stairs. 'I need to close the missing person's report. It will need some kind of explanation about where you were, maybe we just need to say you went on a bender?'

Lucien went upstairs, leaving Will alone with Chris. 'To me, it sounds like he's got involved in things he shouldn't have been meddling with. Someone or something has silenced him. Probably best to leave it at that, I think. He's going to need you by his side, Chris, so if I can get this sorted right now you can be left alone. I'll tell his editor not to bother him. How does that sound?'

'Great, thanks, Will, you are a good friend to us. Maybe you and Mel can come over for dinner one night this week? I want to get things back to normal as soon as possible.'

Will asked Chris if she could fetch Lucien's clothing downstairs, as he wanted to take a closer look at it. Chris disappeared upstairs and returned with the dirty clothing.

Without speaking, he checked with his fingers round the seams of the jacket and the rim of the collar, there he found what he had been looking for, a tiny bugging device, complete with a microphone the size of a pin head. He managed to remove this without Chris noticing. Years of experience working with NCIS, intelligence gathering and working undercover, had taught him the art of surveillance. He wrapped the bugging device in a piece of paper towel and placed it in the freezer compartment of their refridgerator. There was nothing else in the remainder of the clothing so Will handed them back. Chris Palmer looked totally confused by his actions. 'I was looking for evidence of any paint or markings that we could analyse and perhaps identify where he'd been, there's a little bit, so I put it in that towel in the freezer, it protects it from contamination,' he said. Chris nodded but was still clearly confused by proceedings.

Lucien returned to the lounge, wearing a dressing gown and slippers. He didn't look like the type of man that MI5 might be interested in. Will went to work on him, convincing him that he shouldn't repeat or talk about what had happened or he had found out.

'Will, it's not that I could tell anyone anything. I honestly cannot remember what happened until I woke up in the gutter, I feel like I've had my brain wiped clean. I'm worried what my editor will say, I think he might be expecting a mind-blowing story.'

'Don't worry about him, Lucien, take some time out mate, you've been through the wringer. I'm speaking with him first thing tomorrow about the murders, so I'll let him know not to bother you for a few days. If you do remember anything, please call me. You've got to trust me, Lucien, this is your best mate talking to you, not DCI Scott. Keep your head down, spend some time with your wife, and chill out.'

On that note, Will left the couple, and returned to his own home where Mel waited in the kitchen. 'Chris rang to say you were on your way home, so I've made you a mug of hot chocolate. It's good news about Lucien isn't it. Do you think he needs to see a doctor?'

'No, he got some serious bruising but he's walking, moving and talking okay. I expect Chris will arrange a doctor if he's struggling. I've told them both to lock the front door and to chill out for a few days.'

Mel looked lovingly at her husband, 'If only we could do the same, Will. You are a good man you deserve a break too you know.'

Will took a sip from his mug before taking his wife in his arms and holding her tightly. 'I love you, Mel Scott,' he said.

'I love you more,' said his wife. 'Now come on let's go to bed, you've got an early start again tomorrow.' Mel led her husband by the hand to the stairs and instructed him to go up while she checked the rest of the house.

As was usual, Will instantly fell asleep the moment his head hit the pillow. Mel wasn't too far behind. At least one of Will's problems had been resolved, now he could return his focus to the murder investigation, and catching the killer.

The following morning, Will took a call at his home, the caller was reluctant to identify themselves. It was woman's voice, a woman with a Lancashire accent. 'Good work, Will, very commendable, you did well. So well, that you may well be hearing from us again. Your friend, Lucien, he won't be able to remember a thing, so don't worry about his welfare too much.' The call ended before he could respond. It sent a shiver down his spine, since it meant that the all seeing eye not only knew where he lived and his telephone number, they had listened in to his conversation earlier that morning with Lucien and possibly Chris Palmer. It unnerved him, but he recognised that when MI5 were involved in something, there could be no secrets, everything was likely to be heavily monitored. For now at least, it was over, Felicity Harvey had the decency to confirm that. Before he left for work, he made a call to the Chief Constable, and explained that he had accomplished all that he promised, Lucien had been silenced. The Chief sounded relieved and congratulated him on his excellent work.

'That was a good shout, Will. Keep an eye on him just in case, we don't want any loose cannons dropping us in it. Best chalk this one up as experience I think.' Will agreed it was time to move on, and to return to what now bizarrely seemed altogether safer investigations.

CHAPTER NINETEEN

No one in the investigation unit dared suggest it, however, there was a brief lull in the murders. This allowed Will and his team some time to play catch up. Various discussions surrounding a serial killer's desire to continue to kill were central to trying to determine and understand the driving force behind the crimes. Clearly, the victims weren't randomly chosen, they had been specially selected, showing that the killer knew their movements and potentially their past. Mandy Ward believed that the victims had likely been groomed by the killer. This assumption meant the killer might be personable and approachable in having the ability to put each victim at ease and off guard. It was ironic that in each case, the hunter had become the hunted.

The press had embraced the killings, portraying the killer as a figure of justice, effectively doing the police's job for them, and at the same time keeping children across the UK safe. Curiously, the tag that Lucien had given the killer, 'the paedo preyer' had featured as a front page headline in the printed press across the globe, as different countries became aware that the victims were paedophiles. It had somehow become common knowledge that each victim had been tortured before meeting their death, the sanguinary details making the slayings all the more newsworthy.

In a televised political debate, members of the Conservative Party condemned the murders, appealing to the people of the UK to remain calm, and to understand that what was happening was morally and legally wrong. No one has the right to murder another human being just because their predilections are different. The Prime Minister, speaking of the murders on national radio said, 'As a government, we have nothing to hide, we don't support the killings, they are barbaric acts of murder. We condemn them, the killer is dangerous, he must be caught and correctly tried for his crimes through the British Judicial system.'

Labour politicians were equally as damning of the killings, and blamed Tory party cuts to policing numbers as one of the driving factors behind them. The BNP were much more forthright with their beliefs. 'This killer should not be maligned, or judged as being sick or mentally ill. This is an act against the establishment, the people of this country are sick and tired of the excuses and lies spouted by those in power. The killer is making the world a safer place by killing off the cancer that rots our society, paedophiles deserve no justice, just death,' they claimed.

In pubs, clubs and bars across England, people of all adult ages, men and women, were privately supporting the killer. In a televised news story, one man said, 'Whoever is doing this deserves a bloody medal, he's showing the police up for the continual failure to address these problems. People are fed up with weak or no justice. If these crimes help save one child from harm, then he's done his job.'

A woman, a mother of two, commented, 'This is the justice we lack in this country. The police aren't proactive in this area, councils don't care, and the social services haven't got a clue, they are frightened to refer children at risk, in case they make a mistake. Why we have useless do-gooder charities claiming they can make these people better, I really don't understand. It's lunacy, what planet are these people on? Honestly, believing they can help cure a paedophile? The only way to cure or stop a paedophile is to put a bullet in their head, they deserve no kindness or support.'

Despite there being just one murder committed in the town, for some reason the media and the public had decided that the epicentre of the killings was Bridlington. The town was already busy, it was summer season, however a whole new identity of tourist flocked to the town. Ghouls, wishing to visit the murder site and see the key streets where the killer and the victims might have walked, were as busy as the sea front promenade.

One enterprising writer produced pamphlets that he sold around the town. These discussed such gruesome details as the story of the Acid Bath Murderer's visit to the town and showing where he was married and the hotel where he and his wife stayed for their honeymoon. How Peter Sutcliffe, the Yorkshire Ripper, came to Bridlington on his holidays and would drink in the railway station bar. There was a chapter donated to Jimmy Savile, and his unusual visits to the town and his good friend Allan Roberts, which of course linked very nicely to the current day murders. He was brought in by the police for questioning. He claimed he wasn't glorifying the actions of these criminals, he was writing the town's sinister history. In the local press, he later apologised to the public for any distress his pamphlets may have caused.

The local authority, although pleased to have a greater influx of visitors to the town, didn't appreciate that many visitors wished to learn about the darker side of humanity in the town. Ironically, the council leader condemned what he described as exploitation of the murders. He himself had been photographed speaking to members of the local communities at the local crime scenes, and splashed these along with a weak statement offering his political support for the police on his facebook and twitter pages.

He lost any sympathy when he stated in an interview, 'Innocent people have been killed by this murderer, who when caught, deserves the book thrown at him and to be locked away for the rest of his life, allowing us to get on with ours without fear of retribution.'

The national press seized the opportunity to suggest that this inferred that the councillor 'had something to hide' since the killer wasn't troubling normal people, he focused on paedophiles. A public scandal had been narrowly avoided as news of the death of a high profile entertainer hit the headlines temporarily distracting attention away from Bridlington, and from the curious statement associated with the local authority. A second statement was released, this one had been properly vetted and prepared leaving no ambiguity in its content. The entire world it seemed was following the murders through the media on and off line, with enthusiastic interest. Central to every news story was two main protagonists, DCI Will Scott, and his now arch nemesis, the paedo preyer.

Will described the media attention to a news programme, 'It's like being in a huge glass goldfish bowl, on which the eyes of the world are focused. My every action is analysed, every lead is investigated by armchair detectives across the planet. And, it seems, everyone thinks they know who the killer is, except us, the police. I have the press follow me everywhere, they are outside my home at night, they are still there when I leave for work the following morning. Intrusive is an understatement, and would be putting it mildly. It's got so ridiculous, that one television programme discussed my wardrobe and fashion sense.'

Within the sanctuary of the police station, the investigation team continued to analyse every detail and piece of evidence. From the outset, the victims' laptop computers were recognised as being important and integral to help the police catch the killer. On each of the seized laptops there had been a word document containing a list of names. The lists were identical, and it was believed had been added by the killer after each murder. The team had spent dozens of hours investigating every name on the list, and where possible, physically visiting such persons bearing the name and questioning them. None were known paedophiles and none were on the sex offender register. To the contrary, when the team decided to dig deeper the list was positively identified as being victims who had been subject of what was now termed historical child abuse. In each case the victim had reported the matter to the police at the time and several years after the abuse. Unfortunately, on each occasion the police had dismissed the allegations and took no further action. Leaving each victim mentally scarred and lacking faith in an establishment which had turned its back to them, and left them feeling alone, vulnerable and disbelieved. The list of police forces failing these people stretched the length and breadth of the UK, just one force was obvious by its absence, Eastborough.

Mandy Ward was of the opinion that the killer had selected the Eastborough Police area because of this fact. It was her belief that the killer believed that the force was more sympathetic to victims, and in more recent times, had shown an excellent record in catching and convicting paedophiles. 'He is highlighting that paedophiles are not few and far between, they are everywhere, and they walk among us right now. They don't look like monsters, they are ordinary people. In all too many cases they are people who hold powerful positions. They can be your next door neighbour, your work colleague, a family member. That's the overarching message this guy is sending to us and to society in general.'

DS Smith discussed the panic that was running through the paedophile and child sex community. 'My informants tell me that the sicko's are shitting themselves, because they are frightened and can't come to us for protection, as it would be an admission that would change their lives and their families lives forever. The bastards don't think of how their actions affect the poor kids they abuse, selfish twats. Apparently some paedophile helpline charity is offering to provide confidential support via telephone. They are asking the paedos themselves, if they hold any suspicion whatsoever about the identity of the killer, to pass his name to them and in turn they will pass it on to the local constabulary to investigate. What the fuck is that all about? Why haven't we been made aware of that?'

Will agreed with DS Smith and instructed one of the team to contact the charity to see if any names had been proposed. 'It's ridiculous, yet typical, that these organisations don't engage with the police. It's not that bad an idea, but it requires proper policing, the fact that they might hold such information is equally of concern, we need to see what level of information they do hold.'

The telephone on Will's desk rang out. It had become something of a standing joke among the investigating officers that every time that telephone rang it brought bad news, namely that another murder had occurred. As a result, it had been called 'the death phone.'

Will looked at Daisy who was closest to it, 'Answer that please, Daisy,' he instructed. The room fell silent in anticipation of what news might be forthcoming. Daisy covered the handset with her hand and looked up at Will, 'Sir, it's for you. It's Interpol, they believe they have a dead body, a murder victim in Germany, that might be of interest to us. They think it could be one of ours.'

Will took the receiver from Daisy and spoke into it, introducing himself to the caller. It was Detective Inspector DeGraunge from Interpol. He explained that a body had been found in the town of Lahnstein, Germany, it had been partially destroyed by fire, and was badly burnt. Further enquiries by the German Polizei had revealed it was a known paedophile Franz Schimmacher. Will asked his international counterpart to send over images of the body and the crime scene, asking if a small silver angel trinket had been found close to the body? 'Nothing of that nature has been found, I'm sorry, the body has been dead for a long time, maybe a month, the flesh is literally dripping from the bones,' replied the Inspector. Will agreed to send two officers over to Lahnstein to carry out joint investigations in collaboration with the local Polizei.

When the call ended, Will selected who would travel to Germany, and asked them to provide daily updates to Daisy. Travel vouchers were arranged, and the flights and accommodation booked by the station's admin office. In the meantime, the images of the body were emailed through. The mass laid upon the floor barely looked human. Blow-ups of the images were created, when it became clear that the victim was fully clothed and he still had his eyes, fingers and some head hair. The clothing had been set alight and a police note commented that cause of death was suffocation. 'It's not one of ours, if it is, the killer has murdered in a different manner. I think this might be a copycat killing,' Will said.

Mandy Ward again took to the floor to add her thoughts to the matter. When she stood up to speak, most of the room stopped and listened to her. It wasn't every day that the officers got to work with a forensic psychologist, so what she had to say had some gravitas and always seemed important.

'Copycat killings are one of the downsides to having a serial killer on the loose. There could be a spate of them, though hopefully, not in this country. It's often difficult to determine a copycat from the original killings, so it's just as well that our killer leaves a calling card, and kills in such a uniquely gruesome manner. Looking at those crime scene images from Germany, I question whether it is our killer, there are far too many discrepancies. Let's face facts, in each of our murders, the killer wanted us to know it's his work, why would he suddenly act differently when killing overseas?'

Will's phone rang again, and abruptly ended the discussion. It was Interpol. 'DCI Scott, regarding my previous communication with you, abort all enquiries. We have our killer, he's walked into a police station and confessed to the murder. The men were lovers and it was apparently a sex game that went wrong, nothing at all to do with his sexual liking of young children. Please accept my apologies for the confusion.'

Will instructed Daisy to recall the two officers from the flight to Germany without delay. A quick call to their mobiles determined they were at Leeds Bradford Airport waiting for a connecting flight to Germany. When directed to return to Bridlington, Daisy could hear the disappointment in their voices as they reluctantly agreed to do so. The brief introduction to Interpol showed the team how widespread the interest and awareness of the murders actually was. The fact that he had so readily interacted with European based colleagues, on what might have been an international murder investigation, caused the hairs on the back of Will's neck to stand up. However, Germany had their man, England was still looking for theirs. The investigation, Will reasoned, needed one lucky break.

The check of the three types of vehicle seen in the area of some of the killings, revealed nothing. The police in Kettering had arrested a man on suspicion of murder, when he was seen breaking into the home of the murder victim. Further investigations into his movements showed that he was not the killer, since he had been incarcerated in HMP Bedford during the time of the murder. He was heading back to prison having been later charged with burglary.

In Romford, there had been a public demonstration through the town centre, demanding that the police reveal the identity of all known sex offenders and paedophiles in the area, so protecting innocent members of the public who might live close to or have some association with such people. In Bridlington, an anonymous letter had been received by the police, requesting police protection for paedophiles and sex offenders and an amnesty from arrest for those individuals who came forward. This request was formally denied by the police, who advised anyone in fear of attack to purchase security locks and CCTV for their premises, along with a strict reminder that they, the paedophiles, were not to use violence as a form of self-defence.

Officers in Driffield had found three witnesses who had caught sight of someone, a stranger, seen loitering outside the victim's home, around the time of the murder. The individual was described as being male, slim build, and wearing a grey coloured hoodie and blue jeans. He was carrying a rucksack on his back. This description was circulated locally and nationally but was too vague to be of any real use.

Mark Daniel, the forensic team manager, had been invited by Will to discuss where they were with their own investigations and findings. 'This case is unique in many ways,' said Mark. 'For the first time in my professional life I have been unable to find traces of alien fibre, fingerprints or random DNA at the scene of a crime. Whoever our killer is, they have been careful not to leave any trace of their presence. On each occasion where the body had been found inside the victim's home, there was no sign of forced entry. This could mean one of two things, the caller was expected, or the killer was known to the victim. We had hoped to find something for you to work with, sadly we haven't been able to locate anything other than latex glove powder on some of the instruments of torture. The laptop computer at the first crime scene had latex powder on the keyboard, this is the one real piece of evidence we have. A memory stick had been uploaded to transfer the names document. We have been unable to retrieve anything relating to the memory stick, which the killer must have removed from the scene since no such item was discovered. This is repeated across each of the murders. We do know that the killer wears latex gloves during the commission of the crime, so it's likely he will be wearing a full body suit and shoe coverings throughout, explaining the complete lack of any evidence being found.

We considered that anyone seen approaching a house, wearing such items would stand out and be instantly recognised as suspicious, therefore we believe the suit and tools of his trade, were carried into the house and he changed once inside. Thorough checks of the hall and vestibule areas of each property were carried out, with no alien traces found.

'You already have the report into the internet activity. We have recovered in the region of 270,000 images of child pornography, most of it is level four or five on the SAP scale, and the worst Category A, in the Sexual Offences guidelines, so the victims have been seriously involved in that deviant world.

'A cheese grater was utilised in the earlier crimes, this was used to inflict injury to the victim's skin and to rip out body hair. The make and manufacture of these items is not unique, it's a mass production that is commonly sold around the country.

'The staples in each of the victims eyelids are likewise, mass produced and available at most big DIY stores and online, as is the staple gun used to fire them. We have identified the brand of staple gun as a Stihl battery powered device. By the markings on the fired staples recovered from the bodies, I believe the same gun has been used at each crime scene. I understand that inquiries are being carried out into local sales of such a tool at DIY outlets. I can confirm that should we locate the staple gun we will be able to uniquely match it to the staples fired into each victim.

'From a wholly personal perspective, I would think we are looking for a male perpetrator based solely on the injuries inflicted on the victims. In one instance we had a claw hammer used, that would need force delivered from a height above that of the victim, (he's likely to be taller). The back of the victim's skull in that instance was smashed open, with pieces of bone impacting deep inside the brain tissue, this shows the measure of the force and impact. Other victims were stunned by a Taser type weapon, circular marks found on the rear of the neck indicated that this was likely to have stunned and caused temporary paralysis of the victim, allowing the killer time to secure them in the killing position.

'Six inch nails have been used in several cases, this again would take powerful force to drive them into place through bone tissue and wood. In essence, I think what I'm trying to suggest to you, is that our killer might work in the DIY retail business, since the tools used are all readily available in such an industry.'

It felt as though a real breakthrough in the case had just taken place. Mark Daniel had highlighted the potential occupation of the killer and it was based upon sound judgment. Will didn't delay in sending officers out to every DIY or ironmongery/hardware store in the region, obtaining lists of employees and checking them through the PNC. Further to this, he suggested as an option the mass fingerprinting of every such employee.

He discussed the matter with the Chief Constable and received approval to commit to the fingerprinting of all DIY shop staff including management.

The media, believing the murderer was going to be exposed, managed to get their hands on similar lists, photographers visited stores and shops, taking digital images of employees, so that when the killer was revealed, they would be able to produce a copyright image for their scoop storyline. What they hadn't realised was that no fingerprints had been found at the crime scenes. The police were on a fishing expedition, trying to identify previous criminal behaviour among the staff, which in turn would produce a list of suspects. This all being based on the assumption that the killer had a previous police criminal record. The staff union called for an all-out strike by personnel working at such stores, and claimed a breach of article 8 of the Human Rights Act. This resulted in counter claims being made against the police for loss of income by many of the businesses involved. It took two full days to resolve the situation, whereupon all employees had a legal obligation to provide fingerprints and DNA samples to the police, on the written proviso that once cleared they would be permanently destroyed.

The results were less than impressive. Three staff at one superstore had previous records for exposing themselves in a public place, in another two were convicted child sex offenders, and elsewhere there was a number of convicted thieves, fraudsters and disqualified

drivers. Amazingly, not one employee across the region had a record
of violence. The investigation produced similar results across Leeds, Kettering and Romford.

The positive aspect of the higher intensity of investigations, was that no further murders had occurred for almost a week. Team meetings began to conclude that the killer was either in prison, or hospital, or had come perilously close to being caught so had gone to ground. Checks of hospital in and out patients were carried out with no useful leads coming to light. Will, Daisy and Mandy discussed the hiatus and the very real prospect of the investigation being wound down because of it, and of course there was the issue of financial austerity. As a forensic psychologist working for the prison service, Mandy recognised that she was an expensive commodity to the investigation. She proposed that it would be better if she returned to her usual position at Wakefield Prison, since there was little else for her to work on. 'I'm quite prepared to go back to the prison, if it helps with your budgeting. I'm going to be urgently recalled anyway, my psychology report is required for a hearing I must attend early next week.'

Will was reluctant to release Mandy, he still believed she had a huge part to play in helping identify and catch the killer. In truth, she had proved to be a real asset, her presence and experience had got many officers thinking differently about the way they investigated crimes and sought offenders. She had been like a breath of fresh air with her enthusiasm and professional attitude. 'I'm not going to release you just yet, Mandy,' he said, 'I've no problem with you fulfilling your commitments to the prison, but I really need you here. How long do you think you will need to complete your report for the hearing?'

'A good couple of days. It's the weekend tomorrow anyway so maybe you could release me for that? I haven't seen my partner for weeks, so it would be good to spend a little bit of time with him as well. Just give me this weekend, boss, please.'

Will agreed and told her to go home straight away. After collecting a few items from her part of the desk, Mandy disappeared through the office door, wishing everyone a peaceful weekend as she did so.

'While we are quiet, I want you and me to sit down together this weekend, and write up reports on each of the murders, Daisy. We can pass these onto the Chief and his sidekicks, it'll get them off our backs and show them we are making progress. What's your take on why the killings have stopped? We are going to have to give the powers some kind of explanation for this lack of activity. I think he's gone to ground because we are somehow getting close, maybe he's been spoken to by a uniform officer about something completely detached from this.'

Daisy sucked thoughtfully on the top of her black biro, 'I don't know, but something inside tells me that we shouldn't be counting our chickens just yet. The murders seemed to happen so quickly, one after another. I can't believe he's just stopped because he got fed up or satiated his appetite for killing. It's more likely that he's gone on holiday or something. He's got to be some kind of psychopath or sociopath or something along those lines. The severity of the kill got progressively worse, whoever killed our victims was out of control during the kill, he must have been surely? I can't believe he was so cold and calculating that he could torture somebody and calmly enjoy it. There must have been some element of frantic emotion during the kill.'

'I think you could be right, Daisy. He has to be a sociopath to survive daily routine without drawing attention to himself. I attended a course on this a few months back, I've got classroom notes depicting the personality traits of a sociopath.' Will reached into his desk drawer and withdrew a blue ring binder folder. 'Here they are, now let's see. Sociopaths are charming and intelligent, they never show remorse or guilt. They seek to win at everything they do. Emotionally, they are incapable of love, and can be inventive liars. They speak poetically, don't ever apologise, and have a belief that they will make into the truth.'

Daisy began to nervously laugh.

'What are you laughing at, Daisy?' asked Will.

'Nothing really, sir, it's just that it sounds like most of the blokes I have ever had in my life. Maybe I attract sociopaths. One bloke told so many lies, he couldn't remember the last time he spoke the truth. I'm also thinking we have a fair few in the police as well. How many coppers do you know that won't ever apologise, even when they know they are in the wrong? Don't even get me started on the inventive lying aspect.'

Will smirked. 'Daisy, I think we can tick another box of our suspect profile. He's a sociopath, but then so is 30% of the population.' Will took to his feet and grabbed his coat, 'Come on, let's go home, the night shift are in. I need to quickly speak with Ian Simpson, then I'm finished for the day.'

Daisy waited for her boss to handover to DS Simpson and walked with him to the police station car park. 'I think it'll do us good not having our psychologist friend around for a couple of days. She's a bit prim and proper and I'm finding I have to watch my p's and q's all the time. Do you trust her boss? She's an outsider, she's not like us, no understanding of police procedures or canteen humour. She's a bit of a liability I think, maybe naive even.'

Will was laughing. 'Now, now, Daisy, don't be like that. I think she's a good asset, she's probably a bit nervous being on the front line with us, she doesn't know us, and I don't think she really likes us, but that doesn't worry me, she's professional and knows what's expected of her. That's all we can ask of her really. It did make me laugh when she threw up at the crime scene last week. I thought she was going to pass out and fall on top of the body.'

'She wasn't alone there, boss, I couldn't really handle it either. Do you reckon we'll get counselling after this is all over?, I think we are going to need it.'

'I expect not,' said Will, as he opened the door of his Audi and climbed inside. As he pulled away, he wound his window down, 'See you in the morning, Daisy, sleep well. Who knows what new adventures tomorrow may bring.'

CHAPTER TWENTY

The weekend had gone by with no activity whatsoever. The game of cat and mouse between killer and police had suddenly stopped. With enquiries into the seven murders almost exhausted, Will and his team were reviewing each case over and over, desperately looking for a clue or something that might progress the investigation. Even the press had lost some interest, all that remained outside the police station was a skeleton crew of local reporters and newshounds. The murders had fallen from front page headlines to filler paragraphs on page four or five of the national papers. In the absence of outside influences the investigation was altogether less pressured and Will felt he was in control of every aspect of the case. It was almost a week since the death phone had rung out and in an obscure way Will thought that was a good thing. It was tangible evidence that the killings had stopped, though whether that was by police intervention or by accident he could never truly know.

Will had given Daisy the Sunday off, she needed a break from being 'Miss Reliable' and time to enjoy her life away from Bridlington Police Station. She looked a different woman, refreshed and buoyant when she returned to duty on the Monday morning. Mandy looked much more spritely too, she was busy imparting her psychological knowledge to some of the male members of the team who hung off her every word. Will knew that one more week of silence and inactivity would sound the death knell for the investigation. The Chief wanted to see a return for his investment. As yet Will had nothing to offer other than the murders had stopped.

Everyone was busy, fresh intelligence had come in over the weekend, very little of which was informed, it was more guess work or rumour. Nothing annoyed Will more than poor quality intelligence reports, which can be a hindrance to any police investigation, such submissions often revealed detail that is already known and has been investigated. The 'jungle drums' as they were often referred to by police forces across the globe had stopped beating, bringing to an end insider information from the criminal underworld of Bridlington. Will asked one of the DC's to attend every uniform shift briefing for the following week, and to remind patrol officers to submit better standards of intelligence especially if the source was a trusted one.

Throughout the weekend, Will had pored over every detail of the case including the random list of historical child abuse victims found on each of the laptops and tablets. As he mulled over each name something suddenly triggered in his mind. The names, when correctly listed, spelt out a macabre message: '*Vengeance Is Mine They Will Suffer For Their Sins*.' His heart thumping in his chest, he called over to Paula Jay. 'Come here, I'd like you to take a look at this, it's a fucking acrostic puzzle,' he said pointing to the sheet of paper on his desk. Paula carefully studied the list of names, her eyes darting up and down the names to double check what she was reading. 'Christ, boss, I see it straight away. The first letter of the forename spells out a message.

How weird, do you think we might have some kind of religious zealot running amok? The opening words are definitely a quote from the Bible. I'll run a check to see where it comes from. That's bloody clever, you've obviously got an analytical brain.' She pondered for a moment, before adding 'What was it Mandy the psychologist said? You'd have to think the same as the killer to get close to him. Looks to me like you're doing just that, boss.'

Will smiled and began to rock back and forth in his swivel chair, his mind was churning over the provenance of the list of names. 'My problem is, Paula,' he said, 'how has the killer got hold of these names? It's surely confidential information? I'm reasonably sure there isn't a single database in existence with a list of historical child abuse victims from around the UK contained within it.'

Paula was checking her smart phone. 'Boss, I've checked online, 'Vengeance is mine' comes from Romans 12:19-21. So there's no real clue to be had from that source.'

Will nodded his understanding. Leaning forward in his chair, he planted his feet firmly on the ground beneath his desk. 'Paula, I want you to run some checks on where this type of sensitive information might be held. I've checked PNC, it isn't contained there. That aside, some of these victims come from far flung places like Orkney, The Western Isles, Jersey and the Isle of Man. So it's doubtful that any one police force would hold such a database. What's your thoughts?'

'I think I know the answer, sir, what about charities or similar organisations that take calls from survivors of sexual abuse. Surely they would compile a detailed list if the caller was in agreement to them recording their information? Failing that, what about the local authority, social services? They may hold national records. I'll check these out straight away.'

Within the previous 72 hours there had been several incidents of suspected and known paedophiles being severely beaten and left for dead in various towns and cities across the UK. Vigilantes, as they were being described by the police, were taking the law into their own hands. Inspired by the paedo preyer, they were hunting down and attacking those suspected of child sexual abuse. The press picked up on these attacks and classed them as being 'the justice of the people.' This forced the Home Secretary and the Minister of Justice to call for calm. In America, there was talk that the paedo preyer had crossed the Atlantic and resumed his killing spree on child sex offenders across many States.

For Will, matters hit rock bottom when he was approached by two serving police officers who pleaded with him for protection, both admitted possession of child abuse images and to being active on various forums and message boards, one copper had sickeningly given himself the pseudonym *The Childcatcher*.' Both officers were suspended from duty with immediate effect, pending further criminal investigation. Elsewhere across the UK, police officers of all ranks were suddenly being suspended from duty, or instructed to take gardening leave. It was a virtual epidemic that would seriously undermine the police force as a collective law enforcement organisation should these facts ever be disclosed to the public. Will was later called to an emergency meeting of the Association of Chief Police Officers, where he provided an update on the murders, and was also asked to maintain an air of secrecy about the quantity of police officers being relieved of duty pending investigations. One Chief Constable informed the group, 'The enormity of what has happened as a result of these killings is beyond our comprehension. We must close ranks, support our fellows and colleagues, and maintain their integrity. To fail to do so will result in a complete breakdown of law and order. I am talking about those of us in this room maintaining a silence, and crushing any discussion about police officers being active criminals and sex offenders. We must stand together on this.'

Will recognised what was happening, this was a senior officer cover up on a colossal scale. Every force across the British Isles was represented and all voted in favour of suffocating the facts. He was sickened by what he heard.

'As far as I'm concerned, in the worst cases, dismissal and cancellation of police pension will suffice, without the need for any criminal prosecution,' said another senior officer. A suggestion which received a generous round of applause.

Back in the investigation room, you could hear the sound of a pin drop when suddenly, the death phone burst into life. Everyone in the room froze, including Will. Part of him wanted to ignore the ringing, but with all eyes on him he had no option but to pick up the receiver. His heart was beating like a steam train thundering down a track, and he became slightly breathless. The voice on the other end of the telephone was abrupt.

'This is Detective Chief Superintendent Connor from the Major Investigations Team at New Scotland Yard. To whom am I speaking?'

'DCI Will Scott sir, how can I be of assistance?'

'Are you the SIO covering these so called 'paedophile preyer' murders?'

'I am indeed the SIO, sir.'

'We've got a bit of a delicate situation down here in London, and we need your assistance. I'm talking about a highly sensitive matter that for a variety of confidential reasons cannot be dealt with by our officers. We need detectives from an outside force. Since it clearly relates to your murders, it's been suggested by the office of the Home Secretary that you are the right officer to deal. Are you available to come down here for a few days? You can bring two of your own officers with you as support. The Home Office will supply full forensic support.'

Will stuttered, 'Sir, erm, I'm not sure I can make that kind of decision. That would have to be decided by my Chief Constable. Are you telling me that you have a murder you suspect has been committed by the same killer we are looking for?

'That's precisely what I'm saying. Yes. Listen, I'll get my boss to contact your Chief as a matter of urgency. We need you down here as soon as. Do you have any outstanding commitments up there that would prevent you coming here later today?'

'No, sir, other than I'm heading a murder investigation with cross county boundaries.' The call went dead. Will wasn't sure what to make of it, so to cover himself he called the Chief Constable's office. Barbara, the Chief's secretary answered Will's call. 'Can you get the boss to call me urgently please, Barbara?' asked Will.

'Gosh you'll be lucky, Will, he's had calls from the Home Secretary, the Director of Public Prosecution and the Commissioner of the Metropolitan Police already this morning. I haven't got a clue what's going on, but it's something big.' Will replaced the receiver and decided to grab some fresh air, so took a walk down to the street outside the police station.

'Daisy, come walk with me,' he instructed his right hand woman who had just returned from an external enquiry.

Outside the station, away from the presence of the investigation team and nosy ears, Will explained what had just happened. 'Something's happening in London, it's something major by the sounds of it, Daisy.' The pair were suddenly interrupted by a police civilian worker who rushed out of the station and told Will he had an urgent telephone call waiting at his desk.

'It's the Home Secretary's Office,' said the young girl excitedly. Will ran up the stairs taking two at a time, and reached his desk before Daisy had entered the office.

'DCI Scott? It is I, Felicity Harvey. We spoke a few days ago regarding those murders you are investigating?' Will felt a tinge of anger at the patronising manner in which she spoke to him. 'We've had a murder down here in London. Neither the Met nor the City boys can deal with it. Since its likely to have been committed by your killer, I thought you would be the right person to investigate. I've cleared it with your Chief Constable, you are to get your arse down here pronto. I'll sort overnight accommodation for you and two of your fellow officers. You can expect to be here for three to four days.

'Before you start asking questions, I can assure you that this is a direct instruction from the office of the Prime Minister and the Home Secretary. A police helicopter will collect and bring you here, they'll be in touch with you directly regarding timings. Be aware, you will be meeting with MI5, the DPP and the Lord Chief Justice at 3.00pm, at the Royal Courts of Justice in the Strand. Once you are here, we will provide you with more detail.'

The phone line went dead as the caller hung up. Will stood in silence, his face felt numb and devoid of any expression. 'Daisy, Mandy, you need to go home and pack a bag, we are going to London for a few days. A police helicopter will be picking us up very shortly. Meet me back here in an hour. I can't say anymore because I don't know what this is all about myself. The only thing that's been divulged is that this is a direct instruction from the Prime Minister, so bring some decent dress clothes with you, we might well be meeting her. I'll give Mel a ring and get her to check all the news channels to see what's breaking in London. That way we can be forewarned and forearmed.'

Will placed DS Smith in charge of the day shift during his absence, and made his way to his car. He rang Mel during the journey home and told her what was happening. She was shocked and a little bit worried by the secrecy of it all. By the time Will got home, she had not only checked out all the news channels, she had also packed a small suitcase for him. One of his best suits was ready and waiting for him to change into. 'There's nothing breaking in London, Will, I think it must be something very secret.' Will barely had time to drink a cup of coffee, before he was kissing Mel goodbye and driving back to the police station.

Daisy and Mandy arrived a few minutes behind him, perplexed and worried. They questioned their boss on every aspect of the call, analysing every word and trying to second guess what it might be about.

Daisy's phone rang in her pocket, answering it she was told to go to the playing fields at Headlands School, Bridlington, close to the library building, where a helicopter would be arriving to transport them to London within the next half hour. Mandy offered to drive to the school.

'I haven't got the foggiest idea what's going on, ladies,' said Will, almost apologetically.

'I'm just so excited to be going in a helicopter,' said Daisy.

'Me too,' added Mandy.

As the car pulled into the school gates its occupants could see the police helicopter landing, it's huge rotor blades spinning round like a giant whirling dervish. The three ran across the playing field towards the black and yellow aircraft, carrying their luggage with them, it was noticeable that Will had the bigger suitcase, a detail that wasn't missed by the co-pilot who greeted them and packed away their bags.

'Got all your make-up in there have we, sir?' he said laughing. Will was far too nervous to answer and climbed into one of the three rear seats and buckled himself in. He was shaking.

The pilot went through the safety regulations and advised them not to speak into the microphone attached to the green helmets they each wore. 'Only speak when instructed to or if you are asked to answer. We'll use your Christian names, is that understood?' The trio confirmed their understanding and sat nervously waiting for the helicopter to lift off. Will was sat next to a door and had a window view, Mandy sat in between her two police officer colleagues. Will's legs were now shaking uncontrollably, he was terrified as the rotor blades suddenly picked up speed and the deafening sound of the aircraft's engine increased. Moments later, they were in the air, looking down on Bridlington which rapidly disappeared beneath them as they were propelled upwards and forward towards London.

'Have you any idea why you are being brought down to London, Will,' asked the pilot.

'No not a clue. I think it must be something big though, do you know anything?' he inquired.

'No, something's going on though. You're being met at City Airport by the secret service, I believe. You're not spies, are you?'

The journey took around an hour as the pilot gave his passengers an aerial guided tour of the metropolis with plenty of photo opportunities. Daisy and Mandy settled down and enjoyed the flight, whereas Will dared not move a muscle. By the time they landed at City Airport, his legs had gone into spasms caused by tension. He couldn't wait to get out of the helicopter and stretch them. As he collected his luggage, a black sleek looking Mercedes 'C' class pulled alongside the group. Two men got out and opened the rear doors, ushering the Eastborough team into the rear seats, scanning their luggage before placing it in the boot, they drove off before anyone could thank the helicopter crew.

Will asked the two men sat in the front seats if they knew why they had been brought to London? Neither man spoke, causing a tangible feeling of concern among their passengers.

Thirty minutes later the car arrived at a police cordon blocking access to the Strand at St Clement Danes Church. Several uniform police officers were carrying out traffic control diverting it towards Waterloo Bridge. There was chaos. The black Mercedes was waved through and travelled a couple of hundred yards before turning left into one of the gated car parks of the Royal Courts of Justice. An overweight, serious looking security officer who manned the gate checked the driver's identification and allowed them to enter.

As the car stopped, the two men in the front seats alighted and opened the rear doors inviting the three passengers to step out. Their luggage was removed from the boot of the vehicle, which left the car park and drove out into the Strand, leaving them stood by a flight of stone steps.

'Charming,' said Daisy sarcastically, 'Rude set of bastards they were. I'm so glad I don't work down here, everyone takes themselves so seriously,' she added.

'Will, thank you for coming down at such short notice,' said a voice from behind them, it was a woman who sounded vaguely familiar to the DCI. He turned round to see the tall elegant figure of Felicity Harvey walking towards him. 'I've organised accommodation for you all for three nights. I don't expect you'll be here that long, but just in case. Your booked into the *Savoy*, it's handy and is literally just up the road. Absolutely nothing will come out of your budget, so don't think about that. We need you to remain professionally focused on what matters,' she said, smiling at Will's two companions.

'Come with me. I'll take you up to the Lord Chief Justice's office, that's where our meeting is being held.'

'It's very quiet here. I expected the building to be really busy, bustling with clerks and barristers rushing into the different courts,' said Daisy curiously.

Felicity snapped back, 'It generally is, however, it's closed for special reasons today.'

As they climbed various stone staircases within the Royal Courts of Justice they soon arrived at a red carpeted corridor. The walls on each side were lined with wooden panelling and original antique oil portraits of the Judiciary throughout the years. It smelt fusty and old. Felicity lowered the tone of her voice to a whisper. 'These are the Judges corridors. On the left are the back of the courts, the Judges' entrance, on the right are the Judges' private chambers.'

Reaching a dark solid oak door, Felicity knocked twice and entered, instructing the others to remain where they were.

Moments later, the door opened and there stood before them was the Home Secretary. She stepped forward and greeted the visitors offering them a seat inside the huge office with walls lined from floor to ceiling in beautifully bound law books. It was all Will could do to stop himself exclaiming 'wow' at the sight. This was a very different world from Bridlington Police Station. Sat around an oval shaped, highly polished dinner table, was the Director of Public Prosecutions, The Lord Chief Justice of England and Wales, the Commissioner of the Metropolitan Police and two other people, both of whom were wearing expensive looking suits and were clearly from MI5. Felicity Harvey sat next to the Lord Chief Justice.

Each party introduced themselves and their respective roles, before the MI5 officers opened proceedings. 'Ladies and gentlemen, you are reminded, that under the terms of the Official Secrets Act, you must not reveal anything you are about to witness or hear, outside these walls. Is that understood by all present? If so, I require you to sign this declaration,' he said, pushing an official looking sheet of paper in front of everyone. It was an acknowledgement relating to the Official Secrets Act, which everyone signed.

The Commissioner of the Metropolitan Police was the next to speak. He looked directly towards the Bridlington based officers. 'Thank you for coming here. This is an extremely delicate situation which cannot be compromised. I'm sure you want to know why you have been brought here. It's as simple as this. There has been a double murder. It is our belief that it is linked to the killings you are currently investigating. Let me assure you, this is no ordinary murder, and I won't go into any detail because I do not wish to cloud your professional judgment with my own opinions. What you're going to see with your own eyes, is a crime scene like no other in the history of law and order anywhere. The main issue we have is that of confidentiality. The press must never know, nor the public. It's that serious. The Home Office have provided a select team of forensic experts to assist you. Aside from the individual who found the bodies, there has been only one other person enter the crime scene, the police surgeon who, in both instances, declared life extinct. Beyond that, there is absolutely nothing else I can tell you that might assist your investigations. The bodies were found at 9.30am this morning. Your killer, it seems, has come to London.'

Will asked what had happened. This caused the Lord Chief Justice to lean forward across the desk and in a solemn voice he replied, 'It is your responsibility to find out exactly what has happened, how it has happened, and why it has happened and tell us. That's all we can say on the subject. Catch whoever committed this atrocious crime.'

One of the MI5 officers stood up and asked Will, Daisy and Mandy to follow him. They moved swiftly out of the Judges' corridors, and down to the main public foyer and area. It was a maze of similar looking corridors with more paintings and even more secure doors. Everything was made all the more eerie by absolute silence. Five minutes later they were stood outside the entrance to Court number 13. 'The crime scene is in here through these double doors. You are to enter and exit through this door only. A forensic team is ready and waiting for your instructions. The remainder of this vast stone building has been checked by tracker dogs and search teams. It's clean, but we do not know how the killer entered or exited the building. There is no CCTV in any of the Judges' corridors, which are located at the rear of the court room behind the bench and the Judges' throne. I'll leave you to it. Here is my telephone number, call me when you have carried out your own cursory examination of the scene, you'll need to update us in the office. Can I remind you, this is a sterile crime scene, so it's down to you to thoroughly work it.'

Daisy asked why the Met Police weren't investigating?

'Because many of those officers are in and out of these courts on a regular basis. They live in London. Therefore cross contamination is a real possibility, so we have opted for you, since in principle it's your investigation anyway. I've put my neck on the line and convinced those people upstairs that you would be the right team to investigate this. Trust me, this isn't just any double murder. You will never forget what you are about to see, not least because it is undermines every aspect of what British justice stands for.' The man walked away, pointing at a neat pile of sealed bags containing the forensic Tyvek suits laid upon a stone bench, for the team to wear.

The double doors to the court room were half glazed, with half a dozen small square windows providing a scant view of the court interior. Peering through these they realised that it only showed a few feet beyond the door, and not a clear view of the inside. They would have to physically enter to see what all the fuss was about. None of them could imagine what it was that would make this crime scene so important to the establishment.

Will was first dressed and through the doors, he waited for his colleagues to join him. 'I think we'll make decisions once we are inside, and can get a full view of what it is we are dealing with here,' he said. The group stepped forward beyond a pillar that obstructed the view from the door. They were now inside the main body of the court room. The first thing Will noticed was the ornate marble flooring. Then he smelt it, the disgusting stench of death. The shocking scene laid out before them caused each of them to take a deep intake of breath.

CHAPTER TWENTY ONE

Stood in the cold court room none of the three knew whether to laugh or cry. Will looked around him and shook his head in total disbelief. Sat behind the bench was Mr. Justice Steven Tibbs, a High Court Judge who was globally recognised for his often outspoken comments regarding criminals and punishment. He believed the punishment should fit the crime and that no two cases were alike, therefore the presiding Judge should deliver a tariff or sentence he felt correct. He had been severely criticised in the past for his leniency in sentencing convicted paedophiles who he believed were not criminals but mentally ill people who needed help. In one case, he accused a child victim

of concocting details as a form of revenge upon her uncle with whom she did not get along. As a result of his summing up the jury found the uncle innocent and he was allowed to walk free with an apology from Mr. Justice Tibbs for putting him through such an ordeal. There followed media and public outrage against the judiciary as a whole. Two months after his release the girl's uncle was caught in the act of raping a six year old child, this time he was found guilty and given the paltry sentence of three years imprisonment.

Will slowly walked towards the bench looking for any sign of the silver angel trinket. As he reached the well of the court, he looked up towards the Judge sat in his high backed red leather chair which resembled a fancy throne. His gaunt, white face looked down on Will. He was wearing his grey court wig and a red gown. He had an almost clown like appearance sat there in all his finery, yet absolutely exposed and vulnerable. Beneath the gown, he was naked.

Will looked back towards Daisy and Mandy who stood very still and hadn't moved from the spot. 'I'm going to go up behind the bench. Daisy, can you please take photographs of this victim? Walk the same route as I have. If you spot anything out of place or untoward capture it, please.'

He moved round the side of the raised bench which stood several feet above him and climbed four stairs until he was fully able to survey the scene from the judge's position.

As he approached the chair in which the dead man sat he saw it swivel slightly, under the vibration of his footsteps, causing him to tread more lightly so as not to disturb anything.

'There's something laid out on the bench before the judge. It looks like photographs,' he added. As he neared the body, he recognised images of the dead bodies relating to his investigation. Nine independent piles of them, neatly lined up in rows. The piles consisted of five images, the top one reflecting the precise pose that each victim had been in. They could almost be crime scene photographs. The photographs beneath were an overview of the various stages of torture each victim had suffered during the attack. Will carefully went through each pile, replacing them precisely where he had found them.

Pile number eight covered the murder of Mr. Justice Tibbs.

Momentarily Will had forgotten that a ninth victim existed in the very court room where he now stood. He looked at the graphic images of this victim, before lifting his eyes towards the dock, at the far side of the court, and seeing a man also dressed in a court wig but wearing a black university graduate type gown. Both Daisy and Mandy let out faint screams when they realised Will looking behind them, towards the dock, where the second body sat.

Mandy called out to Will, 'This is symbolic boss,' her voice echoing in the cold empty court room. 'The killer is making a statement here, showing a complete disrespect for British Justice, perhaps highlighting the fact that paedophiles exist in all walks of life, and that nowhere is sacred, there is no limit to who or where he will kill.'

'Fucking hell, Mandy, that's one hell of an assessment, you have a way of putting things that completely sums everything up,' replied Will. 'Can you both join me up here, please, I want to get a closer look at the judge and his injuries, so we need photographs before I move him. He looks like a big bloke so he's going to be difficult to move. We can then move round the court room towards the second victim. Do either of you recognise him at all?'

'Not me, boss,' said Mandy briefly glancing towards the man sat in the dock behind her. 'He has the appearance of a Halloween skeleton. So thin and gaunt, a bit like the child catcher from *Chitty Chitty Bang Bang*, I think' she added. Daisy confirmed that she didn't recognise the judge, let alone the man sat in the dock. She continued to capture images of the court room and the crime scene so that a comprehensive gallery would be available once the area had been cleared.

'There's no sign of the Malakim,' reported Will, 'I've looked all over the bench, but there's nothing here. It's definitely our killer, so why not leave his calling card?' he wondered.

Daisy and Mandy joined Will in his delicate fingertip search of the bench. 'Other than the photographs, there's nothing on here, so maybe there is something in his gown?' Will reasoned.

As they tried to pull the swivel chair containing the judge from beneath the bench they found it was stuck and wouldn't budge as though caught on something. Will bent down crouching by the dead man, he looked underneath the bench and revealed the reason why the chair wouldn't move. 'His hands have been pinned to the underside of the bench. He's stuck here for the time being.' Will then searched the robe, feeling through the velvet material for any sign of items left in the garment. It was empty. Folded neatly on the floor, was a pile of clothes presumably the murdered man's.

Will asked Daisy to search through these for any useful evidence that might have been left by the killer. In a pair of black corduroy trousers she found a black leather wallet. She opened it and laid the contents out on the bench well away from the body. Inside, she found his driver's licence bearing his full title and name, and a security pass for the Royal Courts of Justice. 'Christ, boss,' she said,' did you know he is a proper 'Sir', he's been knighted by the Queen', she said.

Mandy revealed yet another credible piece of information when she revealed 'All High Court Judges are knighted once they move over to the RCJ, quite a few of them go on to be Law Lords.'

Will brought the topic of conversation back to the murder. 'Forget the heritage, stick to what we are here to do. I have some serious questions for you both; do you think he, the judge was a paedophile? How the hell did the killer get into this place? Finally, how did he lure his victims here? I can see why this is a matter of utmost secrecy, a serial killer has infiltrated the very place where legal justice, the law of the land, was created. There are religious connotations attached to this place, then there's the Knight's Templar as well, for fucks sake, he's desecrated it all.' The sheer magnitude of what they were dealing with, in these latest two murders, suddenly hit Will.

'Okay, let's take a look at his lordship's body shall we? Record this please, Daisy. As with the other victims, the eyelids are stapled open, and we have the customary two wooden skewers through the eyeballs. Beneath the wig, his hair has been burnt back to the scalp. It's obvious, without opening the mouth, that a penis is protruding from that orifice, bulbous end projecting out. His face appears to be covered in some kind of white make up powder, giving him a strange complexion, to me his face has the appearance of a clown. Moving down to his blooded chest region, his heart has been crudely cut out of the body, causing haemorrhaging of blood which is covering the torso of the body. This is a bit like a scene from a Jack the Ripper movie, didn't he remove a victim's heart? Fuck me, look at this, his nipples are pierced, he's got a small silver ring in each of them. The piercing isn't new, it's got all the signs of being old, a regular piercing, with no scarring present. The dirty old bastard, I think he might have been into kinky stuff.'

'I can see looking down to his lower abdomen, the penis and testicles have been removed, I believe the penis may be inside the mouth, and if typical of other victims, the genitals will have been eaten and digested. The pathologist will be able to confirm this detail in the post mortem examination. His legs and feet appear to be intact.'

'What about his fingers, Will?' asked Daisy, 'are they still on his hands?'

The DCI bent down and took a further look at the dead man's hands pinned to the underside of the bench. 'Well that's weird,' he muttered, 'the skin on his fingers has been sliced to the bone, the skin is drooping towards the floor, it looks like dead flowers.'

Daisy moved to photograph every detail before coming up with the idea of an overview of the court room taken from the public gallery which was raised above the floor of the court, immediately opposite the bench where the judge sat.

'Good idea, Daisy,' prompted Will, ushering her to go and do it immediately.

Daisy climbed the stairs that gave access to the gallery from the floor of the court, as she turned to walk along the seated gallery, she stopped dead in her tracks. 'Err, boss, I think you better come and take a look at this, it's freaky to say the least.' Will rushed up the stairs to join his colleague, and like her, he was stopped in his tracks. Before them, every folding wooden seat in the public gallery had been opened out, sat in each seat, was a silver angel trinket. In all there was twenty six of them.

'It's the Malakim. A relative army of them. Remember, they inflict double the damage to those who are guilty of child abuse. So what the fuck is going on?' he wondered, looking somewhat forlornly at the rows of tiny silver objects as though they were real breathing entities. 'Right, make sure you photograph these please, Daisy, exactly as you found them. Maybe forensics can lift some fingerprints off these seats, maybe fibres too, the seats are close together and he will have had to literally squeeze through to be able to open each one. Once you've done that, I want to examine this second body that's sat in the dock.' Daisy set her work phone to continue photographing the Malakims, when she heard a beeping sound. Looking at her phone she realised the battery was dead. 'Shit, the bloody thing is always doing that to me.' Retrieving her own phone from her pocket, she carried on recording this aspect of the crime scene. Once this was completed Daisy decided to gather the Malakim up, and put them in an evidence bag which she popped inside her handbag. 'We don't want these forgotten just because they are up here,' she said to herself.

'Mandy, what are you thinking about right now? What's your opinion of this crime scene?   What is the killer trying to say to us?' Will asked the forensic psychologist.

'It's all about power and control, he's asserting his power over the criminal justice system and the establishment. The Judge has been deliberately posed to look like a clown. He's been left exposed, emasculated of all of his authority. His sins have been laid out before him, in the form of the photographs of each murder victim. He is helpless to do anything, his hands nailed to the bench, his fingers stripped bare. The ultimate act is the removal of the heart, the power over life and death. To be honest, I don't really understand why he has done that. Who do you think the other victim might be?'

'My guess it's a convicted paedophile.   It's like he's passing judgment on him as he's sat in the dock. We'll soon see,' said Will carefully climbing into the dock beside the ice cold deceased man.

As with the judge, a pile of neatly folded clothes sat on the floor close to the body. Will was forced to wait until Daisy was ready to photograph these before searching through them.   A wallet was found in the rear trouser pocket. Removing this, he looked inside. 'Right, on his driving licence, it says his name is Ulrich Vivien Wilcox, he's from an address in Somerset, Yeovil.   There's a membership card and some sort of business card relating to the Middle Temple. What the hell is that, sounds very Masonic to me.'

'That's an area's where most of the barristers chambers are, maybe he's a barrister?' said Daisy.

'Of course, that's why he's wearing the wig and the black gown,' replied Will.

'This is getting extremely spooky,' quipped Mandy, 'I'm not liking this at all. It's giving me the jitters. The injuries don't worry me anymore, it's the other stuff, the connections these people have to sordid stuff that most folk wouldn't believe existed or happened. The freaky way those Malakims have been lined up on each seat, like they are watching over us and everything we do. It's freaking me out a little bit. I feel like the killer is in here with us, watching us. Let's be honest, this guy isn't some run of the mill serial killer, he's got the ability to access seriously secure places like the RCJ, and then be able to persuade a High Court judge and a barrister to come to a closed court room to meet him. How has he managed that? My immediate suspicion would fall on the security guards, they have the means and the ability. We should check their past, maybe one of them lives in our neck of the woods and has connections to Leeds, Romford and Kettering? Whatever, I think we are getting closer to solving all of this. I must admit, I can't wait to interview our killer, I've got a thousand and one questions to ask him. He's one smart bastard.'

Will was just about to begin his examination of the man sat in the dock, when Mandy Ward cried out, 'I've found his business address, it's printed on an envelope, he's based at Zenith Chambers.' Will told Mandy to place it in an evidence bag and turned to Daisy, again asking her to record his comments. 'The body is seated in an upright position in the dock, as though facing the judge who is sat at the bench. Beneath the court wig, the man's hair has been burnt to the scalp, this has blistered. A small kitchen blow torch, presumably used to inflict this injury is sat on a shelf in front of him. Both of his hands have been nailed to the shelf through the centre of the back of the palm. His fingers have been skinned to the bone, and the flesh laid back over the upper facing part of the hand, in a symmetrical pattern. His eyes have been pierced with two wooden skewers and the lids stapled open. His ears have been removed. It appears as though they have been cut off with a pair of scissors which are on the floor by the dead man's feet, alongside the outer parts of the ears. A penis has been inserted inside his mouth, bulbous end protruding between the teeth and lips. Beneath the black gown he is wearing, the heart is absent from the cavity in his chest, which is covered in blood. The rest of his genitalia has been removed, and his feet have been pinned or nailed to the floor.'

Mandy took a seat in the well of the court and began to analyse the scene and her findings. 'So, we have two bodies with no hearts. Why would the killer remove and take away the heart? He hasn't taken trophies from any of the previous murders. So why these two?'

Daisy stopped Mandy's flow, 'I think I have the answer to that. How the hell did we not see this when we came into court?' She pointed towards the clerk of the court's bench, which was situated directly below the judge, close to where Will had stood. Two brass balanced weighing scales sat at the far end of the desk, these were purely for ornamental purposes, and were supposed to depict the scales of justice. Both scales were laid out in an identical manner, on one side of the balance sat a human heart, on the other, a pure white feather. 'There's our missing hearts,' cried Daisy. 'What kind of lame arse would try to balance a human heart with a feather. It's obvious which is the heaviest,' she said rather hastily.

Will, immediately recognised the significance. 'In the *Egyptian Book of the Dead,* the body of the dead pharaoh has to overcome certain quests before entering the afterlife. The final test is the most difficult. His heart is weighed on a scale against a feather. If it is shown to be lighter than the feather, he can cross safely into the afterlife. If it is heavier, then he has sinned during his mortal life, and his soul is tossed to the demons. I guess both of these guys were sinners. We are going to have to dig into their lives to find out exactly how they have sinned, and against what were they judged.'

'I think we need to go back upstairs and report back to the powers that be. I'm not certain how we proceed with this, maybe they can enlighten us. Can you give them a call to come and get us, please, Daisy?'

Will made an excuse to leave his colleagues and go to the toilet. Once inside, he made a call to Mel, he didn't want anyone else to hear. 'Mel, can you do me a favour, search the following two names on the internet for me, please.' Will passed over the names and titles of the two latest victims and waited. Mel found what she had been searching for and came back almost immediately. 'Will, there was a high profile child abuse case a few years ago, the judge you mention presided over it. The defence was led by that barrister. The three accused men were known in the press as the X-Men, because their names were withheld, and they were referred to in court as Mr X, Mr X2 and Mr X3, they were all found not guilty on a technicality. The judge apologised to each of them for suffering the trauma of arrest and detention, before releasing them. There is no mention of victims, but he did state 'that this verdict should be a warning for all those parties who falsely accuse innocent people of child sex abuse, justice will always prevail.'

Will, the other thing you should know, all the major news channels are reporting a security issue at the Royal Courts of Justice, and that disruption to court hearings will occur for the remainder of the week.'

Will fell silent. 'For fuck sake, security incident, it's a bit more than that. Can you print out the reports on that trial for me, please, and don't speak to a soul about anything to do with it, okay. I'm keeping this quiet for now, at least until I can research the trial in more depth.' He thanked his wife, and told her to expect him home in a few days' time. 'I'll call you tonight from the hotel, it's the *Savoy* don't you know!'

For now, the trio temporarily left the crime scene, and carefully removed their forensic suits. Within minutes they were being escorted back through the corridors of power and up to the office of the Lord Chief

Justice of England and Wales. The MI5 officer had been right, it was a crime scene the like of which had never been seen before, and it was never likely to be seen again. This was a unique set of circumstances, and whilst it had some kudos attached to it, it also carried a wealth of heavy responsibility, and an expectation that, in the short term, might be difficult to aspire to.

CHAPTER TWENTY TWO

As they entered the office, the pressure placed upon them to deliver something, anything, was made absolutely clear. Will took it upon himself to deliver their initial findings, with the caveat that a more in-depth examination of the bodies and crime scene would be necessary later that day. He described the morbid scene, and the gruesome manner in which the killer had tortured his victims to death. 'I have quite a few questions I need answers to,' he told the meeting. 'I need to speak to whoever found the body, and identify how many people had access to the court building over this last weekend. I'm assuming, by the condition of the bodies, that they were murdered yesterday. This place is heavily secured, so it should be a simple enough exercise, finding out who came into the building yesterday, and at what time they left. It's fair to say at this point in time, the killer is likely to be within this building. Perhaps a judge's clerk, or a court clerk, it may even be one of your security personnel. Whatever, we are going to drill right down into everyone's movements within the building.

The Lord Chief Justice spoke. 'None of us want you to rush this investigation, God forbid, we have a difficult task ahead of us in trying to keep these murders under wraps. I'd like us all to meet on a daily basis until such time as you have exploited every avenue, Detective Chief Inspector. With the resources of MI5 available to you, I would hope we would be able to identify the offender quickly. I should add, that any offender will be dealt with by the most appropriate authority and not necessarily the police. We shall meet again tomorrow, at 6:00pm, here in my office.'

Will asked one last question before the meeting was wrapped up. 'Do any of you know of any reason why these two men would be targeted by our killer? Is there any suggestion that they might have been paedophiles?'

The Lord Chief Justice was first to react. 'That's enough of that, it's not your place to question whether they were or they weren't. That's 100% confidential. So far as we know, there is no connection between either man other than they both work in the field of criminal justice, and manage that within this building. I seriously doubt they have ever met.'

One of the MI5 officers added, 'We've checked, they have never been involved in the same trial or worked together. They were comparative strangers.'

With that, everyone stood up and left the office. Will was accosted by Felicity Harvey, who handed him a piece of paper containing details of their hotel booking.

'Security here will create new passes for you all to come and go whenever you like. The courts have been closed down for the week, so you have the freedom of the place. If anyone like judges or barristers ask any questions, let me know. We'll handle all enquiries. I believe the forensic team manager is waiting for you downstairs. Don't make any decisions without first consulting with us, naturally this is a situation we need to control, so keep us informed. Here is a list of telephone numbers for you. They are listed in priority order, so if you uncover something, start at the top and work your way down the list.'

Will looked at the piece of paper. 'I see your name is at the very top?' he remarked with more than a hint of sarcasm in his voice.

'Naturally, who do you think pulls the strings? That'll be me. Stick with what you are good at, catching criminals and stop being so paranoid about how the system operates.'

Without any further comment, Felicity left them and walked down the corridor, disappearing through a swing door to the right.

'Well, that's us told,' said Will with a laugh. 'Come on, let's go find these forensic people and get this investigation rolling. I have to admit, I'm not comfortable with the way this is panning out, I think we need to cover each other's backs at every step we make. Who are we answerable to?' Neither of his colleagues answered, they were as bemused as he was over the entire affair.

Downstairs, they met with Grace Wyatt, the forensic team manager. The woman had an air of authority about her and clearly didn't suffer fools gladly, or northerners. As they introduced themselves she reacted in a less than pleasant manner. 'Can you speak slowly, I can't understand your accent,' she barked. 'I've been waiting here for over five hours now. I appreciate this is your crime scene, however, it's not good practice to ignore your most powerful assets. By leaving me and my team out in the cold, as it were, you have allowed time to pass at the crime scene potentially compromising evidence.'

Will apologised and tried to explain why they had not contacted her before now. She wasn't really interested and began to ask questions about the scene and what was expected of them. More importantly, was there anything specific they were looking for. To which Will had responded, 'Evidence that will help us catch who committed this crime might be useful.'

Daisy led the forensic team to Court 13 and as they dressed into Tyvek suits, informed them of the areas they had moved through, and what they were interested in.

'There are nine sets of polaroid prints on the judge's bench, they are laid out in front of him. Can you analyse them and see if we can be more specific about time of death. The police surgeon, from his cursory examination of the bodies, has estimated it to be sometime yesterday, Sunday morning. We are trying to hone that down if possible, that's why I wondered if it would be possible to get some kind of reading from the chemicals on those prints?'

Grace Wyatt wasn't certain that was possible. 'All I can do is ask our guys back at the lab to take a closer look at them and see what they can do. Maybe we can do something by analysing the shadows cast on the prints, that might help gauge where the sun was and give us a more defined time. We'll see.' With that, she turned her back and began to speak with her team instructing them on procedures and what to expect once inside the court room.

Daisy turned to her boss and said, 'She's friendly, good luck with her boss. While forensics are in the court, I'm going to interview the first contact, the person who found the bodies.' She wandered over to a central console positioned in the middle of the foyer area. A skinny greasy haired security guard sat lounging behind the desk. 'Can I help you, love,' he said in a coarse cockney accent.

'Yes,' replied Daisy. 'I'm looking for the person who first reported the incident in Court 13 this morning.

'Ah, that'll be Jane Lovell. Poor cow, she got the shock of her life. What's going on in there, we've not been told a thing. Rumour has it, we've been burgled, the bloody night shift will cop for it if that's the case.'

'Yes, precisely,' said Daisy 'where's Jane Lovell now then?'

'She's in the clerk's office, waiting to be interviewed by the police, that's you ain't it? You can find her through that door there.' He was pointing to a wooden door further along the foyer.

Daisy walked to the clerk's room, knocked on the door and entered. There she saw a short dark haired woman, dressed in a matching two piece plain cream skirt and jacket stood smoking a cigarette. She was visibly shaking.

'My name is Detective Sergeant Daisy Wright, are you Jane Lovell? Are you okay?'

'No, I'm bloody well not. I found those bastards this morning. I feel sick to the pit of my stomach at what I saw.'

'You don't seem sad by the deaths?'

'Sad, why should I be sad. Those pair were the biggest perverts in the courts, they were into anything, kids, foursomes, prostitutes the lot. That judge, he was as

285

seedy as they come, couldn't keep his hands to himself. We reported him time and again, but nothing ever happened. The clerks talked about what the judges got up to on circuit, that one in that court, he would be out until all hours taking advantage of his position with kids. Sick he was, sick. He's got what he deserved, I think. So has the other fella, it's common knowledge throughout the chambers that this pair were paedophiles.'

'Jane, can you tell me what you saw when you went into the courtroom, please,' asked Daisy.

'I didn't see much in there, just the judge sat there at the bench, looking like a zombie. I saw the blood and left, as I turned, I saw the bloke sat in the dock. I didn't know what to do so I locked up the court and reported everything to the clerk of the Lord Chief Justice.'

'Thank you, Jane. If you can just sit tight here for a few more minutes, I'll get a full statement from you. Have you had a hot drink? If not, now would be a good time to make yourself one, but please don't leave this room, okay?'

Will and Mandy appeared at the security desk in the foyer, and questioned the supervisor who had just returned from his rounds.

'How many access doors leading directly into the building are there?' asked Will.

The supervisor looked a little uncomfortable with the question. 'There are quite a few. There are judges' entrances, delivery entrances, public entrances, staff entrances. Not all are guarded though. Quite a few people, like the judges' clerks, have keys that will open most of the entrances.'

Will attempted to tease more details from the man. 'Okay, well approximately how many keys are officially signed out or issued to the court staff?'

The colour in the supervisor's face drained away, and before Will's eyes, he saw him turn green. 'I don't feel very well, can I sit down please?' the man asked.

'Yes, yes, of course you can, what's up?' responded Will helping the security officer onto a nearby wooden bench. Mandy asked the security officer who was sat at the desk for some water for his unwell colleague. He promptly handed her a small plastic bottle of the liquid to give to his manager. Will was crouched down in front of the seated supervisor. He was still probing and sensed that the supervisor wasn't being open with his answers. Mandy handed the supervisor the drink and he instantly took a large mouthful and swallowed it.

He looked back at Will and said 'I'm really sorry, I don't know how many access or pass keys have been handed out. It's something we don't vet. The clerks can, and do, get their own keys cut, so do the judges. We have no way of knowing a precise figure or number. It could be fifty, it could be two hundred and fifty. The important thing is, once inside the building, anyone entering would have to have an electronic pass key to get through to some of the judges corridors and have access to the back door to the court rooms.'

Will stood up and pondered for a moment before replying. 'So the electronic pass key allows access to the inner confines of the courts, the non-public areas? How many passes have been issued?'

'A total of 117. However, people retire or resign and don't hand them in, so in theory there might be another forty to fifty unaccounted for. The electronic tag inside the pass key has its programme changed every few months, so those passes would not permit access after that time.'

Will then asked the guard if he could take them to the nearest building entrance door to Court 13, so they could potentially see the route the killer had used to get in and out of the building. As they walked through the labyrinth of corridors, some carpeted in deep red lush pile, and some with a marble floor, they reached one of the rear entrances of the building. The door was locked and showed no sign of being tampered with. Looking outside into the street, Will noticed that there were no CCTV cameras, ruling out any chance of camera recognition of the offender. As they traversed the route within the building, they found three of the six access doors leading into the judges' corridors, and the rear of the court rooms, were inactive. Anyone could push them open and walk through. The security system was fatally flawed. Will let out a scream of frustration, causing the supervisor to turn and look at him.

'I'm sorry, sir,' he said, 'you must think we are remarkably lax with our security arrangements. You don't expect anyone to try to break into the courts, it's really made us look like a set of numpties, hasn't it?'

'Too right it has. While I'm at it, can I ask you how often and at what time Court 13 was last checked by security, prior to the bodies being found?'

'I can check that from our logs, it should be every three hours, I can definitely confirm that for you though.' He sounded relieved that for once he could provide a professional response to police questions. As they made their way back to the security desk, Will saw Daisy taking a statement from the witness who first found the bodies.

'We'll need to get a statement off you about some of this stuff,' Will informed the supervisor. 'You aren't going to come out of it very well, however. I'm certain things will change after this.'

The supervisor pulled out a ring binder filled with the security check logs. 'Here we are, Court 13 was last checked at 9.00am, this morning. It was all clear. The keys to the court were issued to J Lovell at 9.25am.'

'That's impossible!' said Mandy looking at Will, 'Are you certain your security log is correct?' she asked.

'What is the name of the officer who carried out that check?' added Will.

'It was me. I'm sorry, you're going to find out anyway, but I faked this check time, we all do it. I'm in big trouble now, I'm really sorry,' reiterated the supervisor.

'My colleague will take a statement from you. All of this detail will have to be included, I'm afraid.'

Will was clearly disturbed by what he had discovered in these preliminary enquiries. He walked away and sat on one of the wooden benches that lined one side wall of the foyer, he was deep in thought. Mandy followed.

'I think you ought to ring one of those numbers for that Felicity woman, and tell her what has happened. Remember, we need to cover our own backs here, Will, because sure as hell no one else will do that.'

Will agreed and made the call. Felicity responded as he expected her to. She was angry and screaming for heads to roll because of the situation. 'How the hell can security at the Royal Courts of Justice be so pathetic? This is not going to help the situation one iota. I'll pass this on, thank you, Will,' she said ending the call.

By the end of the first day of the investigation, the team had confirmed that the victims had been killed in the court, the identities of both victims had been established, and of greater concern to the judiciary, the building security had been found wanting on almost every front. Will provided a bullet point update to the office of the Lord Chief Justice. To the team's surprise, the security issues appeared to be the major concern to the assembled group and not the victims. 'We can't have anything of that nature discussed anywhere, so wipe it from the investigation please,' said one of the MI5 officers. The rest of the group nodded their agreement and approval.

Will wasn't happy with this decision. 'I'm sorry, but I believe it's of primary importance to our investigation. If we ignore the fact that anyone with a key to an external door could simply walk in and out of the building, undetected, it opens up countless avenues of enquiry. No stone should be left unturned if we are to catch the killer,' he said. It was clear his appeal was falling upon deaf ears, it seemed his opinion didn't matter. Felicity Harvey butted in, 'Detective Chief Inspector, may I ask on behalf of all those convened here, what the hell you are talking about? We haven't got time for silly talk about leaving no stone unturned. This isn't a bloody press release you're compiling, or an episode of CSI, it's the real world.'

Daisy and Mandy could only sit and watch as Will was blocked at every turn by the powerful authorities sat around the table. Nothing he was saying was making the slightest difference. Instead of being dictated to, Will took control of the situation and stated, 'This is very early stages of our investigation. Tomorrow we will have a pathology report on the two bodies, as well as feedback from the forensic team. We have requested from the Metropolitan Police recordings of any CCTV footage in the streets surrounding the building. Our killer must have changed clothing twice while inside the building, he would be covered in blood after the murders, therefore he is unlikely to leave here dressed like that. From blood spatter we can confirm that both victims were killed inside the court room. What we have to figure out is how the killer managed to lure both victims there and overpower both of them, and if he was acting alone? The other thing is, why didn't either victim scream out for help or assistance? It has to be someone who knew the movements of both victims. Someone who perhaps they both knew and recognised, all importantly, it has to be someone they would trust.'

The older of the two MI5 officers was first to respond to Will's synopsis. 'Are you suggesting that someone inside this building killed those two men? That's totally ludicrous, everyone who works within these walls is vetted and tested before they can work here. It's disturbing that you can consider such a thing. The killer isn't an employee of the Royal Courts of Justice. It's more likely to be someone with a vendetta, maybe a criminal who has been prosecuted by the barrister, or jailed by the judge. That supposition would make far more sense than to blindly claim 'it's an inside job guv'nor'.'

Will was having none of it. 'You have placed me in charge of this investigation, I'm not going to sit here and be told what to do. There is a seriously deranged killer out there, maybe walking the streets of London, or some other city, wherever. He needs to be caught before more people are killed. I suspect everyone until they can prove their innocence.' No one replied. The meeting was ended, leaving Will and his two colleagues with concerns about the interference of this group on the investigation. They left the office and walked down the corridor leading them into the public area of the court building.

Mandy was first to speak out. 'British Justice indeed, it's as though they are determining the route our investigation will take. I don't feel as though we have any decision making authority here, everything we suggest, well, you suggest, is being dismissed. I'm not one for conspiracy theories, however, I think we might just be patsies here. It's like we are being used as a front for something else. I know it sounds daft, but it all seems a little sinister.'

Will laughed, 'Mandy, have a word with yourself, these sort of people want black and white results, no grey areas, they don't like ambiguity, they can't handle it. These people live in a different world to us, they've no concept of reality. For now, we are going to have plough on, and do all we can.'

CHAPTER TWENTY THREE

After what seemed like a surreal night of luxury and a five course breakfast at The Savoy, the team walked the short journey to the Royal Courts of Justice first thing the following morning.

'Talk about extravagant,' exclaimed Will excitedly. 'My room was amazing, I've virtually filled the memory of my I-phone with photographs I have taken of everything to show Mel.'

The two women laughed at his boyish charm and behaviour. Daisy typically put things into perspective. 'Well it may be The Savoy, but it ain't like home. I miss my own bed, and I hardly slept a wink because of the traffic noise. Bloody city never sleeps. Don't get that in Bridlington,' she said with a wink.

As they arrived at the Court building, it was clear that security had already been stepped up and was much more professional and effective, for a start they were uniformly dressed. As they moved through security, their bags were searched and each of them had their clothing frisked by stern looking security officers. Once inside the great hall of a foyer, they made their way to Court 13.

On arrival there, they were stunned to find the crime scene gone, the court room had been professionally cleaned from top to bottom and the evidence they had highlighted had been removed. Will signalled his displeasure by slamming the side of his clenched first against a wood panelled wall. 'Damn it! Who's authorised this? How can we be expected to investigate a double murder when the bloody crime scene has been extinguished? I'm fed up with this, I'm going to call that Felicity bird, I wouldn't mind betting this is her doing.'

Will made the call. He was incensed. It was brief. Rather than answer his questions he was instructed to attend the office of the Lord Chief Justice without delay. His walk to the office was more like an angry stomp, with Mandy and Daisy following behind.

Arriving at the office door, Will showed no respect and threw it open and stepped inside. 'What the hell is going on? Why has the crime scene been cleaned? You brought us all the way down here, allowed me SIO status then manipulate the entire bloody investigation. You can't just wipe clean what has happened here, two men were butchered in that court room,' looking at the Lord Chief Justice he commented, 'one of your own, a judge, a Knight of the Realm, you care more about the reputation of your useless bloody court system than you do about the murder of two men?'

'Detective Chief Inspector Scott, shut up and sit down,' shouted the Lord Chief Justice. 'You're bang out of order making such comments, remember who you are talking to. I'd like to thank you for your professionalism in dealing with this investigation. As a result of your efforts, MI5 have detained someone, our killer. He's under lock and key at a high secure location in the city. He's being interviewed by officials as we speak. From what we're told, he had a grudge against paedophiles, and so ran amok, primarily in your neck of the woods, before moving down to the city, where he killed those poor men in the court room. He thought they were paedophiles. You deserve to be made aware, this individual has been on the MI5 watch list for some time for his allegiance with overseas criminal gangs. His status changed, as he dropped off their radar. He was originally wanted for creating faked images of senior public figures in sexually explicit situations. According to the evidence MI5 hold, he was stalking our victims. He had gone as far as tapping into the home landline of Mr Justice Tibbs and he was blackmailing him and many others too. The images look authentic, however, I assure you they are fake. They portray dignitaries in compromising situations with young children. By compromising I am of course relating to sexual acts. Do you have any questions, Chief Inspector?'

Will was stunned into silence, every ounce of his intuition told him that what was being said was bull shit. He resisted the temptation to speak out against the group. Instead, he asked, 'Can you tell me, how certain are you that the man in custody is the man we are looking for?'

'He's admitted everything,' piped up one of the MI5 officers, 'absolutely everything. The individuals name is Raymond Sproutt, with two t's. Because of the delicate nature of this man's crimes, you'll be given no access to him, he'll be questioned about your murders, we've already been provided with dossiers from your Chief Constable. You'll be able to sign the crimes off as detected. The Home Office will be advised to record such an outcome in their official figures.'

Will disrupted the officer's flow. 'So why the hell have we been brought all the way down here for this pantomime? There is not one thing that we have achieved during our brief stay London that would assist with the arrest of this man Sproutt with two fucking t's.'

'Chief Inspector, our number one priority is to safeguard the integrity of the establishment, we've done that and also solved your series of murders. It was our initial belief that your journalist friend had met with him, and that he may have shared some of the images, thanks to your intervention, we are no longer actively pursuing that line of interest. I hope everything is falling into place for you now?

'You were brought down to investigate these murders because we felt, collectively, that you were the right people to do so, mainly because of your knowledge and awareness of the killer's behaviour. Last night, we found him inside the RCJ, like so many killers, he'd returned to the scene to revel in the chaos he had created. He was hiding in a corridor, security detained him as an intruder until the police arrived. So it's job done, fait accompli.'

Will's jaw dropped open in disbelief, and he shook his head reflecting his thoughts.

'I think you've taken us for a ride here, I'm finding it hard to believe that you'd go to all this trouble then stop us from interviewing what is effectively our prisoner.'

Felicity Harvey stood up. 'He's not your prisoner, he's been arrested in London, the Metropolitan Police area. The Met won't be interviewing him, MI5 will, that's where this discussion ends. You can pontificate all you like, your work is over here. We require you to hand over to us all the paperwork and images you have collected, they are legally the property of the Crown, and like everything else in this investigation, are covered by the Official Secrets Act. Once we have collected those from you, you can get on your way back to Bridlington.

'We'll be sending through letters of commendation to your Chief Constable for each of you. For you, Amanda, there'll be a letter from the Minister of Justice to the Prison Governor at Wakefield. You'll have to organise your own way back to Bridlington. We will, however, reimburse all expenses. Thank you for your co-operation.' With that, she ushered them from the room.

Before they could speak, a bald headed bruiser of a man, dressed in a cheap black three piece suit and plastic shoes approached them. 'I need you to give me your mobile telephones and any camera equipment you have. We need to clear them of any images and recordings relating to the Royal Courts.'

Will and Daisy not only had work mobiles, but also their own private ones. They gave each other a knowing glance and elected not to hand their private phones over. They handed the man their work mobiles as requested, and were then told to go downstairs and wait in the main foyer entrance hall, where they would be reunited with their property within a few minutes.

'What the fuck,' whispered Will. 'This is so, so wrong. Have you ever known anything like it?'

Daisy was equally as perplexed by it all but tried to justify what had happened. 'Will, to a certain extent,

Mandy was right. We were patsies. Somehow, I don't know how, we have got ourselves entangled with the secret service, MI5. All I can think is our investigations must have crossed and we have been used for their dirty work.'

Mandy joined in the debate. 'Well I for one don't think that this guy Sproutt or whatever he's called, exists. Unless of course, he is connected to the court service and the powers that be needed to surpress everything because of that?'

'That's true, Mandy,' said Will. 'They were quick to disconnect all talk of it being an inside job. How the hell will they keep all of this quiet though? There's quite a few people know what's happened, that court clerk for one.'

Daisy was beginning to think suspiciously about the entire affair. 'Will, how do we know that any of those people we interacted with were what they said they were? We didn't see any forensic report, nor did we speak with the police surgeon who allegedly carried out the post-mortems. In addition, they've taken all our documentation from us, there's nothing much to show that any of this happened. I have a weird feeling about all of this. The more I think about it, the worse it seems. How many organisations would book two coppers and a forensic psychologist in town on a criminal investigation, into the *Savoy Hotel* for fucks sake. It's normally a bed and breakfast we get to stay in.'

Will looked momentarily confused, 'Certainly, nothing adds up, and I doubt we'll get any answers from this lot.

Let's get our phones and get the fuck out of this place. Maybe we should have lunch at The Savoy, heaven only knows we deserve it. Then we can see about catching a train back home.'

'Sounds like a good plan to me,' added Mandy.

Deep inside, all three were seething. It had been a complete waste of their time coming down to London, each believed they were part of a larger cover-up.

Back in the office of the Lord Chief Justice, the establishment team, minus the Commisisoner of Police, were nervous. Felicity was pacing around the room, and stopped at a window overlooking The Strand below, she wore a supercilious grin on her face. 'I think we've plucked ourselves from the verge of real disaster here. I still find it unbelievable that his bloody honour Mr. Justice Tibbs and his barrister pal Wilcox were going to drag us all down the pan. The murderer, whoever he is, did us a real favour in snuffing out those two. Keeps MI5 clear of any involvement in their demise. Imagine if it ever got out, two bloody paedophiles employed within the English Judicial system, threatening to take down the entire Judicial system and government through whistleblowing about high level deviant behaviour. I hate to say it, but they were traitors, I honestly feel they got what they had coming. Thank God, I say, miracles do happen.

Nothing now exists that can repeat this ludicrous situation ever again. All the evidence has been destroyed, computers wiped clean of images and diaries destroyed. The press are satisified with the reason for the closure of the Courts, so we're covered there. It's a matter of reporting the sudden deaths of our blackmailers now. Thankfully, neither were married, so there's no bereaved family to deal with. The Times will receive a notification of death and obituary of both, later this week. We should be able to contrive a suitably subdued tale, to keep the interest minimal, car accident or something along those lines. By tomorrow, both men will have been cremated in a private service outside London and we can all move on.'

The MI5 officers nodded in agreement, however, they remained concerned about absolute closure. 'What about the Eastborough officers, can they we rely upon them to keep quiet?'

'Yes absolutely. Give it a couple of days and we'll reveal to them that Sproutt died in custody, hung himself. They'll get their commendations and glory and this will soon be forgotten.'

'I wasn't alluding to that, Felicity,' said the officer. 'What if the killer strikes again? He's struck in London, where next? We'll have some difficult questions to answer then?'

'From who? If you mean from the Eastborough lot, then forget it. Any questions they ask will be rebuffed. They'll be heavily influenced to believe any future killings are copycat crimes. They're likely to run with what we suggest, otherwise it makes them look professionally stupid for revealing their killer to be dead. We can manipulate everything to serve our interest, we can control press coverage should that be necessary. Gentlemen, the top and bottom of this situation is, we cannot allow anyone to start digging around the lives of the Judiciary, there's far too much national integrity to be lost. This situation has to be buried, right here and right now. Everyone carries on with their own lives.'

With that, the meeting was closed. Felicity Harvey gathered up the documentation relating to the investigation, and placed it inside a brown manilla box file. She left the building, smiling at security as she passed through their operations desk. Outside, in the Strand, a few reporters had gathered by the main entrance, none of who were aware of what had taken place. Felicity put her head down and confidently strolled past them and away from the Courts. As she put it 'her job was done.'

On the rail journey back to Bridlington, Daisy and Mandy were soon asleep. Will couldn't sleep and remained deep in thought. He had far too many questions on his mind, not least, why the establishment had lied to him? There was something that didn't sit right with him about the whole 'Sproutt with two tt's' story. Then there was the trial that Mel had discovered online, why was that never mentioned? It was a rock solid motive for murder if Sproutt had been one of the abuse victims in that trial? Then there was the key used to gain entry into the RCJ, how had the killer got hold of that? He blinked and looked out of the carriage window at the lush green fields and pleasant countryside the train cut through on its way to Doncaster, this was a far cry from the hectic streets and roads of London. Maybe he was being paranoid about everything, after all he had been through a lot in the space of a few weeks, he thought to himself. He sat back, and for the first time in days, he allowed himself to relax and think of home. Sure, the investigation hadn't turned out how he expected, but the establishment had insisted the killer had been caught, so he was in no place to argue with that fact. Outwardly, he smiled and faked his understanding of Sproutt being the killer. Internally, in a dark place within his own mind, there were too many unresolved issues relating to the murders for him to be entirely convinced. He put such thoughts out of his mind, and took a slow drink from the glass of Shiraz which sat in front of him.

CHAPTER TWENTY FOUR

Back at Bridlington police station the following morning, Will walked into the murder investigation room to a rapturous applause. Officers from the day and night shift had congregated to celebrate the successful conclusion to the investigation. Such celebrations were normally put on ice until an offender had been found guilty and sentenced in court. However, everything about this case had been unique, therefore, the post investigation party was starting straight away. The Chief Constable was expected at the station within the hour. Will instructed everyone to continue with their work, and to go about officially closing down all enquiries relating to the investigation. Such activity would ultimately take a couple of weeks to achieve and would be handled by a skeleton crew of detectives, including Will.

Minutes later, the Chief Constable of Eastborough arrived at the police station and entered the investigation room. Behind him were three of his finest bag carriers, Chief Inspectors and Inspectors all carrying crates of beer and several magnums of champagne. The mood was electric as the Chief coughed out loud to bring silence to the room, before speaking. 'Ladies and gentlemen, I wish to congratulate every one of you for your hard work and determination in bringing, what the press are claiming to be, the most morally acceptable series of murders to occur in the United Kingdom. Your efforts will go down in the annals of criminal history as a huge success. I'd like to give special recognition to a number of individuals whose efforts went above and beyond that expected. Miss Amanda Ward, Forensic Psychologist for the Prison Service, your efforts in helping profile and determine the mind-set of the killer is recognised with a commendation from the Home Secretary and the Minister of Justice for England and Wales. Detective Sergeant Daisy Wright, for outstanding police and detective work, you too receive official commendations from the Home Secretary and from the Minister of Justice. Finally, to Detective Chief Inspector Will Scott, you are highly commended by the same authorities and you are now confirmed in the rank of Chief Inspector. Sergeant Daisy Wright, you will instantly assume the duties of the rank of Detective Inspector, working with DCI Scott. The entire room burst into cheers and a chorus of 'for they are jolly good fellows' rang out. Will was hoisted from the floor and raised above the investigation teams heads, where an unsuccessful attempt at crowd surfing saw him fall unceremoniously to the floor. The Chief Constable asked that the team respect peace, since the rest of station was still hard at work. 'I'll leave you all to celebrate your success, thank you one and all.' He left the office, and the building wearing a broad grin, since the success of the team reflected on his career too.

Will looked over towards Mandy, she was stood alone peering at the original local crime scene images. He walked over to her and calmly placed a reassuring and friendly arm around her shoulder, causing her to jump and pull away from him.

'Oops sorry, Mandy, I didn't mean to scare you. I know we haven't always seen eye to eye, but I want to personally thank you for what you did and for your support throughout this investigation. We got there in the end though, didn't we?'

The forensic psychologist took another step back from him, and looked at him squarely in the eye. 'Did we?' she replied, placing the champagne flute she was holding, down onto his desk, and walking out of the room for the last time. Will stood motionless, his expression blank, he was in a temporary state of shock. After everything, the last thing he expected to hear from her was what she had just said.

Daisy approached Will and tapped her glass against his. 'Come on, boss, it's time to celebrate! We bloody well did it and we gained promotion. Who'd have ever thought, Detective Inspector Wright. I'm well chuffed.'

Will gazed into nothingness with Mandy's final words going round and round in his mind. He finally snapped back to reality and gave Daisy a cuddle. 'Congratulations, mate, I'm proud of you, and the whole team. We are a force to be reckoned with.'

Daisy looked at her boss, something was troubling him. 'What is it, boss? What's upsetting you?'

'Daisy, do you honestly believe that our killer has gone away, he's been caught and that it's all over?'

Daisy pondered for a second before replying. 'Yes, boss, I do. That Felicity woman from the government, she told us that Sproutt was our killer. We've got to trust what she says, otherwise, who the hell can we trust?

Boss, think about it, the fucking Chief Constable's accepted it.'

'I needed a body, Daisy, I don't like all this accepting the word of others in authority, its bull shit. I wanted to look at this fucker right in the eyes, I wanted to see what drove him to kill like he did. I wanted to put a name and face to a monster. It doesn't feel like we've got any closure without the killer being sat in front of us.'

'Boss, you are going to have to accept it. Go take some leave, take your family away for the weekend, you deserve it. After all, I can officially cover for you now I'm an Inspector, whoopee.'

Will smiled, and celebrated a little more with his team, before going home and taking a full seven days off. Other than the lies he had been told by the establishment, he never fully discussed what happened in London with Mel, it was too difficult for him to comprehend let alone his wife with her sense of morality. Mel never questioned the link with the judge, the barrister and the murders. It was dismissed, as though it had never happened.

The family took a break in Scotland, renting a croft overlooking Loch Ness. This time he was investigating a different mystery, helped by his children, they went in search of the Loch Ness monster.

The week flew by, and the break helped Will get his head around everything. He returned to work at Bridlington Police station to find he had his own office, bearing his rank and name on a smart plaque on the door. A pile of paperwork for him to review and sign off sat on his desk. The office was large, and overlooked the town, in the distance he could see the harbour and the sea front. It felt good having his own office, a private space where he could think. Despite that, he missed the camaraderie of the investigation room, where everyone worked as one. He remembered that he had to write a formal letter of appreciation to the prison service commending Mandy Ward for her work and for her professionalism. He made a mental note to himself to do this as a priority. Looking out of the window, he wondered if he would ever see Mandy again, or work with her? He needed to get the investigation wound up and closed as quickly as he could. All of that was history now, and not even the local newspapers or media could muster any interest in the matter.

As he wandered through to the investigation room, he saw four plain clothes officers filing documents and storing some of the seized evidence in boxes marked in large black letters on two sides 'Detected - Paedo Preyer.'

'How long until we can officially close it down fellas?' he asked.

'By the end of today, boss', said DS Barry Smith. 'It's been a blast, boss, don't you think? The death phone has got dust and cobwebs on it now. It hasn't rung for over three weeks. That's all that will be left in here from the investigation, unless you want it on your desk, boss?' he added with a laugh.

'Go fuck yourself, Barry. I never want to touch that thing again let alone answer it. That phone is my nemesis. Our nemesis. We should send it down to the

Black Museum at New Scotland Yard, to put on display. Poxy bloody thing.'

'Did you know sir, DI Wright worked it out, that telephone rang eight times during the murder investigation, every time, it was a report of another body. Isn't that something, eight times, nine bodies, a 100% call rate.'

Will turned to leave the room, 'That's enough, Barry, I don't want to discuss it any further. Can you come and let me know when you're all finished in here, I'd like to have a few moments alone in here before I lock the place up.'

'No problem, boss, I'll let you know. Everything is going into the archives at Headquarters, including the evidence. We've sealed that under the prescribed terms for storage, and future DNA sampling. Not that we'll need it, but you never know someone someday might want to take a look at it.'

Will returned to his new office and rang home. He wanted to share the news about his new office with Mel. 'Hiya, darling, guess what, I've got my own office. It's well nice, got my name on the door and everything,' he told her.

Mel was thrilled to hear an enthusiastic tone in her husband's voice. 'Wow, that's great, Will. So come on, tell me the truth, what's up? Are you bored or something?' she asked.

'Bored? Never. This is the modern day police force we are talking about, it's hectic, all go, go, go,' he said laughing. 'Actually, I'm a little sad, I know the murder investigation took its toll on me, but it's going to be formally wound up today, and I feel a tinge of sadness about it.'

'It's no surprise, Will, you all worked like Trojans. You were living and breathing it every day, but it's gone now, it's over, so it's time to put it where it belongs, into the archives. Time to move onwards and upwards. Don't forget what you said this morning before you left here, you promised to write a personal thank you to every officer who worked the inquiry with you, so get that done, then it's closure for everyone.'

Will did as he was told, and spent four hours hand writing the individual thank you messages. He felt guilty since there were 101 other things that needed his attention, however, he wanted to let each of them know his appreciation, so he figured it was right to spend time committing to the task. He dropped each sealed memorandum into the relevant internal post boxes of the officers concerned and returned to his office.

The ringing of his new desk telephone made him jump, picking it up, he introduced himself. 'DCI Scott, how can I help?'

'Will, hello, it's Felicity Harvey here from the Home Secretary's Office. I apologise for intruding, however, there is something I must let you know. This morning, prison officers found Raymond Sproutt dead in his cell, he had hung himself with his bedding sheets. They tried to revive him, but were too late, he was dead. He's left a note, confessing everything. Will, I think this gives everyone some closure, you might want to convey the news to families or relatives of his victims?' With that, she hung up.

'Yes, how comfortable, everything is nicely gift-wrapped up and can be lost in the mists of time,' said Will speaking to himself. The call made him feel tense, every suspicion he held came flooding back to him. He continued with his own conversation. 'I doubt whether Sproutt with two fucking t's was our killer, or if he even existed. The bastards have used us.'

DS Smith interrupted Will's thought process when he knocked on the slightly open door to attract the DCI's attention. 'That's it, boss, all done. We've notified all police forces and organisations that the investigation is now closed. The evidence has been bagged and sealed and placed in archives along with the paperwork. Seventy-six boxes of documents and reports. We've returned the white boards back to the uniform briefing room, so it's all clear now. I'll leave it with you, boss. Thank you again for involving me in the investigation, you know where I am if you need me.'

Will stood up and shook Barry's hand. 'Cheers, Barry, you're a top man,' he replied.

As he walked into the investigation room for the last time, Will remembered how busy and hectic it had once been. Crime scene photographs lining the walls, things to do lists on each officers desk, the constant ringing of telephones. The photocopying room where he held private, out of ear shot discussions, now stood empty, the photocopier itself being returned to its rightful original owner.

At the far end of the room stood Will's desk, on which sat the dreaded death phone. He slowly walked up to the desk, and picked up the telephone receiver and placed it to his ear. It made a burring sound. The line was more or less redundant, this fact alone gave Will some assurity that the killer was gone, presumably now laying in some prison morgue.

As he turned to leave the room for one last time, he slipped the key into the door lock and began to pull it closed. Then it happened ... Will's heart sank as the death phone began to ring!

Will raced back into the room, his heart pounding as he picked up the receiver. 'Hello, hello, this is DCI Scott.'

'Hello, DCI Scott, this is agent Penelope Brawn from the Federal Bureau of Investigation headquarters in Washington DC. How are you today, sir?'

Will stuttered his reply, 'erm, yes, I'm fine, I'm good, er, how about yourself, how can I help?'

'I understand you are investigating a series of murders over there in England, I saw it detailed in a recent FBI bulletin. Is that correct, sir, am I speaking to the correct officer?'

'Yes, you are, I am that officer. Please call me Will'

The tone of the American voice on the other end of the line took a slightly more serious sound. 'Sir, I've been asked to contact you by senior FBI officials, to liaise with you, we have two bodies over here. Our examination of each corpse and crime scene indicate that these victims are likely to be connected with your series of crimes. Your killer has crossed the Atlantic, sir! Our victims, one male, one female, have both been tortured to death within their own homes. Both individuals had convictions for child sex grooming and indecent sexual offences with children as young as four years old.'

Will took a deep breath before asking, 'Penelope, can you tell me, were they found in the same household or at independent murder sites?'

'They were totally independent, sir, one victim lived in Windermere, Florida, the other in Miami, Florida. That's quite a distance apart if you aren't aware of the state. Our CSI teams haven't found one trace of forensic evidence. They did find a tiny little angel figure from a key fob which had been inserted inside the mouth of both victims. Does that sound at all familiar to you, sir?'

'Yes, yes, it does. That was our killer's signature, we didn't reveal it to the public or media over here, so it might be pertinent not to mention it.'

'Sir, you said the word 'was,' as though your killer isn't currently active, is that correct?'

'It's a long story, but we understand that our killer was incarcerated, and during that period he confessed to the killings and hung himself before being questioned about them.'

'Well, sir, unless we have a copycat killer over here, I guess your guy wasn't the killer, especially with this freaky angel signature left at the crime scene. It's too much to be a coincidence, unless of course, someone else knew of that detail and is continuing the behaviour over here?'

'I doubt that very much, Penelope, it has always been my thought that our killer might still be active. I was emphatically told that the man in custody was the killer and since then, we've been told he was dead. For your info, Raymond Sproutt, with two t's, is his name, you might want to check with customs to see if that name comes up with anything over there.'

The FBI officer fell silent for a moment. 'Sir, my senior officer has requested that we invite you out here to work with us on this case. We aren't into conspiracy theories over here I'm afraid. These two people, our victims, they were killed within the last few days. The state of the bodies, it matches the description in the FBI Bulletin. Does that timescale fit with your supposed killer's date of death?'

Will was visibly shaking and was pale, beads of sweat ran down his face from his temple. 'No it doesn't fit at all, he's been incarcerated for over three weeks, so it cannot possibly be him. I don't know what to say or how to proceed with this, Penelope?'

'Sure, I understand, sir, I'll get our Chief to speak with your own people, and they can sort it out between them. Can I ask you to give your boss a heads up and to expect the call please. Nice talking to you, Will, I'll send over an email outlining what we've got, and hopefully we'll see you very soon.'

It was Will's worst nightmare, having to tell the powers above him that the murders had apparently continued in the USA, with the same MO throughout was going to be difficult. He slowly made his way back to his office, and picked up the telephone and informed the Chief Constable of this latest development. The Chief had already expressed an opinion that the English case was closed, so the opinion of the FBI wasn't likely to change that. The leading Eastborough Police official told Will to inform Felicity Harvey of the details, and to request an official response from her. The situation was potentially dangerous for both the police and the Government and it had to be addressed before the media got hold of it. Will wasn't happy at playing the political messenger.

As he made the call, he wanted to demand from her, the truth. However, he was too astute to open himself up like that. If he was to find the truth, then it wouldn't be through official channels. The call to Felicity Harvey was brief, on hearing of the American link, she was anything but helpful. 'Will, our killer is dead, you know that, therefore this has to be a copycat killer active over there. There is no genuine evidence connecting their killings to ours is there? It's just another dead paedophile who has been butchered by a vigilante or nutter over there in the States.'

Will had kept the finding of Malakim at each crime scene, private. Felicity, nor any of the establishment figures were aware of this detail, he guessed even fewer knew what a Malakim actually was. Their placement within the court room crime scene wasn't at all obvious, they had been hidden on the seats in the public gallery. Not once had any of them asked to see the figures, nor were they interested in them. Indeed, by their own admission, the evidence from that crime scene had been taken away and destroyed, apart from, that is, the property Daisy had removed, the 26 Malakim. He decided not to mention the importance of the Malakim to this series of crimes to Felicity.

'DCI Scott, I think it's very much a decision for your Chief Constable to make. I'm certain it would be good for policing relations to show international collaboration. It will serve as a bit of kudos, showing how you, because of your outstanding reputation in this case, have been called upon to help an overseas force in their own investigation. I know the Home Secretary will agree and support that, I'll speak with her and get a press release ready for distribution once your Chief has spoken with the head of the FBI, okay?'

Will was being railroaded, the situation being manipulated by the government to their own advantage, he was a pawn in a piece of pro-government propaganda. Despite this, he said nothing controversial and agreed with Felicity, thanking her for the support, before replacing the receiver on its cradle. Sitting at his new desk, he opened the top right hand drawer, and removed a small silver Malakim, it was the one found at the Hooton crime scene. He had this because it helped keep him focused on the impact the death of that victim had on his own daughter, Ellie. She saw a different person, a kind caring teacher who she respected, rather than the filthy digusting pervert Will and other police officers saw. Will recognised, that personally, he owed it to Ellie to catch her teacher's killer. He could never tell her of the forced circumstances that caused him to lie to her, it would be damaging to their father daughter relationship.

Clutching the Malakim tighly within the palm of his right hand, he rang Mel. Their conversation was disturbed by the ringing of Will's work mobile.

'I'll have to answer that, darling, this is a real fucking nightmare,' he said.

His wife, forever a wise and level headed person told him, 'Will, it's a nightmare for the establishment, those people who have not been honest with you, it's not a nightmare for you. All I would say to you, is commit to whatever your head and heart tells you, don't be brow beaten. If you get the chance to go out to the USA, take it, catch the bloody killer, if not for the victim's sake, for that of your own daughter. You're a good man, Will Scott, don't grow old and have doubts. Sort it now while you can. Of course I'm not happy you are being pulled in different directions by all and sundry, it's always away from home, but I think this is something you have to do, Will.'

'Thanks, Mel, I really do love you,' he said before ending the call.

Will answered his mobile, it was the Chief Constable. 'Will, I've spoken with the FBI, they clearly want you out there, I've also spoken to Felicity Harvey, the Home Secretary thinks that you'll be a marvellous ambassador for British policing. She has cleared you to go out there with one staff member. I'm assuming it will be Detective Inspector Wright? If so, you better speak with her. My understanding is that the FBI want you out there pronto, so liaise with them and arrange it. A reminder, it will be paid for by them, not us, so get them to organise your flight and accomodation bookings. Let me know when it's sorted.'

A pinging noise at his computer, alerted Will that he had received an email. It was from the FBI agent, he opened and read it. The message confirmed everything, he was to provide personal details to them and flights would be arranged within the next 48 hours. Will then made one final call. The phone rang out several times at the home of Daisy Wright, who was settling down to watch some mind numbing daytime television that helped her relax. She answered the phone with a brief 'Hello,' when she heard the voice on the other end of the line she recognised it was a serious call. It was her boss.

'Daisy, how you doing, mate? I really hope you haven't got anything planned, because we are going to the USA, just you and me. We'll be working with the FBI, so pack your bags, girl, we've got a serial killer to catch. They've had two murders over there, complete with Malakim. Don't ask any questions now, I'll brief you during the flight. Are you able to come with me?'

'Too right I am, boss, I've been thinking a lot about what happened in London, none of it sits right with me. I've tried to locate Raymond Sproutt in voters registers across the UK, then check the corresponding age. I've made countless telephone calls, to people called Sproutt. The only one I've not been able to physically speak with lives in Orkney, and he's in his seventies, so he's hardly likely to be the paedo preyer. All the others, I've spoken to, they are leading normal lives, not been in prison or

318

arrested. So who the fuck is the Raymond Sproutt with two t's we were told was our killer?'

'Christ, Daisy, that's some research you've achieved there. I thought you were supposed to be on leave? I was told earlier today, by our friends in high places, that Sproutt has hanged himself in his prison cell and is now dead.'

'That's bollocks, boss, and you know it. I'm coming to the conclusion that there's some kind of cover up going on. For what, I do not know. So let's go to America and nail our killer, once and for all.'

CHAPTER TWENTY FIVE

Lucien Palmer hadn't been the same since he returned from his four day disappearance. His wife, Christine, was concerned that he had never talked about what had happened, nor would he discuss anything about the story he had been researching. Instead, he sat staring into space, seemingly not prepared to interact with her nor friends and family. The doctor had advised that he be allowed to rest and had written a sick note covering his absence from work for three months. His diagnosis was that Lucien was suffering from Post-Traumatic Stress Disorder, he had suffered huge trauma during the time he was missing. Lucien was to attend specialist one to one counselling sessions that would help him cope and move on. In the meantime, Christine was to ensure that he led as normal a lifestyle as possible, and to encourage social inclusion.

Will Scott, was Lucien's best friend, that's the way it had been since they were at primary school together. There was few secrets between them and those that did exist were enforced as a result of Will's police career. Lucien's disappearance had frightened Will, because he knew how tenacious he could be with his journalistic investigations. However, this was the first time their professional career paths had clashed, both men were taking different routes towards an identical goal. Both were in dangerous territory. The Paedo Preyer, as Lucien had referred to the killer in a newspaper article, was on a nationwide killing spree that had most recently ended in

Court Room 13, of the Royal Courts of Justice, in London. There was no trial, instead, the killer had somehow entered the innermost sanctum of the British criminal justice system and wreaked havoc and mayhem.

With clearance granted, Will and his trusted sidekick, newly promoted DI Daisy Wright, travelled across the Atlantic Ocean for a joint international murder investigation. It was an eight hour flight, during which both officers relaxed as best they could, as each officer imparted what little knowledge they had uncovered since the official closure of the paedo preyer crimes in the UK.

'We've been had over, Daisy,' remarked Will. 'They've literally created an identity for our killer, someone who wasn't even real! Why the hell would they do that unless it was to cover something far greater?'

'I tried doing online searches for the judge and barrister, there's nothing anywhere. It's as though they never existed.'

'We have to focus ourselves on this current investigation, Daisy, I'm really looking forward to working with the FBI. If we can't crack this case between us, then no one ever will.'

On arrival at Orlando International Airport, the pair were greeted by two smartly dressed FBI Agents. Officers Walters and Lopez were vastly experienced female officials, who were specialists, not only in murder investigations but ritualistic crimes also.

'Welcome to Orlando, and thank you for coming over here at such short notice, we really appreciate it,' said Agent Walters. 'My name is Shelley and this is my colleague, Beth Lopez.'

Will and Daisy introduced themselves as the group made their way through the busy airport, past customs, where their English passports were stamped, and out into the main reception hall. Beyond the smoked glass sliding doors that led to the outside world, Will caught sight of a huge, candy apple red Chevrolet Equinox parked in the drop off zone. 'That's our vehicle right there,' said Beth pointing at the mean machine Will had seen. 'We'll take you to your hotel first, it'll give you time to settle in, and for us to talk and get to know each other.' Will and Daisy were both tired as the jet lag associated with long distance travel hit them simultaneously. Despite this, both were keen to get started and to learn more about the two murders.

Having booked into their hotel rooms, they were soon travelling again, this time through the ultra-busy roads that crossed Orlando, eventually arriving at the police department headquarters building some twenty minutes later. It was late afternoon US time, and the precinct was busy with dozens of people who had gathered in the main reception area, all wishing to speak with the police.

Behind a long wooden reception desk, a solitary uniformed police officer attempted to promote calm and coordinate appointments with local officers and the public. A crowd of other people looked particularly menacing, their discomfort at being inside a police station was obvious, they appeared nervous and shifty.

The two Eastborough officers were taken through to the squad room, where several plain clothes officers were sat at desks, some with piles of official looking paperwork beside them, others were busy either writing or on the telephone. At the rear of the room sat two empty desks. Shelley Walters pointed to these and said, 'These are your desks, we've left the most recent, up to date files covering our investigation and the crime scene, for you to look at and go through. I believe the City Mayor is in the building, he's here to welcome you. There is likely to be some media coverage of you being here and working with us.'

With that, a pair of wooden full length doors swung open, as the Chief of Police, the City Mayor and an entourage of photographers marched into the room. For the following twenty minutes Will and Daisy were the centre of media interest, with the Mayor seemingly making up new words during his speech, embracing what he called a 'transcontinental police investigation' alluding to the fact that the President, Mr Trump himself, would welcome such 'inter-country collaboration.' It was all something of a circus for Will and Daisy, political propaganda that would be unlikely to enhance the murder investigations.

After the press machine had gone, Will sat at his desk for the next few hours, barely speaking a word to Daisy, who likewise, was studying every aspect of the murder files. Shelley Walters reappeared, and placed on both officers' desks, a silver Malakim in an evidence bag. 'Guys, we found these at the crime scenes, I understand they hold some significance to your own investigation?'

'Yes, they do,' responded Will, picking up one of the bagged Malakim and closely examining it. 'These are our killer's signature, his calling card.'

Beth Lopez joined in the discussion, 'We have carried out research into these tiny figures, they are available online, there is no wholesaler or manufacturer here in the US. Therefore, we believe the killer brought them with him, he had an intention to kill out here. Listen, the law of averages state that this is the same killer, there's no such thing as coincidence, right?' Will nodded in agreement.

Daisy interrupted, 'Our killer is dead, that's if we are to believe what we've been told by our own Government officials, then this can't be him murdering over here.'

Will shook his head. 'I don't for one minute believe Sproutt was our killer. Please keep this to yourselves, however, we, as in Daisy and I, believe we were set up by Government hierarchy who wanted us to believe that this guy Sproutt was the man we wanted. There's a lot more to this than we can currently fathom. When I look back, so many questions remain unanswered. Like, why didn't the Met, or the City of London cops deal with it, it was on their patch? Why did we have no access to the killer once he'd been caught? Why was the crime scene destroyed? Why did we never see any documentation relating to the London crime?'

Shelley Walters looked confused by the talk of Government cover-ups. 'Surely, if that's the case, what about when, or if, the killer struck again in the UK? How could they cover that up?'

Will smiled, 'It's all too easy for them, Shelley, they'll write them off as copycat killings, spill the story to the nationals and its job done for them. When we eventually catch the killer, I guarantee he will be taken away from us and he'll probably disappear.' Beth Lopez tried to put some sense into the discussion. 'Well, you're in the USA now, our jurisdiction. If we catch him on our territory, then we will interview him. I'm sorry, but these things don't really happen, it might in television shows, or in books, but not in the real world.'

Shelley and Beth were both laughing at their English counterparts. 'I'm only kidding, you folks, we have cover ups out here all the time. The CIA or whichever organisation, take our prisoners and we don't see or hear of them again, they just disappear. Once someone crosses that threshold of becoming dangerous, or a threat to the 'illuminati' or whoever it is that runs our damn country, they are cut loose by society and the powers that be sweep them up and make them go away. We don't tend to ask too many questions, and neither should you. Do what you're paid to do, and do it in the best way you can and your conscience will be clear.'

Beth Lopez picked up the Malakim from Daisy's desk, 'Deep down inside, do you genuinely feel that someone over here could leave one of these tiny figures at the scene of not one, but two different murders. This is no copycat, it's your killer. He's come out here, maybe because you were getting too close, or maybe because he fancied a change of scenery, I don't know. Whatever, I guarantee, it's him. That's the sole reason why you are out here to help us catch the bastard.'

Daisy switched the conversation back to what she viewed as more solid ground. 'Why don't we have the victims' names in the files?' she asked.

'That's an oversight on our behalf,' added Shelley. 'Until definite confirmation of identity is received, we always refer to dead bodies as John Doe, if it's a male victim, and Jane Doe if it's a female. I have their names right here for you. The female is Kimberley De'ath, that's one hell of a surname to go through High School with. Before you ask, she didn't work for an undertaker either.' added Beth laughing at her own comment.

Shelley continued, 'Our male victim is Malcolm Andrews, both victims were convicted child sex offenders, and were known and active paedophiles. There is no connection between either victim, other than, they share the same sexual perversions. Andrews in particular was one nasty piece of trash, he was convicted in 2014 of raping a six month old baby. Six fucking months old. The stupid idiot of a judge gave him an eighteen month prison sentence, with good behaviour, he was out after 12 months. His murder gives us reason to believe that this was a revenge killing, so our killer may be aware of the case.'

Daisy turned to Will with a look of horror on her face. 'Boss, we never did consider that our last two victims might have been involved in trial proceedings. What if the QC was defending the paedophile and got him off, or the judge prescribed a ridiculously low sentence tariff. Fuck me, that would have been a real motive.'

Will nodded and smiled. 'Daisy, as a matter of fact I did carry out some covert investigations into that very idea. I knew that both the judge and the QC were involved in a trial, and as you say, the QC was defending three paedophiles. It was known as the trial of the three Mr X's, because the judge banned the press from revealing the three suspects identities. The case was thrown out on a technicality, and the Judge apologised to each defendant. He also condemned the victims for making up their stories. That case single handedly damaged relations between victims of child sex abuse and the authorities. Reported cases dropped by 35% as a result of what the idiot judge said. You might remember, during our discussions with the Lord Chief Justices' office, he told us there was no connections whatsoever between the judge and the QC. He lied to us, Daisy, I should have listened to Mandy at the time, we were patsies.'

'Sounds like you two are gonna have some phenomenal biography to write when you both retire,' added Beth with an intonation of understanding in her voice.

'Boss, why didn't you tell me at the time?' asked Daisy, 'that was important, didn't you trust me or something?'

Will stood up. 'Daisy, it wasn't about trusting you, I thought I was being paranoid and that perhaps I was wrong. It wouldn't have been right to force my paranoia onto you, so I left it where it was. I had to accept what those bastards told us and tried to move on, despite my gut instinct and Mel telling me differently. I firmly believe our killer might be here in the States, right now as we speak. Somewhere, within our investigation, we must have looked at him, he got past us, Daisy, we missed him. My belief is, he was over here within days of the last killing, and had been carefully watching and selecting his victims.'

Will reassured Daisy that he trusted her implicitly. 'I wouldn't want to work with anyone else, Daisy, you are the best copper and the best detective I know.' This caused a round of applause from the two FBI agents who stood smiling at their British counterparts. 'Come on, you two, no more questions, we all want to catch this bastard, so we work together, as a team and keep nothing from each other, no secrets and no paranoia Will Scott,' said Shelley in a distinctly strict school mistress manner, Will blushed and felt suitably admonished.

With that, the FBI agents checked the time, it was gone six in the evening. 'Today's work is over, you two must be exhausted, so come on, I'll drop you at your hotel, and will collect you tomorrow morning at 8a.m. sharp, okay,' said Beth Lopez picking up the keys to the Chevrolet.

That night, after dinner, the two English police officers slept soundly. Will had briefly spoken with Mel on the telephone. 'I'm missing you, darling, and the kids, tell them won't you? I'm exhausted with all the travelling.

America is so in your face, everything seems to happen at superfast pace here, but the cops are all really helpful and we've kind of struck up a good relationship, I think.' That literally was the extent of his conversation, before he started to drift off into a much needed deep sleep. The following morning, he couldn't remember saying goodnight to Mel, so sent her a text message in which he apologised for falling asleep. Mel responded with three kisses.

CHAPTER TWENTY SIX

Beth Lopez was outside the hotel and waiting for the British detectives, who had both shared a table over a cooked breakfast. As they emerged into the sunshine, they had the lost look of tourists visiting Florida for the first time. Everything seemed to amaze them, the size of the roads, the cars and most of all the people. Will was already feeling uncomfortable, dressed in his thick cotton suit, shirt and tie, he was beginning to feel the heat.

'Gosh, it's so hot,' said Will. 'Everyone is so smiley and friendly. We don't get this in Bridlington, sunshine and lots of happy people.'

Beth was quick to inform Will that not everyone was so kind, 'We have one hell of a drug problem here, what with Disneyland, and the attraction that holds, our transient population is huge. That makes it difficult for us to get a real hold on drug smuggling and their mules. Attached to that we've got gun crime, we get masses of shootings and I'm ashamed to say our unsolved murder rate is rising every year. It's a great city on the surface, scratch beneath that and it's like anywhere, prostitution, drugs and gang crime are all around you. Tourists don't really notice it too much, but you two will see it very differently by the time you go home.'

The ride to the precinct took about half an hour, rush hour traffic and a couple of vehicle accidents causing the delay.

Once there, they were met by Shelley Walters, who had coffee and pastries waiting for them.

'We've got a suspect we need to pull in, he's British and has been over here for five weeks. His green card says he is over here on vacation, he was stopped last night in the red light area, chatting up an eleven year old child prostitute. The officers took his details and decided to let him go, as they were called away to a crime in progress. His name is Patrick Baines, he's from Leytonstone, London, England. The motel he's staying at is well known for prostitute activity, he's in room five.'

Minutes later, the team were on their way to the Waverley Motel, just south of Central Orlando. As they pulled into the car park, the two FBI agents checked their weapons, which sat in their shoulder holsters. 'We go to the door first, you two stand behind us, don't get drawn into any potential firing line, this guy may be armed, we don't know.'

Shelley Walters gave three loud knocks to the door of room number five. As the door opened, Beth Lopez forced her way in, knocking to the ground a curly haired middle aged man who was slightly built and as thin as a racing snake. He offered no resistance. 'Sir, we have some questions we'd like to put to you at the police precinct about your activity last night. You have the right to remain silent ...'

Will and Daisy stood in awe, the swiftness of the operation and how quickly the FBI agents had it under control had surprised them. What came as more of a shock was when six marked police vehicles arrived in the parking lot and armed uniform officers with their sights trained on the arrested man, arrived as emergency back-up. Beth Lopez barked into the police radio, 'officers stand down, stand down,' causing the officers to jump back into their patrol cars and leave the scene. One marked car transported the handcuffed prisoner to the police precinct its blues and twos alerting drivers of its presence for miles around.

'We don't take risks here, I'm afraid folks,' said Shelley Walters. 'Every suspect is potentially dangerous, so we are proactive in disarming them, better that than being shot.'

The hotel room was searched, and nothing out of the ordinary was found. Back at the police precinct, Will and Daisy were present as Baines was questioned and interrogated. He was a complete wet, a wimp. To their surprise he admitted knowing the girl he was accosting was a juvenile, and said that he preferred them young, because they were more open to his personal predilection. He wasn't the paedo preyer, however, he was an active paedophile, a person of interest that the British police force would have to monitor when, and if he ever returned to the UK.

The next piece of work involved taking the Eastborough officers to both murder scenes. 'Windermere, you'll like it there. It's a really nice place. There's lots of Disney employees live out there, and crime isn't all that common. Saying that, a couple of years back, we had a uniform cop shot dead there. So as cops, we have to tread carefully even in the decent places.

As they pulled up outside the single storey estate home, the first thing that struck Will and Daisy was how middle class the area was. The house was well kept with a picturesque swimming pool sitting beneath a large landau. There was no litter, and it was hard to believe that a grisly murder had taken place within this type of neighbourhood. Inside, the crime scene had been cleaned up, however, there were tell-tale signs of violence, with blood staining and spatter still evident on some of the walls.

'There was no sign of forced entry, so we think the killer was invited in by the victim. This was the home of Kimberley De'ath. As you can see, it's only a few hundred metres to the main freeway into Orlando Central, the killer can easily disappear in that amount of traffic,' said Agent Walters.

The following crime scene was less salubrious, it was in a rundown part of Orlando, a ground floor apartment. The cleaning of this crime scene had been less careful. The smell of death still filled the air inside, small pools of dried blood remained on the wooden floor, the holes in this indicated where the body had been pinned down. 'This was Malcolm Andrews' home, this fucker was depraved. We found nothing in any of his mail or documentation that we didn't already know. To be honest, neither of these victims will be missed. Least of all by the families living in the area,' added Agent Lopez. 'Typically, no one saw anyone or anything suspicious at either crime scene. The killer came and went without drawing attention to himself.'

'Just as the bastard did in England,' said Daisy.

'We'll take you to the city morgue next, you can view what's left of the remains, then we can go grab something to eat maybe,' said Agent Walters with a smile.

'Do you have access to CCTV footage of the area surrounding the crime scenes?' asked Will.

'Yes, but it's grainy, almost impossible to see anything. We've had it cleaned up, but still there's nothing. We've got it back at the precinct. We can take a look at it after lunch,' replied Beth.

The drive to the city morgue was incident packed. First, an armed raid on a jewellery store had caused the closing of an entire street, meaning a lengthy detour. Stuck in the resultant traffic jam, a young boy was knocked to the ground and injured by a taxi which had deliberately mounted the kerb to pass a parked vehicle. With the rest of the traffic at a standstill and going nowhere, Shelley Walters had jumped out of the police vehicle and gone to assist at the scene. Paramedics were quick to arrive, and the injured boy was wheeled along the sidewalk on a stretcher to a waiting ambulance. The driver of the taxi was detained and taken away by traffic patrol officers. As Shelley returned to the Chevrolet, she dusted herself down and climbed back inside explaining to the team that the taxi driver was driving under the influence of alcohol. 'He was pissed, can't stand drunk drivers, they should be punished more severely. That kid has broken his leg and may have spinal injuries, all because that reckless bastard liked a drink,' she added.

An hour later, they arrived at the morgue. 'I hope you are okay with cadavers?' asked Beth. 'Our victims are in an awful state, they are unrecognisable as human beings.'

'Yes, we've seen some grotesque bodies in the past few weeks, it's the smell I hate,' added Will. As the team moved through the cool dark corridors of the morgue, the smell of death was unmistakable. No one spoke, until they reached a secure double door with an intercom outside. Shelley Walters spoke into it. 'FBI Agents Lopez and Walters here, with two British Detectives, to view bodies of Andrews and De'ath.'

There was a loud click as the security bolt moved back and one of the doors swung open. As they walked inside, Shelley handed round the vapour rub, Will and Daisy wiped copious amounts of the stuff on their upper lips to help disguise the stench of rotting flesh.

The mortician was equally as weird as his chosen profession. A tall, skinny man, with a distinct stoop and rounded shoulders, he had lank greasy hair and looked like he hadn't washed for several weeks. As Will shook his hand it was more akin to that of a dead body, weak and cold. 'My name is Clemence, I'm the head mortician here in Orlando. Kindly change into those items hanging up over there before entering the morgue,' he pointed to a row of white coats hanging from a wall, and slip on booties and hats laid out beneath.

The group were soon dressed in the requisite attire and walking through another corridor. This one was short, with windows on both sides that allowed an unobstructed view of the room inside. Bodies, laid on

335

stainless steel gurneys, and covered in white sheets filled the rooms. 'These are our new arrivals, fresh from their everyday lives,' said Clemence in a weird, seedy kind of way. 'We have six murder victims here at the moment, I take it you wish to see Malcolm Andrews and Kimberley De'ath. I just love that name, so fitting to the surroundings, don't you think? Curiously enough she's my first ever De'ath,' he said giggling to himself like a naughty schoolboy.

Shelley Walters clearly didn't like the man, she kept her distance from him and privately whispered to Daisy, 'This guy gives me the shivers, he's so sinister. Can you imagine the conversation over a meal with him?'

Clemence darted into a room on the left, and was followed by the group of police officers. As he weaved in and out of the parked gurneys, each one holding a body, he suddenly stopped. 'Right, he we are, the final remains of Mal. I knew him when he was alive, you know. Real creep he was.' The group laughed at the irony of the statement.

Beth leaned over the body and using a pen as a pointer, she highlighted the various injuries inflicted upon the body. 'He really suffered in his final moments, I expect that's just what the killer wanted. Poor bastard had his tongue cut out and shoved into his throat, so he couldn't scream.'

'That's virtually identical to the injuries inflicted upon the UK victims,' said Will shaking his head at the grotesque form that lay before him.

'Are you saying that the UK killer has travelled across the pond and started killing here?' asked Clemence looking slightly agitated and moving his body weight in a sideways motion, from foot to foot.

'That's precisely what we are saying Clemence, but don't you go shooting your mouth off about it, it's not our intention to broadcast it at this time. The last thing we need is for every freakin' paedophile in the state to panic and ask for police protection,' added Shelley. Clemence nodded his understanding.

'The body on the next gurney to you, officer,' said Clemence looking at Daisy, 'that's Kim. Ooh, I just realised, wasn't there a 90's pop band called Mel and Kim? Whereas we've got Mal and Kim here.' No one laughed.

Will, however, suddenly cried out. 'That's it, that's the message from our killer, letting us know it's him. Don't you get it?' he asked the group who shook their heads in unison. 'Look at the names of these victims, it's another cryptic clue he's giving us, Mal and Kim, it's Malakim,' he said convincingly.

'Hang on a moment,' said Shelley, if you add the word De'ath to that we've got Malakim De'ath, or Death dependent upon which way you say it.'

Beth Lopez didn't agree with Will's conclusion. 'I think you're getting a little too carried away with you anagrams and puzzles, Will. I agree, it's a strange coincidence, but it's unrealistic surely?'

Daisy added her thoughts, 'There is no such thing as a coincidence,' she said solemnly. 'This is the same killer, right down to the play on words.'

The officers thanked Clemence for taking the time to show them the bodies, 'Be sure not to say a word about what you heard today, not to another living soul, understand?' Beth reminded Clemence before leaving the morgue building.

Clemence laughed, 'Living soul, did you mean to say that, it's quite funny in the circumstances,' he added before disappearing back through two swing doors and into the inner gloom of the morgue.

'I tell you, that guy gets freakier every time I see him, he's one odd ball that's for sure,' laughed Shelley as they climbed back into the parked Chevy.

'Right, who's for lunch, I know a great little restaurant where we can sit and talk, are we all up for that?' asked Beth, slamming her seat belt shut and firing up the Chevy's V8 engine. The drive to the restaurant was quiet, everyone in the vehicle was deep in thought about Will's latest discovery.

Over lunch, the officers discussed various investigation techniques and the way forward in trying to identify and catch their quarry. The sad fact being, the killer was leaving no evidence at the various crime scenes. Trying to identify and locate a suspect in an area as large as Florida, assuming he, the killer was still there, was very much akin to finding a needle in a haystack.

'I think we need to work with immigration and passport control at the airports and ports, checking and verifying the authenticity of identification for each visitor. I'm thinking no one with a criminal record in the UK should get into the country, they would be weeded out at passport control,' said Shelley Walters.

'That's correct,' confirmed Beth Lopez, adding, 'so if our immigration control systems are working correctly, to get through, the killer has used a fake passport and identity. Failing that, he doesn't have a criminal record. Judging by the manner of the killings, I find the latter hard to believe.'

Daisy pointed out how laborious and time consuming such work would be. 'How far do we go back date wise? And more to the point, how many UK citizens visit Florida every week?'

'I think we are looking at several thousand a week, most fly in, so I think that would be a good place to start, at the airports,' added Shelley. 'There is a central hub where all the passport details are recorded along with the eye and thumb recognition facilities operated by immigration. We should go there next.'

Will pointed out that the last murder occurred in England almost four weeks previously. This meant the killer was in the UK at that time, therefore records going back one calendar month needed to be checked for all flights into Florida. 'In the meantime, we've got to hope there are no more murders,' he added.

The team worked tirelessly for two weeks, with no obvious connection between criminality and visitors to Florida being found. Back in the UK, Eastborough Police force were becoming a little edgy over the length of time two of their officers were spending in America. The force were already under strength complement wise, so couldn't justify an extended stay for Will and Daisy. CID resources were beginning to suffer as a result of their absense, investigations back home were building up. Much to the relief of both Eastborough officers, the Chief Constable requested that both officers return to the UK within the week. Life in the States was great, they both enjoyed the experience and had learnt a great deal from their FBI counterparts. Yet Will missed his family and Bridlington, for all its faults was home.

'We've got you booked on your return flights to the UK in two days' time,' said an attractive red haired female FBI administration official. 'We'll settle both your hotel bills and any other expenses you have incurred. If you can let me have your receipts by noon tomorrow please. I'll give you your flight tickets then, too.' Will and Daisy nodded.

'Will, we've got one more check to carry out before you leave, it's CCTV footage from passport control at Orlando airport for three weeks ago. It'll take a couple of hours to run through the visuals of those people singled out for closer attention by immigration control officers,' said Shelley Walters, picking up her holster and gun, and strapping them over her shoulder. 'We should go now and get it done, are you ready?' Will picked up his jacket which hung over the back of his chair and moved to leave the office.

'Daisy, you and I should stay here and check through the files one last time, to see if we've missed anything,' said Beth Lopez.

It took less than an hour for Will and Shelley to reach Orlando Airport and gain access to the CCTV footage. 'For flights from the UK and Europe only, we have 1000 hours of footage. This includes footage in the arrivals area and the queues to get through passport control.'

'Can we hone that down to UK flights only?' asked Will.

'Sure, of course we can, give me a moment and I'll get that loaded for you,' replied Officer Grant of Immigration Control. 'You can reduce that footage time again if you only want to see passport control filming. Would that be better?' Will and Shelley agreed.

For the next few hours, Will diligently sat staring at the monitor showing the faces of hundreds of British tourists as they entered the country. After a time, each face looked the same as the one before, it was only when someone with a curious moustache or a dodgy hair-do went through that the images stood out.

'Who'd have ever guessed that human beings could look so similar?' commented Will as yet another flight of passengers appeared in the footage on the monitor.

'This is the last one, Will, my eyes are tired, I guess yours are too, I doubt we are really able to concentrate after this length of time,' remarked Shelley.

'I confess, I'm struggling, Shelley,' confirmed Will, who stood up and stretched his arms upwards, letting out a yawn as he did so.

'I think we are done here then, I'll get the guy to come and turn the footage off and we can be out of here,' said Shelley leaving the room.

Will glanced down at the footage for one last time, the final few passengers were passing through immigration. His eyes widened as he recognised someone in the footage. He bent down to look more closely at the image on the screen. 'For fucks sake, look who that is,' he laughed, but it was only for a second. 'Jesus Christ, never, it couldn't possibly be?'

Shelley re-entered the room and looked over at Will. 'What's up with you, you look like you've just seen a ghost?' she asked.

'Oh it's nothing, Shelley, just my imagination playing tricks with me. Do you think you could give me a copy of this footage to take back to the UK to look through again please. I'm interested in these particular frames,' he added as he scribbled the timings down onto a sheet of paper. 'I also need to know when those people who appear in the frame, left here on the return trip to the UK.'

'Have you got something, Will, why are you interested in those particular frames and people?'

'It's probably innocuous, I don't want to cause a fuss here and now by making rash claims, I need to check things out back in the UK first. A few enquiries to make there and I'll come back to you straight away.'

Shelley asked Immigration Officer Grant to provide copies of the footage and the requested information and details of the people highlighted in the frame. He confirmed that he would have it with them within a few hours and it would be dropped off at the police precinct.

Will's mind was all over the place, not only through the monotony of peering at CCTV footage for such a long period of time, but also because he thought he recognised a figure in the arrival hall footage.

He elected to play it down as nothing, however, he also knew that it might well prove conclusive to the entire investigation if his suspicions were proved right. 'We should head back to the precinct now, speak with Beth and Daisy and see if they've picked up on anything.'

Will agreed and soon they were venturing through the busy Orlando traffic towards the police precinct. 'We've got a nice surprise for you both when we get back to the office,' said Shelley sounding extremely excited about something. Will's mind remained fixed on the footage he had just viewed, he needed answers, but those would only be found when he returned to Bridlington.

Back at the police precinct, Beth and Daisy were in deep conversation about serial killers, whether those in the UK were more evil than those in the US. The arrival of Will and Shelley halted the conversation. 'Find anything?' asked Daisy.

'Something and nothing,' added Shelley, 'your boss thought he might have recognised someone in one piece of footage, but he's uncertain, so he's taking it back to the UK with you to look at and make enquiries over there.'

'Wow, cool,' said Daisy, 'Who is it, boss?'

'I'm not certain to be honest, it's just a face I thought I recognised.' None of those present believed Will, he was too dismissive of the question and avoided all comment on the matter. 'We'll check it through when we get back, if I'm right, then we might be onto something significant.' He pulled out the chair from beneath his desk, and sat down on it with a heavy thump.

Shelley Walters spoke up. 'Right guys, tomorrow is your last full day with us, so we want to make it a memorable one. We've organised day tickets for each of us to go to Disney tomorrow, so you can end your stay here with good memories and not dark ones. We'll get you back to your hotel early so you can get a night's sleep before your flight the following day. So make sure you leave nothing behind here in the precinct, you won't be coming back after this evening. How does that sound?'

'Amazing,' replied Daisy. 'How exciting.'

Will laughed in agreement. 'I can't wait,' he added, 'How long until that CCTV footage arrives, Shelley? he asked.

'It won't be long, Will, lets grab a coffee, then sit down and write up the report covering your visit and our joint investigation, you'll need one, so will we, so I suggest we commit to a joint one. Sadly, it's going to be fairly negative, so we must ensure that we cover every aspect of our investigation to show we were thorough.'

Will hated bureaucratic paperwork, however it was a requirement and would show that they hadn't been on a holiday, but show their professionalism working alongside the FBI. Two hours later, it was done. Daisy took a photocopy of the report and in case it was lost, sent a copy to her Eastborough Police email address. Shelley

344

handed Will a sealed box containing the footage and information he requested. 'Will, this is me pulling rank on you now,' said Beth Lopez. 'You don't open this until you get back to England, is that understood. I've deliberately sealed it so you can enjoy the last 24 hours of your stay here. So that's it, folks, time to wrap up, come on we'll take you back to your hotel, and we'll collect you at 8am sharp tomorrow morning.'

The day spent at Disney was amazing, albeit, there was too little time to see everything, they had a taste of what it was like, with Will declaring, 'I'm definitely booking a holiday for my family over here later this year. It's totally different from what I expected, my kids will love it here.'

As Beth Lopez pulled the Chevy to a halt outside Will and Daisy's hotel, it was clear that everyone in the car was feeling more than a little emotional. Hugs and kisses and friendly embraces continued for several minutes, contact details exchanged. The group said their final farewell. Will and Daisy had booked a taxi for the early morning trip to the airport, and as they waved goodbye to their new found FBI friends, tears ran down their cheeks, before they bid each other goodnight for the last time in Orlando.

The next day's flight back to UK went as planned, Will and Daisy both slept for much of the journey. In the intervening hours when they were awake, Daisy badgered Will about the person he thought he had recognised on the CCTV footage. 'Come on, boss, spill the beans, you're going to have to tell me some time, why not now?'

'Daisy, for heaven sake, stop going on about it. Firstly, I won't know until I can confirm it is the person I think it is, and secondly, they explain why they were in Orlando? It's routine stuff to be honest, nothing to get overly excited about.'

Back in England, the pair never once discussed the matter during the journey home. It was late into the night when they arrived back in Bridlington. 'I'll be back in work tomorrow morning, Daisy, I'd like you in at 8.00am, please, report to my office. If I'm not there, I'll see you in the CID office. I hope we can find some answers then.'

On arriving home, Will was met with the greatest greeting anyone could expect. Mel, Ellie and Daniel grabbed hold of him and squeezed him so tightly that his arms started to tingle with pins and needles. That night, Will told of his American adventure, of his visit to Disneyland and a promise that he would take them there in a few months' time. Very little had occurred during his absence. It felt good to be home and surrounded by people he loved and cared for.

CHAPTER TWENTY SEVEN

The following morning, Will arrived at Bridlington police station and was met by Daisy, who had a coffee waiting for him on his desk. 'Morning boss. What have we got this morning then?' she asked.

'I just need to check through some of my emails and paperwork. It'll only take a couple of minutes. Can you pop downstairs and speak with the duty uniform Inspector, tell him we need uniform back up and a couple of dog handlers on standby at this address,' he handed Daisy a piece of paper, which she immediately looked at.

'For fucks sake, boss, you've got to be kidding?'

'Sadly, Daisy, I'm not. We have an arrest to make, I don't expect a ruck or any kind of resistance, so we only need a couple of patrols to be on standby nearby. I'd like at least one dog handler to be at the rear of the premises too. Everyone to be in place by 8.45 a.m.'

Daisy rushed down the stairs and into the duty Inspector's office, where she conveyed the DCI's request to the officer. 'Not a problem, I'll let the control room know and ask them to inform and deploy those units.'

As Daisy returned to Will's office, he was on the telephone, in the process of notifying the Chief Constable's office of the impending arrest. She noticed that her boss had drunk his coffee, so refilled his 'I Love Brid' mug. When the call ended, Will sat back in his chair, looking a little uptight. Daisy, meanwhile, was pacing up and down his office, clearly nervous and wanting further details from her boss.

'Daisy, I'll make the arrest, however, for obvious reasons I need you with me.' Will didn't have the chance to say anything else, as the police radio sparked into life. It was the control room notifying elected units to deploy to the address stated by Will, 'An arrest is to be affected at that address by CID, so remain on standby, until confirmed.'

Will leapt out of his seat, 'What the fucking hell are they playing at?' he yelled at Daisy. Announcing all that detail over the radio. There's no bloody need for that.'

'Boss, we're on Tetra, no one can listen in, there's no problem,' confirmed Daisy.

'It's not that I'm worried about, Daisy, I just don't like uniform being so open with details like that. It's reckless, what if an officer was stood next to a member of the public, they'd overhear that transmission.' Daisy nodded accepting that Will's concerns were not without foundation. 'Ring the bloody control room for me now, tell them not to discuss address details over the air again.' Will was angrier than Daisy had ever seen him, tiny drops of spittle fired from his mouth.

'I don't want anything to mess this up, not even the woodentops, do you understand, Daisy? Now get them fuckers in the control room told,' he said pointing to the telephone on his desk. Will left his office, grabbing his coat as he did so. Daisy made the call, reminding them of the need for confidentiality.

'Boss, listen, it's a genuine mistake, all kinds of data gets mentioned over the radio with no detrimental outcome. The Tetra system can't be hacked, its safe, you know that.'

This time it was Will's turn to nod in agreement. 'I know, I apologise for yelling at you, Daisy, none of what we've been through on this case has been easy, straight forward, or simple. I've said all along, I'll know we've genuinely got our killer when I look at them straight in the eyes. We both deserve that, along with a shed load of answers, don't you think.' Daisy saw a cold steely look in Will's eyes, he was like a predator hunting down his prey. He could literally smell the blood and wasn't about to let it escape.

'Too right, boss,' said Daisy, 'I've certainly got a lot of questions I need answered.'

As Will and Daisy pulled up at the head of the street where their suspect lived, they asked control for confirmation that all requested units were in place.

The familiar voice of the uniform Inspector responded to the request. 'We are awaiting for the arrival of the dog unit to the rear, it was diverted to a burglary in progress, stand by.'

Will and Daisy sat waiting for what seemed like an eternity, but was only fifteen minutes, before the control room contacted them. 'Bravo Zero One, can you confirm that entry has not yet been made into the target's house?'

'What the fuck? What are they going on about now? I told you uniform would fuck it up,' Will said to Daisy.

Speaking into the radio, he responded 'Negative, no entry has been made, we are awaiting arrival of the dog unit.'

The response he received sent a cold chill through his body as time momentarily stood still. 'Bravo Zero One, we are receiving a signal from a police radio within the target property.'

'This is Bravo Zero One to control, we are going to enter the property with immediate effect. Stand by all units,' instructed Will.

It was drizzling as Will and Daisy ran up the neat red bricked path leading to the front door of the target property. Will took a deep breath and gave his customary heavy triple knock on the door, and nervously waited for it to be answered. After a few moments, he rapped at the door again, there was no answer. Daisy peered through the front ground floor windows. In between the vertical blinds, she could see a smartly furnished living room, clean and tidy, but no sign of life.

Will wasn't going to delay entry a second more, he leaned his left shoulder against the door and gave it a heavy shove. The door swung open into the hall, which had a staricase leading to the upper floors on his left. Will had barely called out, 'Hello, this is the police, is there anyone here?' when he saw a body dangling from a piece of blue rope attached to the upper staircase bannister.

It was the body of Mandy Ward, her head flopped at an awkward angle, almost resting on her right shoulder. Her red, bloodshot eyes were bulging from their orbits, her face was blue and her tongue grotesquely protruded several inches from her mouth. She was clearly dead.

Daisy rushed upstairs to check if anyone else was in the house. It was all clear. Returning partially down the staircase, she reached over to touch the body which was still luke warm checking for a pulse. Will joined Daisy and slapped Mandy's face in the vain hope of getting some reaction. There was nothing. He slowly slumped to a seating position on one of the stairs. Both officers were silent, staring at the slightly swinging corpse in disbelief.

'You stupid bloody cow,' Will said speaking to the dead body. 'Whatever it was that caused you to do all of this, it must have been hellish for you. Were you the killer? We'll never know. You selfish bitch, you've taken that control from us, you've carried your secret to the grave.'

Daisy made the radio call for one uniform unit to attend the property. 'No entry is to be made, the scene is to be externally secured. In addition, can we have the police surgeon and a full forensic team here as a matter of urgency. All other units to stand down, resume normal duties,' she commanded. Daisy couldn't quite take in what she was seeing, she sat with her head in her hands.

Will was trembling, he could feel a cold sweat on his brow. He wandered down the stairs and closed the front door to shut out the outside world.

'Boss,' said Daisy, 'what if she isn't the killer?' she asked.

'It was her, Daisy, I saw her on the airport CCTV footage. I double checked everything, dates and times of each murder, she had the opportunity at each one, even the two in the States. I'm well fucked off that we'll never hear her confession. Bitch.'

351

He moved into the lounge, he saw a police radio laid on the floor. He carefully side stepped this and considered that if Mandy was the killer, then he and Daisy were deep inside her lair. Looking around further, he saw, laying on a glass topped coffee table, a manilla envelope. In neat handwriting, it said:

'For the attention of DCI Will Scott only.'

Will felt his heart thumping wildly in his chest, and he became breathless, the cold sweat on his brow suddenly felt like ice. He collapsed to the floor, striking his head on the solid glass table top as he fell. Will was out cold.

'Boss, boss, wake up, are you alright. Come on, Will, wake up, don't you dare give up on me now,' said Daisy trying to revive her closest friend. Rushing into the kitchen, she poured some cold water into a mug, before returning to Will's unconscious body and carefully throwing the contents into his face. Will coughed and spluttered, and opened his eyes as he slowly sat up.

'Daisy, what happened? Jesus, I must have blacked out or something.' He tentatively rubbed his right temple and saw blood on his fingers. 'I must have banged my head on the glass table when I fell.' Will was anxiously looking around the floor. 'Daisy, did you see a letter?'

'What letter? I haven't seen a letter,' she replied.

'It's from her, I think, it's got my name on it.'

Looking on the floor around him, he saw the letter beneath his legs, where he had dropped it. He moved to his knees and retrieved it.

'Boss, leave it for now, an ambulance is on its way here for you. Relax, you've hurt yourself, give me the letter and I'll keep it safe.' Will handed her the envelope and its contents. 'I'll make sure you are the first to read it, okay, boss,' she said placing it inside her jacket pocket. 'Boss, you do remember, don't you?'

'She's dangling from a piece of rope in the hall out there The bloody psycho bitch, how could she do this. The perfect liar, no wonder the killer was always one step ahead of us, she was part of our investigation team. The cow knew every fucking thing we were doing. She played us all like real fools.'

Will woke up in hospital, Mel and Daisy were standing by his bedside.

'Will, thank goodness you're awake at last. We've all been so worried about you.'

Will was groggy and confused. 'Where am I? What's happened?' he asked.

'Don't you remember, you collapsed inside that Mandy's house and banged your head,' said Mel. 'You've been unconscious for nearly two days.'

'What?'

'The doctors have been carrying out all kinds of tests on you, to make sure you are okay. They think you initially collapsed from exhaustion. As well as that, the shock of finding that woman hanging, caused you to black out, collapse and bang your head.'

Will gave the hint of a smile. He was pleased to see his wife. 'Where're the kids? I don't want them worrying about me,' he replied.

'They're fine, they're having sleepovers with Gemma and Luke at Chris and Lucien's, so don't worry about them. I've told them you're going to be okay and they're fine about it. You need to relax, Will, give your brain a rest. The specialist thinks you may have a slight concussion, so she's got a few more tests to conduct before you can be discharged and allowed to come home.'

Will was restless and fidgeting in the bed, trying to sit up. 'I want to come home now, Mel, I don't need any more tests, I know better than anyone how I feel. I'm fine. I've got things I need to do, can you get a nurse or someone to bring my clothes please?'

'No, I won't, and you'll stay where you are.' Mel reached forward, and placed her hand on Will's shoulder, gently and reassuringly pushing him back into his pillow adding, 'Will, you must rest,' as she kissed his forehead.

'Boss, let me tell you, you're something of a local, national and international police celebrity. You got the bitch, you solved the case. Well, according to the Government press release, you caught a 'copy-cat killer' who you tracked to the USA and back. That media statement has got Felicity Harvey written all over it. In the bigger scheme of things, none of that matters, because we'll always know the truth.'

Will looked thoughtful and started to focus. Suddenly everything came flooding back to him. 'What about her house, has it been searched, did they find any incriminating evidence, Daisy?'

'Sure did, boss. Forensics have recovered a shit load of evidence from her home, six taser guns, a small sack of Malakims, rolls and rolls of gaffer tape, hammers, six inch nails, you name it. She had the lot. There was even a fake pass for the Royal Courts of Justice, and a key. We also found loads of trial transcripts from paedophile cases, including the X-men trial.

'The best piece of evidence we currently have, is a photo album with images of each victim immediately before, during and after death. Honest, it's the stuff of nightmares. The Government have requested full access and control over it, so it's likely to disappear into the ether fairly soon.' Daisy leaned forward and whispered to Will, 'I've taken copies of every image and page so don't even ask. No one but the three of us here knows about the letter, so you'll get to read it first. She certainly was one for documenting everything. There was a diary that covered the murders and her perceptions of our handling of them. The woman was one psycho bitch I can tell you. Oh, and before I forget, we carried out an inventory check of police radios, one was missing along with a small charger unit. No one noticed because our housekeeping was crap. All sorted now though. She must have taken them when she was working with us. Everything about her was fake, there never was a boyfriend, she lived alone, had few friends apart from her sister who occasionally visited, but she apparently lives abroad. Interpol are looking for her as we speak.' Daisy took a deep breath and continued.

'By all accounts Mandy was an extremely private person according to neighbours and her colleagues in the Prison Service. Speaking of which, that organisation is presently distancing itself from her.'

Will was overcome by a wave of tiredness and for a few seconds, closed his eyes as he tried to fight off his exhaustion.

'I've said too much for you to take in already, boss, sorry I blurted everything out at once. You need to rest. Before you ask, I've locked the letter away somewhere safe.'

Will could barely process what he was hearing. 'I need to read that letter, can you get it now?'

'No, Will. It's wrong that you should ask that of Daisy. You are in no fit state to work, let alone read a letter from a serial killer. That can wait until you're discharged and back at home. For now, you rest and you recover,' instructed Mel.

'Boss, Mel has the letter, it's safe, it's at your house okay?'

Will nodded and drifted off into another deep sleep.

The following morning, after a further examination of his head wound, he was allowed home. The journey from hospital to Marton Gate seemed to take an eternity. Mel was trying her best not to talk about work, or the paedo preyer. 'Lucien and Chris have been really worried about you, I told them to pop over to see us this evening. The kids are at school, so you have peace and quiet until this afternoon, when they get home. I expect you'll want that if you are to digest the letter.'

'Thanks, darling, are the kids both alright? I've missed them I don't know what I'd do without you all.'

Mel gave a smile of contentment. 'Yes the kids are fine, they've missed their dad too.'

As they pulled up outside their home, a bright red Royal Mail van was about to pull away. It stopped, and the driver jumped out and opened the side sliding door. Mel stepped out of the Audi and went to meet him.

'Glad you're home, we've got a stack of mail and cards for the local celebrity cop. Most were addressed to him at the police station, however, we've agreed with them that it would be better to deliver them all to your home for now. Is that okay with you?'

Mel laughed out loud. 'Yes, I expect so. I'm struggling to understand all of this to be honest. Maybe we need to employ a press secretary to open and read them. We are going to need a lot of stamps if he's going to reply to all of that lot.' She shook her head in disbelief at the size of the sack the postman carried into the house, 'It's all quite unbelievable,' she said shaking her head.

'I know it's not the right time, but when is there ever a right time, is there any chance I can have a selfie with your husband, please?'

Mel laughed. 'You'd better ask him, I don't think he'll mind too much'

Will stood next to the beaming postie, unsure whether he should smile, wave, or cry. He opted for a serious face.

The postman shook his hand and thanked him, before driving off for the rest of his round.

Will and Mel took great delight in closing their front door to the world, sitting down and holding onto each other. They felt safe and protected in each other's arms, especially so in the sanctuary of their own home. Mel got up to make a coffee for them both, she could see Will was still tired. On her return, she dropped an opened manilla envelope in front of her husband. He immediately recognised it as the one he had found inside Mandy's house.

Carefully, he pulled several sheets of cream paper from the envelope, and laid them out on the coffee table in front of them both. 'Will, do you want me here, or would you prefer to read that in private?'

'I need you beside me, Mel, I want you to listen to what she says.'

To DCI Will Scott,

Since you are reading this, I'm assuming you have found my body. I knew you were closing in on me, but didn't expect it to be so soon.

I've had this letter prepared for a few days now, I took the decision to finally end my life this morning, when I heard over the police radio that you were coming to arrest me. It will save the tax payer and the criminal justice system time, and money, on a trial that would achieve nothing more than lining the pockets of lawyers and barristers. It's as full a confession as you are likely to get, no holds barred, Will. I thought you might need this to satiate your own ego and for closure of the case in full. It's a self-diagnosis.

My innocence and childhood was taken from me when I was sexually abused by a number of monsters. One was my father and there were other people too, including: a council worker, a school teacher, a nurse, and a policeman, all people in authority and in whom we all place our trust. The only person I ever told of my abuse, was my doctor, the family GP. He didn't believe me. The impact this had on my life was devastating.

As I grew up, during my teens, I read a newspaper report about a mother who had sought revenge on a paedophile who had abused her daughter. She removed his sexual organs before setting him on fire. She gave herself up to the police. At trial she admitted the crime and made a statement in which she damned British Justice. The same paedophile had abused other children, and had been put away for 18 months only. He was released within a year and moved into the same street as two of his child victims. The authorities did nothing about it, so she took justice into her own hands. He had a caravan at the rear of his house, the abuse still happened in there.

One evening, she watched him go in there and followed him inside, where she maimed him and set him on fire. The judge sentenced her to 8 years. The imbalance in the sentencing is obvious, every abused child suffers torment on a daily basis for the rest of their lives, everything, trust, love and relationships is lost. It takes great strength and courage to overcome these issues. It's the equivalent of a life sentence. Judges don't take this into consideration when sentencing paedophiles, because they don't understand.

The sentencing in that case has remained with me all of my life. I cannot forgive or forget. I see it as my responsibility to expose and take action against paedophiles, to stop them from committing further sick acts on innocent children. I'm not a bad person, I wasn't born evil. The establishment created me, transforming me into what I am today. I feel no guilt or remorse when I kill these people, they deserve it, every right minded person will agree with that.

I didn't start out to kill. Instead I did my utmost to be accepted by my peers. This is why I studied and worked hard at my education, passing out with a Masters Degree in Forensic Psychology. I wanted to know why paedophiles acted in such a vile way, and tried to identify triggers or character/personality defects that would cause them to abuse children. I soon learned that it isn't an illness, or any kind of sickness, nor is it hereditary. They are paedophiles through choice.

I quickly found employment within the Prison Service, dealing with psychological aspects of serious category A offenders. I learnt a lot from those prisoners, everything I needed to know, techniques to make someone suffer before I kill them. I understand the importance in staging the body to deliver an offensive message to all who view it, and of course instil fear into a certain type of person.

I know I possess psychopath and sociopathic tendencies, I'm a chameleon, I adapt with ease to my

360

surroundings. The people I killed were all carefully selected, all were convicted paedophiles. The two legal bods down in London were different, they were never going to be brought to justice by their own, many of who are of the same inclination. The establishment, to the very highest levels, sweeps up all indecent activity committed by those who will damage it. It hides their crimes and wrongdoings. You witnessed such behaviour first hand, it was immoral, reckless and deceitful. I was deeply offended when they tried to write those two murders off as being committed by someone else, Raymond Sproutt with two bloody t's. That, I believe, was my finest work. It sent shock waves through the Judiciary and the legal world which is rife with all kinds of corruption.

You were perplexed by the riddle of how the killer gained access into the Court building. It was in fact relatively easy to get hold of the door key that allowed me access. The drunken Clerk to the Judge handed it over after a few drinks and a bit of flirting in the nearby Knights Templar pub. The idiot didn't notice that I also removed from his jacket pocket the security door pass that gave access to the Judges' corridors. With those, I could come and go as I pleased.

Getting the two perverts to come to the Courts on a Sunday was equally as simple. I instructed them to meet me there, separately. If they chose not to attend, then I would publicly expose them as predatory paedophiles, I had photographs to support my blackmail.

I despised them both, they abused their legal expertise and power to their own advantage all too often they protected paedophiles. Tibbs had thrown out 47 individual cases of paedophilia during his years as a Judge. No one ever recognised this failing, I did, that's when I discovered barrister boy Wilcox was at it as well. He excelled in defending paedophiles at trial. The bastard had a 100% record in this field and bragged about it. Both of them deserved to die, they served no useful purpose to civilisation. The fact that the establishment lied about and disguised their deaths says it all. In life and in death, they were little more than numbers in a book, worthless pieces of shit.

As for the others I killed, I would befriend each one before I got up close and personal and attacked, I dressed into a full Tyvek suit. That apparel is so easy to take to and from a crime, dropped nicely into my handbag. It was easy to watch and study their every movement. Creatures of habit, they thought they were so clever, their conceit made my work much simpler. I wasn't randomly killing paedophiles at will. Everything was carefully planned and executed. You were so wrapped up in ephemeral detail, like finding the Malakim that you failed to notice that each murder had an alphabetical format to it. This allowed me freedom to seek out further victims. Let me explain it more clearly to you.

A-B was victim Allan Roberts in Bridlington. Being my first killing, he took a bit more time to die. I got hold of a number of taser guns through contacts in the Prison Service. I practised on Roberts, right down to the level of electrical power it took to immobilise someone. Two long shots stunned him, the third sent him into seizure allowing me to handle and restrain him. That's when I stepped things up a notch. I gave him something very real to focus on. It wasn't only him, I took my time with each victim, making sure they would never damage or harm another child. When restrained, I stapled open their eyelids, making the eyeball dry and uncomfortable. This allowed them to see what horror was coming next. I then took their eyesight away from them by impaling the barbeque sticks into their eyes, I used a small hammer I bought from a pound shop, to drive these into the eyeballs.

Next, I took away their ability to speak and taste, either splicing or cutting off the tongue. Sense of touch, I fucked their fingers up good and proper, stripping the skin off or removing them all, dependent upon my mood. The sexual organs, penis and testicles, I removed these to totally immasculate the males, some of them were made to eat these or I popped them into their open mouth, or inserted it into their anus. I found that by splicing the fingers open, and folding back the skin, it created a sort of neat flower pattern. This was a bit of artistry I added to make them slightly less grotesque for you to view.

C-D: was Charles Hooton in Driffield, what a horrid little man he was. He genuinely thought he was going to make love to me. He was the only one who had my mobile phone number, so I had to switch his phone for an old one with no sim card. His stature was small, everything about him was small except his ego. It took less time to incapacitate him than any of the other victims.

E-F: is covered by Enid Shuttleworth in Flamborough. Poor cow, she begged for mercy after I hit her on the back of the head with a lump hammer. I took special care with her because she was my first female. Women aren't generally recognised as paedophiles, she was a nurse, compassionate and caring about vulnerable people. She raped and abused dozens of kids, as part of a Northern paedophile ring.

G-H: Gary Tilley. I disliked this man so much. The caravan brought back memories of my childhood, both my sister and I stayed with my uncle in school holidays in his Hymer caravan. Tilley was an out and out sleezy bastard. You might wish to note, the manager at Sandskipper, Andy Hanson provides kids on site for these fiddlers. He advertises bespoke holidays with 'discreet amusement for adults' on forums of the dark web.

I-J-K-L: I opted to move location for this murder. Irene James in Killingbeck, Leeds had been on my radar for some time. The evil witch that she was, was enticing kids as young as five to her home, for her husband to abuse. Then she filmed it. Through her lawyers, she arranged a deal with the police that got her off all charges if she gave evidence against her husband, which she did. There's no loyalty among abusers. As bait, I faked being a freelance journalist, offering her money for lurid stories about her husband. She couldn't wait to meet me. In the end, she wouldn't stop blubbering, so to shut her up. I filled every orifice of her body with expanding foam. Boy did she get big.

M-N-O: Martin Newell in Oldham Street, Kettering. Newell was well known across the East Midlands as a paedophile. I found him online on a dark web forum. I made him suffer most, because he spat in my face. I was half way through finishing him off, when I heard a crying noise from behind me. When I looked round, I saw a dog and its puppies. I felt so guilty that those poor creatures had to witness what I was doing. I quickly finished him off, then fed the dogs and gave them some fresh water. It wasn't their fault their owner was such a vile person. I seriously worried about those dogs. Twice I returned and fed them. I expected the body to be found much sooner than it was. Ultimately, when you, Daisy and I officially attended the scene, the bloody dog recognised me and came running over. Daisy noticed that I believe, because the dog had acted aggressively towards anyone approaching her puppies. Everyone except me, because she knew I was kind and I looked after her when her pups needed it the most.

P-Q-R: Patty Quinn in Romford. Least said about this cop shagger the better. It was the uniform and the power she liked most. She had a passion for young boys, she forced them to be intimate with her, then raped them in return. She plastered photographs of the abuse onto the internet. One photograph showed a view out of her window, with a street sign on it. I tracked the address down, before befriending her online and offering to visit and bring a boy with me. She jumped at the offer. Later, the silly woman threatened me with the police, just as I was about to drive the stick into her eyeball.

S-T: That's the pervert Judge Stephen Tibbs. He abused his power and position to aid paedophiles and abuse children. He terrified them with threats of throwing them and their parents and families in prison, for life, if they ever told anyone. And they say British Justice is the best in the world!

U-V-W-X-Y-Z: Our Barrister boy. Ulrich Vivien WilcoX of Yeovil. He worked from Zenith Chambers in Middle Temple.

Unless you kept it from me during the investigation, you didn't recognise this pattern. I recall you saying that it was your wife, Melanie, who was able to point you in the right direction regarding the Malakim figures that I left at each crime scene. You saw it as a breakthrough, whereas, in reality it took you nowhere, but at least you gained an understanding why I was doing what I did. Double the damage in return for child abusers.

Incredibly, you did manage to work out the acrostic puzzle in the list of names, and I'm assuming, someone, somewhere in America, must have recognised my 'Malakim Death' message - MALcolm Andrews KIMberley De'ath. It took me less than half an hour to identify and find those two freaks out there.

It is my belief that I've done humanity a great favour in getting rid of each of these vile people. In making them suffer prior to death, I gave them some understanding of the pain and torment their child victims have to endure every single day of their lives. They won't hurt children anymore, I'm doing what everyone would privately want to do. Delivering true justice.

Just because I'm gone, it doesn't mean there will be no further paedophile murders. I'm certain there'll be many others delivering their own justice in the future. I was simply a catalyst to inspiring innocent victims and people, to take a stand against perverts and paedophiles everywhere. Exposing them at every level of society and across all professions and callings. Monsters are not only found in dreams, they lurk in the shadows all around us, in every street, everywhere. We simply need to acknowledge their existence, and open our eyes if we are to see them. To all of mankind, I say, 'You think you know your neighbours, but are they who they seem?' You might want to consider having my remains cremated.

Knowing the human psyche as I do, it's likely that any grave will become a memorial for those of a similar emotional inclination to me. I'm certain the police have better things to do, than stand guard at a grave. Things like catching genuine criminals and paedophiles.

Amanda Ward

Will was choking back his tears, the missive covered every aspect of their investigation and a whole lot more. It gave cause for a good deal of thought.

'I don't know whether to be pleased or scared after reading that, Mel. To think I worked closely with that woman. Yet behind the mask of normality that she wore on a daily basis, she was this smouldering, enraged, psychopathic vigilante. How could I not notice that? The worst thing about all of this, she's probably right, there will be others after her. The whole thing is about monsters, but who was the biggest monster? The paedophiles, or her?

'We have to open our eyes to this sort of deviant behaviour, not least, the judges. They have to deliver the correct level of punishment, they should be banged up for life if they interfere with kids. They should have no privileges, let the prison population sort them out. If not, there will be more Mandy Ward types walking the street, randomly killing off the paedophile community and driving it further underground. Was she doing humanity a service by killing these perverts off? It seems to me that most people privately agreed with what she was doing. Who'd have ever guessed that it was a psychopathic psychologist all the time.'

Mel sat expressionless. 'That's such a sad letter, Will, she must have been hurting every day of her life, who, or how, could she trust in anyone or anything ever again?'

Will reached out and took hold of Mel's hand, gently squeezing it, he reassured her.

'I'll never let anyone hurt our children, darling, if anyone ever tried, well, justice would be mine.'

The story of

THE GROOMING PARLOUR

continues in

THE DARK WEB

to be published by

WILLIAMS & WHITING

SUMMER 2017

Made in the USA
Charleston, SC
12 March 2017